GUARD DOG

GUARD DOG SERIES - BOOK 1

KATT ANDREWS

CRIMSON QUILL
PUBLISHING
LLC

GUARD DOG

Guard Dogs Series - Book 1

Paperback

ISBN 979-8-9991952-1-0

CONTENT WARNING

Guard Dog is a mature, high-heat dark cartel romance with characters who are sometimes very irredeemable with extreme proclivities towards violence. It contains situations that some readers might find offensive, distressing or triggering. Reader discretion is advised as this book contains:

- Sexually explicit content, including detailed sex scenes and sex toy use
- Physical abuse, emotional abuse, and psychological manipulation
- Drugging/attempted drug-assisted assault
- Attempted kidnapping/abduction
- Past intimate partner violence
- References to childhood trauma and domestic abuse
- Blood, gore, violence, torture, and graphic injury
- Use of firearms, knives, explosives, and other weapons
- Death including remembered death of a sibling, death of parents
- Remembered childhood trauma

- Remembered car accident involving drunk driving
- Criminal activity including murder, assault, hacking, surveillance, and theft
- Invasion of privacy via hidden cameras, microphones, and other means
- Cartel-related violence and organized crime
- References to drug dealing, human trafficking, and forced prostitution
- Power imbalance in romantic dynamic (bodyguard/client)
- Themes of trauma, PTSD, and survivor's guilt
- Mentions of alcohol abuse/addiction
- Alcohol consumption
- Plagiarism and theft of intellectual property

1

THE CONTEST

Email to Crimson Quill Press, LLC Email List Tagged "All"

Subject: Win a Dream Dinner with Amira Zadegan, Author of the Smash-Hit Tennis Fixation Series!

Do you adore love stories that make your heart race and your cheeks flush? Are you still swooning over the steamy romance, unforgettable characters, and hilarious banter in Amira Zadegan's *Tennis Fixation* series? Then this is your chance to meet the literary sensation herself!

Crimson Quill Press is thrilled to offer one lucky fan an exclusive evening of fine dining and fabulous conversation with **Amira Zadegan** at San Antonio's premier Riverwalk restaurant, *La Cascada*. You'll enjoy a once-in-a-lifetime opportunity to pick Ami's brain about writing, hear the behind-the-scenes inspiration for her iconic scenes, and maybe even get a sneak peek at her next project!

. . .

How to Enter: Submit a short essay (500 words or less) telling us:

1. Why the *Tennis Fixation* series is your favorite romance series.
2. What you'd love to ask Ami during your dream dinner.

Essays will be judged on creativity, passion, and originality. Make us laugh, make us cry, or just tell us why Amira's books mean so much to you—we want to hear it all!

The Prize Includes:

- Dinner for two with Ami Zadegan at *La Cascada*
- A signed hardcover set of the *Tennis Fixation* series
- A Crimson Quill Press swag bag packed with exclusive goodies

How to Submit: Email your essay to **contests@crimsonquillpress.com** with the subject line "Dinner with Ami Contest."

Don't wait! Whether you've dreamed of asking Amira how she creates such sizzling chemistry or want to gush about your favorite romantic moments, this is your chance to make it happen.

Get those entries in now and let your love for romance shine!

———

Email from Natalie Morris to Amira Zadegan

Subject: Top 5 Entries for the Dream Dinner Contest

Hi Ami,

Hope you're ready for some fun reading! I've just finished narrowing down the over 300 entries we received for the Win a Dream Dinner contest to my top five picks. Let me tell you, romance readers are passionate. You've got superfans who wrote their hearts out, a few aspiring novelists seeking mentorship, and at least one person who seems convinced you're the reincarnation of Jane Austen (flattering, but a little much).

I think you'll enjoy reading these. Each one stood out in its own way, but one in particular caught my attention—and I'm curious to hear your thoughts.

My favorite is Maria Sandoval. Her essay is equal parts heartfelt and dramatic. She credits your *Tennis Fixation* series with helping her through a tough time, and her passion is palpable.

She also hints at having a unique family dynamic, which might make her story relatable for you as a fellow strong-willed woman navigating life on her own terms.

Here's the thing, though. Her name stood out immediately. I mean, Sandoval. In San Antonio. Could she be related to *those* Sandovals? Honestly, if she is related to that family, she probably deserves dinner just for the courage to write to us!

Of course, this could all just be a coincidence. Either way, her email was thoughtful and moving, so she earned her spot fair and square.

Let me know what you think. I'm curious which of these entries speaks to you the most.

Talk soon, Natalie

P.S. I'll make reservations at La Cascada for the last night of SpicyLitCon. It's got that perfect "straight out of a romance novel" vibe I know you'll love!

2

———

MARCO

LA CASCADA on San Antonio's Riverwalk wouldn't have been my first choice for this assignment. Too public. Too many exits. Too many obstacles between me and a clean shot if something goes wrong. The restaurant's open-air patio is exposed to the Riverwalk, where tourists drift by in slow-moving boats, phones out, cameras flashing. The main dining area is worse—cluttered with unevenly spaced tables, blind spots created by the floor-to-ceiling waterfall, and just enough ambient noise to muffle approaching footsteps.

A place like this? It practically invites trouble.

The only reason I agreed to this location was Raul's assurance that the owner is a Sandoval client—a man who pays handsomely for protection. That, and Maria's persistence. She wanted this fucking dinner. And Raul always gives Maria whatever she wants.

Which leaves me here, running security while she fawns over her dinner guest.

I have two of my team with me.

Elias is on the patio. It's a good position—gives him a full view of the river and the guests outside while keeping an eye on the doors leading back inside. Tall, lean, and always calm, Elias has the kind of quiet presence that makes people assume he's in charge wherever he stands. Dressed in a tailored suit, he looks more like the restaurant's manager than security. Which is exactly why he's posted there.

Chuck is at the front entrance. Where Elias blends in, Chuck does the opposite. He's big, blond, and built like a tank. A presence meant to be noticed. Anyone thinking about causing trouble takes one look at him and rethinks their life choices.

And me? I'm inside. Close enough to stop anything before it starts.

From my seat one table over, I keep my hands loosely wrapped around the glass of water I'm not drinking, my gaze sweeping the room every few minutes, tracking every movement. The restaurant is quieter than usual for a Saturday night —exactly how I arranged it.

Four occupied tables. Ten diners. Two servers moving between tables. A bartender behind the counter. The math is easy. The variables aren't.

Even with the controlled setting, unease lingers in the back of my mind. The layout is bad. The patio is worse. And the back kitchen door? That's a problem.

I touch my communications earpiece. "Report."

Chuck answers. "Front door's clear, boss. No movement."

"Copy."

Elias's voice is smooth, quiet. "Patio's normal. No one looking twice." A pause, then, almost amused, "Maria making your life difficult?"

I don't answer, because Maria's delighted laughter carries across the dining room before I can.

She looks completely at ease. No sense of caution, no awareness of the security risks surrounding her. Dark eyes wide with excitement, leaning forward, practically bouncing as she listens to the woman across from her.

Amira Zadegan. Also known as Ami.

She's not what I expected.

The dossier was thorough. Bestselling romance novelist. Writer of "spicy" books about tennis players and their tournaments. Clean record. No criminal ties. No history of violence. On paper, she's ordinary.

But this woman? There's nothing ordinary about her.

She's chaos wrapped in a red dress.

Wild brown curls tumble from a too-loose bun, refusing to stay pinned up. Hands that gesture too big, too fast, nearly knocking over her wineglass—again. And her scent hits me even from the next table—light and clean, something floral. Jasmine, maybe. Not perfume. Shampoo?

Her voice carries across the room, loud and warm. She's completely unaware that everyone within earshot is listening intently.

Maria is enthralled.

Ami leans in, clearly mid-story, voice animated. "—as he pressed hard into her back, kissing the nape of her neck, and licking her earlobe slowly. Then he said, 'I plan to taste your pussy until you forget your own name.'"

The glass in my hand freezes halfway to my lips. *What the hell are these two talking about?*

Maria gasps audibly, clasping her hands together like this is the greatest thing she's ever heard. "Oh my God, that's so hot! So she could definitely feel how hard he was, like she could feel his dick pressed against her?"

I set my glass down with deliberate care. Neutral expression. Straight spine. No reaction.

Ami grins, more curls escaping her bun as she nods. "It's about the build-up, Maria. The slow burn." She says it loudly, unapologetically. As if she isn't aware of—or doesn't care about—the handful of diners now openly eavesdropping. "You can't just jump into the action—you've got to tease them. Make them beg for it."

Maria nods, completely absorbed in the discussion. "Yes! That's why the blow job on the tennis court worked so well. It's iconic."

A blow job? On a tennis court?

I shift in my seat, jaw tightening. Eyes forward. This is not the conversation I expected to be monitoring tonight.

Chuck's voice comes through over the comm, amused. "You getting an education over there, boss?" Apparently, even he can hear their conversation through the earpiece.

I ignore him.

I should be scanning for threats. Watching Maria. But instead, I'm hyper-aware of Ami's mouth. *Make them beg. Blow job. Taste your pussy.*

Jesus Christ.

I roll my shoulders, refocus. Nothing is out of place. Just the soft hum of the waterfall, the clink of glasses, and then—

Something shifts.

I don't see it, not at first, but I feel it. A presence. A movement that doesn't belong.

The bartender. He stiffens. His hands slow where he's wiping a glass.

The server closest to the kitchen glances over his shoulder. Twice.

My gut goes tight.

The kitchen doors slam open.

Three men storm into the dining room. Masks. Guns.

"Everyone stay where you are!" the lead man barks.

No one stays where they are.

Chairs turn over. Glasses shatter. Panicked screams fill the air.

And the man with the gun?

He strides straight for Maria.

3

AMI

THE SOFT HUM of cascading water fills the air at La Cascada, blending with the distant strum of a mariachi band playing somewhere along the Riverwalk. Twinkling lights reflect off the slow-moving water, casting rippling gold patterns onto the stone pathways that wind alongside it. Couples stroll hand in hand, tourists float by on boats, sipping margaritas while a guide rattles off historical facts no one is listening to.

It's enchanting, the kind of place that belongs in a romance novel.

Which is exactly why I love it.

Inside the restaurant, candles flicker on crisp white table-cloths, lush greenery spills over wrought-iron railings, and the scent of citrus and tequila lingers in the warm night air. Everything about this place feels designed for a perfect, cinematic moment.

Normally, I'd be cataloging every detail for my next book— noting the glow of candlelight, the way the waterfall's soft rhythm makes everything feel more intimate, how the distant hum of conversation adds warmth to the space.

But tonight? Tonight, everything feels too perfect.

I can't quite put my finger on it. Maybe it's the fact that, for a Saturday night, the restaurant is too quiet. Only a handful of tables are occupied, and the waitstaff moves with the kind of measured precision that reminds me of stage actors hitting their marks. La Cascada is supposed to be a foodie hotspot, the kind of place people drooled over on Instagram. But tonight, there's something calculated about it, something that makes the back of my neck prickle.

I shake it off.

This dinner is supposed to be a celebration, not the setup for a thriller.

The real reason I'm in San Antonio is the Spicy Literature Convention, aka SpicyLitCon, a four-day whirlwind of panels, book signings, and cocktails with my favorite people in the world—romance writers. We spend the days debating trope hierarchy, TikTok thirst traps, and the logistics of historical corset removals. We spend the nights dancing, gossiping, and drinking enough margaritas to make bad decisions feel like good ones.

It's heaven.

And tonight is supposed to be the highlight for me—a "Dream Dinner with Your Favorite Author," with me as the guest of honor.

I wasn't entirely sold on the idea at first.

"We're hosting a contest? With a dream dinner? With me? Who dreams about that?" I had asked when Natalie Morris—my best friend and publisher—pitched it.

"Don't be so self-deprecating," she'd replied, rolling her eyes. "You're building a brand, Ami. This is marketing gold. Plus, free food. You love free food."

She wasn't wrong.

And now, sitting across from Maria Sandoval, the contest winner, I have to admit Natalie was right.

Maria is pure energy—bubbly, enthusiastic, and completely obsessed with my *Tennis Fixation* series of spicy romance novels. Which, honestly, is kind of amazing. I just wish I could relax enough to enjoy it.

"I still can't believe I'm sitting here with you, Miss Zadegan," Maria gushes, her dark eyes sparkling as she leans forward. "Do you know how much your books mean to me? I've read all of them—like, multiple times."

Her excitement is contagious, and I can't help but smile. "Well, first, call me Ami—like Amy, but with an 'i.' And second, it just so happens..." I reach into my oversized purse and pull out a hardcover copy of *Volley Girl*, the final book in the series. "I want you to have this. It's signed. I hope that's okay."

Maria gasps, her hands flying to her mouth. "Oh my God, Ami! This is incredible!"

As she flips through the book, running her fingers reverently over the title page, I feel a flicker of pride. Fans like her remind me why I write in the first place.

See, Chad? There are people who love my work. Lots of people. My books are successful. They're even in Portuguese, Chad. Portuguese!

Unfortunately, that small, petty victory over my ex-boyfriend doesn't distract me from the unease curling in my chest.

I glance around the restaurant again.

The two waiters move too smoothly, like they've been rehearsing their steps. A bartender wipes down a glass, his movements too slow, too precise. Something is off, but I can't quite name it.

I shift uneasily, trying to brush off the feeling—until my gaze snags on the man sitting at the next table.

Tall. Broad-shouldered. The kind of man whose presence shifts the air in a room. Makes it hard to breathe.

His charcoal suit fits like it was made for him, crisp and sleek in a way that screams control—not flash. But it's the contrast that hits me. The tattoos just visible at his collar, curling over deeply tanned skin. Black hair slicked back with deliberate precision, streaked with silver at the temples. A five o'clock shadow frames his jaw, more salt than pepper. And when he moves—because I swear, he barely moves—he does it like everything he does is calculated. Efficient. Like a man trained to kill and trained not to show it.

Even from here, I can smell something faint. Not cologne exactly—cleaner than that. Soap, citrus, something earthy. A scent that's sharp and absolutely not forgettable.

But it's his eyes that make my breath hitch—dark, piercing, too damn observant.

He's not staring outright, but I keep catching him glancing at our table, his gaze flicking between Maria and me.

Something in my gut clenches.

"Maria," I whisper, leaning in. "Don't look, but the guy at the next table keeps staring at us."

Maria immediately turns to look.

"No, don't—!" I hiss, but it's too late.

She turns back, grinning. "Oh, that's Marco. He's with me."

"Marco?"

"My bodyguard," she says casually, like it's the most normal thing in the world for a twenty-two-year-old to have a bodyguard.

"Your bodyguard?"

Maria waves a hand dismissively. "My dad's a little overprotective."

Before I can ask what "a little overprotective" means, the kitchen doors bang open.

Three men storm into the dining room, faces obscured by ski masks.

"Everyone stay where you are!" the man in front barks, brandishing a gun.

The restaurant erupts into chaos.

And the man with the gun strides straight toward us.

"You," he says, pointing at Maria. "Let's go."

He grabs her arm, yanking her to her feet.

The second his hand closes on her, I don't know why but I'm furious. Something inside me snaps. I don't think. I react.

My purse—a massive thing stuffed with hardcovers, notebooks, and my laptop—swings up in a wide arc, colliding with the underside of Ski Mask No. 1's chin. His head snaps back. His grip on Maria loosens. The gun slips from his hand, clattering to the floor.

"Let her go!" I shout, my voice sharp and furious. *Oh my God. Who am I right now?*

Ski Mask No. 1 staggers. And because I can't help myself, I kick him. Hard. Right in the crotch.

He crumples with a pained groan.

Before I can even process what I've just done, Marco is next to me.

He moves with terrifying speed. No hesitation, no wasted motion. He pulls a gun from beneath his jacket and slams the butt of it into Ski Mask No. 2's face. The man goes down hard.

Ski Mask No. 3 bolts for the front door.

Marco's voice is calm, controlled. "Chuck. Front door. Coming to you."

"Copy that." I hear the reply.

I stand frozen, heart hammering, as the chaos settles. Two men groan on the floor, their weapons discarded.

A guy—who I'd assumed was the restaurant manager—is now standing over them, gun drawn, expression unreadable.

The third ski mask? Gone. Apparently taken care of by someone named Chuck.

Marco barely spares the men on the floor a glance. "Elias," he says sharply, "you're in charge of cleaning up this mess."

Elias—who is definitely not the restaurant manager—gives a single nod, calm and cool.

Marco then turns to Maria, his gaze hard. "Are you okay?"

Maria nods, pale but unharmed.

Then his dark eyes shift to me. "And you, Miss Zadegan? Are you okay?"

"I'm... fine?" I stammer, my voice shaky. My wrist throbs, and my pulse still roars in my ears. But Marco's steady voice, his controlled movements, the way he'd reacted without a second of hesitation—it all makes me feel... safer than I want to admit.

I'll process the fact that he knows my name later.

"Fine?" Maria says, gripping my arm. "You're not fine, Ami. You're coming home with me."

"What? No. I—"

"I'm not asking," Maria interrupts, her voice firm. "You saved me, and now it's my job to make sure you're safe. I'm not letting you go back to your hotel alone."

"I'll be fine," I protest. But my voice is breathy now, edging on panic.

Maria's grip on my arm tightens. "Please. We don't know who those guys were or what they wanted. I need you to trust me. My family can protect you better than anyone else. Just until we figure this out."

I hesitate, my chest heaving as the adrenaline begins to wear off. My gaze darts to Marco, who is speaking into his phone, but his eyes are locked on mine.

I exhale sharply, my shoulders slumping. "Fine," I mutter. "But I hope someone can explain what the hell just happened."

Maria smiles, relieved, as she puts an arm around me and begins guiding me toward the front door.

For some reason, I keep looking back at Marco who follows us, silent and formidable, his movements calculated and controlled, quiet authority in every step.

And I notice that his dark eyes are still on me.

4

MARCO

THE STEADY HUM of the Suburban's engine fills the cabin, but the silence is anything but calm. It's tight, charged, stretched so taut it feels like one wrong move might snap it in two. Adrenaline from the ambush still thrums under my skin, sharp and insistent. My grip on the armrest is firm, my knuckles brushing the edge of my holster.

From the driver's seat, Chuck breaks the tension. "Where do you even buy ski masks in San Antonio? I mean, it's not like we're in Aspen."

I shoot him a look sharp enough to carve into steel. "You think this is funny?"

The grin vanishes immediately. "No, boss," he mutters, sitting straighter, like a school kid caught passing notes in class.

Good.

I let the silence settle over us again, but Chuck's presence is impossible to ignore. He's big. Blonde. Built like a goddamn Viking in a designer suit. All muscle, all brute force when needed, but somehow always in a good mood.

He's been this way since the day I met him, back in the Marines, when he was Charles Edward Hamilton, III, a cocky-as-hell Golden Gloves boxer from Dallas. We trained together, fought underground matches together, ran missions that should've gotten us both killed more than once. I was his team leader back then. He never questioned an order. Still doesn't.

When I left the Marines, he followed. Said civilian life would be boring without me. I warned him working for the Sandovals would be different. Definitely not boring. Didn't scare him off.

Chuck is charming and absolutely convinced he's hilarious. The jury's still out on that.

Elias is still at the restaurant, handling the fallout. He's meticulous, dependable, and charming in his own way. By now, the scene will be contained. The staff and diners will be... encouraged to forget what they saw. And the three masked idiots? Restrained. Waiting to be transported to the warehouse.

"No cops," I told Elias before leaving. "Pay whatever needs paying. Make sure those three are ready to talk when I get there."

But the longer we drive, the heavier my decisions feel. The night had gone to hell in record time, and irritation simmers beneath the calm I force myself to project.

Raul Sandoval will want answers the moment we arrive at the compound. Maria is safe but Raul will want assurance that the situation is under control. And an explanation as to why a civilian—a romance novelist, of all things—is now tangled in his family's business.

I flick my eyes to the visor mirror, catching a glimpse of the backseat. Maria is on the phone with her father, her voice bright and unbothered, as if she wasn't just nearly kidnapped.

But Ami Zadegan? She's a different story.

She sits stiffly, her wide hazel eyes darting between the window and each of us, every muscle locked tight, like she's waiting for the next blow to land. Her body radiates tension. And for some reason, I can't stop watching her.

She's cradling her wrist against her chest. She must have hurt herself when she took that wild swing.

Who the hell takes on a guy with a gun and a hundred pounds on them—with a purse?

She could've gotten herself killed. Christ, she should've. And I can't decide if that pisses me off or scares me.

She's stupid. Reckless. And hot as hell.

I shove that thought aside. That kind of reckless bravery is bad. It gets people killed. She doesn't belong here.

And I don't have time to be impressed—or distracted.

Maria ends her call with a cheerful, "I love you, Papa," and turns to me. "The doctor will meet us at the house to check Ami's wrist," she announces matter-of-factly.

"I'm fine," Ami says immediately, holding up her hand like she's demonstrating a magic trick. "See? No big deal. I don't need—" Her voice cracks, just a little. She sounds like she's trying hard to sound casual.

"Ami." Maria's tone leaves no room for argument. "Your wrist might be worse than you think. And you're staying the night. For both our sakes."

"I'm not staying the night," Ami snaps. But her voice wavers. She's starting to realize just how dangerous what happened in the restaurant was. But anger's easier right now. "I don't even know what's going on, and I'm not about to just—"

I twist slightly in my seat, cutting her off with a calm, measured tone. "She's right. You're hurt, and Mr. Sandoval will want to meet you. You're coming to the compound. Non-negotiable."

Her eyes widen. For a second, she just blinks, like she's trying to process the fact that I just gave her an order. I see the confusion first, her gaze flicking between Maria and me, like she's waiting for someone to tell her this is a joke.

The comes the defiance. Her shoulders square, her chin lifts, and the fire in those hazel eyes flares hot and bright.

Yeah. I don't think Ami Zadegan lets herself get ordered around too often.

Her glare hits me like a slap. "Non-negotiable? Non-negotiable? Are you kidding me? You don't get to tell me what to do! You're not my... my... boss!"

A smirk tugs at the corner of my mouth before I can stop it. "Good thing I'm not your boss. You seem terrible at following orders."

Her cheeks flush pink, and she leans forward, jabbing a finger in my direction. "Next time someone tries to kidnap my *friend,* I'll be sure to check in with her *giant bodyguard* for instructions!"

Chuck clears his throat from the driver's seat, his voice carefully neutral. "ETA five minutes."

"Good," I say.

The tension in the air thickens, but I let it hang, leaning back against the seat. I shouldn't enjoy needling her so much, but the way she pushes back—unrelenting, unafraid—is impossible to ignore.

Most people in my world know better than to challenge me. Ami Zadegan doesn't.

And maybe it's not bravery. Maybe she's learned to fight back to survive.

She glares at me, those sharp hazel eyes practically daring me to say something else.

I turn my attention back to the road. For now, this woman is part of the equation. I just need to make sure she's not the variable that gets us all killed.

5

AMI

My throat feels tight, like there's not enough air in the car, but I keep it together.

Breathe in. Breathe out. It's fine. You're fine.

I cradle my throbbing wrist against my chest, fingers clasped tightly together, but it doesn't stop the shaking. It's not the dramatic kind—the kind you see in movies where someone gasps and collapses into a heap. No, this is smaller, more humiliating. A constant, irritating tremor I can't seem to control.

Honestly, I expected the shaking to stop by now. I thought once the adrenaline wore off, I'd feel better, not worse. But it's like it's settled in instead, buzzing under my skin, making everything feel too fast, too bright, too much.

I press my back into the seat and fix my gaze on the window, watching the streets of downtown San Antonio blur into streaks of neon and shadow. Bars spill light onto the sidewalks, their signs glowing in bold reds, blues, and greens. Clusters of people wander in and out of restaurants, laughing, carefree. A group of women in matching t-shirts stumbles past, margaritas in hand, screaming the chorus of a song I can't quite place.

Normally, the noisy, chaotic energy of the city would comfort me. But then the neon fades.

The sidewalks give way to concrete overpasses and looping on-ramps, the sprawl of downtown funneled into the blur of headlights and taillights. The Suburban merges onto the highway, the towering skyline shrinking in the rearview mirror.

The further we go, the more the bright storefronts and packed parking lots turn into scattered strip malls and half-empty gas stations, their buzzing fluorescents casting long, artificial shadows.

And then even that's gone.

The highway narrows. Exits become fewer, the occasional roadside diner or distant ranch entrance the only signs of life. The city melts into something darker, quieter, emptier. Streetlights are rare now, the glow of fast-food chains replaced by rolling hills, thick clusters of trees, and long stretches of nothing.

The landscape outside the window looks wild, untamed—the kind of place you don't wander into without knowing exactly where you're going. This is just how Texas is—sprawling cities dropped into the middle of nowhere, surrounded by miles of nothing.

I swallow hard, my pulse quickening. *Where the hell are they taking me?*

Maria looks utterly unbothered.

She sits beside me in the backseat, casually scrolling on her phone as if she didn't just survive an attempted kidnapping by armed men in ski masks.

She's still on the phone with her father—her Papa, apparently—but her tone is breezy, almost bored. Like she's giving a recap of a slightly inconvenient night out instead of a near-death experience. From what I can make out, she's telling him what happened, who she's bringing home, and what to expect.

My fingers tighten around my wrist. *Who she's bringing home?*

Something cold slides down my spine. She's talking about me.

And then there's Marco.

Marco the bodyguard. Marco with the unreadable stare and ironclad composure. Marco who had taken over the night with the kind of calm that made it clear this wasn't his first time handling chaos. He didn't even blink. Just handled it. Like everything that happened was a typical night out.

Maybe it was for him.

He's in the front seat, all broad shoulders and tense jawline, speaking into the mic attached to his ear. His voice is steady, deep, maddeningly unhurried. I don't want to be obvious about eavesdropping, but certain phrases stick.

"No cops."

"Take them to the warehouse."

I freeze. That is, without a doubt, the most crime-syndicate-y thing I've ever heard in my life.

A chill prickles at the back of my neck. Maria Sandoval, contest winner... Maria Sandoval, girl who fangirled over my books... Maria Sandoval, criminal underworld heiress?

No. No way. That's insane.

But my brain won't stop spiraling.

Maria had an armed bodyguard sitting in a restaurant with her tonight like it was totally normal. Maria had almost been kidnapped, and instead of panicking, she'd just rolled her eyes and called her father. Maria was way too casual about whatever the hell "the warehouse" was.

I shift in my seat, pressing myself further against the door like that's going to help. *What the hell have I gotten myself into?*

I'm a 30-year-old romance novelist, for God's sake—not some action hero. I should be back in my hotel room, drunk-texting my best friend Natalie about how I nearly died tonight. Instead, I'm here.

In a black Suburban.

With a cartel princess and her tattooed bodyguards.

Headed to a compound where I've just been told my presence is "non-negotiable."

Because I swung my purse at a guy in a ski mask.

Every so often, my gaze flicks up to the visor mirror, where I catch glimpses of Marco's face. Half-shadowed, sharp features unreadable. But his dark eyes? Impossible to miss. They scan the road. The mirror. The road. The mirror.

And every time I look, it feels like those eyes land on me.

My heart kicks faster. *What is this guy's problem?*

I try to retrace the night, to make sense of how things spiraled so fast.

Dinner with Maria had been normal. Fun, even. We'd talked about romance novels, tennis smut, and our mutual love of ridiculous tropes over margaritas like old friends. For the first time in months, I'd felt comfortable.

And then—

A gun.

Ski masks.

Maria being grabbed. That man's hand clamping down on her arm like she wasn't important—just a problem to be handled.

The heat and rush of adrenaline flooding my veins.

I hadn't thought. I'd just acted.

And now?

Now I was here. Shaking like a leaf. Spiraling, while Maria scrolled Instagram.

Chuck's voice breaks the silence. "ETA five minutes." His tone is neutral, like he's reporting on the traffic.

"Good," Marco replies, clipped, unreadable.

I glance at Maria. Completely unfazed.

Meanwhile, I'm losing my goddamn mind.

I glance at Marco's reflection in the mirror again. This time, his eyes flick up. Our eyes lock.

My stomach flips. Caught.

"Stop staring," I mutter under my breath, hoping the hum of the engine drowns it out.

No such luck.

"I'm not the one staring, Miss Zadegan."

His deep voice cuts through the quiet, sharp and precise.

Heat rushes to my cheeks.

"Excuse me?"

He doesn't turn around. Doesn't look at me again. Just shifts his attention back to the road, dismissing me completely.

"Just saying what I see."

I grit my teeth. Smug bastard.

The Suburban passes through a pair of towering gates, sliding open like something out of a high-security thriller.

A long, winding driveway stretches ahead, flanked by massive oak trees looming like silent sentinels. The city is gone. Civilization? A distant memory.

Scattered lights dot the landscape ahead, too few, too far apart to be even remotely comforting.

I don't know where I am. I don't know who these people really are.

And the worst part? The sinking feeling that I'm completely alone—that if things go bad, no one's coming.

For the first time tonight, real fear settles in.

6

AMI

THE BLACK SUBURBAN rolls to a smooth stop. I lean closer to the window, trying to process what I'm seeing.

This isn't just a house. It isn't even a mansion. No, the Sandoval estate is a fortress—an absurdly elegant, Italian villa-inspired fortress.

A massive stone fountain dominates the center of the circular driveway, its centerpiece an imposing statue of some mythological figure I absolutely cannot name but assume is important. Behind it, the mansion sprawls wide and unbothered, all pale limestone, wrought iron, and money.

Balconies jut from the facade in precise intervals, their intricate railings so ornate they probably cost more than my annual income. Arched windows gleam under soft golden lighting, casting an intentional warmth over something that otherwise looks completely impenetrable.

Wide terracotta steps lead up to a pair of carved wooden doors so massive they could belong to a medieval castle. Those doors could withstand a battering ram.

What the hell am I doing here?

The Suburban idles softly, the engine's hum filling the silence. Chuck twists in his seat with a grin.

"End of the line, folks."

Marco is out first, moving with a maddening mix of grace and precision. Even now, his sharp gaze sweeps the property, scanning for threats like he expects a sniper to pop out from behind the fountain.

Maria climbs out next, effortlessly poised, and I follow. Or try to. My wrist throbs as I fumble with the door, biting back a wince.

The last thing I want is to look weak in front of these people. But before I can get my bearings, Marco is there, holding out a hand.

"This way," he says, clipped and impatient.

I freeze for a moment, caught off guard. His dark eyes meet mine, unreadable, but something about his expression leaves no room for argument.

Reluctantly, I give him my good hand, trying not to notice how warm and solid his grip is. He helps me out with brisk efficiency, stepping back the second my feet hit the ground. That brief contact sends a weird prickle through me.

Maria loops her arm through mine as we start up the wide staircase.

"Wait until you see the inside," she says, practically buzzing. "It's even better."

I glance around the driveway, picking up details I'd missed before. Security cameras discreetly perched on wrought-iron railings. Shadows near the tree line—men stationed at strategic points, rifles slung casually across their backs.

This isn't just a home. It's a compound.

As if on cue, the massive double doors swing open, spilling warm light onto the stone steps. A man in a suit stands there, gesturing for us to enter. *Is that what a butler looks like?*

Inside, the opulence is staggering.

Polished marble floors gleam under the soft glow of a wrought-iron chandelier the size of a small car. An enormous oil painting of the Texas Hill Country dominates one wall, so life-like I half expect to smell wildflowers.

Maria's heels click on the marble as she darts ahead.

"Papa!" she calls, her voice ringing through the cavernous space.

A man steps into view from a side hallway, a crystal glass of dark amber liquid in his hand.

I stop breathing.

This has to be Raul Sandoval.

The Raul Sandoval.

His name flashes in my brain like a neon sign, dredged up from every half-whispered news article and crime blog I've ever read.

Alleged head of a sprawling criminal empire. Suspected links to cartel operations stretching across Texas and into Mexico.

Untouchable. Never convicted. Immensely powerful.

The details are always vague, wrapped in rumor and careful omissions. No one ever says exactly what he does—only that he owns San Antonio, and much of Texas, in ways no politician ever could.

And now, he's standing ten feet away from me, watching.

My stomach clenches instinctively.

He isn't imposing in the way Marco is. Marco's presence is all coiled tension, an unsheathed knife waiting for an excuse to be used.

Raul Sandoval? He doesn't need a weapon.

He is one.

His tailored gray suit fits perfectly, the fabric molding to his lean frame with precision. A gold tie gleams against the crisp white of his shirt, and gold cufflinks flash at his wrists. His tan face is clean-shaven, his silver hair thick and slicked back with effortless authority.

But it isn't his appearance that commands attention.

It's the way he carries himself. Utterly still, completely in control, like the world bends to his patience.

Maria breezes over to him, wrapping him in a brief hug.

"Papa," she says, soft with affection.

Raul returns the hug, but his eyes stay on me. When he finally speaks, his voice is polite, but edged with something unreadable.

"Miss Zadegan." His gaze pins me to the spot. "My daughter tells me you were hurt while defending her tonight. Please accept my thanks."

I stare at him, my brain stuck in a loop of:

Sandoval... cartel boss... crime family.

The words flicker behind my eyes, loud and impossible to ignore.

For one horrifying second, I think I might actually say them out loud.

Instead, I force a shaky response past the lump in my throat. "Uh... yes. Defending her. Exactly."

What am I supposed to say? *It was nothing? Just swung my laptop bag at a guy with a gun like an idiot?*

I clear my throat. "But I'm fine."

Raul's expression doesn't change.

"Let's let the doctor be the judge of that."

Then his focus shifts to Marco, his voice sharpening.

"Dr. Rodriguez is waiting in the sitting room. Take them to him first. Then go to the warehouse and handle the matter. We'll speak when you've finished."

"Yes, sir," Marco answers. Tight, clipped. A professional soldier.

Raul turns and strides down the hall, footsteps echoing, before pausing.

"You will, of course, stay the night with us, Miss Zadegan," he calls over his shoulder, not even turning to look. "Maria insists, and so do I."

Before I can protest, he's gone.

Maria hooks her arm through mine again, warm and steady.

"Come on," she says brightly. "Let's get your wrist checked."

We enter a sitting room that is no less intimidating than the foyer. Dark wood paneling covers the walls, while plush gold velvet couches and leather armchairs are arranged around a massive stone fireplace. A fire crackles in the hearth despite the August heat. A fire. In August. In San Antonio. Maybe it's a crime lord thing.

A Persian rug sprawls beneath the furniture, its shimmering shades of gold and gray adding to the room's subdued opulence. Above it all hangs another wrought-iron chandelier, casting a warm glow over the space.

Maria guides me to one of the couches, where a man in his sixties—Dr. Rodriguez, I assume—is already rising to greet us.

"Miss Sandoval, Mr. Cedillo," he says, clasping hands with Maria before turning to me.

"Miss Zadegan," he says, gesturing for me to sit. "It is a pleasure to meet you despite the circumstances." His tone is brisk but polite, like he already knows everything about me and isn't particularly impressed.

"I really don't think this is necessary," I start, but Maria silences me with a look.

"Humor us," she says firmly, her tone leaving no room for argument.

Sighing, I sink onto the plush couch and hold out my wrist

for the doctor to examine. He carefully manipulates it, asking a series of questions about the incident. How I'd swung the bag. How much weight had been inside. Whether I'd felt anything snap.

"It seems to just be a strain," he says finally, securing one of those snug, black braces around my wrist that screams *middle-aged desk worker* with practiced efficiency. "You might have a bit of bruising tomorrow, but giving it a little support will help. Rest it, and you'll be fine. I'll leave something to help with the pain and something else to help you sleep tonight."

"There, see?" I say, glancing at Maria. "Not a big deal."

"I'll follow up in a few days," Dr. Rodriguez adds, gathering his bag.

"Oh, I won't be here—" I start to protest, but Maria cuts me off again.

"Thank you, Dr. Rodriguez," she says smoothly. Then she turns to Marco. "Can you see the doctor out? I want to take Ami to her room."

Marco nods without a word, leading the doctor from the room. I watch him go, the way he moves like he owns the space around him. No shouting. No barking orders. Just... steady. And for some ridiculous reason, it's not intimidating. It's weirdly comforting.

"You're staying in one of our guest rooms," Maria announces, breaking into my thoughts. "Right near me."

"Maria, really, this isn't necessary," I say, my voice slightly edged with frustration.

"It is," she replies simply. "Your things are already being brought over from the hotel."

I open my mouth to argue, but the serene confidence in her tone makes it clear there's no point. I'm starting to realize that fighting Maria is like trying to swim against a tidal wave—pointless and exhausting. I'm too tired. And somewhere nearby,

Marco is probably lurking like a tattooed shadow, waiting to pounce on my next protest.

Sighing, I nod. "Fine."

Maria smiles, looping her arm through mine again. "Good. Come on. I'll show you to your room."

7

MARCO

THE DRIVE IS QUIET.

Chuck drums his fingers on the steering wheel, his usual cocky grin subdued. We drove south, back through town, then passing through a stretch of low-slung warehouses and run-down businesses—auto body shops, storage units, shipping depots. But now, even those fade out. The last traces of San Antonio civilization disappear, replaced by empty stretches of road and low, rolling hills. The streetlights grow sparse, leaving only the Suburban's high beams cutting through the darkness.

I let the silence stretch, replaying the night in my head.

This was too sloppy. Too reckless. An attempted kidnapping of Maria was not on my radar. Who the hell were these guys? Hired guns? Some idiot crew trying to make a name for themselves?

One thing is certain—they weren't professionals.

No real exit strategy. No secondary team in place. Nothing but three men in ski masks, walking into the ambush they didn't even know was waiting for them.

Which means either they were stupid. Or they were desperate.

Chuck lets out a low whistle. "Three guys. Ski masks?" He shakes his head. "They were on a goddamn suicide mission."

I stare out the window. "Then someone sent them to die."

Chuck frowns but doesn't argue.

And that's the part I need to figure out.

Who sent them? And why?

Chuck pulls off the main road and onto an unmarked gravel path, the tires crunching over loose stone.

The warehouse looms ahead—a sprawling, fortified structure built for one purpose: moving weapons.

It's one of several storage facilities the Sandovals operate across Texas. This one is close enough to the city for convenience but isolated enough for what needs to happen inside.

Floodlights bathe the exterior in harsh white light. Armed guards patrol the perimeter, some stationed at the gates, others pacing near the loading docks. As we roll up, one of them waves us through without a word.

Inside, the space is vast. Tall industrial ceilings, steel shelving units stacked with crates of firearms, ammunition, explosives. The air smells like gun oil and metal. Overhead, flickering fluorescent lights hum softly, casting long shadows across the concrete floor.

At the center of it all, three men sit tied to chairs under the glow of a hanging lamp.

Elias stands nearby, calmly cleaning a knife, his movements slow, meticulous. Rafe leans against a crate, arms crossed, watching the prisoners with bored disinterest. Elias must have brought him in to help at the restaurant and with the transport of these guys. Good call.

Rafe doesn't talk much, but he doesn't need to. He's my cousin but he's also a former Marine Scout Sniper—trained to wait, watch, and end a threat with a single shot. The kind of guy who never blinks at a scene like this. I've known him my whole life. Lived with him and his mother at times. In high school, Rafe and I took up boxing, then no-rules brawling, fighting in San Antonio's underground circuit, in shitty backroom rings where the air stank of sweat, blood, and cigarette smoke.

He deployed around the same time I did. Different unit, different missions, same war. Iraq. Afghanistan. Before the Sandovals, we'd spent time breaking bones for money and handling problems the quiet way. Rafe's a soldier—quiet, efficient, trained to kill.

And Elias? Grew up in the foster system. Aged out onto the streets of San Antonio. A born con man, brutal with a knife. Tried to pickpocket me once. Got the shit beat out of him and then ended up working for me.

Rafe and Elias don't look like they have a whole lot in common, but when it comes to work, they speak the same language.

Elias doesn't look up as I approach. "Took you long enough."

I don't respond. My eyes flick over the scene, assessing.

The man on the left is trembling, barely holding it together, his pants wet with piss. The one on the right is passed out, face bloody, looks like his nose is broken. Rafe's work, no doubt. The one in the middle—the one Elias must have carved up—shudders with each breath. Blood is already pooling under his chair, spreading across the concrete.

Rafe grunts. "The guy who pissed himself? He cracked first. Told us the plan but no names. The guy in the middle was useless, so Elias made an example out of him."

The middle guy is covered in blood. He shifts slightly, letting out a hoarse, pained groan.

Elias is flicking a butterfly knife between his fingers. "Still alive. For now."

Chuck lets out a low chuckle. "I'm guessing the piss guy is our best bet."

The man flinches.

I take a slow step forward, letting the silence stretch. The weight of it does more damage than any fist.

The pissing-himself guy looks up, and when his eyes meet mine, he starts shaking harder.

Good.

I pull up a chair, straddling it backwards, elbows resting on the backrest. Calm. Controlled. I don't need to yell.

"You had one job." My voice is even, almost quiet. "Grab a girl. Make it clean." I tilt my head slightly. "Instead, you fucked up."

No one speaks.

I sigh, shifting my focus to the bleeding one in the middle. "You. Look at me."

He lifts his head, barely able to hold his gaze steady.

"Who sent you?"

No answer.

A beat passes before I nod at Chuck.

Chuck doesn't hesitate—gripping the man's collar and slamming a fist into his ribs.

The man lets out a strangled gasp. His head lolls forward again.

I turn back to the guy on the left. "Don't waste my time," I say, voice steady. "Who sent you?"

The piss guy has tears in his eyes when he blurts out, "It was the Calderóns!" His voice is raw with panic. "Diego Calderón! He—he put the job together. Paid us upfront."

My chest tightens. The Calderóns? I don't let my expression change.

Chuck glances at me. "You gotta be shitting me."

"Paid you for what?" I ask.

"To grab the girl," the guy stammers. "That's all we know. We —we weren't supposed to kill her. Just bring her back."

I lean forward slightly. "Back where?"

A flicker of hesitation. Chuck grabs the bleeding man by the hair, wrenches his head back. "Answer him."

"Del Rio!" The man gasps. "They—they were taking her to Del Rio."

Del Rio. Far west Texas. The middle of nowhere.

The Calderóns' home turf.

Rafe lets out a breath, shaking his head. "The Calderóns don't have the balls for this."

And he's right.

The Calderóns deal in drugs, human trafficking, forced prostitution. Raul Sandoval has strict rules about what his organization won't touch, and the Calderóns cross every line on that list.

But they're small-time. They don't have the manpower or the resources to pull something like this off. So why now?

I turn back to the piss guy, voice low. "Who else was involved? I want names."

"I—I don't know!" The man's breathing turns erratic. "They just told us where to go and who to grab! We were supposed to deliver her, get paid, and leave. That's all I know."

I study him for a moment. He's not lying. He's too scared to. Someone in the Calderóns is making a move.

I glance at Rafe. "What do you think?"

Rafe shrugs. "They don't know anything else."

I stand, brushing off my hands.

"Get rid of them."

The piss man starts to shake his head frantically, but two of the Sandoval soldiers step forward out of the warehouse shadows to assist.

Chuck lets out a low whistle. "You guys really fucked up tonight."

I don't wait to see what happens next. I already know.

As I walk toward the warehouse doors, my mind is already turning.

The Calderóns shouldn't have the resources for this.

So what changed? Who inside their ranks decided to take a shot at Raul Sandoval?

8

___

AMI

The "guest room" Maria leaves me in feels more like a luxury suite in a five-star resort than an actual bedroom.

I stand in the center of the space, slowly spinning in a circle, trying to process it all. The plush ivory carpet beneath my feet is so soft I have the bizarre urge to lie down and make carpet angels. The four-poster bed draped in silky white linens could belong to a European royal. And the ornate dresser, one that looks like it was hand-carved by an army of underpaid artisans, stands proudly against one wall.

My suitcase sits open on a luggage rack in the corner, along with my other bags and the now-infamous purse.

Everything about the room screams wealth. The kind of effortless, generational wealth that makes it all look understated but absurdly expensive.

I've already peeked into the en suite bathroom which is even more ridiculous. Marble counters, a rain shower big enough to host a dinner party, gold faucets, and a bathtub so oversized it could double as a small swimming pool.

Yet, despite all of it, the anxiety twisting in my chest doesn't budge.

Because as stunning as the guest room is, it's still a crime lord's guest room.

I exhale slowly, pressing my hands against my face, asking myself again—*What the hell am I doing here?*

Less than twenty-four hours ago, I was sitting in a fluorescent-lit conference room, half-listening to an editor drone on about the forced proximity trope and visualizing the mechanics of sex scenes. Now? I was in the mansion of a man powerful enough to make his enemies literally disappear.

I flop onto the bed, kicking off my shoes and letting my braced wrist rest on my stomach. The silky bedding is cool against my back, but nothing can soothe the chaos spinning in my head.

I haven't just stumbled into Maria Sandoval's life. I've cannonballed into it.

I'm here. In her father's home. Raul Sandoval's home.

The name alone carries weight. Power. Fear. Stories whispered in dark corners.

I've seen his name before—news articles, speculative blog posts, reports that never quite have enough proof to pin anything on him. A ghost in the legal system, always just out of reach. He's the kind of man people know better than to cross.

And now I'm under his roof.

A fresh wave of unease rolls over me, curling around my ribs like a vice.

My phone buzzes beside me, and I groan, already knowing who it is. I've been ignoring my phone all night, but Natalie Morris is not the kind of woman you ignore without consequences.

I grab it with my good hand and swipe to answer.

"Ami Zadegan, what the actual hell is going on?"

Natalie's voice explodes through the line, sharp and brimming with sass and concern.

Natalie Morris isn't just my best friend. She's the reason I have a career. With her long honey blonde hair, an arctic stare, and six-foot tall runway model energy, she looks like she could run a fashion empire—or a covert operation.

The owner and founder of Crimson Quill Press, Natalie has built her own publishing empire by taking risks on bold, fresh voices, especially authors who mainstream publishers have ignored. Her instincts are razor-sharp, her business acumen legendary. She took my *Tennis Fixation* series from a few quirky indie romance novels to a bestselling powerhouse, and somehow, in between launching careers and shaking up the industry, she finds time to be my personal hype woman.

Right now, she sounds one second away from driving to San Antonio herself.

"I've been texting and calling you all night, and you didn't respond! Do you have any idea how many terrifying scenarios I've imagined?"

I sigh. "Hi, Natalie. Nice to hear from you too."

"Don't 'nice to hear from you' me! Are you okay? Did you fall into the Riverwalk? Are you kidnapped?"

"Funny you should mention that last part."

A pause. Then Natalie's voice shoots up an octave. "Excuse me?"

I sigh, leaning back against the headboard. "It wasn't me they were after. It was Maria."

"And just who the hell is Maria?" she demands.

"The contest winner," I explain. "Remember? Maria Sandoval, my superfan who lives for the *Tennis Fixation* series? Well, plot twist: she's also Maria Sandoval, as in Raul Sandoval's daughter. You know, San Antonio's resident crime kingpin."

"Wait, wait, wait." Natalie's tone sharpens with disbelief. "She actually was *that* Maria Sandoval? So you had dinner with a mafia boss's daughter, who happens to be one of your biggest fans, and during that dinner, someone tried to kidnap you? Ami. What the actual hell?"

"Well, I'm pretty sure they were trying to kidnap her. I just... happened to be there."

"Oh my freaking God, Ami! Are you okay?"

"Mostly." I wiggle my braced wrist. "I strained my wrist taking one of the bad guys down with my purse. I had a couple of books in there. And my laptop. God, I hope I didn't break it."

There's a long pause before Natalie bursts out laughing, the sound equal parts disbelief and admiration. "You're telling me that you, Ami 'I'm too weak to carry more than two books' Zadegan, took down a kidnapper? With a *purse*?"

"An armed kidnapper," I correct, smirking despite myself. "And I also kicked him in the general groin area. Really hard. Like, 'he might not have kids' hard. So, how about that?"

"Girl." Natalie's voice is breathless with laughter. "I've always said you were a badass, but this is next-level."

"I don't know what happened," I admit, chuckling softly. "One second, I was connecting with Maria—who, by the way, is incredible—and the next, these ski-mask-wearing assholes showed up and ruined our dream dinner."

"Wow. Just wow." Natalie exhales, clearly trying to process the absurdity. "Okay, so where are you now? At the police station? Back at the hotel?"

I hesitate, my gaze sweeping across the ridiculously opulent room once again. "Not... exactly."

"Ami..." Natalie's voice sharpens. "Where the hell are you?"

"Well..." I draw the word out, my voice tentative. "I'm at the Sandoval mansion."

Natalie screams, her reaction so loud I have to pull the phone away from my ear. "You're telling me you're *currently staying* in the home of one of the most powerful crime families in the country?!"

"Trust me, this wasn't my idea. But Maria insisted, and her dad..." I hesitate, searching for the right words to describe Raul Sandoval. "Let's just say he doesn't seem like the kind of man you say no to."

Natalie's tone sharpens. "Ami. You're staying with the Sandovals. Do you hear yourself? This is a terrible idea."

"I know," I admit, exhaling. "Believe me, I know. But it's just for one night, two at most. I'll be out of here before anything bad can happen."

There's a pause, then Natalie sighs. "This is seriously sketchy. I hate it."

"Yeah, me too."

Another beat of silence. Then, her voice drops into something almost conspiratorial. "Okay, I'm still freaking out, but I need to know—how hot is this guy? Please tell me he's a silver fox crime lord."

"Oh my God, no! He's Maria's *dad*, Natalie."

"That doesn't answer my question," she says, her voice practically dripping with mischief.

I groan. "You are impossible."

As I try to steer the conversation away from Raul Sandoval's hypothetical hotness, my gaze falls on my suitcase again, and a horrifying realization hits me like a freight train. I freeze. "Oh my God."

"What?" Natalie asks, suddenly on high alert. "What's wrong?"

"They brought all my stuff here. From the hotel."

"Of course they did," Natalie says, clearly unimpressed. "And?"

"And..." I lower my voice to a horrified whisper. "Do you think they packed my vibrator?"

There is a moment of silence on her end, followed by a loud cackle. "Ami, you *did not* just say that."

"I'm serious! It was on the nightstand in its little bag!" I sit up, panic creeping into my voice. "Someone might've opened the bag and *touched* it. Oh my God, I'll have to sterilize it. How do you even sterilize a vibrator?"

Natalie dissolves into laughter, gasping for air between her words. "This—this is amazing. Ami, you've officially landed yourself in the middle of a dark crime romance novel. You realize that, right?"

I groan, flopping back onto the bed and covering my face with my free hand. "I just wanted to meet Maria, talk about books, and have some good Mexican food. I didn't sign up for... this."

"Correction," Natalie says, recovering from her laughter. "You've signed up for the best research opportunity of your life. You told me you were ready to move on from tennis books. No more sports romances. You even said you were thinking about trying a dark crime romance. Well, guess what? You're living one. You better research your heart out."

I groan. "Ugh. No. Maybe. I don't know." I hesitate, guilt creeping into my voice. "There's... more. There's this guy..."

"Yes!" Natalie practically shouts. "Please tell me there's a guy. Let me guess. He's a big, broody bodyguard with tattoos and a bossy attitude?"

"That's... disturbingly accurate."

"Of course he's obnoxious," Natalie says, her amusement unmistakable. "A real take-charge kind of guy. And I bet you already think he's hot."

"I do not!" The denial shoots out of me too quickly, too loudly, and even I wince. "Jesus, calm down," I mutter under my breath.

Natalie bursts into laughter again. "Ami, you sound way too adamant. And that's how I know you're into him."

"I'm not adamant," I say, flustered. "This is exactly why I didn't want to give you all the details."

"You're so adamant," she teases, her voice sing-song. "Ami Zadegan has the hots for the broody, tattooed bodyguard."

I huff. "Even if he is hot—and I'm not saying he is—it doesn't matter. You should see him. He's the hero who sweeps the damsel off her feet and saves the day. I'm the quirky side character who spills coffee on the hero's shoes and apologizes for existing."

Natalie's voice softens, the teasing slipping away.

"Don't do that to yourself, Ami. I know as well as anyone that you've been hurt, but you can't keep beating yourself up for that. You've got to give someone a chance."

I close my eyes, her words hitting a sore spot I don't like to acknowledge. "Yeah, well, for now, it's easier to avoid men altogether," I mutter.

"I know that Chad was a manipulative, stupid shit," Natalie says, her voice sharpening with anger. "You know I never liked him from the moment I met him. And guess what? I was right."

Her words bring a flood of unwelcome memories. Chad, my ex, with his smug superiority and those carefully veiled jabs at my self-worth. At first, he'd seemed charming and intellectual—a "serious writer" who threw around terms like *gravitas* and *zeitgeist*. But his charm had curdled quickly into condescension. And worse.

I can still hear his voice in my head, dripping with derision. *"You're just playing dress-up as a writer, Ami. All that fluffy romance drivel? It's not real literature."* He'd skim my pages like they were beneath him. *"I wonder if you even have the depth for anything serious."*

The worst part? A tiny, insidious part of me still wonders if he was right.

"I know, Natalie," I say quietly. "But sometimes I think...

what if I really don't have what it takes? What if I'm just an impostor?"

"Ami," Natalie says firmly, her tone no-nonsense. "Do not do this to yourself. You're one of the smartest, most talented writers I know. And your readers? They love your work because it's good. And because it matters to them. And to me."

I stare up at the ceiling, the words sitting heavy. "You know the worst part?" I whisper. "It's not just that Chad was a liar. Or that he... hurt me. It's that I let all of that happen because I wanted so badly to believe he loved me... that we were building something together."

My throat tightens, the words scraping out. "I gave him my manuscript, Natalie. The one I poured everything into. And then I stood there and watched him tear it apart, critique it, and make it into a joke."

I suck in a shaky breath. "And the worst part? When we finally blew up, I still thought maybe it was *my* fault. Like, maybe I really didn't deserve him. Maybe he was right and I was some kind of impostor pretending to be an author."

Silence hums on the line until Natalie's voice drops, low and lethal. "He gaslit the hell out of you, Ami. He made you doubt your own talent, your own memory. You didn't deserve any of that."

I close my eyes, swallowing hard. "I don't know if I trust myself anymore, Nat. Not with men. Not with... anything. Sometimes I feel like I don't know anything about romance or love," I say softly, my voice cracking just a little. "I'm supposedly a romance writer and I don't even know what good sex is, Natalie. I told you. Chad and I weren't exactly... exciting in bed."

Natalie snorts. "Of course you weren't. He was a self-absorbed narcissist. You could've had fireworks going off and sucked his dick in time to the Star-Spangled Banner, and he still wouldn't have noticed."

I laugh despite myself. "Yeah, it definitely wasn't fireworks with him."

"Exactly," Natalie says, her tone warm now. "So stop letting that idiot live rent-free in your head. He didn't appreciate you then, and he sure as hell doesn't deserve to be part of this conversation now."

I take a deep breath, forcing myself to let go of the heavy weight Chad's voice always carries in my head. "You're right. He's not worth it."

"Damn straight he's not. And for the record? You're amazing. Don't let one crappy guy make you doubt that."

I stare up at the intricate molding on the ceiling, trying to hold onto her words. Natalie is right. Chad doesn't deserve to occupy any part of my mind.

"Thanks, Natalie," I say softly. "I'm working on it."

"You better be," she say, her voice lightening again.

"Goodnight, Natalie."

"Goodnight, badass purse ninja. Stay safe."

I hang up and let her encouragement settle around me. But as I burrow under the covers, Chad's words still linger, clinging to the corners of my mind like a stubborn shadow.

What if it's not just writing I can't trust myself with anymore? What if it's everything?

9

MARCO

RAUL SANDOVAL SITS behind his massive oak desk in his study. The room is a testament to its owner—imposing, calculated, and meticulously curated. Floor-to-ceiling bookshelves filled with leather-bound volumes, more decorative than read. A framed oil painting of cattle on a Texas range hangs above a stone fireplace, its pastoral serenity at odds with the tension humming in the air.

Despite the fact that it's almost 3 a.m., Raul is impeccably dressed. His suit is pressed to perfection, his tie neatly knotted. A crystal glass of tequila rests in his hand, the amber liquid catching the light as he swirls it with lazy precision. To anyone else, he might seem to be a well-to-do businessman enjoying his drink. But I know better. Raul Sandoval's ease is as calculated as his empire.

I stand across from him, my back straight, hands clasped behind me in the stance that was drilled into me during my years in the military. I'm exhausted but, with Raul, I never let my guard down.

Raul doesn't look up right away. He lets the silence do its

work. I've seen him use it on men who don't realize they're already dead. But I've known him too long to be baited.

Finally, he lifts his gaze, his eyes dark and sharp. "So tell me what happened this evening."

"The men who attempted to kidnap Maria were interrogated. We've learned the Calderóns hired them," I say, my voice steady. "I believe they're making moves. They're sloppy. But dangerous. My guess is that they're trying to send a message, hoping to rattle us."

Raul leans back in his chair, his eyes fixed on me. "And what message shall we send in return?"

That's Raul. Straight to the point. No wasted words. No room for hesitation.

I inhale deliberately, keeping my tone even. "I've already taken steps. Reinforcements from Austin and Houston have been called in. Chuck is coordinating their arrival tomorrow to bolster the compound and cover our other properties in San Antonio."

Raul leans back in his chair, fingers tapping against his glass. He doesn't nod. Doesn't offer approval. Just watches me, weighing my words like a jeweler inspecting a cut diamond.

"The Calderón men were low-level grunts, barely worth the time it took to interrogate them," I continue. "Their orders came directly from Diego Calderón, Eduardo's nephew. I believe he's trying to build a name for himself. Maybe seize leadership from Eduardo."

Raul exhales through his nose, something between a sigh and a laugh. "A boy trying to be a man."

"A boy who is a problem," I reply. "Kidnapping Maria was supposed to either force your hand or humiliate you. Either way, it's a power play."

Raul's lips curve faintly. Not quite a smile. More like the

baring of teeth. "And yet, you don't sound convinced. You think there's something more."

I hesitate, choosing my words carefully. "The Calderóns are small-time, reckless. This move is too big for them. It's desperation on a scale that doesn't track. Kidnapping Maria? Trying to muscle into San Antonio? They don't have the resources to pull this off. Not on their own."

Raul's gaze sharpens. "Then who's bankrolling them?"

"That's what I'm trying to figure out," I admit, my jaw tightening. "The men we captured were scared—scared enough to talk—but they didn't know much beyond their orders. Someone's either feeding them resources or feeding them lies. Either way, it doesn't add up."

Raul cocks a brow at me, wordlessly ordering me to continue.

"I don't have anything solid yet but we're working on it. My men are reaching out to their contacts, monitoring online chatter and surveillance feeds, looking for any connections. I'll get answers."

Raul swirls the liquid in his glass once more before setting it down with a deliberate clink. "Be sure you do."

"Yes, sir."

The words are automatic, drilled into me over thirteen years of running his security and sitting at the right hand of this man. Longer, if you count the years before I began working for him.

I was sixteen when my mother began working in the kitchen for the Sandovals, when Raul became a permanent fixture in our lives. I was eighteen when I joined the Marines and left to fight a different kind of war. Twenty-five when I came home to a sister in the ground and a life I didn't recognize.

And twenty-six when Raul gave me a job.

I built the Guard Dogs for him. His security team. Spent a decade shaping them into something ruthless, efficient, unshakable. And in return, Raul gave me what my life after the Marines was missing—a purpose.

But Raul doesn't give without expecting something in return.

"I want the details of this attack and our response laid out in tomorrow night's video conference. If this isn't an isolated move, everyone needs to be aware and ready. Have contingency plans in place and be prepared to present them."

"Yes, sir."

He leans forward now, resting his forearms on the desk, voice calm but weighted. "And what of the attempted kidnapping? What of Maria?"

"She's safe," I say immediately, my voice leaving no room for doubt. "The compound is secure. The additional guards will ensure it. Chuck, Rafe, Fidel, and Elias will rotate through her detail personally."

"And the writer?" Raul's tone sharpens, the shift making my pulse tick faster. "Ami Zadegan."

"She's Maria's guest," I reply evenly, keeping my expression neutral. "Maria likes her. That's rare enough to matter."

Raul's fingers tap against the desk. A slow, measured beat. "Yes, a friend for Maria." He pauses in thought. "But she's a stranger. An unknown."

"She's been vetted," I say carefully. "And she immediately picked up on the threat at La Cascada. She acted in Maria's defense and helped her escape unscathed."

Raul studies me for a long moment and then leans back, reaching for his glass again. His movements are casual, deliberate. The ease of a man who knows he doesn't need to raise his voice to be heard. "I don't like unknowns, Marco. I never have." He takes a slow sip. "Keep Miss Zadegan close. Watch her."

I nod once, the weight of his words settling heavily on my shoulders. She's a variable. An unknown. And I know how to handle unknowns.

But something about the way Raul says it puts me on edge—like he's already seen a crack I haven't.

"Yes, sir."

Raul watches me for a beat longer, then adds, "I trust you to keep your priorities straight. Follow orders. The Calderóns appear to be watching us. The last thing we need is for you to be watching the wrong thing."

It's a warning.

Ami Zadegan isn't just an unknown to Raul. He thinks she's a distraction. And distractions get people killed.

As I leave his office and step into the quiet hallway, his words stay with me, curling around my thoughts like smoke.

I've given him the answers he wants. Laid out the plans to keep Maria safe and the Calderóns off balance. I'll take additional steps by the time the video conference happens.

But there's one variable I can't shake.

Ami Zadegan.

She *is* my responsibility. Raul made that clear. But every time I think about her—her fire, her defiance, the way she stepped into chaos—it feels like she's something else entirely.

Raul's warning echoes in my head. *I trust you to keep your priorities straight.*

He's right. The Calderóns are out there, waiting for a single misstep.

I know my priorities. I don't make mistakes. And I sure as hell won't get distracted.

10

AMI

THE RHYTHMIC KNOCKING on a door drags me out of sleep. For a moment, I flounder in the haze of half-formed dreams and unfamiliar surroundings. Sunlight spills through sheer curtains, illuminating a room that is definitely not mine. Ornate furniture. Plush bedding.

Yeah, this is not the Riverwalk Marriott.

Then, the events of last night come crashing back. Maria. The kidnapping attempt. The unnervingly intense Marco Cedillo. And my decision—or more accurately, Maria's decision—to spend the night at the Sandoval mansion.

I sit up too fast, my dress tugging uncomfortably, a reminder that I hadn't even changed before collapsing on the bed.

The relentless knocking persists.

"Okay, okay! I'm awake!" I croak, my voice dry and raspy. "Come in."

The door cracks open, and Maria's head pops in, her grin too chipper for whatever ungodly hour this is. "Good morning! Did you sleep well?"

"Well enough," I mumble, rubbing at my face. My eyes feel

53

gritty, contacts still in. Fantastic. "Why didn't you wake me earlier?"

Maria steps fully into the room, balancing a tray holding an assortment of pastries and a carafe of coffee that smells divine. "You looked like you needed the sleep. I figured famous authors don't have to wake up early."

I snort. "I'm not famous."

She arches a brow. "You're kidding, right? *Smash Girl? Volley Girl?* My whole book club devoured those like chocolate-covered strawberries."

"Your book club?" I try to picture Maria Sandoval—heiress to a criminal empire—sitting in a cozy living room, surrounded by twenty-somethings, debating the finer points of romance novels. It doesn't fit. At all.

Maria grins as if reading my mind. "Okay, full disclosure: there's no book club. It's just me."

I laugh and take the coffee she hands me. The mug is warm in my hands, and the first sip is pure heaven. "I'm starting to think you might be my biggest fan."

Maria perches on the edge of the bed, her excitement dimming slightly. "Ami, I have to be honest with you. I know it's weird, but I don't really... have a lot of friends. Not real ones anyway. It just doesn't work with all of..." She gestures vaguely around her. "This."

There's something raw in the way she says it. Like she's used to people assuming she has it all, but no one bothers to ask. She suddenly seems vulnerable. Even lonely.

"That's part of why winning your contest meant so much to me," she says softly, her eyes meeting mine.

I hesitate, then tell her truthfully, "You don't need to explain. I'm glad I'm here. And you deserved to win that contest. What you wrote was amazing. I loved it."

Maria's smile returns, brighter this time, like a weight's been lifted. "Good. Because now I'm going to tell you a secret. A *big* secret, and I need your help."

I pause mid-sip, already bracing myself. *Please don't tell me you've recently murdered someone and need help disposing of the body.*

"I need your help, Ami Zadegan," Maria continues, her voice dropping conspiratorially. "Because I want to write... a romance novel."

My mouth falls open. "You... what?"

"A romance novel," she repeats. "I was going to tell you about it last night before the whole kidnapping thing."

I stare at her. She is definitely *not* fazed by the whole kidnapping thing.

Maria leans in, lowering her voice. "But you can't tell my dad. He'd lose his mind if he found out. He thinks stuff like that is way too public."

"Well, it's not like I'm going to announce it in the mansion newsletter," I say, grinning.

Maria laughs, but it fades fast. "No, really, Ami. This has to stay between us. My dad has..." She hesitates. "Very specific expectations for me."

"Specific, huh?" I sip my coffee, debating whether to reveal my own deep, dark secret. Finally, I settle on the direct approach. "Maria, I need to tell you something."

Her brow furrows. "Okay...?"

I lean closer, whispering. "I think I know who your dad is."

Maria freezes, her expression unreadable. She glances around as if the walls might have ears before leaning in even closer.

"First rule," she whispers sharply. "Don't talk about my dad if you can help it."

"What?" I whisper back. "Because your dad's a crime boss?"

Maria flinches, pressing a finger to my lips. "Shh!" she hisses, her eyes darting around the room. "And *definitely* never say anything like that. In this house, you don't talk about business. Or what my dad may or may not do." She looks around again. "You call him Mr. Sandoval and leave it at that."

"Got it. Mr. Sandoval," I say, raising my hands in mock surrender.

She exhales, then straightens, though her voice remains hushed. "And for the record, he's not a... crime boss. He's a savvy businessman and serial entrepreneur with a wide range of investment portfolios, primarily real estate, throughout all of San Antonio, most of Texas, and parts of the southwest United States and northern Mexico."

I stare at her, suppressing a laugh. "Uh-huh. Very convincing and not rehearsed at all."

Maria ignores me. "Anyway, now that we've cleared that up..."

"That's not all, Maria," I say, shifting uncomfortably.

She raises an eyebrow. "What else?"

I hesitate, then plunge ahead. "Well, you know how I'm a writer?"

She rolls her eyes. "Uh, yeah. I'm kind of your biggest fan, remember?"

"Right, well... I've been thinking about my next series. I think I want to do something darker. More intense. Like a dark crime romance series..."

Her eyebrows shoot up. "Wha—"

"And I was wondering," I rush on, "if you'd be okay with me, uh, taking some notes? About your family?"

Her expression sharpens. I raise my hands. "Not real names or anything! Just general dynamics. For research. Your family's, uh, unique situation would be the perfect setup for that kind of romance series."

Maria blinks, tilting her head to the side. Then, to my surprise, she grins. "Ami, you're lucky I like you."

"I swear. Just notes," I say quickly. "Super careful. No one will ever know about you or your dad or any of this." I wave my hand dramatically around the room.

Maria sighs, then drops her voice further. "Fine. But you have to swear—*on your life*—that no one finds out what you're doing. Not my dad. Not the bodyguards. No one. They wouldn't... like that."

I nod solemnly. "Stealth-level careful. Got it."

Maria's smile turns mischievous. "Good. Now get dressed, sweetie. Workout gear. You must have some. You're about to experience a 'day-in-the-life-of-Maria-Sandoval.'"

"What does that mean?" I ask warily.

She grins. "Just trust me. Fifteen minutes."

As Maria stands to leave, she pauses in the doorway, glancing over her shoulder. "Oh, by the way, the staff already took care of your laundry. If you need anything else—clothes, shoes, a tiara, whatever—just let me know. I've got closets full of stuff."

Her words make me laugh, but they also leave me wondering what, exactly, I've just signed up for.

"Wait! Where are we going?"

"To the gym," she replies. "And after that, shooting practice. Trust me. You're going to love it."

I nearly choke on my coffee. "Shooting practice?"

"Yeah, shooting. Welcome to the Sandoval family," she replies, as if it were the most normal thing in the world.

And then she's gone.

11

MARCO

IF AMI ZADEGAN hadn't been there...

I shake my head sharply, stepping back and rolling my shoulders. Don't think about her. Not now.

But the memory of her refuses to stay buried. Her wide hazel eyes, flashing with anger. The wild tumble of her curls coming undone. The reckless defiance in the way she'd swung her purse like it was a goddamn weapon.

Stupid. Dangerous. Infuriating.

And impossible to forget.

She shouldn't be here. Not in this world. The Calderóns aren't playing games, and the Sandovals can't afford a single misstep. I have to be five moves ahead. Anything less is a liability. Anything less is failure.

And yet, despite the Calderóns, despite Raul's expectations, despite everything that demanded my attention—

Ami is here. And I can't stop thinking about her.

Rafe's right hook slams into my ribs, bringing me back to the present. I absorb it, feet steady, lungs burning as I push forward, closing the distance and answering with a jab to his jaw that snaps his head to the side. He grunts but grins through it, fists up, weight shifting smoothly as he circles me in the ring.

The bastard lives for this. The fight. The burn. The chance to knock me on my ass, even if it doesn't happen often. We do it to stay sharp.

And I need to stay sharp.

Outside the ring, the gym hums with quiet movement. The Sandoval estate might look like an opulent retreat to outsiders, but I know better. It's a fortress. And after the sloppy, desperate, but dangerous attack last night, I'm not taking chances. Desperate people make reckless choices, and reckless choices get people killed.

All of the Dogs are here this morning. Chuck has already gone a few rounds with each of us and is standing outside the ring, arms folded, watching. Elias sits nearby, posture relaxed but eyes scanning, the way they always do. He doesn't love this kind of fighting—his skill set is quieter, sharper—but he still shows up. Still fights. Training is training.

Fidel is stretched out on a weight bench, looking like he has nowhere better to be, one foot propped up as he scrolls through something on his phone. Probably security footage. Maybe something more interesting. With Fidel, you never know.

He looks effortless, relaxed. But that's just the surface. My little brother is *always* working. Always on a device, always running calculations, always monitoring something. He's gotten tall these last few years, taller than me, but he's lean. All wiry muscle instead of bulk. No ink—so not like me. If anything, he's the clean-cut one in this group, the quiet one.

Running the Sandoval security systems isn't just about monitoring cameras and alarms, though he's always doing that. It's about going deeper, breaking into anything and everything that gives us an edge. If there's a back door into a system, he's already found it and gone through. If there's intel worth knowing, he's two steps ahead of whoever thinks they're keeping secrets.

And right now, he's tense. He won't show it. Fidel never does. But I know him. This kidnapping attempt shook him. Anything involving Maria always does. They grew up together, here on the compound, like siblings. So he's even more protective of her than the rest of us, and considering our job description, that's saying something.

But none of us have fully shaken what happened last night.

I don't let the thought slow me down. I push forward, cutting off Rafe's movement, forcing him into a tight exchange. Our fists meet, quick, punishing strikes, sharp bursts of pain that keep me grounded in something physical instead of the frustration twisting through my head.

The Calderóns shouldn't have the means to pull off something like last night. Their operation is small. Underfunded. Undisciplined. Clinging to a territory that barely stretches beyond Del Rio.

But they had men last night. They had weapons. And they had the timing.

That's what doesn't sit right.

Rafe lands a shot to my ribs, but I barely register the impact. My brain is still in that goddamn warehouse, replaying every second of the interrogation. The thugs we caught were nothing. Low-level enforcers, sent to do someone else's dirty work. They gave up Diego Calderón's name fast. Too fast. It wasn't loyalty keeping them quiet. It was fear.

But fear of what?

I feint left, drive a hook into Rafe's side, then catch him with an uppercut that snaps his head back. He stumbles, breathless, then spits out a laugh. "Jesus, you trying to kill me?"

"If I was, you wouldn't be standing."

Rafe snorts, shaking out his shoulders, bouncing on the balls of his feet as he resets. "You always get mean when you're over-thinking shit."

I don't answer. Just push forward again, because if I stop, my mind will go places I don't want it to.

Raul had been calm when I gave him my debrief. He listened while I laid out the attack, my response, how we handled cleanup. He absorbed every detail, nodding when I told him Maria was safe, when I told him Ami Zadegan was one of the reasons she was still breathing.

He barely reacted to that part, except for a slight narrowing of his eyes.

Rafe throws a quick one-two, his fists a blur, but I block both, shoving him back with my forearm. He staggers, shaking his head. "And here I thought Chuck was the *pendejo* today."

Chuck smirks from the sidelines. "I had my turn."

Rafe groans. "Yeah, and my ribs still feel it."

I don't smile. I don't joke back. My focus is fractured, tension winding through my muscles that even this fight isn't unraveling.

Because if last night was a test, it means someone else is watching. Someone bigger than the Calderóns.

And Maria was the target.

Why her?

There are a thousand ways to disrupt the Sandoval empire, and taking Maria isn't the most obvious one. Unless it was meant to be personal. Unless it was meant to send Raul a message.

I see the next punch coming, but I don't move fast enough. Rafe's fist clips my jaw, just enough to jolt me out of my thoughts. I roll with it, but it still stings.

He grins. "Yeah, you're definitely distracted."

The word sticks, hooks into something Raul said last night. *Keep your priorities straight.*

Ami Zadegan.

I hear the echo of her voice in my head, sharp and defiant, the way she looked at me last night, like I had no goddamn right to tell her what to do. Even as she shook, adrenaline crashing, she hadn't backed down. She should have been running. Instead, she was swinging a fucking purse at an armed man.

It was reckless. Stupid.

And I can't stop thinking about it.

Rafe moves in again, but this time, I see the opening. I feint left, then catch him hard with a right hook to the ribs. He grunts, doubling over slightly, then straightens with a groan. "Fuck. Okay, I'm tapping out."

I step back, rolling my shoulders. The fight is over, but the tension isn't gone.

Rafe climbs out of the ring, wincing as he stretches. "You're in a real mood today, man."

Fidel, still sprawled on his bench, doesn't look up from his phone. "*Jefe's* brooding. As usual."

Elias finally speaks, his voice low and calm. "He's thinking about the Calderóns."

Chuck snorts. "Yeah? Or is he thinking about the woman?"

I shoot him a glare.

Fidel grins, flicking his gaze up from his phone. "Called it."

I grab my towel, ignoring them as I wipe the sweat from my face.

They're not wrong. I am thinking about her.

Ami Zadegan is my responsibility now.

Raul made that clear. *Keep her close. Watch her. Make sure she doesn't become a problem.*

But something about her already is a problem.

Because I can't stop thinking about her.

12

———

AMI

THE GLASS DOOR to the gym slides open with a soft whoosh, and Maria breezes in like she owns the place. Which, technically, she does. I follow hesitantly, my sneakers squeaking faintly against the polished floor as I step into what looks like a high-end fitness catalog come to life.

Treadmills and ellipticals line one wall, their glossy screens blinking like they're waiting for orders. Free weights gleam under sleek overhead lights. The faint smell of disinfectant lingers in the air, mingling with the quiet hum of the air conditioning. And in the center of it all, like a king presiding over his court, is a boxing ring—ropes taut, corners padded, daring someone to step in.

Maria told me to wear workout gear, and thank *God* I'd thrown in some leggings and t-shirts when I packed for SpicyLitCon. I feel marginally more prepared for whatever it is we're doing in my *Metaphors Be With You* t-shirt, though the brace around my wrist is a glaring reminder of last night's chaos.

"Good morning, Marco!" Maria chirps, her voice entirely too chipper for this hour.

I barely register her enthusiasm because my attention snags —and sticks—on the lone man across the room. Marco.

He's hammering a heavy bag hanging from the ceiling with a ferocity that makes my pulse tick up a notch. His bare fists move in a brutal, unrelenting rhythm, every punch landing with a solid *thud* that echoes through the cavernous space. He's shirt-less, wearing black sweatpants slung low on his hips, and he's soaked in sweat—every hard line of muscle glistening beneath the overhead lights.

He's enormous. Not just tall. Built. Dense with strength. Broad across the shoulders, thick through the chest, his entire body honed and battle-ready.

There is something hypnotic about the way he moves, fluid and controlled, yet raw with power. Each strike makes the bag swing violently, its chain rattling against the ceiling. *Thud. Thud. Thud.* Each blow is a reminder that this man can—and probably has—taken someone apart with those hands.

His back is a map of ink and muscle, black tattoos twisting over tan skin like they've always belonged there. Some are brutal and sharp, others surprisingly artistic. Black roses unfurl across his right shoulder, sweeping down his arm and moving in perfect motion with the twist of his torso. On his other arm, I catch the Marine Corps emblem inked deep into his bicep—an eagle, globe, and anchor—with the words *Semper Fidelis* wrapped beneath it. Always Faithful. A vow.

There's a bulldog inked onto his back, snarling mid-lunge, and something else, just above his heart. I can't see it fully, but it looks like a single word in script. Elena?

My gaze skims lower, catching a glimpse of a skull etched beneath the name, ornate, almost decorative, like a Day of the Dead calavera. A symbol of remembrance, maybe. Of grief.

And the scars. Pale slashes that cut across muscle like faded war stories. The kind of marks that tell me this man has survived things I can't even imagine. I want to know who gave them to him and what they got in return.

I realize he looks like he belongs on the cover of a dark crime romance novel. Like every woman's fantasy come to life.

"And this is the gym!" Maria announces, dragging my focus back with a cheerful flourish. "Marco, Ami and I are going to work out. Don't mind us."

Marco doesn't even glance our way. He grunts in acknowledgment but doesn't break his rhythm. His laser focus on the bag makes the air feel heavier somehow, like his intensity has its own gravitational pull.

Maria starts pressing buttons on her treadmill. "Where is everyone, anyway Marco? I figured we'd be walking into some kind of testosterone-filled fight club."

"If you didn't sleep so late, you would've seen them," Marco says, his voice rough from exertion. He lands another brutal punch before stepping back, rolling his shoulders. "They've already showered and gotten to work."

He grabs a towel from a nearby bench, dragging it over his face, biceps flexing, lats shifting with the movement. He's still breathing heavily, still wired, and I get the sense he needed a little longer here. Needed to punch something more.

Maria waves me toward a treadmill. "Come on, Ami. Stress relief."

I hesitate, clutching the water bottle she handed me in my good hand. The gym feels both impossibly large and suffocatingly intimate at the same time. "I'm not sure this is a great idea," I mutter, casting a glance toward Marco.

He still hasn't stopped moving, stretching out his arms now, shaking out his hands. His presence is tangible, radiating across the room like heat from a furnace.

Maria waves me off. "You'll feel better, I promise."

With a sigh, I step onto the treadmill next to her, fumbling with the controls. Just walking feels impossible with Marco in the room. My gaze keeps straying back to him, like my brain can't process anything else. Everything about him is both unsettling and mesmerizing.

"So," Maria begins, already breathless as she powers up her treadmill, "let me tell you about my romance novel. There's a duke with a dark secret. And I'm thinking a love triangle. Oh, and an evil count. But maybe the count is secretly in love with the duke."

Despite myself, I laugh softly. "Bold move. You're really leaning into the Regency drama, huh?"

"Always," Maria replies with a grin.

Out of the corner of my eye, I see Marco glance our way. His brow furrows slightly, and he drapes the towel around his neck as he moves toward us.

"Is this a workout or a book club meeting?" he asks, his tone sharp.

Maria smirks, unbothered. "Oh, here we go."

"It's called brainstorming," I shoot back before I can stop myself. My gaze locks on his, and I lift my chin slightly, feeling the challenge in my own voice. "Maybe you've heard of it."

He wipes his face with the towel as he stands before us, his movements slow and deliberate. "Brainstorming? About a duke and a count having sex? Sounds sordid."

Maria leans toward me, her grin widening like we're in on a joke that he isn't. "I think he's interested in our little romance project."

Marco jabs a finger toward her treadmill controls. "Go faster, Maria. You've got energy to burn."

She sticks her tongue out at him but obediently cranks up the speed. "You're no fun, Marco."

Then he turns to me, his dark gaze locking onto mine. His

expression is unreadable, but the weight of his stare is enough to make my pulse skip.

"Don't hurt yourself. Again," he says flatly, though there's a flicker of something—amusement? concern?—in his tone. No, impossible. Probably just irritation.

Before I can fire back, he turns away, heading toward the locker rooms.

"Don't worry about me," I call after him, steadying my voice despite the way my cheeks burn. "I can handle myself."

The door swings shut behind him, but I can feel the tension he leaves behind.

"Oh, Ami," Maria shouts after him, laughing. "If this were one of your books, you'd have kissed him by now—on a tennis court!"

I stare at the door, my cheeks flaming as I bite back a retort.

Not that he would've heard it anyway.

13

———

AMI

AFTER OUR WORKOUT, Maria decides the tour isn't over and drags me through a glass door into another part of the building. The moment we step inside, my eyebrows shoot up.

"See? It's not just a gym. It's a bowling alley, it's a spa, and it's this!" She pushes open the soundproof glass door, revealing a private shooting range.

Of course. A private shooting range. Because why wouldn't there be a private shooting range?

I try not to roll my eyes as I follow her in. The faint squeak of my sneakers is swallowed by the hushed hum of the room's high-tech ventilation system. The space is sleek, modern, and gleaming. Soundproofed walls absorb every noise except the muffled *pop, pop* of gunfire coming from the far end of the range. Glass display cases line the walls, showcasing an arsenal of weapons that would look more at home in an action movie than on a private estate.

The faint metallic tang of gunpowder hangs in the air.

At the far end of the room, a wiry man with close-cropped hair stands firing a sleek handgun, his movements methodical and precise. Each shot hits the center of the target with unnerving accuracy, shredding it into paper confetti.

"That's Rafe," Maria says casually, as if she's introducing someone delivering pizza. "Guns are kind of his thing."

The man in question lowers his weapon, clears it with quick efficiency, and sets it on the counter in his booth before turning toward us. His sharp gaze sweeps over me, cool and assessing, before landing on Maria.

"Maria," he greets with a nod, his tone calm and measured. Then his focus shifts back to me. "And this is?"

Maria beams. "This is Ami Zadegan, famous romance author and our houseguest for the foreseeable future. Ami, this is Rafael Moreno—Rafe. He's one of the Guard Dogs and, as you can see, basically a human sniper rifle."

"It's... nice to meet you," I say, feeling awkward under his scrutiny. "But what's a Guard Dog?"

Maria shrugs, breezy as ever. "The guys who protect the family. Marco, Rafe, Chuck, Elias, and Fidel. They're the best at what they do—bodyguards, enforcers, security, whatever needs to be handled. And since 'the security team' is boring as hell, I call them the Guard Dogs. I think they like it!"

Rafe's lips quirk into a faint smirk, but he doesn't confirm or deny it. Instead, he stands watching us with quiet amusement as Maria leads me to one of the display cases along the back wall.

She pulls open a glass door and lifts out a small black handgun, holding it out like she's offering me a cupcake.

"This," she says, grinning, "is for you."

I freeze, staring at the weapon in her hands. "Is that... loaded?"

Maria rolls her eyes. "Not yet. Relax, silly." She grabs a box of ammunition and then reaches over to a nearby rack and grabs two pairs of clear protective glasses and heavy earmuffs.

"You're going to need these," she says, handing me the gear before leading me toward an open shooting booth.

I put on the glasses and earmuffs, trying to ignore the weight settling in my stomach as she loads the gun's magazine with practiced ease. The soft *snick* of the magazine locking into place makes my hands tighten around the water bottle I'm still holding.

"Now it's loaded but the safety is on," Maria says. "Here, take it." She holds the gun out, grip first, barrel pointed safely downrange. "And always keep it pointed at the target. Not at anyone. Ever. Even if you think it's not loaded. Safety first."

I place my water bottle on the counter and take the gun, keeping it pointed downrange. Maria stands to my side, adjusting the fit of the glasses on my nose. "You're going to do great," she says cheerfully, stepping back to admire her handiwork. "Trust me, it'll be fun."

"Fun," I repeat flatly, staring at the gun in my hands. "Sure. Fun."

Behind us, Rafe crosses his arms, unimpressed. "You realize her wrist is in a brace, right?" he says, his tone neutral but pointed.

"It's a Ruger LCP," Maria replies breezily. "Super lightweight. Barely any recoil. Perfect for a beginner."

"Hi, still here," I interject, glancing at the small pistol. "And this still doesn't feel like a great idea. My wrist and I would like to formally object to this entire scenario."

Maria huffs out a breath as she carefully helps adjust my grip. "Relax. You're just going to aim at the center of that target down there. Deep breath, exhale, gentle squeeze, and don't jerk the trigger. Just let it break clean."

I swallow hard and step forward in the booth, the tang of gunpowder sharpening in my nose as I line up the sights with the paper target at the end of the lane. My heart thuds as I adjust my stance.

I've never shot a gun before. I've never even held a gun before. Something about it makes me feel... weirdly powerful.

I shift awkwardly, my good hand tightening around the grip as my braced wrist offers shaky support beneath it. It's clumsy, but it's the only way I can hold steady. The weight of the gun feels all wrong, but I grit my teeth and refuse to back down.

Deep breath. Exhale. Gentle squeeze.

The sharp *pop* of the shot startles me, and the recoil jolts up my arm, forcing me to stumble back. Before I can even process what's happening, I collide with something solid behind me. Something warm. Unyielding.

A clean scent of citrus and sandalwood fills my senses.

Strong hands steady me at my waist, firm and grounding, their heat searing through the fabric of my t-shirt. My breath catches as I turn—

And find myself face-to-face with Marco.

His dark eyes lock on mine, sharp and intense, tension crackling between us like a live wire. His hands shift from my waist to gently guide the gun I'm still holding downward.

"Careful," he murmurs, his voice low and steady.

My pulse thuds in my ears. His hands linger, just for a second, before he steps back. The loss of contact is jarring, like I've been yanked back to reality.

"I—I'm fine," I stammer, my cheeks burning.

Marco's gaze flicks to Maria and Rafe. "What's going on here?"

"She's learning to shoot," Maria replies, as if this were a perfectly normal activity for a houseguest.

"With her wrist in a brace?" His tone is calm, but there's a hard edge of disapproval beneath it.

"That's what I said," Rafe mutters, deadpan.

"She's fine," Maria insists, waving them both off. "It's barely a gun."

Marco doesn't look convinced. His dark eyes return to mine, holding my gaze like a physical weight. "You don't need to do this," he says quietly.

I straighten slightly, tightening my grip on the pistol. "Maria thought it was a good idea," I say, lifting my chin. "I thought it was a good idea."

After a long moment, Marco exhales and turns to Rafe. "If she's going to do this, make sure she does it right. Help her with her stance."

As Marco strides toward the door, Maria leans toward me with a wicked grin.

"Did you notice? He's giving you tips now. That's basically foreplay."

14

AMI

THE LIBRARY IS MASSIVE, its towering shelves lining every wall and stretching to the ceiling. A rolling ladder leans against one wall of shelves, like something out of a fairy tale, just waiting for someone to glide across the room on it, singing while holding an armful of books.

There are leather-bound volumes that scream old money, sure, but there are also shelves packed with well-worn paperbacks, their spines creased from years of use. Dog-eared classics sit beside modern bestsellers. Stacks of books—not neatly arranged—litter the side tables and reading chairs, as if someone abandoned them mid-chapter. There's even a small pile of romance novels near one of the armchairs, their covers a stark contrast to the more somber tomes around them.

Maria has declared this the perfect spot for us to work on her historical romance novel and, as she put it, to help with my "research."

After our shooting lesson, we showered in the gym's ridiculously luxurious locker room and then shared an incredible lunch with the mostly Russian house staff in the mansion's sprawling kitchen. They speak heavily-accented English, and between bites of chicken pesto pasta salad, I picked up bits and pieces about their lives.

According to Maria, they'd arrived two years ago as part of a shipment of weapons, which apparently wasn't a big deal to anyone at the table. And somehow, instead of leaving, they had stayed—taking over the kitchen and the motor pool, and settling into the Sandoval compound like they belonged.

Maria, of course, had been in her element, chatting with the cooks like they were old friends, laughing as she mapped out an itinerary for my stay—though "mapped out" was a generous term. It was less of a schedule and more of an onslaught of half-formed plans that shifted with every other sentence.

"Okay, so mornings are for workouts," she announced, ticking off her fingers. "You need self-defense, shooting, basic survival stuff. Then lunch. Sometimes in the kitchen, sometimes by the pool. Ooh, or the tennis courts! Or maybe I'll plan a picnic somewhere. I'll figure it out."

I raised an eyebrow but let her roll with it.

"Afternoons are for work," she continued, gesturing dramatically between us. "Writing, brainstorming, whatever. Late afternoon, we'll have a snack. Churros, maybe? Or green smoothies would be healthier. And then evenings are for fun! Games, gossip, movies. Do you like Harry Potter? Anyway, I've got ideas."

It was a lot to take in. But as I watched her ramble, practically bouncing on her toes, something clicked. Maria wasn't just excited. She was giddy. The sheer joy radiating off her was almost tangible.

And for the first time, I truly saw it. How lonely she must be.

For all her confidence and charm, Maria's world was a gilded cage. She was constantly surrounded by people—family, staff, bodyguards—but how many of them did she actually get to be herself with? She didn't just *want* me here. She *needed* me here. Someone to laugh with. Someone to plan ridiculous days with. Someone who didn't see her as Raul Sandoval's daughter first.

And *that,* I understood. Wanting to just be yourself with someone. I really understood.

The thought made me smile, even as her itinerary overwhelmed me.

I barely had time to process it all before she dragged me to the library.

Now, I'm sitting at an oversized oak table in the middle of the grand room. Maria's laptop is open in front of me, its cursor blinking mockingly on a blank document. So far, the only thing we've managed to accomplish is titling the file *Maria's Novel.*

Meanwhile, Maria is a storm of energy, darting between bookshelves and the table, tossing out ideas faster than I can type.

"Okay, what if the duke realizes he's in love with her—no, wait, she realizes she's in love with him first, but she's too proud to say anything. Or maybe they're both in denial?"

She stops mid-pace, turning to me with wide, questioning eyes.

"Maria," I say, holding up a hand to slow the chaos. "Take a breath. You've got so many amazing ideas, but we need to start with the basics."

She blinks at me like I've suggested we invent a new language. "The basics?"

"Yes, the basics," I say firmly. "Let's outline."

Maria tilts her head. "Outline?"

"We need to figure out who your characters are, what they want, and what's standing in their way. You can't just toss a duke and a love triangle onto the page and hope for the best."

With an exaggerated sigh, Maria flops into the chair across from me. "Fine. Outline me."

I bite back a grin. I know how to do this. I'm good at this.

Maria might resist now, but I have a feeling she's going to love this process. "All right. Let's start with your heroine. Who is she? What's her name? What's her backstory?"

Maria taps her chin thoughtfully, then her eyes sparkle with inspiration. "She's strong, independent, but secretly vulnerable. Her name is... Lady Penelope Hargrove. She has a tragic past—her parents were betrayed by the crown, so she hates the aristocracy but has to pretend to be one of them. Or maybe her father gambled away the family fortune and sold her off in an arranged marriage to the rakish duke."

I type as she speaks.

"How's that for outlining?" she asks, grinning.

"We're getting there," I say. "Now, what does your heroine want more than anything?"

Maria leans forward, her enthusiasm sparking again. "Revenge. Or justice. No, revenge. Definitely revenge."

I nod, fingers flying over the keyboard. "Revenge. Got it. And what's standing in her way?"

Before she can answer, the library door swings open.

Elias strolls in, smooth and self-assured. His tailored pearl-gray suit is immaculate, his pink tie perfectly knotted. He moves like he owns the place. Or at least, like he doesn't need anyone's permission to be here.

"Ladies," he greets, his deep voice tinged with amusement. "Marco sent me to check on you two. Make sure you're not causing trouble."

Maria rolls her eyes. "Of course he did."

Elias chuckles, picking up one of the books Maria has stacked on the table. "Let's see... *Love All* by Ami Zadegan. *Volley Girl* by Ami Zadegan. *Break Point* by Ami Zadegan. You've been very busy, Miss Zadegan."

When his gaze flicks to me, there's a glint of something

calculating, like he's learned something about me that he's filing away, just in case.

I open my mouth to respond, but Maria cuts in. "Yes, she's famous. And now she's helping me with my book." She waves at the laptop. "She's making me outline. It's what real writers do."

Elias smirks. "And this book is... secret, I take it?"

"Very," Maria says, glancing towards the library door. "Papa cannot know."

Elias raises a brow but nods. "Got it. But you know Marco's going to find out eventually, right? He always does."

Maria groans. "Yes, I know. But let's just try to wait on that a little longer. Until I really have something to tell everyone about."

Elias holds up his hands in mock surrender. "Understood." His grin softens, and for a moment, he looks more like a protective older brother than the suave liaison I'd seen before. "So, what's the story?"

Maria immediately launches into an impassioned explanation of Lady Penelope, the brooding duke, and the villainous count. I watch, amused, as Elias listens—his brows furrowing, his expression shifting from skeptical to genuinely intrigued.

"What if the duke's secret is tied to her father's betrayal?" he suggests, tilting his head thoughtfully. "Maybe he knows something about it but can't tell her because it would put them both in danger."

Maria claps her hands, eyes shining. "Yes! Ami, write that down!"

Biting back a laugh, I type as instructed. "Got it. Anything else, Elias?"

He leans back, crossing his arms, considering. Then he smirks. "If you really want drama, make the heroine choose. Trust the duke and risk everything, or walk away and lose her chance at revenge."

Maria gasps like he just handed her the Holy Grail. "Elias, you're a genius."

Elias shakes his head, amused. "You're lucky I like you, *niña*. No one else could drag me into this."

Maria grins, utterly unfazed. "You love me, and you know it."

Elias sighs dramatically. "Unfortunately." But there's warmth in his voice, and when he glances at me, I see it again—that fond exasperation, like he's given up trying to resist whatever whirlwind Maria pulls him into.

And as the brainstorming continues, I glance at her, watching as she spins wild ideas with uncontainable excitement, drawing Elias further into her creative storm.

And I finally get it.

Not just why everyone loves Maria.

But why no one ever tells her no.

15

MARCO

THE LATE AFTERNOON sun slants across the compound, throwing long shadows over the grounds. From where I stand on the second-floor terrace, I can see everything—the swimming pool, the tennis courts, the patrols moving in quiet, disciplined pairs. Beyond the perimeter wall, the Texas Hill Country stretches out in rolling waves of green and limestone, the gnarled live oaks dense enough to hide anyone who wants to watch from a distance.

Not that anyone would get far. The estate is locked down. Gates secure, cameras covering every angle, guards stationed at every key point. The Sandoval compound might look like luxury from the inside, but from out here, it's a fortress.

And it still doesn't feel like enough.

The Calderóns aren't finished. The kidnapping attempt had been sloppy. But they'll come back, and next time, they won't make the same mistakes.

Luck saved us last night. And I don't believe in luck.

Footsteps approach from behind, steady and familiar. I don't need to turn.

"Boss."

Rafe steps up beside me, leaning against the iron railing like he has all the time in the world. Even though we're the same age, cousins who've been together since we were born, he defers to me. Knows I'm in charge. "Perimeter checks are clean. Everyone's sticking to the schedule."

"Double the rotations at the gates," I say. "No one gets in or out without clearance."

"Already done." He crosses his arms, a faint smirk tugging at the corner of his mouth. "You've been out here all day. You think staring in the Calderóns' general direction is gonna make them drop dead?"

I shoot him a look. "Don't you have something better to do?"

"Plenty," he says, his smirk widening. "But watching you stand here looking pissed off? Always entertaining."

I ignore the jab, my gaze still fixed on the property. "The Calderóns aren't done. They'll come back. It's just a matter of when."

Rafe's smirk fades, his expression sharpening. "You think they'd be stupid enough to hit the compound? That's a hell of a risk."

"They seem desperate," I say. "And desperation can get someone killed. Us if we're not ahead of them."

He nods, his posture shifting as his eyes scan the property. The teasing is gone. This is the side of Rafe I've always relied on—the strategist, the fighter.

"And what do you make of what we got from the interrogation?" he asks. "They talked fast."

"Too fast," I say, my jaw tightening. "They gave up Diego Calderón too easy. Like they were just waiting to say his name. They weren't scared of him."

Rafe frowns. "Then who?"

I exhale slowly. "That's the question. The Calderóns are small-time. They don't have the manpower or the resources to pull something like this off on their own. Diego's not smart, but he's not that stupid. I think someone's backing them."

"Funding them?" Rafe's tone darkens.

"Maybe. Or feeding them lies. Either way, there's more going on here than we're seeing."

Rafe leans against the railing, the weight of the conversation settling between us. "So we're watching Calderón pawns while someone else moves the pieces?"

"That's the theory," I say. "Or maybe the Calderóns really are dumb enough to think they can take Raul on their own. Either way, we don't take chances."

For a moment, we stand in silence, the weight of the situation pressing between us. Then Rafe glances at me, and the smirk creeps back onto his face.

"What about Miss Zadegan?"

My jaw tightens. "What about her?"

"She's an interesting guest," he says lightly, amusement threading through his voice. "Shooting for the first time ever with her wrist in a brace? Not sure if that was stupid or smart."

"She's Maria's guest," I reply evenly. "Maria likes her."

Rafe raises an eyebrow but doesn't push. Instead, his smirk turns knowing. "You know, she kind of reminds me of Elena."

The name hits like a punch, but I don't flinch. Can't flinch. My grip on the iron railing tightens, the cool metal biting into my palms.

Rafe is my oldest friend. He knew me before any of this. Before the Sandovals, before the Guard Dogs. My mother was his aunt. My sister, Elena, was his cousin. He knew both of them. And he remembers how they died.

My sister before her time. My mother, a year later, from a broken heart.

"She's nothing like Elena," I say quietly.

"Not how she looks," Rafe clarifies, his smirk fading into

something softer. "But she's got the same fire. The same way of pushing back, even when it's not in her best interest. When she went ahead with the gun. Well... I just thought you might have noticed too."

I exhale through my nose, my gaze locked on the horizon. "She's not Elena."

"Didn't say she was," Rafe says easily, holding up his hands. "Just saying she's got that same spark."

The way she gritted her teeth, wrist shaking, and pulled the trigger anyway...

Yeah, Elena would have done the exact same stupid thing.

The conversation is over. I make that clear in my tone.

"Anything else, Rafe?"

He pushes off the railing, taking the hint. "Chuck's got the house patrols squared away. I'll oversee the rotations tonight myself. You should get some rest."

"I'll rest when this is over."

Rafe mutters something under his breath—probably about my stubbornness—but doesn't argue. He starts to leave, but I call after him.

"Rafe."

He stops, glancing over his shoulder. "Yeah?"

"Stay sharp." My voice is quieter now, but the meaning is clear.

His smirk returns, easy and confident. "Always, boss."

I watch him disappear through the terrace doors, his words still echoing in my head.

Elena. Ami.

The sun dips below the limestone wall, the compound cast in shadow. Below, the patrols move in tight, methodical lines. Everything in its place.

And I still feel that knot in my chest. The one that never loosens.

16

———————

A PODCAST

Excerpt from Blood and Bullets: A True Crime Podcast

Hosts: Marty Chang and Darren Short
Episode 127: The South Texas Ghost

[PRE-ROLL NOTE FROM MARTY]

Marty (voiceover): Hey listeners, Marty here with a quick note before we begin. We apologize for the poor audio quality in this episode. The original master file was somehow deleted from our cloud storage, and what you're about to hear is a recovered backup that's clearly been tampered with. You'll hear moments of distortion, bleeped-out names, and abrupt jumps in audio.

We left the episode up because the topic matters. And because we think someone doesn't want you to hear it.

· · ·

So grab your tin foil hat and hang on tight. It's about to get weird. This is *Blood and Bullets*. Cue the theme music.

[BEGIN EXCERPTED TRANSCRIPT]

Darren: I'm just saying nobody makes that much money in South Texas real estate without getting dirty. Like... actually no one.

Marty: We're talking about a man—no, screw it, an entity—who owns more of South Texas than the state government does.

Darren: Dude came out of nowhere in the '90s, buys up blocks of downtown San Antonio. There's no way this guy's not laundering something.

Marty: He came up through real estate, private security, urban development—you know, squeaky clean fronts. But if you peel back one layer?

[DISTORTION – 2 SECONDS OF STATIC]

Darren: A private security firm that trains with ex-military. Like, legit special ops types. Why does a real estate developer need guys who can disassemble an AR-15 blindfolded? And, Martyl, let's be honest. This guy's not just rich. He's insulated. I'm talking black ops, MK Ultra, Operation Northwoods type insulation.

Marty: Look, here's what we do know. Born 1962. Acuña, Mexico. Crossed the border at fifteen. No family, no papers. Worked kitchens, picked crops. Then, somehow by twenty-five, he's running crews. Chop shops.

Darren: Like overnight, he's in with a cartel in [BLEEP]. Not just some lookout or driver. Like all the way inside. Learning the system. Smuggling routes, bribery chains, crypto before crypto even was crypto.

Marty: And then in '93, something happened. A fire. An explosion. A dead boss.

Darren: And suddenly? The kid who used to strip stolen cars is buying half of San Antonio?

[AUDIO GLITCH - WORDS REPEATED - BLEED TO STATIC]

Darren: Real estate. Nightclubs. Executive protection firms. All legit. On paper.

Marty: But what do you need "executive protection" for when your clients are politicians, judges, and goddamn oil execs?

. . .

Darren: And let's not forget the disappearances.

Marty: Remember the zoning lawyer who blocked his downtown casino deal in 2008? Yeah. That guy—

[BLEEP]

Marty (cont'd): —then no trace.

Darren: Another one—union rep, filed a complaint about unsafe working conditions at one of his sites. Disappeared on a Tuesday. Totally disappeared. SUV found idling in a Walmart parking lot with the engine running. Like WTF? Did they grab him out of his car?

Marty: This guy isn't flashy. He's not out there waving AKs and filming rap videos in gold-plated jacuzzis. He's not that kind of crime lord.

Darren: He's worse. He's smart. He's strategic. He's...

[BLEEP]

. . .

Marty: And no one will say his name. Not in the press. Not online. No leaked texts or emails. No court cases. Just clean spreadsheets and obliterated history.

Darren: Well, I'll say his name. It's—

[FIVE SECOND BLEEP]

Darren (cont'd): There. Done. So if you're listening to this and you've got theories—speak now. Because we don't know how long this episode's gonna stay up.

Marty: And if we vanish?

Darren: Play this episode at our funeral.

[LAUGHTER]

[HARD CUT TO SILENCE]

[END TRANSCRIPT]

17

AMI

Despite hours of brainstorming—and some unexpected help from Elias and Chuck, who also had "dropped by" under the guise of checking on us but stayed to enthusiastically contribute—Maria's so-called outline is still a chaotic swirl of ideas.

The document on her laptop looks like the aftermath of a brainstorming hurricane: half-formed characters, sprawling plot twists, and more questions than answers.

Maria, it turns out, is not a planner. At all.

"I think," I say carefully, scrolling through the mess on the screen, "we've officially entered full pantser territory."

Maria blinks. "Panster?"

"Someone who writes by the seat of their pants," I explain. "No plan, no outline. Just chaos and vibes."

Maria groans, slumping back in her chair with a dramatic flop only she could pull off. She draws her legs up, resting her chin on her knees like a sulking teenager. "Why do people outline, anyway? It's so boring. Why not just let the characters do their thing?"

"Because that's how you end up with three dukes, a secret

baby, and a time-travel subplot all crammed into one chapter," I reply, arching a brow.

She laughs, and for a moment, the tension of the day dissolves. Maria's energy is infectious, so unapologetically bold and creative that I can't help but enjoy her excitement, even as I try to corral it into something resembling structure.

Eventually, though, even Maria has to admit defeat.

"Okay, fine," she sighs dramatically. "I think I've officially hit the wall."

"You and me both," I say, closing her laptop with a decisive click.

Maria tilts her head, studying me. "Well, Miss Zadegan, since my creative tank is empty, I think it's time for me to help you with your research."

I hesitate. "We don't have to do that now. If you're too tired—"

"A deal is a deal," she interrupts, her voice firm. Then, with a mischievous glint in her eye, she adds, "But before we start, just know there are security cameras in the house."

I freeze. "Excuse me?"

Maria waves a hand like it's no big deal. "They're mostly on the first floor. Papa doesn't want them upstairs. But they're monitored from the guardhouse. Usually by Fidel." She tilts her head toward the corner of the room, where a tiny red light blinks.

I glance at the camera, trying not to look like I'm looking at it. "Not upstairs. Good to know," I murmur, pulse suddenly quicker.

Maria grins. "Relax. They're not listening. Just video."

"Oh, sure. Totally fine. Nothing unnerving about that."

She laughs, and somehow, I can't help but smile. Maria has this way of making everything—cameras, mansions, armed guards—feel almost normal.

Almost.

She straightens in her chair. "All right, Ami. You said you

wanted the inside scoop on what it's like growing up around a crime family. So, ask me anything."

I hesitate. Because, honestly? I have questions. A lot of them.

After last night, I'd spent way too long falling down a true crime rabbit hole, trying to understand exactly what kind of situation I'd walked into. And what I'd found was... unsettling.

The official news barely scratches the surface. Articles about the Sandovals' high-rise developments, their security firm, their luxury nightclubs. All perfectly legitimate. But the deeper I dug, the messier it got.

The podcasts and Reddit threads painted a different picture: Raul Sandoval, a ruthless kingpin who allegedly built his empire through weapons trafficking, and crypto-laundered millions through real estate. A cartel-adjacent crime syndicate that ran more like a Fortune 500 company than a street gang. A "businessman first, criminal second," if you believed the podcasts.

And if you betrayed him? You didn't live long enough to regret it.

So, yeah. This should all be setting off massive flee-for-your-life instincts.

But strangely? I feel safe here.

Maybe it's because Maria is so casual about everything. Maybe it's because, for all his terrifying intensity, Marco made it clear last night that he wouldn't hurt me.

Or maybe I'm just delusional.

I shake off the thought and clear my throat. "Okay, let's start with something easy. Why is every guy in this house walking around in a suit jacket? It's August. Don't they get hot?"

Maria grins, clearly amused. "Oh, Ami. You're so sweet."

I frown. "What?"

"They're all carrying guns under those jackets."

"Guns?" My voice cracks, and Maria's grin widens.

"Of course. Elias probably has a couple of knives tucked in there, too. And Rafe? He's probably carrying something ridiculous, like a grenade." She shrugs. "Fidel's a tech guy, so I wouldn't put it past him to have some app that can remotely blow something up."

I open my mouth, then shut it again. "Right. Guns. Totally normal."

Maria's laughter rings out, and despite myself, I laugh, too.

"Okay, moving on," I say, trying to recover. "What about your family? Do you have siblings?"

Her smile softens. "Yeah. Raul Jr. and Carlos. But they don't live here. RJ's in Houston, Carlos is in Austin." She twists a strand of hair around her finger. "They're a lot older than me. By the time I was old enough to care, they were already working for my father. And now... I guess it's just one of those things, you know? I love them so much but, somehow, you can grow up in the same family and still end up worlds apart."

"And your mom?" I ask gently.

Maria's gaze drops to the table, her smile dimming. "She died when I was three. I don't really remember her. Just pictures and stories." She exhales. "When I was old enough, Papa sent me to boarding school. Vermont. He said it was for the education, but I think he just didn't want me too close to... all of this."

My chest tightens. "That must've been lonely."

Maria shrugs. "I came home for summers and holidays. Those were the best times. I practically lived in the kitchen with Miss Ana—Marco and Fidel's mom. She treated me like one of her own."

Hearing Marco's name perks me up. "Wait. Marco and Fidel? You've known them since you were all kids?"

She nods, her expression softening. "Marco was older. Always the protector. Fidel was closer to my age. And their sister, Elena..." Her voice falters. "She was my big sister and my best friend."

Her gaze goes distant for a second. "She used to do my hair in these ridiculously elaborate braids. Painted my nails with glitter polish she wasn't supposed to have. Gave me my first lipstick—stole it from Miss Ana's purse and told me red was *my* color. I was eight."

She smiles, but there's grief tucked in the corners. "I thought she was magic."

I hesitate. "So, they were like siblings to you?"

"Totally," Maria says quickly. Too quickly. "Like Fidel and I did everything together—caused trouble, played pranks, all of it. He's still like a brother. Just... a really good-looking, infuriating brother." She pauses. "Why do I feel like you're analyzing that relationship for one of your romance novels?"

I smirk. "No comment."

Maria rolls her eyes but keeps talking. "Anyway, Marco and Fidel started working for my father when they were old enough. Marco runs security but he's basically Papa's right hand, especially when it comes to San Antonio. And Fidel, well, he's the tech guy, but he's a genius. He could probably hack into NASA if he wanted to. Probably already has."

"And Marco's background?" I ask, keeping my tone casual.

Maria frowns. "I don't know all the details. He joined the Marines right after high school. Whatever he did, Fidel says it's classified. Something with terrorists? But when he would come home, he was different. Changed. And when Elena..." Her voice falters, and she takes a deep breath. "When Elena died, I think it broke him. And Miss Ana, too."

The air shifts, heavy with a name I know matters more than Maria's saying. Elena. I don't know the whole story yet—but I can feel the crack it left behind.

I swallow hard, my stomach twisting. "That must've been awful."

"It was. For everyone." Maria's voice is quieter now. "Fidel and I were just kids, trying to stay out of the way," Maria says quietly. "And Marco... I know he blames himself. He never talks about it, but you can see it in the way he does his job. Like he's trying to make up for something."

The room falls silent, heavy with everything Maria has shared. For the first time, I feel like I'm starting to understand her. Like I'm seeing beyond the sparkle and chaos to the girl underneath. Someone who'd grown up different. Lonely.

Just like me.

Maria lets out a breath, breaking the quiet with a grin. "Anyway! I'm pretty sure this is all going to end up in one of your books. And if it does, I better be in the acknowledgments."

I laugh, shaking my head. "We'll see."

As we leave the library, my thoughts stay behind, swirling with everything Maria said. Marco's past. Fidel's loyalty. Her own resilience.

Maybe we're not so different, after all.

18
____

MARCO

THE SECURE VIDEO call is already live when I step into the conference room, its multiple screens flickering with encrypted feeds. Raul sits at the head of the long, polished table, the overhead light casting sharp shadows across his face.

On the wall-mounted monitors, the rest of the Sandoval leadership waits. RJ calling in from Houston, leans back in a leather chair, his suit crisp despite the late hour. Carlos, streaming from his high-rise office in Austin, swirls a glass of tequila as he listens. Elias sits across from me, as cool and unreadable as ever, while Fidel is in the seat next to me, typing something on a separate screen, probably running background checks mid-meeting.

This is how it works.

Raul insists on these weekly status checks, and no one—no one—misses them. It started as an in-person meeting years ago, but once Raul accepted the security and ease of encrypted video calls, he tolerated zero excuses. Everything that impacts the family, legal or otherwise, gets discussed here. Finances, security, expansion, political alliances. If you don't have an answer ready when Raul asks, you shouldn't be on the call. And you better be on the call.

Tonight, the Calderóns are the priority.

Raul steeples his fingers, his expression unreadable. "Marco. Report."

I lean forward. "The kidnapping attempt was a desperate move. But that doesn't mean it wasn't dangerous."

RJ lets out a low whistle. "Desperate? Maybe. But they had the balls to try it in public. That's a hell of a leap from their usual low-level shit."

"We're thinking they may have backing," Elias says, his voice smooth as ever. "We caught their men too easily. They gave up Diego Calderón's name fast. Either they were following a script, or they were more afraid of someone else than they were of us."

Raul nods, his gaze sharp. "Then we assume this wasn't an isolated event. What's our response?"

"We lock it down," I say without hesitation. "We increase security at every access point—no movement in or out without clearance. We keep Maria guarded at all times. Patrols are doubled, and I want our men in every club, every casino, every contact point listening for whispers. We find out if the Calderóns are acting alone, or if someone's feeding them resources."

Carlos tilts his glass slightly, considering. "They don't have the money to bankroll this themselves. Either they've got a silent investor, or they're making plays they can't afford. That makes them unpredictable."

"Unpredictable gets people killed," I say bluntly.

Raul exhales slowly. "RJ, what about our Houston operations?"

"Quiet," RJ replies. "Business is steady. Clubs are moving money as usual, real estate investments are stable, and our security firm picked up two new contracts last week—private sector, nothing that touches government. We're making headway with the oil and gas expansion, but it's slow. Lots of red tape, lots of people who need convincing. No ripples from the Calderóns on our end."

Raul nods and turns to Carlos. "Austin?"

Carlos takes a slow sip of his drink before answering. "A little heat on the car business. A shipment got flagged at the border, but nothing that can be traced back to us. Other than that, money's moving clean. We've been shifting more through crypto, just like Fidel suggested. Harder to track, faster returns. The tech sector's been useful for some quiet investments, but it's a long game. Politicians still need wining and dining before they're fully on board. And I'm looking into opportunities in entertainment—clubs, venues, maybe even production. Still early, but the money's there if we move right. "

Raul turns to Fidel. "And security?"

Fidel barely glances up from his screen. "All systems are stable. No breaches, no outside attempts to access our network. I ran a deep scan earlier. Everything looks clean. But I'll keep digging."

Raul leans back, nodding slightly.

"For now, we keep everything running as usual. But we don't underestimate the Calderóns. We push deeper—find out who's whispering in their ears. And if it's just them?" He exhales sharply. "Then we remind them who the Sandovals are."

RJ smirks. "Finally. Some fun."

Carlos nods. Fidel still has his head down, staring into his laptop screen. Elias, as always, watches quietly.

"One last thing," Raul says, shifting his attention back to me. "The girl. The writer."

I keep my expression neutral. "Ami Zadegan is Maria's guest. Maria trusts her."

"And do you?" Raul's voice is deceptively calm.

There it is. The real question. Not about security. About me.

I meet his gaze evenly. "She's not a threat."

"Make sure she stays that way." Raul's tone leaves no room for misinterpretation.

I nod once. Raul scans the room, satisfied.

"That's all for tonight. Stay focused."

One by one, the screens flicker off. RJ disappears first, followed by Carlos. Fidel shuts his laptop with a snap. Elias rises smoothly, already adjusting his cuffs.

Raul is the last to move. He watches me for a beat longer than necessary, then stands. "Handle this, Marco."

I nod. "Yes, sir. I will."

As he leaves the room, I roll my shoulders, exhaling slowly.

We don't have the full picture yet. But we will.

And when we do, the Calderóns won't like what comes next.

19

AMI

Dinner in the kitchen with Maria, Rafe, Chuck, and the Russian staff is as lively and warm as it is surreal. The kitchen feels like a pocket of normalcy tucked inside a sprawling, high-stakes world. It's bright and bustling, filled with teasing banter, bursts of laughter, and the homey smell of fresh-baked bread.

Maria perches on a stool by the counter, chatting animatedly with the cooks, Katya and her mother, Arina. Maria's energy is magnetic. She isn't the boss's daughter here—just Maria, part of the crew. Even Rafe, with his sharp eyes and no-nonsense demeanor, seems softer in her orbit.

But the kitchen's warmth feels like a distant memory now, swallowed by the heavy, gilded silence of Raul Sandoval's study, where I've been summoned.

The room radiates power and control. Dark wood paneling gleams under the golden light of the massive wrought iron chandelier. A solid block of black marble serves as a coffee table, dominating the seating area, its glossy surface free of even a speck of dust. Luxurious couches upholstered in deep black leather flank it, as if daring anyone to sit too comfortably. The walls are lined with floor-to-ceiling bookshelves

98

filled with books, and massive oil paintings of Texas land-scapes hang in gilded frames. A carved stone hearth anchors one wall, a fire crackling faintly within, casting flickering shadows across the room. Does Raul ever *not* have a fire going?

Raul sits behind his massive oak desk, as composed and unreadable as ever. His navy suit is immaculate, his yellow tie knotted with surgical precision, his fingers steepled under his chin in a pose that seems almost too practiced. He looks every inch the king surveying his court.

Marco is already here, seated in one of the leather chairs in front of the desk. His posture is sharp, his presence commanding without effort. He doesn't glance my way as I step inside, his focus locked on Raul like a soldier awaiting orders.

Dr. Rodriguez greets me with a warm smile, standing near the side of Raul's desk with his medical bag in hand. His calm, professional demeanor is the only thing keeping my nerves in check as I take a seat on the edge of the other chair.

"Let's have a look," the doctor says, taking my braced wrist in his hands. His touch is clinical and efficient as he rotates my wrist gently, examining the range of motion. The soft rip of the Velcro echoes in the stillness, absurdly loud in the heavy silence.

"There," he says with a satisfied nod. "Good as new, Miss Zadegan. You've healed nicely. But no heavy lifting for a few more days, just to be safe."

"Thank you, Doctor," I say, forcing my voice to sound lighter than I feel. My shoulders remain tense, my entire body on edge.

Dr. Rodriguez gives a polite nod to Raul and quietly excuses himself. Marco stands briefly to shake the doctor's hand—his movements brisk but respectful—before sinking back into his seat. The moment the door clicks shut behind the doctor, the atmosphere in the room shifts. The silence thickens, charged with expectation.

Raul leans back in his chair, his eyes sharp as they settle on me.

"I've enjoyed having you as a guest in my home these last few days, Miss Zadegan," he begins, his voice smooth and deliberate. "And it seems you've made quite an impression on Maria."

I offer a faint smile, unsure if this is a compliment or a prelude to something heavier. "Thank you, Mr. Sandoval. Maria's great. And I'm happy to be here. For now."

Raul's lips curve into the faintest smile, but his gaze doesn't soften. "Maria's happiness is what matters most to me. And lately, with you here, she's been... happier. For that, I am grateful."

I open my mouth to respond, but he doesn't give me the chance.

"But happiness and safety are not the same," Raul continues, his tone dipping lower, heavier. "You saw that for yourself the other night, at the restaurant."

The air feels colder suddenly. My gaze flicks to Marco. He hasn't moved, but there's a tension in his shoulders now—a stillness that feels like a coiled spring.

Raul leans forward slightly, his voice taking on a quiet intensity. "This family lives in a... complicated world. That complication brings risks. Risks you may not fully understand. I admire your courage in staying, but courage without caution is dangerous."

I swallow hard, forcing myself to meet his gaze. "I understand," I say, my voice steady despite the chill creeping up my spine.

Raul studies me for a moment longer, his silence as unnerving as his words. His gaze lingers, cool and deliberate, and for a fleeting second, it feels like he's looking straight through me—to my name, my background, and every detail about me a man like him could unearth with ease. The reality of this man hits like ice water: Raul Sandoval doesn't just handle problems. He eliminates them. So, whatever I am to him, I can't afford to be a problem.

When he speaks again, his tone is smooth, measured, but the weight of it presses down on me like a warning.

"Marco will ensure your safety while you are here. It is his responsibility to see that nothing happens to you, Maria, or anyone else in this house." He glances at Marco, who gives a small, deliberate nod. Then Raul's attention snaps back to me, his eyes sharp enough to pin me in place. "And, Miss Zadegan, please exercise discretion. Do not speak of what you see here. Ever. Be mindful not to inadvertently complicate matters."

"Of course, Mr. Sandoval," I say quickly, my words coming out almost too fast. My gaze flicks to Marco, hoping for some kind of anchor, but his jaw is tight, his expression locked in that unreadable calm. Still, I catch the subtle clench of his fists resting on the chair arms, as if Raul's words carry a weight only he understands.

"Marco?" Raul prompts.

Marco's eyes meet mine for the first time since I entered the room. His voice is low, firm, and entirely unimpressed.

"Just do as you're told, and everything will be fine."

I exhale slowly, forcing my tone to stay even. "Right. Just sit quietly and breathe. Got it."

The corner of his mouth twitches—the faintest hint of a smirk before he schools his expression.

"See? You're catching on."

Raul's deep chuckle breaks the tension. "I trust you two will find a way to get along. For Maria's sake." He rises gracefully from his chair, signaling the end of the conversation. "Miss Zadegan, your are welcome here but I suggest you make sure your time here is... uneventful."

His words hang in the air like an unspoken warning.

Marco and I stand, clearly dismissed. As we turn toward the office doors, his hand presses lightly against the small of my back, guiding me out.

My breath hitches. The touch is fleeting, barely there, but it sends a shiver racing down my spine. His hand is warm, steady, grounding in a way that makes my pulse skip. And then, just as quickly as it appeared, it's gone.

In the hallway, Marco speaks to me, his voice quieter now. "Just stay out of trouble. Please."

I square my shoulders. "I'll do my best. But trouble seems to have a habit of finding me lately."

Something flickers in his eyes. Annoyance? Amusement? But instead of snapping back, he gives a single, curt nod.

"Fair enough."

Without another word, he strides away, leaving me alone in the quiet hallway. And for a long moment, I just stand there, waiting for my pulse to settle.

20

MARCO

I STEP inside the guardhouse at the edge of the compound and the glow from the monitors washes over me. Screens line the walls, each showing a different live feed: the tree-lined driveway, the perimeter wall, the tennis courts, and every other angle of the compound. Motion detectors, infrared sensors, cameras with person and vehicle recognition—all feeding into the security system Fidel built from the ground up. Everything runs through a central hub, with a state-of-the-art app he coded himself. I can access it from my phone, shutting down cameras or activating privacy zones for areas like the upstairs bedrooms or Raul's study, where nothing and no one is allowed to snoop.

It's flawless. Meticulous. Just like Fidel.

He doesn't look up as I enter, but the corners of his mouth twitch. "Took you long enough."

"I was busy," I say, letting the door click shut behind me.

"Babysitting Maria and her new sidekick?" I can hear the smirk in his voice.

I ignore him and step closer to scan the bank of monitors. "Anything I actually need to know?"

He spins in his chair to face me, his tone sharpening. "Plenty.

I've been tracking Calderón communications. There's talk of an attack. Big and soon."

I still. "How soon?"

"Days. Maybe less." He taps one of the screens. A map of San Antonio is lit up, red dots clustering around key Sandoval properties. His finger lands on one in the northeastern quadrant. "The warehouse complex where we store the heavier shipments —guns, ammo, grenades, the high-dollar stuff. It's the most likely target. Strategic, high reward."

I cross my arms, my jaw tightening. "And you're sure?"

"Eighty percent sure," Fidel says with a shrug. "Patterns line up. The Calderóns have been sniffing around. But they're being careful. Sloppy enough to notice, not sloppy enough to confirm."

"Eighty percent isn't good enough," I snap.

Fidel bristles, eyes flashing. "It's what I've got for now. But feel free to apply your psychic powers to come up with something better."

I glare at him, but he doesn't flinch. He never does. Not anymore. Fidel was three when he moved onto the compound with my mother and sister—just a quiet kid clinging to my mother's skirts while she settled into this new life. Maria was a newborn and my mother was here to cook and help raise her. Our father was long gone, out of our lives, maybe dead, maybe not. I moved in with Rafe and his mother. That made it easier. So Fidel grew up here, in Raul's house, with Maria as his shadow.

Now, he's someone I rely on. A genius with computers. A master with explosives. And a sarcastic shit who never knows when to quit.

I exhale slowly. "Fine. Reinforce the warehouse. But keep up the patrols here, too. If they're planning some kind of diversion, I don't want anyone slipping past the compound's defenses. Eyes everywhere."

"Already on it." Fidel turns back to his monitors. "Cameras upgraded, blind spots covered, motion sensors calibrated. Plus, Rafe and I rigged... a few surprises."

I arch a brow. "Explosives?"

His grin is unrepentant. "Maybe."

"You and Rafe are going to blow yourselves up one day."

"Not if we blow them up first," he shoots back, his tone light, though his eyes stay sharp. Beneath all the bravado, Fidel is thorough. Diligent. Every detail matters.

"Anything else?" I ask, already turning toward the door.

"Yeah," he says casually, his fingers tapping a few keys. "I did a little more digging on our writer guest."

I freeze. And then turn back. "What kind of digging?"

Fidel shrugs, but it's forced. "Started simple. Sales, social media. She's bigger than you think. Sixty thousand books sold. Another fifteen thousand internationally. TikTok's obsessed. But... that's not the part you need to hear."

I say nothing. Wait.

Fidel leans back, staring at me. "It's her ex. Chad Bennett."

The name scrapes something raw. "What about him?"

"Well," Fidel says, swiveling to face me fully. "Chad was on track to be a big-deal novelist. Big advance, splashy debut, the works. Until it all fell apart. Plagiarism."

My frown deepens. "Plagiarism?"

"Yeah. Turns out he copied huge chunks of someone else's work. Word-for-word, ripped from another author's unpublished manuscript."

Fidel shoots me a look, eyebrows raised. "Guess whose?"

My stomach sinks. "Ami."

He nods. "Publisher buried it to avoid scandal. The agent made sure Chad's career disappeared. But here's the kicker—I don't think Ami knows."

My jaw clenches as I lean back against a desk. "Doesn't know?"

"Nope." Fidel leans back, crossing his arms. "She was the victim, and no one even bothered to tell her."

The hum of monitors is deafening. Ami—writing stories because it's who she is. And her boyfriend, someone who should have protected her, used her instead.

Fidel's voice drops lower. "There's more."

I don't move. "What?"

"I kept digging, once I connected him to her." He pauses. "You won't like this."

"Tell me."

Fidel doesn't answer. Just pulls up grainy surveillance footage.

"University of Texas. They were in school together. Ami was getting her Master's."

He hits play.

It's night. Two people arguing under a campus light. He's towering, looming over her. She's smaller, arms wrapped around herself. Defensive.

Then—he hits her. Hard. A slap across her face, open-handed. Her head whips to the side. She stumbles. He shoves her. She falls back, hits the ground.

And he walks away.

I flinch. My fists clench so tight my knuckles crack.

She pushes up slowly, looking around like she's worried someone might've seen. But knowing there's no help coming for her. Then, she follows him.

"This was all I could find," Fidel says, voice flat. "One camera caught it. But... well, you know..."

I do know. I know exactly what Fidel doesn't want to say. This probably wasn't the only time.

I know because I've seen it happen before. I lived it. With Hector Cedillo, my father.

My voice turns cold. "Did she press charges?"

Fidel shakes his head. "Someone saved this video. Probably thought she would. But... no. Nothing."

I shove away from the desk. My chest is tight. "Fucking son of a bitch."

Fidel exhales slowly. "I don't like this. It's too much like... Dad."

His words hit hard. I knew he saw it. Even as a small child, he saw what Hector did to all of us. But I told myself he was too young to remember, too young to understand. But he wasn't.

Fidel's voice softens, almost a whisper. "You were the one who stopped it back then."

First time I fought back, I was thirteen. Broke Hector's nose. Didn't stop him. But it made him think twice. After that, fighting became survival. Then instinct. Then the only thing I was good at.

The weight of Fidel's words land heavy. I'm still his big brother. Still the one he's looking at like I'll fix this. Fix everything.

"What are you gonna do?" he asks quietly. "Are you going to tell her about what he did? The plagiarism? She should know."

"I... it's not my place."

Fidel exhales, gaze dropping. "I get it. It's not our problem." He looks back up to me.

I drag a hand down my face. "I can't, Fidel. I barely know her. This... it's invading her privacy.'

Fidel doesn't argue. He just studies me—quiet, steady. Like he already knows how this ends.

"So... we just pretend we don't know?"

Silence stretches. Heavy. Drowning.

And in that silence, I hear everything I want to shut out—my father's rage, my mother's sobs. I couldn't save my family. I can't save Ami Zadegan.

Finally, I rasp, "Yes. For now, we pretend."

I turn, hand on the door. My voice is low. Rough. Meant only for him.

"But while she's here, while she's under our protection, no one touches her. We protect her."

Fidel almost smiles, but it doesn't reach his eyes. "Okay. We protect her while she's here." He turns back to his monitors.

I step out into the cool evening air. I hear a patrol radio crackle nearby. The house looms ahead.

Ami's in there. Probably pacing. Probably dreaming up some ridiculous plan that'll make me insane.

Because somehow she survived. She survived everything that this asshole Chad put her through. She's stronger than I thought.

I drag in a slow breath, forcing myself back to the fight in front of me. The Calderóns are closing in. I need to be sharp. Focused.

And yet—

All I see is that video. All I see is her.

No one stopped my father. No one stopped Chad.

But I won't stand by and allow it to happen to anyone I protect. Not again.

21

AMI

THE COMPOUND IS quiet at night. Not peaceful, just... still. The kind of stillness that feels loaded, like the air itself is holding its breath.

I'm sitting cross-legged on the bed, notebook balanced on my knees, staring down at the blank page. The overhead light is harsh, but I don't want to turn it off. Darkness makes it too easy for my thoughts to go places I don't want them to—tonight especially.

I should be working. Researching. Taking notes for the dark crime romance I'm supposed to be writing.

But my mind keeps going back to that moment in Raul Sandoval's study, the weight of Marco's hand steady against my back as he guided me out. The heat coming off of him. It was just a touch. Barely anything. But it felt like so much more.

I glance at my computer case sitting useless in the corner, the mangled remains of my laptop still tucked inside. I wrecked it the night of the attack, when I swung my purse like a weapon. I need to deal with it, probably replace it, but right now the idea of going shopping, of walking around in public like none of this is happening, feels impossible.

So I'm back to old-school pen and paper. It feels weird—primitive, almost—but the scratch of the pen against the page is grounding in a way I didn't expect.

I tap the pen against my thigh, then start writing, slow at first.

Hero: Ex-military. Security. Quiet. Dangerous.

I stare at the words for a beat, chewing my bottom lip. That sounds good. I keep going.

The kind of man women should run from. A man who's seen too much. Done worse. A man built for violence, for survival. Tattooed. Scarred, inside and out.

I pause, heart ticking up.

Tall. Broad shoulders. Strong hands, rough from work. A body built for fighting, but a mouth that rarely bothers with words. Eyes like they're always watching, calculating. Protective. Possessive. He's safe. But you know he would burn down the world for the one he loved.

My stomach flips. I read the description again, slowly, and this time, there's no pretending I don't know who I'm writing about.

I swallow hard and set the pen down, staring at what I've written. It was supposed to be character work. A placeholder for some fictional alpha antihero in my dark romance. But every word on the page is him.

Marco.

God. I close my eyes, but it doesn't help. Because now I can see him. The way his muscles flex in the gym. The way his dark eyes track every movement like he's always calculating risk, weighing what it would take to break someone if he had to. The way his voice stays low and calm, always, even in the presence of Raul Sandoval.

And that stupid, fleeting moment—his hand at my back.

Steady. Warm. Strong. Not grabbing. Not controlling. Just...
there.

It should've made my skin crawl. After Chad, most men touching me would've sent me straight into fight or flight mode. But Marco? Instead of flinching, I'd leaned into it. Some part of me, buried so deep I didn't even recognize it, had felt safe with his touch.

And that scares the hell out of me more than anything.

I stare down at my notes, swallowing around the lump forming in my throat. I should stop. Should rip the page out, crumple it, burn it if I have to. But instead, my hand moves almost without thinking, pen gliding across the paper.

He's the kind of man you don't realize you're already trusting until it's too late. The kind of man who makes you wonder what it would feel like to be wanted by him—not owned. Touched by him—not controlled.

My breath catches, pulse thrumming low and steady.

God, what am I doing? What am I even thinking? I don't know him. I don't know anything about him.

I close my notebook, pressing my palm flat against the cover like that might stop me. Stop what I'm feeling. My skin feels too tight, my body too aware of itself.

I shift restlessly, thighs pressing together. There's a hum under my skin now, a low, insistent pulse that has nothing to do with fear and everything to do with how he looked in that gym. Muscles flexing with every movement, like his whole body was made for work and war and, well, let's just say it—sex.

And the tattoos.

They'd been seared into my brain the moment I saw them. Black ink against golden skin, coiled over muscle like armor. The bulldog on his back. A skull over his ribs. The word "Elena" in script, inked near his heart.

I can't stop thinking about them. Wondering what they

mean. Wondering what kind of man carries stories like that on his skin.

I grab my phone and start searching: "Marine Corps tattoo." It pops up immediately—eagle, globe, anchor. It's the one I saw on his arm.

I keep scrolling. "Day of the Dead skull meaning." Article after article. Memory. Protection. Grief. A way to honor the dead.

I pause. Elena. The name tattooed near his heart.

Maria had mentioned her. Marco's sister. I don't know what happened, but I can feel it. She's gone. And he carries her with him, every day. Right over his heart.

I want to know what it all means. The roses down his arm. The bulldog on his back. All of the others. Every piece of him feels like it has a code I haven't cracked yet.

Jesus. I feel like a stalker.

I never Googled anything at all about Chad. Not once.

With Chad, I hadn't thought like that. Wondered about him, wanted to know more. Maybe because none of it had been about me, always about him.

Keeping him happy. Keeping him calm. And the sex? Same. It wasn't about connecting. It was mechanical. Clinical. Like I was something for him to control, to use. A body he owned, not a person he touched.

But this feeling? Thinking of Marco? It's heat curling low in my belly, awareness prickling along my skin. It's wondering what it would feel like to have his hands on me. To feel that strength turn gentle. To see him—this man built for violence— slow down, just for me. Rough palms sliding over my skin like I'm something precious. Something desired.

I shudder and shove the notebook aside, sinking back against the pillows. This is ridiculous. I barely know him. And, just looking at him, I can't imagine him choosing me, wanting me.

And yet, I already feel like I know him in ways that matter. The kind of knowing that lives in your gut, not your head.

After Chad, I learned the hard way: I trust my gut now. And my gut is telling me that Marco Cedillo, the big, brooding, dangerous, tattooed bodyguard, is safe. I trust him.

Marco, the most unattainable man I've ever met, is the first man in years who doesn't make me want to shrink away or armor up.

I blow out a slow breath. I should sleep. I should stop this. Stop thinking like this.

But my hand drifts absently down the curve of my thigh, like even my body's tired of pretending I'm not already imagining it —what if would feel like if it were his hands instead of mine.

Jesus, Ami. Stop.

I force myself to stare at the ceiling. Focus. Tomorrow, I'll get it under control. I'll figure it out. I'll do the research, take the notes, write the next damn book. And remind myself that none of this means anything.

And Marco? He'll keep being exactly who he is. Dangerous. Distant. Off-limits.

But right now? He feels like the safest thing I've known in a long time.

22

MARCO

THE SHARP *THWAP-THWAP* of my jump rope hitting the gym floor echoes through the cavernous space, steady and deliberate. Each slap of the rope syncs with my heartbeat, forcing tension from my muscles. Sweat traces a slow path down my chest, running over the scars and ink etched into my skin. The burn in my calves grounds me, pulls me out of my head. At least for a little while.

But last night still lingers.

Raul's voice rings in my ears—*Marco will ensure your safety... please do not inadvertently complicate matters.*

And then—Ami. That grainy video looped in my mind, the hard slap across her face, the way she hit the ground. And then she followed him. A man who used her, broke her... and she still doesn't know how much.

None of that was meant for me to see, to know.

And yet, here I am. Knowing.

I can't stop thinking about her, and that pisses me off. She's not my type, not even close. I'm used to women who know exactly what they want. Money. Power. Access. The game's always the same.

The sex—easy. The attachment—nonexistent. That's the way I've always wanted it.

But Ami isn't playing that game.

She's not trying to be sexy. She's not trying at all. And somehow, that makes her impossible to ignore.

And after last night, after what Fidel showed me, I see her differently. He slapped her. Pushed her down. But she didn't just take what Chad did. She made herself into something more. I know she did because i saw her swing that purse. She's a survivor. She took Chad's hit and got back up. Didn't let him define her. I know something about that—about how fighting back isn't always about throwing punches. Sometimes it's just about standing up again.

And fuck if that doesn't twist something in me.

The whoosh of the gym door snaps me out of it. My rhythm falters, the jump rope slapping the floor in an uneven beat. I glance over my shoulder.

Maria breezes in first, all energy and confidence, her gym bag slung carelessly over her shoulder. She looks at home here, bounding into the space like it's her personal playground.

And then there's Ami, trailing behind. She looks less at home but determined not to show it. Messy ponytail. Yoga pants. A t-shirt that reads *Plot Twist: I Need More Coffee.*

It shouldn't be remarkable. But somehow, it still pulls my focus like a magnet. And makes me smile.

Her gaze sweeps the gym, landing on me. For a split second, our eyes lock, and her chin lifts—just enough to say she isn't going to let me, or anything else, intimidate her.

Maria drops her bag onto a bench, grinning wide. "We're here! And ready to learn self-defense!"

I glance at the clock and raise an eyebrow. "You're late."

Maria waves a dismissive hand. "Barely."

I knew this was happening. Maria cornered me last night, all wide eyes and determination, and somehow convinced me to do this. But I now see she conveniently left out one key detail. That Ami had no idea. And yeah, that could be a problem.

Ami crosses her arms, her expression wary. "Wait. What?"

Maria waves her off. "Trust me, you need this." Then she turns to me with an easy grin. "She'll catch on fast, right?"

I've already made up my mind—first, this woman has experienced physical abuse. So I need to be careful. She probably won't like a lot of physical touch from someone like me. But she should be able to defend herself. And while she might already know how to throw a punch or take a kickboxing class, I can show her some moves they're not allowed to teach at the local YMCA.

Second, this isn't about pushing her or proving anything. Not with Ami. She doesn't need me to hold back, but I want her to know she's in control. That I'll respect any line she draws. And that I'll stop the second she tells me to. I just need to keep it casual, so she doesn't feel pressured.

I exhale, tossing my jump rope to the floor and wiping the sweat from my face with a towel. *Keep it casual.* "That depends. Is she actually going to listen?"

Ami shoots me a look. "Am I the 'she' you're talking about? Because I'm standing right here."

Maria just laughs. "Yeah, she's going to listen."

Ami's head whips toward her, eyes wide. "I didn't agree to this."

"You're going to love this." Maria pats her on the arm. "You'll see."

Ami's gaze is lingering on me, just a moment too long. Her cheeks flush. But something in her face shifts, not just nerves now. Curiosity?

I pull my t-shirt on, ignoring the heat that flares in her stare —and the fact that it makes my pulse kick up.

"Let's get started," I say gruffly, jerking my head toward the mats.

Maria practically skips onto a mat, bouncing on her toes. "This is going to be so fun!"

Ami stays planted at the edge of the mat, arms crossed and gaze wary. "Define 'fun.'"

"You won't learn anything standing over there, Miss Zadegan," I say, keeping my tone firm.

Her brows shoot up. "It's Ami," she corrects sharply. "And I didn't ask to be here."

"Well, *Ami,*" I say, deliberately drawing out her name, "you're here now. Might as well make the best of it."

Maria claps her hands. "Basics first! Let's go!"

I start with the stance.

"Balance is everything," I say, planting my feet shoulder-width apart. "If you're not grounded, you're an easy target. Knees bent. Weight even. Got it?"

Maria mimics me perfectly, her grin smug. Ami hesitates, then steps onto the mat.

"Bend your knees," I instruct.

She throws me a sideways look. "Aye aye, Captain." Then gives a stiff little salute. "Should I drop and give you twenty while I'm at it?"

Maria snorts. I don't.

I smirk. "Well, Ami. Can you actually do twenty push-ups?"

Ami glares at me.

"That's what I thought."

She mutters something about boot camp under her breath, but she adjusts her stance.

Once she has it, I move on. Keeping my voice even, I tell her, "Let's try breaking out of a hold."

I gesture for her to stand in front of me. She hesitates, but then steps closer.

"Someone grabs you from behind," I explain, moving slowly in place behind her. "Is this okay?" I ask, voice low so only she hears.

She hesitates but then takes a deep breath and nods. I wonder if a man has been this close to her since... Chad.

I wrap one arm around her, slowly, hyper-aware of every inch between us. I ask her again, "Is this okay? Do you want me to stop?"

She takes another deep breath. "It's fine." A small pause. "I want to do this."

"Okay." I slowly pin one of her arms to her side. Not tight. Just enough.

"Your first instinct is going to be to struggle, to fight. Don't. Go for the pain points."

She stiffens slightly at the closeness. My stomach knots, but she doesn't pull away from me. Doesn't flinch.

As if she trusts me.

"Where do you think the pain points are?" I prompt.

Her voice is quiet but steady. "Uh... eyes?"

"Good. What else?"

She shifts against my hold, testing it. "Throat? Groin?"

I nod. "Right. Knees, too. And if someone's holding you like this, you've got options."

I tighten my grip just a little—not enough to hurt, just enough to let her feel the difference. She goes still.

"Now," I say, lowering my voice again, "your best move is to shift your weight forward, stomp down on their foot, then drive your elbow to the ribs."

Ami nods, but she still hesitates.

I wait—give her space, give her time to process. Then, "Try it."

She hesitates a second longer. Then does exactly as I said.

Shifts her weight forward, stomps hard on my foot, and drives her elbow into my ribs. Hard.

I grunt, loosening my hold. Maria whoops. "Yes! Ami, that was amazing!"

Ami whirls, eyes wide. "I—wait. Did I actually hurt you?"

I roll my shoulder, more surprised than anything. "Not bad."

Her lips press together like she's not sure if she should be proud or apologetic.

Maria beams. "See? You're a natural!"

Ami shakes her head. "Well, I'm pretty sure if this were real, I'd still be kidnapped."

"You would have bought yourself time," I tell her. "And time is everything."

And that... that lands. I see it in her eyes, the way she squares her shoulders just a little.

Maria claps her hands together, delighted. "Marco, do another one!"

I sigh. Of course, Maria wants a show.

"Fine," I say. "What to do if someone tries to choke you."

Ami sighs, shooting Maria a look. "Are you enjoying this?"

Maria just grins.

I motion for Ami to face me. "Hands up."

She lifts her arms, looking wary. She should be.

I move slowly, wrapping my fingers lightly around her throat, not squeezing. Just letting her feel the weight of it.

Her pulse jumps—faster, harder. But she doesn't flinch. She holds my gaze.

"Someone tries this on you, you don't panic," I say quietly. "You go for the weak spots. Grab my wrist. Stomp on my foot. Knee to the groin if you've got the angle."

Maria snorts. "Groin. Always."

Ami exhales sharply, but I catch the flicker of focus in her eyes.

"Try it," I say.

She doesn't hesitate this time. Her hands snap up, grabbing my wrist with surprising force. She drops low and slams her knee toward my midsection. I block it just in time, catching her leg before it connects, grabbing her waist to steady her.

For a second, we're frozen. Too close. Her breath fans my neck. My hand still on her hip. Her body pressed against mine.

And Christ, my body reacts—half hard already, heat pooling low, impossible to ignore in sweat pants.

Her eyes meet mine, wide, like she feels the shift between us. The desire. My desire. And she's shocked by it.

I let go, fast. Step back. "That's enough."

Maria groans, dragging the moment out. "Ugh, you two are killing me. This is painfully slow-burn."

"Jesus, Maria," Ami mutters, flushed and glaring.

I grab a towel, wiping my face. Then holding it low, hopefully covering myself before either of them can see too much. No way I'm letting them notice what just happened.

Fuck. Get it together.

I force my breath to even out.

"Same time tomorrow?" Maria chirps.

Ami hesitates, then glances at me.

I raise an eyebrow. "Unless you want to quit."

She squares her shoulders and lifts her chin. "Not a chance."

And that right there—that fire? That's going to be the fucking death of me.

23

AMI

THE SCALDING WATER beats down on my back, washing away the last traces of soreness from Marco's coaching session. I lean my forehead against the cool tile of the locker room shower, letting the steam fill my lungs and the heat seep into my muscles.

Coaching. Yeah, right. More like a crash course in surviving being manhandled by a grumpy, tattooed Adonis.

Soap slicks my skin, but my mind isn't on the lather or the way the water slides down my body. It's on him. Marco. The way his hands felt—large, calloused, maddeningly steady—circling my wrists, pinning me in place. That strength, that control, had been infuriating in the moment. The man probably follows orders in his sleep.

But now? Standing under the spray, thinking about him, I feel a slow burn I can't seem to extinguish.

And the tattoos. *God, the tattoos.* The way the ink sprawled across his skin, bold and unapologetic. Lines and symbols I wanted to trace with my fingertips, to learn like a language meant only to be read by touch. And the scars. Raised ridges breaking through the ink, proof of his life. A past written in wounds.

I've never known a man like him. Never touched a man like him.

My breath hitches as the thought spirals further, unbidden but unstoppable. His body pressing against mine, my palms sliding over hard muscle, those tattoos hot under my touch. His hands on my hips, dragging me flush against him. That low, commanding voice in my ear, telling me exactly what to do, leaving no space for hesitation.

I groan, scrubbing at my arms like I can wash the thought away.

What the hell is wrong with you, Ami?

But the image won't leave. The way he stood behind me earlier, his breath skimming my ear, voice dropping low as he told me, *"Shift your weight... elbow to the ribs."* The memory replays, and suddenly it's not my elbow hitting his ribs—it's his hands tightening on my waist, his lips brushing the curve of my neck.

A full-body shiver rolls through me. My thighs clench, heat curling through me in a way that's both humiliating and impossible to stop. For one reckless second, I consider touching myself. Right here. Right now.

The idea slams into me with the force of a freight train, sharp and sudden, leaving my skin prickling with awareness. My cheeks burn. My breath comes too fast.

What the hell are you doing?

This isn't my bedroom. This is a gym shower. *In a literal crime lord's house.*

I squeeze my eyes shut, dragging in a breath, forcing my mind to not wander back to Marco. Marco, who probably already forgot about the way his hands felt on me. Marco, who probably touches a hundred women a year like that.

Except... I don't think he does. The way he looked at me. It felt like it might have meant something.

I slap the water handle off with more force than necessary. Enough.

Grabbing a towel, I dry off quickly, ignoring the way my skin feels too hot, too sensitive. I need to focus. On Maria's book, on my research—on literally anything except Marco Cedillo and his impossible body. I yank on a pair of black leggings and an oversized *Don't Mess With Texas* t-shirt, the faded cotton hanging loose over my frame. Practical. Unsexy. Nothing to feed the fire.

And then, as I step out of the women's locker room, I slam straight into the one person I can't stop thinking about.

Marco.

His hands shoot out, steadying me with a firm grip on my shoulders. Heat sinks through the thin fabric of my t-shirt, his touch somehow both grounding and electric. His hair is still damp from his own shower, and his black dress shirt clings unfairly to his chest.

The scent of soap and sandalwood.

I freeze, staring up at him, brain short-circuiting.

"Careful, Zadegan," he says, his voice low, teasing. "Was that an accident, or are you planning to take me out?"

My mouth opens, but no words come out. I have to pull myself together.

"Depends," I blurt, grasping for control. "Are you always lurking outside locker rooms?"

His lips twitch, the hint of a smile breaking through. "Lurking? You make it sound like I'm stalking you."

"Well, if the shoe fits..." I shrug, trying to seem casual despite the fact that his hands are still on me.

He steps closer and I can feel the warmth of his body. "You're kind of a smartass, you know that?" he says.

My pulse skips, but I force my voice to stay steady. "Kind of?"

His gaze flicks over me—not leering, just looking. Like he's taking in every detail, like he's trying to figure me out. My damp ponytail. My worn t-shirt. My bare face. God, it shouldn't make me feel this... seen. And then his eyes lock on mine, and everything stops.

"You clean up nice, Zadegan." His tone is casual, but there's something beneath it. Something slow-burning and unreadable.

I blink. "What?"

He smirks, stepping back just enough to let me breathe again. "Just an observation. Don't let it go to your head."

I narrow my eyes, crossing my arms. "Noted. Thanks for the input, Cedillo."

His smirk deepens, but I don't give him the satisfaction of lingering. I turn on my heel and walk away, my pulse hammering in my ears.

Don't look back. Just keep walking.

But as I push open the door to leave the gym, I can't help but hope—just for a second—that he's watching me leave.

24

AMI

The library has officially become Maria's "war room," complete with scattered books, empty coffee cups, and a whiteboard she dragged in from God-knows-where. On it are a few scribbled notes in her dramatic cursive: *Lady Penelope—defiant, independent heroine.* Below that, *The Dark Duke??* And beneath that, a lonely question mark surrounded by doodles of little stars and hearts.

Not exactly the most detailed outline I've ever worked on.

I try to focus. Really, I do. But my brain is still back in the gym.

More specifically, on Marco.

On the way his voice had dropped low as he murmured instructions against my ear. On the heat of his breath ghosting over my skin. On the way he'd wrapped his arms around me, pressing me into his chest, his body so solid, so impossibly strong—

No. Nope. Absolutely not.

I am not about to sit here, helping Maria plot her historical romance, while my own brain is running an entirely different kind of scene, a much spicier scene, starring Marco Cedillo.

Maria glances up from her phone, brow furrowing. "Everything okay?"

"Fine," I say quickly, forcing my fingers back to the keyboard. "Just... mentally preparing myself for whatever wild plot twist you're about to hit me with."

Across the table, she stretches out in her chair, scrolling on her phone with one hand while tossing out half-baked ideas with the other.

"What if," she muses, her voice tinged with boredom, "the duke has an identical twin, and the heroine falls for both of them but doesn't know which one is the real duke?"

I blink at her, my brain still trying to scrub itself clean of inappropriate gym thoughts.

"Wouldn't that make her kind of... stupid? Not being able to tell the difference?"

Maria frowns, tapping her phone against her chin. "Okay, good point. Scratch that. I'm thinking..." She trails off, typing something on her phone before dramatically tossing it onto the table like it just personally offended her. Then she sighs loudly, slumping back in her chair.

I exhale slowly.

Focus, Ami. The Dark Duke. Not Marco. Not his voice. Not his hands.

And definitely not the way he looked at you.

The, out of nowhere, Maria bolts upright, eyes blazing with excitement.

"Ami!" she gasps, practically vibrating with enthusiasm. "This is it! I've got it!"

I blink at her, warily intrigued. "Okay..."

Maria jumps out of her chair, launching into a full-on pacing monologue, gesturing wildly as she speaks. "We know the duke has a dark secret, right? What if—stay with me here—what if Lady Penelope discovers that the duke is actually..." She pauses for dramatic effect, her voice dropping to a whisper. "A stranded alien!"

I freeze, my fingers hovering above the keyboard. "I'm sorry. What?"

"An alien!" Maria exclaims, her excitement undampened by my stunned expression. "His ship crashed in the woods, and he's working in secret to repair it so he can return to his planet. But when Penelope stumbles across his ship, he has to eliminate her to keep his secret. But!" She holds up a finger, eyes gleaming. "What he doesn't expect is for her to uncover his heart instead." She clutches her chest, then cocks her head. "Or maybe both of his hearts."

She isn't done. Maria picks up speed, pacing even faster. "Now he's torn—between her and his home! Between duty and desire! Between intergalactic loyalty and the power of love!"

I stare at her, utterly speechless. My brain is stuck somewhere between *are you serious?* and *this is so ridiculous it might actually work!*

"A Regency romance," I say slowly, "with... an alien duke?"

Maria grins, her expression pure mischief. "Yes! Think about it, Ami! Forbidden love, intergalactic stakes, and a heroine who doesn't let a little thing like extraterrestrial anatomy stop her from finding true love. What's not to love?"

"Oh," she adds, her grin turning wicked, "and his alien physique? Totally impressive. You know—*down there.*" She spreads her legs in an exaggerated motion, gesturing toward her crotch with both hands. "Think big, Ami. Huge."

That does it. A laugh bursts out of me before I can stop it, loud and uncontrolled. "Maria, that might be... the most ridiculous thing I've ever heard."

"Ridiculous or genius?" she smirks, planting her hands on her hips.

I wipe a tear from the corner of my eye, my laughter

subsiding into a grin. "Say that again," I say, fingers hovering over the keyboard. "No, really. Tell me everything you're thinking because... Maria, I think you might actually be onto something here."

"See?" Maria says triumphantly, plopping back into her chair. "This is why I keep you around, Miss Zadegan. You see the vision."

"I see something," I mutter, still laughing.

Maria leans forward, her elbows resting on the table, her eyes gleaming with excitement. "Okay, here's what I'm thinking. The duke's crash-landing on Earth has to have a purpose. Like, maybe he's part of an alien royal family who was overthrown, and he's in hiding. Or maybe he's trying to find an ancient artifact on Earth that can save his planet."

"Alright, so we're leaning into the angsty alien duke vibe," I say, typing furiously. "Got it. Does Lady Penelope find out he's not human right away, or is it a slow burn?"

"Oh, slow burn for sure," Maria says, waving her hand dismissively. "She doesn't find out until he accidentally uses his alien powers to save her from a fire or drowning or something. Then she has to wrestle with her feelings—does she love the man or the alien?"

I bite back another laugh. "This is officially the most bonkers idea I've ever worked on, but... it's kind of brilliant."

Maria kicks her feet up on the table, looking entirely too pleased with herself. "Damn right it is. Now start typing, Ami. We've got a masterpiece to write."

And so, with Maria dictating at lightning speed, I begin typing what might just become the wildest, most original romance concept I'd ever had the privilege of working on.

25

AMI

Hours later, the library still hums with the lingering charge of creativity, even though Maria has finally collapsed onto the couch, dramatically throwing an arm over her eyes like she just wrote an entire manuscript in one sitting. The outline for her novel, alien duke and all, is surprisingly coherent, even if Elias and Chuck did their best to derail things with a running commentary of questionable suggestions.

"I can't believe you kicked Chuck out," I say, shutting down the laptop and leaning back in my chair.

Maria peeks out from under her arm, grinning. "He suggested the alien duke should have a cloaking device that glitches in the middle of a ballroom scene. That's genius. Of course, we're using it. I just couldn't let him know that."

I laugh, shaking my head. "This story is either going to be a complete disaster or a masterpiece. I honestly can't tell which."

"It'll be a masterpiece," Maria replies with a self-satisfied smirk. Then, out of nowhere, she sits up suddenly, her expression shifting as she fixes me with a knowing look.

"Now spill. You've been zoning out all afternoon. Is this about Marco?"

The question lands like a grenade in my chest. I freeze for a half-second too long—long enough for Maria's grin to widen.

"What? No! Why would it be about Marco?"

Maria tilts her head, amusement dancing in her eyes. Why can this 22-year-old that I've known less than a week read me so well?

"I'm not blind, Ami. I saw the way you were looking at him in the gym this morning. And the way he was looking at you. And *reacting* to you." She waggles her eyebrows, grinning. "He was a little slow with the towel."

"You're insane," I scoff, but my cheeks betray me, already burning. "He wasn't looking at me. Or reacting to me. He was glaring. It's basically his resting face."

Maria just hums, entirely unconvinced. "Uh-huh. Sure. And when he had his arms around you, guiding you through that move? That was just, what... professional?"

I exhale sharply. "It's not like that."

"Then what is it like?" Maria leans forward, propping her chin on her hand, eyes gleaming with curiosity.

I hesitate, my throat suddenly dry. *What is it like?*

Because the truth is, I don't know.

Marco isn't just some good-looking guy I find attractive. He's something else entirely—something that unsettles me in a way I don't know how to deal with.

Maybe it's the way he watches me, his gaze unreadable, like he sees straight through me. Maybe it's the way my pulse betrays me every time he gets close. Or maybe it's the fact that when he had his arms around me today, I wanted him to tighten his grip, not let go.

I don't say any of that.

Instead, I force a light tone. "Maria, you do realize that your father basically assigned Marco to babysit me, right? He doesn't even like me."

Maria rolls her eyes. "Marco doesn't like most people, so congratulations, you're in good company." Then she shrugs. "Look, I'm not saying he's secretly writing your name in a notebook with little hearts around it. I'm just saying that he's different around you. I've known him my whole life, and I've never seen him look at anyone the way he looks at you."

I open my mouth to argue, but I hesitate. Because... had he?

Had Marco looked at me the way Chad used to?

No.

Chad had looked at me like he owned me. Like he was trying to figure out what I could do for him next. Marco looks at me like he's trying to figure me out. Like he isn't sure if I'm a problem to solve or a temptation to resist.

And somehow... I like that.

I shake my head, trying to clear it. "It doesn't matter," I mutter. "Even if you were right, it's not like I could ever be part of this world. You and Marco, you grew up in it. It makes sense for you. I'm just... visiting."

Maria's expression softens. "Ami, you're a writer. Surely you've figured out by now that the world, even this world, isn't black and white."

I shift uncomfortably. "I know that, but there's a difference between knowing it and being okay with it."

Maria studies me for a long moment, then sighs. "You think I'm always okay with it?" she asks, tilting her head. "That I never struggle with what my father does? With what Marco does?"

I don't answer.

She leans back against the couch, looking up at the ceiling. "It's not about agreeing with everything someone does, Ami. It's about understanding why they do it. My dad doesn't wake up in the morning thinking about being a villain. He does what he has to do to keep us safe. And Marco?" She glances at me, her voice softer now. "Marco's not a bad guy, Ami. He's just spent his whole life making sure people like me don't have to be."

Her words hit me harder than I expect.

Because part of me wants to believe that. Part of me already does.

She stands, stretching. "Look, I'm not saying you should suddenly start rooting for the crime syndicate in your next book. I'm just saying... don't be so quick to put Marco in a box. You might be surprised by what's inside."

She gives me a small smile and pads toward the door. "Think about it," she says over her shoulder. And just like that, she's gone.

I stare at the laptop screen, her words replaying in my mind. Marco isn't the kind of guy I'd ever imagined myself falling for—not with his sharp edges and his shadowed past. And his very morally gray present. But Maria's unwavering belief in him makes me wonder if I'm missing something.

Maybe Marco's not as easy to categorize as I thought. Maybe no one is.

My phone buzzes, and I grab it like a lifeline. Natalie. Thank God.

"Finally! Ami Zadegan graces me with her presence. I was starting to think you'd been kidnapped again."

I laugh, sinking further into my chair. "Sorry, things have been... chaotic."

"Chaotic? Try insane. I'm still processing the fact that you're staying in a crime lord's mansion."

I smirk. "It's more like a fortress. With chandeliers."

"Multiple chandeliers?" Natalie gasps. "Okay, now I'm jealous."

"Also a shooting range," I add. "Oh, and a library that would make Belle from *Beauty and the Beast* weep."

Natalie lets out a low whistle. "Well, you always said you wanted to live in a romance novel. Guess this is your chance."

I open my mouth to argue—but stop.

Because... she's not wrong.

The grumpy, brooding hero. The dangerous, powerful world. The intensity simmering beneath the surface.

I've read this a thousand times. Thought about writing it a hundred times. But I've never lived it.

Natalie keeps going. "Speaking of romance... how's Maria's little book project coming along? Is she still pitching you cuckoo ideas, or has she finally landed on something halfway decent?"

I smile, leaning forward. "You're not going to believe this, but she's actually onto something amazing. A Regency rom-com with an alien duke. It's so ridiculous it works. She's got this hilarious, irreverent voice that's going to be perfect for it. I was going to pitch it to you once we had a full outline."

Natalie is silent for a beat, and then she bursts out laughing. "I take it back. You're not living in a romance novel. You're living in the fever dream of a romance novel. But you know what? I'm intrigued. Tell Maria to keep going. And tell her I want a draft ASAP. You know I'm always looking for the next big unhinged thing."

"Will do," I say, grinning.

There's a pause on the line, the kind that means Natalie is about to shift gears. Sure enough—

"And what's the deal with the scary bodyguard? The one you called 'grumpy and tattooed and infuriatingly hot?' Or am I misremembering that part?"

I groan, slumping back in my chair. "You're not misremembering, unfortunately. And no, there's no 'deal.' He's just... Marco. Stubborn, bossy, and..."

"Hot?" Natalie supplies helpfully.

"Infuriatingly," I correct.

"Uh-huh. And let me guess: you can't stop thinking about him."

I press the heel of my hand to my forehead. "Natalie..."

Her laughter softens, her tone turning thoughtful. "Ami, you've spent so much time writing about love—about chemistry, tension, real connection—but when are you going to let yourself feel it? You deserve that. You know that."

Her words hit harder than I expect, forcing me to confront the mess of emotions swirling in my chest. The truth is, I'm not sure what I deserve. Or what I can even handle.

"Thanks, Natalie," I say quietly, grateful as always for her insight.

"Anytime, babe. Now go write something brilliant. Or better yet, go annoy that hot bodyguard. Sounds like you're good at that."

I laugh, shaking my head. "Goodnight, Natalie."

"Goodnight, purse warrior."

I end the call, the library suddenly feeling a little too quiet.

Maria's words and Natalie's advice swirl together in my head, tangling with thoughts of Marco. *Maybe they're both right.*

I'm starting to realize that Marco is exactly the kind of man I write about. The kind of man I dream about.

But he's real. Not a fantasy on the page. Not a character I can control.

And that thought scares me more than anything else.

26

AMI

OVER THE NEXT FEW DAYS, I settle into the normal rhythms of life at the compound—if you can call anything about this place normal. Maria has managed to carve out a kind of schedule: mornings filled with creative chaos, afternoons spent bouncing between activities, and evenings split between lively kitchen dinners and Marco's infuriating self-defense lessons.

And, of course, sprinkled throughout it all are Maria's increasingly frenzied brainstorming sessions for *The Dark Duke.* That's the title she's finally settled on.

At first, I told myself I was only staying for a day or two—long enough to check on Maria, keep her happy after the attempted kidnapping, and then head home. But somehow, a day or two has stretched into something longer. Helping Maria with her novel keeps giving me reasons to stay. And nothing weird or dangerous has happened since the restaurant. At least, nothing that makes me feel like I should be running for the hills.

So, for now, I'm still here. And, surprisingly, I'm not in a rush to leave.

"Okay, hear me out," Maria says one morning, perched cross-legged on the library couch like a mischievous queen issuing royal decrees. "What if the duke has two tongues?"

I pause mid-sip of my coffee, staring at her over the rim of my mug. "Two tongues?"

"Yes! One for talking and one for... you know..." She wiggles her eyebrows suggestively, her grin absolutely wicked.

Chuck, lounging in a nearby armchair, flipping through a copy of *Volley Girl,* perks up. "Two tongues? That's genius. Think of the possibilities." He spreads his hands wide, as if presenting some great cosmic truth.

I bury my face in my hands, groaning. "Maria, I'm begging you. Can we stick to the plot for five minutes? Just five."

Maria ignores me completely, turning to Chuck. "You're a guy. Would two tongues be a plus or a dealbreaker?"

"Total plus," Chuck says without hesitation. Then, raising a finger like a professor delivering a lecture, he adds, "But only if they're coordinated. Otherwise, it'd be chaos."

From the corner of the room, Fidel glances up from his phone and lets out a long, suffering sigh. "Maria, can we please get back to reality for ten seconds? You dragged me into this to fact-check your alien tech, not debate tongue logistics."

Maria grins, unfazed. "Oh, come on, Fidel. You're my research guy, my security consultant, my voice of reason. It's a vital role."

He shoots her a flat look. "I have an actual role. It's called keeping you and the rest of this circus alive."

Maria waves a dismissive hand. "You're just mad because you don't have the imagination for romance."

A flicker of exasperation crosses Fidel's face. "I have imagination. What I don't have is time to sit here and listen to you debate alien tongue counts."

Maria laughs, delighted. "You used to be way more fun."

Fidel shakes his head, standing to leave. "I'm going back to the guardhouse. Some of us have actual responsibilities."

"You mean watching Ami and me on the security cameras?" Maria teases.

Fidel doesn't turn around, but I swear I see the corner of his mouth twitch before he mutters, "Impossible." And then he's gone.

Maria watches him go, still grinning. "He used to be such a little troublemaker when we were kids. Now he's all serious."

I arch a brow. "You do realize he's serious because his job is keeping you alive, right?"

"Yeah, yeah," she says, waving me away. But there's something almost thoughtful in her expression before she shakes it off. "Anyway, back to the two tongue dilemma."

I focus on the outline, trying to figure out where to work in this new twist on the duke's anatomy. And as I listen to Maria babble on, I have the creeping realization that I'm starting to care about these people.

Later in the day, Maria bails on self-defense training—her official excuse is "needing to recharge for my masterpiece." Her absence leaves me alone in the gym with Marco.

And that feels like... a lot.

"Alright, Zadegan," Marco says, his voice low and steady as we square off on the mat. "Let's see what you've learned."

I adjust my stance, lowering my center of gravity the way he'd shown me. "I'm ready."

His dark eyes glint with something that makes my pulse quicken. He's watching me differently today, not like I'm just another problem he has to deal with. I don't know how he's watching me, but whatever it is, it's making my stomach tighten.

"We'll see," he murmurs.

He moves first, grabbing my wrist, his grip firm but not painful. I twist against his thumb, just like he taught me. My free hand comes up, striking toward his ribs—not hard enough to hurt, but enough to earn a flicker of approval in his expression.

"Good," he says, releasing me. "But don't pause. Follow through. Always assume there's another move coming."

"Got it."

We reset, and this time, he moves faster, grabbing me from behind. My pulse spikes as his arms trap mine against my sides, his chest solid against my back. His warmth, his scent—citrus and sandalwood—wraps around me, disorienting me for a moment.

"First move?" he murmurs, his breath brushing my ear.

I shake off the distraction, drop my weight, and drive my elbow into his ribs. He grunts, loosening his hold just enough for me to twist free. My hands come up in a defensive posture as I step back, my heart racing.

"Better," he says, his voice rougher now. "But don't stop there. Finish the fight."

"And what if I don't want to fight?" I quip, trying to be funny, trying to mask the way his closeness has thrown me off balance.

"Then you lose," he says simply.

I swallow hard. Right.

We keep going, cycling through different moves and scenarios, each one leaving me more exhausted. And more aware of him. The way his hands guide me into the right position. The way his voice drops whenever he's explaining something crucial. Every touch, every word, sends ripples of heat through me that I try—unsuccessfully—to ignore.

By the end of the session, I'm drenched in sweat, my muscles aching in the best way. Marco hands me a water bottle, his expression unreadable.

"You did good today, Ami," he says quietly. "You're tougher than you think."

I blink, caught off guard by the compliment. "Thanks."

He nods once, his gaze lingering on me for just a second too long before he turns and walks toward the locker room.

I press the cold water bottle to my throat, but it does nothing to cool the heat creeping over my skin. My pulse is still erratic, my body still humming, not just from adrenaline, but from him. From the way he moved against me. From the way his voice wrapped around my name.

Being this attracted to him—this is not good.

Because Marco Cedillo isn't just the opposite of every man I've ever been with. He's the kind of man who *never* looks twice at women like me.

As I watch him disappear into the locker room, I exhale slowly, my legs unsteady.

This is really not good.

27

MARCO

THE SUN HANGS low in the sky, spilling gold across the compound and stretching long shadows over the terrace. I move through my rounds, checking guard rotations, scanning the perimeter, making sure everyone is at their post, everything is locked down. The Calderóns are still quiet—for now—but silence means nothing. Silence can be strategy. Silence can be the calm before a war.

I should be focused on that.

Instead, I hear laughter.

Maria's laugh comes first, loud and carefree, followed by Ami's softer, warmer chuckle. The sound of it stops me in my tracks, catching me off guard. I shift, moving toward the pool, and from the shade of the walkway, I catch sight of them.

Maria lounges on the edge of a chair, legs stretched in front of her, waving a glass of something iced and pink as she talks animatedly. But it's Ami who holds my attention.

She sits cross-legged on a lounge chair beside Maria, barefoot, relaxed, her head tilted back as she laughs. She's wearing a tank top, the loose fabric knotted at her waist, the words *Romancing The Words* stretched across her chest. The sight of it nearly makes me groan. Of course. Another bookish shirt. Another reminder that she doesn't belong in this world.

And yet...

She's still here.

That should concern me. I should be wondering why. She was only supposed to stay for a day or two, but the days have blurred together, and somehow, she's still in the middle of it all, still mentoring Maria, still showing up to train with me, still making herself at home in a place that should have sent her running.

She leans back on her hands, stretches her legs out in front of her, her skin catching the last of the sunlight. Her hair is loose, wavy, messier than usual. And fuck me, but I can't stop looking at her.

This is a problem.

Maria's voice cuts through the air, too loud in the quiet space. "Okay, serious question. How do you make clear who the villain is in a story? Like... sometimes the bad guys are obvious, right? Guns, drugs, whatever. But what if it's not that simple?"

I go still.

Ami lets out a soft laugh. Quiet, almost bitter. "It's never that simple. The worst ones? They don't need a gun to hurt you. A real villain... they fool you. Use you. Use your love. Your trust. They make you doubt yourself, question what you know is true. And then they break you—slowly, piece by piece—until you believe it's your own fault, that you deserved it."

Maria's voice is quiet, almost a whisper. "That's... dark."

"Yeah," Ami breathes. "Because it is. Evil isn't violence, not really. Sometimes violence is survival. Self-defense. But cruelty?" She shakes her head slowly. "Cruelty is a choice. It's power used to break someone down so they have nothing, are nothing. That's what makes a villain."

The silence stretches, and it feels like every word she said was meant for me.

Maria sighs. "I guess... I never thought about it like that."

"Most people don't," Ami murmurs. "They think the man with the gun is the threat. But it's not the gun. It's the one behind it. The one who enjoys using it. That's the difference."

I should walk away. I tell myself to walk away. But I stay right where I am, heart pounding, every muscle wound tight.

Because what she's saying—*Jesus.* It's not just some philosophical take on fictional villains. It's her. It's what happened to her. And she survived it.

And worse? It's the first time I realize she might not see me as the monster I've always assumed I am.

Because I've also lived with that kind of cruelty. My father—always telling us he didn't mean it, always coming back with the same lies. Smiling while he swung the belt. That's what a real villain looks like. And that's not who I am.

For one brutal second, I want to tell her. I know. I know exactly what she means. I've seen it. Lived it.

But then her laugh breaks the air—light, unknowing. And I remember she doesn't know I'm here. Doesn't know I'm listening.

Still... her words pull something loose in me. Something I'm not sure I can put back.

I've spent years with women who know exactly what they want. Women who seek out men like me for all the wrong reasons. They touch too soon, lean in too fast, smile in ways they think will trap me. Sex is easy. Meaningless.

Ami isn't like that.

She doesn't try to catch my attention. Doesn't use her body like a weapon. Doesn't search for excuses to touch me. Hell, half the time, she acts like she barely tolerates me. But then there are moments—quick, unguarded moments—when I'll catch her looking. When I'll see something flicker in her expression before she looks away too fast, before she fights it down.

And it wrecks me. Because I want more.

She shifts suddenly, and I see it. The way her shoulders tense, the subtle tilt of her chin, the way her gaze flicks across the terrace like she *feels* me watching.

I step back, pressing into the shadows before she can see me. My pulse is faster than it should be, a dull, insistent thrum in my ears.

Get a fucking grip, Cedillo.

But even as I tell myself that, my mind betrays me. The way she'd felt against me in the gym. The warmth of her skin, the quick flutter of her pulse under my hands. That quiet, breathless moment when neither of us moved, when the air between us turned heavy with something I refuse to name.

I squeeze my eyes shut and drag in a slow breath, but it does nothing to clear her from my head. The heat in my chest rolls lower, sharpening into something darker. My jaw tightens as I try to shove the thoughts away, to focus. This isn't me. Not at all. I've spent years mastering control, learning to compartmentalize, to lock every stray thought and feeling in a box where they can't touch me.

But it's no longer working.

And I know why. Because this woman—this sharp, stubborn, infuriating woman—sees the world the way I do. She sees *me*. And she isn't scared. She hasn't run.

This isn't just a problem. This is dangerous.

I turn, walking away from the pool, from the sound of her laughter, from the impossible pull of her.

But even as I put distance between us, I already know—

It's too fucking late.

28

AMI

THE GUARDHOUSE STANDS at the edge of the compound, a sleek, modern contrast to the sprawling old-world mansion behind me. Maria insisted this was where I needed to go, promising that *"if anyone can help, it's Fidel."*

But now I'm standing at the door, second-guessing myself. I don't know Fidel that well, or at all, and I'm sure he has better things to do.

Still, my poor, battered laptop has my whole writing life on it. And it needs help. So I push inside.

It's quieter than I expected. Screens line the walls, monitors casting cold light across rows of keyboards and tangled cables. It smells faintly of coffee and something metallic. I can't help but notice a copy of *Volley Girl* perched on a table nearby.

Fidel's at the center of it all, headphones slung around his neck, fingers flying across a keyboard. He looks up before I can say a word, a slow grin spreading across his face.

"Well, if it isn't Ami Zadegan, purse assassin."

I blink. "Seriously? You've seen that footage?"

"Seen it?" He leans back in his chair, hands lacing behind his head. "Downloaded it. Saved it. Replayed it at least six times for Chuck."

I groan, eyes rolling. "Great. Thanks." But I give him a smile. "Look, I need a favor."

"You don't say." He gestures to the chair beside him. "Come on then, tell me."

I sit, placing my laptop on the desk. "Maria said if anyone could save it, it'd be you."

"I bet she did." Fidel flips my laptop open, frowning at the cracked casing and the flickering screen. "Christ. Here's how you did all that damage with your purse." He taps a few keys, sighs. "Yeah. It's toast. I'm pretty sure I can pull your files, but that's it."

"Figures," I mutter, slumping back. "That laptop was barely holding together as it was."

"You'll need a new one. Soon," he adds, glancing at me. Something flickers across his face—thoughtful, almost careful. He turns away from the laptop and crosses his arms, locking onto me. "So, looks like you're staying longer than you thought, huh?"

I blink, surprised by the observation. "Yeah... I guess I am."

Fidel shrugs like he's confirming something he already figured out. "Yeah. That's Maria. She's good at latching onto people, making them feel like this place is normal."

He hooks up a cable, pops in a flash drive, and starts the transfer without another word. The silence stretches until I speak. "So, Maria said you grew up here?"

Fidel huffs a laugh. "Mostly. Moved in when I was a little kid. My mom started working for Raul. Cooking. Babysitting." His mouth pulls tight, eyes flicking back to the screens. "Marco was older, almost a man. He was smart. Made sure we stayed here."

There's something heavy in his words. Something he's *not* saying.

"You two seem very close," I offer carefully.

Fidel snorts. "Close?" He thinks for a second. "Yeah. You could call it that. He was sixteen when we got here. He moved in with Rafe back then, but he was around. I was the scrawny little brother too young to understand half the shit going on. But Marco—he already understood everything. And he knew this was the right place for our family."

He turns back to his keyboard, taps a few keys, his jaw clenched tight.

"But that's Marco. Always taking charge. Always making the decisions. Even when he was sixteen." He looks over to me again. His gaze lingers a beat too long, like he's weighing something. "Marco takes on a lot. Always has."

I hesitate, then ask, "That just... who he is?"

Fidel's glance sharpens. "Yes, that's him. He is who he is. He isn't going to change." A pause, his mouth twisting like he's swallowing words. "And sometimes... sometimes he takes on too much. Takes on things he shouldn't have to."

I nod, even though something in me braces.

He stares at me for a beat too long, then shakes his head. "Don't, Ami. Don't get too curious. Not about him."

The warning is quiet. But it's there.

I blink. I can't help myself. "Why?"

Fidel's lips press together, debating. Finally, he leans back, scrubbing a hand through his hair. "Because there's nothing good at the end of that story. There's nothing *romantic* about the shit that made him the way he is."

The words hit hard, and for a second, it feels like he's not just telling me—he's warning me. *This isn't one of your stories. No guaranteed happy ending here.*

I study him, my voice softer now, but there's a flicker of defiance I can't hide. "Honestly? Sounds like the setup to every book I've ever written."

That pulls a surprised laugh from him, quick and sharp. "Yeah, well... maybe stop writing that one."

I just wait. And finally, Fidel sighs. "Look, here's the short version of the story. Our father was a bastard. Violent. Drunk. Raul actually tried to help him, but... you can't fix a man like that. Marco took most of the hits. Always did. Protected us, protected my mom. And when it finally got bad enough, Marco made sure we got out."

He goes still. Really still. He's staring at the monitor, but I don't think he's seeing it.

"I used to wonder if Marco could feel anything," Fidel mutters. "Turns out he just learned real young that feelings don't stop fists. Or death."

I know I shouldn't ask. That Fidel doesn't owe me any of this. But I want to understand Marco—and this feels like my only chance. My throat tightens, but I force the words out. "Maria told me about your sister, Elena. That losing her... was hard on your family."

Fidel nods slowly. "Yeah. You could say that. Elena was... everything to us. She was the golden one. Smart, fearless, stubborn as hell. Going places. The kind of person who lit up a room without trying." He exhales hard, staring past me like he's seeing it all play out. "She had Marco wrapped around her finger. Hell, she had all of us. Even Maria. My mom used to say Elena was her heart walking around outside her body."

His jaw tightens. "When we lost her... it broke us. Not just Marco. All of us. My mom... she was never the same. Dead within a year. Stroke, they said, but we all knew what really killed her." He shakes his head once. "And Marco... he blamed himself for not being there that night. Quit the Marines after that. Came home, walked straight into Raul's world, and never looked back."

He finally looks at me, voice low. "When Elena died, that was the day everything changed. The day we stopped being a family and became... whatever this is now."

I swallow hard, my chest tight. "And you?" I ask quietly. "Did you blame him?"

Fidel's mouth pulls into a humorless smile. "No. Never. I was still a kid but I knew who was to blame—some drunk asshole ran a red light. But Marco... he's been carrying it ever since. Like if he'd been there, none of it would've happened." He glances away. "Like I said, that's who he is. Always trying to take the burden on for everyone else. Doesn't matter if it's his or not."

The weight of that settles hard between us.

"Why are you telling me all of this?" I ask after a beat, my voice low.

Fidel leans forward, resting his elbows on his knees, eyes locked on mine. There's something dark in his gaze now. Something careful. Like he's holding something back.

"Because you're here. In the middle of all of this. And whether you mean to or not... you're in it now. And I need you to understand something."

I hold my breath, waiting.

"Marco will protect you. It's what he does. But... " His voice drops lower. "He's not built to survive another loss. Not again. So if you're gonna stick around for a while? Please, don't make him care."

The words hit harder than I expect.

Before I can respond, the laptop beeps. Fidel yanks the flash drive out and hands it to me. "Files saved. You're good."

I take it, my fingers brushing his. He holds my gaze a second longer than necessary—like he's still deciding if he said enough. Or too much.

"Thanks. For this... and for telling me."

Fidel shrugs like it's no big deal, but his eyes are serious.

"Take care, Ami. And... think about what I said. About Marco. Alright?"

I nod, swallowing the lump rising in my throat.

As I step back into the cool air, the door clicking shut behind me, his warning lingers in my head.

Don't make him care.

29

AMI

LATE AT NIGHT, the mansion is silent. The kind of deep, oppressive silence that hums in your ears if you stay still long enough. I like it.

I shuffle into the kitchen in my pajama shorts and a faded *No, I don't know how my book ends yet* t-shirt—peak author cliché —as I raid the fridge for a midnight snack.

Cheese stick? Check. Carrot sticks? Check. Chocolate chip cookie dough I spot in a perfectly labeled glass container? Double check.

I'm mid-bite when the soft scuff of a boot against tile freezes me. I whirl around, clutching the cheese stick like a shield.

Marco's there—leaning casually against the doorframe, arms crossed like he's been watching me the whole time.

"Seriously?" I hiss. "Do you practice sneaking up on people, or does it just come naturally?"

"I didn't sneak." His voice is calm, almost amused. "You're just distracted."

"Distracted? I'm—" I cut myself off. Arguing seems pointless with him.

He steps into the kitchen, moving like he's got all the time in the world. Smooth. Controlled. It's infuriating. He heads for the cabinets like this is his space, like I'm the one interrupting his midnight snack.

"You looking for something?" I ask, trying to sound casual, but my voice comes out a little breathless.

"Coffee." His eyes flick over me—brief, unreadable—before grabbing a plain white mug.

"Careful," I say, biting back a grin. "That one might not be lethal enough for you."

That earns me the faintest quirk of his lips. "I pick mugs based on size. Not body count."

"Sure," I smirk. "And you're definitely not cataloging which barstool makes the best defensible position right now."

He doesn't answer. Just glances at the barstools. Then, deadpan: "The far one. Clear sightline to the door. Minimal exposure."

I blink. "You're actually serious."

He shrugs like it's obvious. It probably is—to him.

I laugh, shaking my head. "Jesus. You don't turn it off, do you?"

"No." The answer is simple. Honest.

I watch as he turns on the machine to make a cup of coffee. His movements quiet, efficient. The sleeves of his black shirt are rolled up, forearms roped with muscle and ink. There's something so... intimate about the moment, like I'm seeing a version of him no one else gets to see.

His gaze flicks to me. "Glasses?"

I push them higher on my nose. Heat prickles up my neck. "Yeah, nerd alert. Contacts during the day, geek chic at night."

"They suit you," he says, voice low.

I blink. "What?"

"The glasses." He lifts his mug from the machine and takes a sip, his eyes steady on mine. Not teasing. Not mocking. "They suit you."

The silence stretches—comfortable, but charged. My brain scrambles for something to say, anything to ground myself.

"So... about my laptop," I blurt. "It's toast. Damaged during my purse swinging antics. I need to replace it. Where can I go buy a new one?"

Marco's jaw ticks. "I'll take you."

"I didn't ask—"

"You need a new one. It's a security issue," he cuts in, voice firm. "You're not wandering around San Antonio alone."

I cross my arms. "You know, this controlling thing? You like to do this, don't you?"

"It's not about control. It's about keeping you safe. There's a difference."

I stare at him, the words bubbling up before I can stop them. "My ex—Chad. He used to pull this 'I know best' bullshit. Always telling me what I could and couldn't do."

Marco's expression darkens. "He sounds like a dick."

I huff out a bitter laugh. "Yeah. He was. Always made sure, no matter what I did, it wasn't good enough."

Marco is quiet for a beat. Then: "He was wrong."

I stare at him, thrown. "Come again?"

"You're more than enough," he says simply. "Anyone who can knock out a guy with a handbag doesn't need anyone else's approval."

Hearing his words, I feel something warm settle in my chest, spreading slow and sure. "Thanks," I murmur, almost too quiet to hear.

He shrugs, eyes still on me. "Show me what you remember."

"What?"

"The wrist escape." He steps closer, placing his mug on the counter. Then, in a low voice, he says, "Show me."

I hesitate, then extend my arm. He grips my wrist lightly, his thumb pressing against my pulse. The heat of his skin sends a shiver racing through me.

"Focus," he murmurs.

I move—twisting, pulling—but he doesn't let go. Instead, his free hand comes up, brushing against my waist to steady me. His fingers graze bare skin where my shirt's ridden up, and the contact is electric. My breath catches.

"Better," he says, voice rougher now. He releases me slowly, his fingers lingering longer than necessary.

I force a shaky laugh. "Guess I'll survive a kidnapping after all."

His mouth twitches. "Maybe."

He turns, grabbing his coffee, and nods once. "After lunch tomorrow. Be ready."

And just like that, he's gone—leaving nothing but the faint scent of coffee and sandalwood in his wake.

I stand there, staring after him, my heart still racing. My face feels flushed with heat. I flex my wrist where he touched me. The warmth of him lingers, impossible to ignore.

30

TEXTS

Text Message Thread - **Maria Sandoval and Natalie Morris**

Maria: Hi! I hope this isn't weird but I got your number from Ami's phone. Well my IT guy got it

I'm Maria. You might remember—I won the Crimson Quill contest?

Dinner with Ami? Best night ever

Long story. Everything's fine. Mostly...

Anyway, hi!! 😊

Natalie: Hi Maria!!

Yes, I remember you. Ami said you two really hit it off.

And I've heard just a bit about what's going on over there 👀

(Everything's fine is always a dangerous sentence, btw)

Maria: Haha yeah that's fair 😊

So okay—this might be super unprofessional but I think I'm writing a book??

Ami's helping me and she says it's "weird but interesting" which I think means it's amazing?

It's like... Regency romance meets Star Trek

But also with a well-endowed alien

And pheromone duels

Natalie: Ami has mentioned it...Go on 👁️👄👁️

Maria: Tentative title: The Dark Duke of Dartharion

Tropes: enemies to lovers, fated mates, political betrayal, forbidden interplanetary touch

The duke has tentacles. Maybe horns. The heroine has secrets. There's a glitter-based alliance ritual.

I'm 17,000 words in and 11,000 of them are probably about his tentacles.

Respectfully.

Natalie: Maria.

I love you already.

You had me at glitter alliance.

Please tell me you're saving this file somewhere safe.

Maria: Totally!

Ami's typing it on my laptop.

Also one of the security guys emailed it to himself? I think to make fun of it.

BUT whatever—it's backed up and I'm writing more tonight.

(Also I might need help with like... what a plot is. Ami is trying but ???)

Natalie: We can work on plot later.
Right now you're doing the most important thing: writing.
And making me want to publish a tentacle duke trilogy.

Maria: OMG should I write a trilogy???

Natalie: ...Let's finish book one first. 😄

31

AMI

Morning sunlight streams through the library windows, spilling golden streaks across the endless rows of books. I cradle a steaming mug of coffee in my hands, savoring the rare, fleeting calm before Maria shows up and unleashes chaos.

I've already gotten my workout in—an hour on the treadmill, half my mind inventing new characters for a book that doesn't even exist yet. A dark, tattooed, morally gray bodyguard seems like a good start. Totally hypothetical, of course.

My phone buzzes on the side table, pulling me out of my spiral. Natalie's name flashes across the screen, and I can't help the smile tugging at my lips as I answer.

"Good morning, boss," I say, curling up in one of the oversized armchairs.

"Good morning, superstar." Natalie's voice practically vibrates with excitement. "Guess what? You're doing a book signing."

I almost choke on my coffee. "What? When? Where?"

"Day after tomorrow. Net Sports. They're the biggest tennis and pickleball retailer in the Southwest. Huge fans of the *Tennis Fixation* series. They placed a massive order, and when I mentioned you're in San Antonio? They jumped at the chance. Crimson Quill's already blasting it out on socials."

Excitement surges through me—quickly followed by panic. "That's... short notice. Do you think anyone's actually going to show up?"

"Ami," Natalie says, her voice full of the kind of confidence I wish I could bottle. "People love you. This is going to be huge. And think about it—this could open up a whole new market for you. Tennis and pickleball players love your books. Why not put them in the stores where they shop? It's genius, honestly. I should have thought of this earlier."

I grip my coffee tighter, nerves and anticipation tangling in my chest. "It's incredible. And terrifying. Thanks for setting it up."

"Don't overthink it," she says firmly, though her voice softens. "You're going to kill it. I know it."

Before I can respond, she adds, "Oh, and by the way. I've been texting with Maria."

My eyebrows shoot up. "What?"

"Yeah, she got my number from a guy named Fidel. Who, by the way, is hilarious. And I'm guessing might be a hacker? Anyway, Maria's everything. She told me you're mentoring her on this wild Regency alien duke thing? I need that book yesterday."

I laugh, shaking my head. "You'll going to love it. I think. It's hard to say. But Maria's got this amazing voice. Honestly? I think you'll be impressed."

"You're such a good mentor," Natalie says warmly. Then her tone turns sly. "But let's get to the important stuff. Like how's it going with the scary bodyguard?"

I groan, tipping my head back. "Oh my God. Do we have to?"

"Obviously." She's grinning—I can hear it. "Maria said something about you two sparring in the gym. And now you're going shopping together? Spill."

My cheeks flush even though she can't see me. "She told you all of that already?"

"Of course. I live for this now."

I sigh. "Marco is... complicated. He's not my type."

"Uh-huh," she says knowingly. "Go on."

I close my eyes, picturing him in the kitchen last night—tattooed forearms, that calm, lethal stillness. "He's bossy. Controlling. Gives off this... mean daddy vibe."

Natalie bursts out laughing. "Mean daddy? Oh, this is gold. Please continue."

I groan but can't stop the grin tugging at my lips. "I'm serious. He's infuriating. But..." I hesitate, heat creeping up my neck.

"But?" she prompts, softer now.

"But somehow, it works for him," I admit, exhaling. "He's confident. Loyal. Ridiculously attractive. And the way he looks at me sometimes..." My voice falters. "It's... overwhelming."

Natalie gasps, full of glee. "Ami. You're literally living in one of your own books. He sounds like your perfect brooding hero."

I shake my head, but my chest aches at how close she is to the truth. "No. I'm not his type. Guys like Marco? They go for tall, blonde, model-perfect. Not me."

Her laughter softens, turning warm. "Ami. You've got to stop letting Chad's voice live rent-free in your head. That guy was a manipulative asshole, and you know it. I don't know Marco but I know Marco isn't Chad."

I swallow hard, the words hitting harder than I expect.

"It's not just that," I murmur. "Marco's world... it's messy. Dangerous. I don't know if I could ever belong in it."

"You're overthinking," she says gently. "Again. You're not marrying the guy. And you've played it safe for so long. Too long. Maybe it's okay to take a risk. Just imagine what could happen."

I stare out at the gardens, silent for a beat. "Thanks, Natalie."

"Anytime," she says warmly. "Now, tell me about this shopping trip. Maria says Marco's taking you to replace your laptop after you smashed it during your purse-wielding heroics."

I groan. "She texted you that too?"

"Of course. I love her. Now spill."

I laugh. "Yeah... the laptop didn't survive. Marco's insisted on taking me to replace it. Says it's a security thing."

"Oh, honey," Natalie cackles. "One-on-one time with Mr. Mean Daddy? Do not waste this."

"Natalie," I warn, though the smile's already breaking free.

"What?" she laughs. "I'm just saying—enjoy it. Let him buy you a drink. Or dinner. Hell, let him buy you a laptop. You deserve it."

We say our goodbyes, and when the call ends, I set the phone down and sink deeper into the chair, staring out at the sunlight spilling across the library floor.

Her words linger, buzzing at the edges of my mind like a challenge.

I tell myself it's ridiculous. Just a fantasy. The heroine drawn to the last man she should want.

Except this time, it's real. And it's me.

32

MARCO

THE LATE AFTERNOON sun is relentless as we walk through *El Encanto Plaza*, one of those polished, upscale outdoor malls designed to make rich people forget the real world exists. Sunlight bounces off red tile and pale stone, casting long shadows as we weave through well-dressed shoppers.

But I don't see any of it.

All I see is her.

Ami moves beside me like she doesn't care she's out of place here. She's not dressed up—just jeans and a fitted T-shirt that reads *My Weekend Is All Booked*. But somehow that makes it worse. She's real in a way the women I usually see aren't. Effortless. Untouched by all of this.

She chatters as we walk, her voice bright and animated, half explaining laptop specs and half rambling just to fill the silence. Every so often she pushes her curls off her face, her hands moving as fast as her words. I should be focused on the crowd, on the angles. But all I can think about is what those hands would feel like pressed against me instead.

"You really don't have to do this," she says, glancing up. It's the third time she's said it, but this time her voice is softer. Like maybe part of her wants me to tell her again that I'm doing this.

"I do," I say, eyes sweeping the plaza automatically. "You need a laptop. I'm making sure you get it."

She sighs, brushing a stray curl away. "Fine. But I'm paying for it."

I don't argue. I've already decided she's not spending a dime.

The electronics store comes into view—slick glass, all sterile modern lines. Ami's pace picks up as soon as she spots it, that focus snapping into place. I follow, half-expecting her to falter, to ask what to do. She doesn't. She walks in like she owns the place.

I stop just inside, arms crossed, watching as she stalks toward the laptop displays like she's hunting prey.

And that's when it hits me. This is who she really is. Now. Maybe not always. But now. This is Ami.

Demanding. Sharp as hell. The kind of woman who no longer waits for permission. The kind of woman who knows exactly what she wants and is no longer afraid to ask for it.

I don't hate anything about this.

Maybe I should be annoyed by how easily she's slipped into this world, into my orbit. But all I feel is this low, gnawing pull deep in my chest.

"I need something portable but powerful," she tells the sales kid, already pointing to a model. "What's the processor? Graphics card? Battery life?"

The kid stumbles, clearly out of his depth. She doesn't wait, firing off specs faster than I can keep up.

Watching her, I realize again that I've never been with a woman like this. Not once.

I'm used to the ones who bat their lashes and wait for me to tell them what to do. The ones who don't care what kind of laptop they own, if they even own one, as long as it looks good on a café table next to their designer bag. Women who want money and power and are willing to trade sex to get it.

But Ami? She's none of that.

She's stubborn. She's mouthy. She challenges me in ways I don't even know how to name. And every single second I'm around her, it's getting harder to pretend it doesn't turn me on.

She finally picks a model, her whole face lighting up in triumph as she pulls out her wallet. "This is the one," she says.

Before she can blink, I'm there, slapping a stack of cash on the counter. "I've got it."

Her head snaps toward me. "Marco. No."

I meet her glare head-on. "You broke yours protecting Maria. I'm covering it. End of story."

"You're impossible," she snaps, her arms crossing tight over her chest. But there's color rising in her cheeks, and not all of it is anger.

"Yeah," I say quietly. "I get that a lot."

The sales kid fumbles with the transaction, eyes wide like he knows better than to say a word. The second he hands over the receipt, I grab the bag and gesture toward the door. "Let's go."

Outside, the sun's lower now, soft gold catching in her curls. She walks ahead, not looking at me, but every line of her body is tense. I know I pushed her, and I know she's going to stew on it.

Good. I'm stewing too.

Because I can't stop thinking about what she said last night. *"Chad. Always made sure, no matter what I did, it wasn't good enough."*

The words won't leave me. She said them like there was a time when it was just fact. Like she'd accepted it. Like that asshole made her believe it.

And it guts me. Because I know exactly what that feels like. Not just losing, but knowing you could've done something different. Should've done something different. And now you live with that choice. The wrong call that cost you everything.

That's what losing Elena did to me.

I was supposed to protect her. And the one night she needed me... I wasn't there. I made the wrong choice. And she died because of it.

And now here's Ami, standing in the sun, that stubborn chin lifted like she's daring the whole damn world to come for her. Trying so hard to handle whatever life throws at her.

She doesn't even realize how out of place she is here. How dangerous this world really is. But she keeps going. Keeps fighting. Deciding, again and again, what she wants, and chasing it.

And maybe that's what's fucking me up the most.

Because if someone like her—brave, smart, relentless—might still believe she's not good enough...

Then what chance does someone like me have?

Elena's death turned me into this—cold, careful, ruthless. The kind of man who measures risk down to the second because once—just once—I fucked up. And it destroyed everything.

And now Ami's here, dragging all that buried shit back to the surface.

She needs to leave. Needs to get out before this world shows her just how bad it can get. Before I show her.

And yet, God help me, I don't want her to leave.

I watch her as she moves ahead, her hands already in motion as she chatters away.

I'll protect her. From the Calderóns. From whatever comes next. From me, if I have to. Especially from me.

Because I'm not the right man for her. I'm not the man she needs. And if I let myself want her—really want her—I know exactly how this will end.

I'll fail her.

Just like I failed Elena.

But, right now, none of that matters. Because I still want her.

33

AMI

WE STEP out of the electronics store, sunlight glaring off the pavement, and that's when I see it—*Librería Vida.*

The turquoise storefront pops like a jewel, strung with colorful *papel picado* fluttering in the breeze. Through the glass doors, I catch the glow of fairy lights, mismatched tables piled high with books, a barista behind a coffee bar.

This beautiful book store in this high-end shopping plaza? It's... perfect. The kind of place that feels like it's been waiting for me.

I stop dead. "Can we go in? Just for a minute?"

Marco glances over, expression already tightening the way it does when he's calculating risk. For a second, I think he's going to say no. But then he gives me a small nod. "Go ahead," he says, his voice steady—but his eyes are already scanning the plaza, jaw locked tight like he's expecting trouble.

I duck inside, and it's like walking straight into my favorite kind of daydream. The air smells like coffee and new books. Soft indie music plays low, barely covering the quiet murmur of the clerk on the phone behind the counter.

For a moment, I just breathe it in. The rows of books, the

faded armchairs, the haphazard stacks balanced on every surface. My chest loosens. I hadn't realized it was tight.

I let myself drift, fingertips brushing over book spines. God, I missed this feeling, getting lost in a bookstore. In here, the rest of the world falls away. No kidnappings. No Sandovals. No Marco.

Except... I feel him.

Before I even hear his boots on the floor, I know he's behind me, his presence sinking deep into my skin. He doesn't say anything, but I know. My pulse picks up like it always does around him.

I turn a corner—and freeze.

There they are. My books.

Front and center on a bright yellow display table, every cover from my *Tennis Fixation* series stacked neatly, my name splashed across them in bold lettering. A sign sits atop one stack—"Your Next Beach Read."

I stare, my throat suddenly dry. No matter how many times I see it, it still feels surreal—like that version of me is someone else entirely.

Then his voice, low and closer than I expect, cuts through me.

"Well, would you look at that..."

I spin, startled, heart racing. Marco's right there. I expect a smirk, maybe some teasing. What I don't expect is the way his gaze lingers on the books, like he's recalculating me. Like, for the first time, he really sees *me*.

"You weren't kidding," he says, picking up *Volley Girl,* his big hand practically swallowing the book. "Fidel said you were successful... but this?" He nods toward the display. "I'm impressed."

Heat floods my cheeks. "It's... nothing," I mumble, wishing I could disappear behind the nearest shelf. *Why is this making me nervous?*

Marco flips the book over, studying the back cover, and then —*God help me*—starts reading the tagline out loud.

"'She's serving up love... will he be able to return it?'" His eyes flick to mine, dark and amused. "Clever."

I want to die. I want to melt right into the bookstore floor.

"I'm buying this," he adds casually.

"What? No!" I lunge for the book, but he just lifts it higher over my head, grinning now.

"Why not?"

"Because... you'll hate it," I blurt. "It's... it's a romance. A fluffy, ridiculous romance. Not your thing."

His gaze sharpens, zeroing in on me. "No? You think I don't do romance?"

I swallow hard. "It's not just romance. It's... explicit." The word practically chokes me. "Like... really explicit."

Marco's grin deepens, dark and slow. "Explicit, huh?" His voice drops low—dangerous. "Sounds exactly like my thing."

I gape at him, brain short-circuiting. Did Marco Cedillo just flirt with me... *over my own smutty book?*

Before I can recover, he's sliding cash onto the sales counter. The clerk, who's been pretending not to eavesdrop, takes it with a barely hidden smirk.

"Marco," I hiss. "Put it back."

"Too late," he says, tucking the book under his arm. "It's mine now."

Oh. My. God. I can't breathe. I want to snatch the book, run.

But... part of me wants to know if he will really read it. If he'll imagine me writing *those* scenes.

I follow him, shaky, as he pushes the door open. His hand brushes the small of my back—warm, possessive—and it takes everything not to shiver.

We step back into the sun. He glances down at me, smirk still playing on his lips. "Gonna tell me which scene's your favorite?"

"I—what?" My voice cracks.

Marco chuckles low. "I'm just saying... might be helpful to know where to start."

I bite my lip so hard it hurts. My entire body is buzzing.

And the worst part? I don't want him to put it back.

I want him to read every single word.

34

AMI

Los Tíos IS like something out of a romance novel—a charming Mexican restaurant tucked into a corner of the plaza, with bougainvillea spilling over wrought-iron railings and the low hum of mariachi music playing from somewhere inside. The patio is bathed in golden light from the setting sun, the warmth softening the edges of the world.

Note to self: Steal this setting for my next book.

Marco holds the door open for me, his broad frame filling the entrance. "After you," he says, his deep voice low enough to make my skin tingle.

"Why, thank you, sir," I reply with mock sweetness, stepping past him.

The tantalizing scent of sizzling fajitas and fresh lime hit me immediately, and my stomach growls loudly, betraying me.

Marco's smirk appears on cue. "Hungry?"

"Starving," I say, trying not to notice the way that smirk makes my pulse trip over itself. "I'll be right back. Can you order me a margarita on the rocks, salt on the rim? Please?"

His eyebrow arches, but the corner of his mouth twitches upward. "Got it. Don't be long."

In the quiet of the restroom, I splash cool water on my wrists and grip the edge of the sink, staring at my reflection. My hair is a little messy, my cheeks flushed, and there's a wildness in my eyes I don't quite recognize.

"Get a grip," I mutter under my breath. "He's just a guy. A guy who's too good-looking for his own good. A guy who smells like citrus and sandalwood, carries a gun, is covered in tattoos and is way too sexy. A guy who would never, in a million years, go for someone like you."

I sigh, leaning closer to the mirror. "And for God's sake, stop picturing him shirtless every time he smiles."

By the time I return to the table, my margarita is waiting, the rim perfectly salted, along with a basket of tortilla chips and salsa. Marco sits across from me, casually flipping through the copy of *Volley Girl* he just bought.

The sight of him stops me in my tracks.

His hair is slightly tousled, catching the last rays of sunlight streaming through the window. But it isn't just the hair. It's the glasses. *Oh my God, he's wearing glasses!*

They perch on the bridge of his nose, an unexpected addition that somehow makes him look even more devastatingly attractive. He glances up, catching me staring, and his smirk grows slow and deliberate, like he already knows what's happening in my head.

"Glasses?" I blurt, my voice coming out higher than I intend.

He raises an eyebrow, looking amused. "Yeah. Glasses. Nerd alert. They're reading glasses."

He's repeating my words back to me. *Damn him.*

I slide into my chair, reaching for my margarita like it's a life raft. "Well, they, uh... suit you. You look like a mean daddy." *Oh my god, why did I say that?*

His smirk deepens, his eyes glinting with amusement. "A mean daddy? I'll take that as a compliment."

It isn't fair how effortlessly attractive he is—or how much space he seems to take up without even trying. And then I notice what he's doing: flipping through my book, dog-earing pages like he has no regard for the sanctity of the printed word.

"What are you doing?" I ask, narrowing my eyes and leaning over the table.

He holds up his phone, which is propped against the chip basket. "Did you know there's a website that lists the page number of every sex scene in this book?" he asks, his tone perfectly deadpan. "It's called *TennisSexation.com*. Apparently, on page 69, she masturbates with her vibrator. And here on page 107..." He pauses for effect, his smirk growing. "She gives him a blow job. On a tennis court."

My jaw drops. "Oh my God. Stop. Please stop."

He ignores me, flipping to another page. "Page 124," he continues, "features an incredibly detailed shower scene. Paige must be very... " He looks up, his dark eyes gleaming. "Flexible."

I want to crawl under the table. "Oh my God," I whisper, covering my face with my hands.

"It's impressive," he says, leaning back in his chair, completely enjoying himself. "Seriously. The creativity. The detail. It's... thorough."

"You're impossible," I mutter, glaring at him through my fingers.

His smirk doesn't budge. "I'm impressed." He leans forward, his elbows resting on the table, his voice dropping to a teasing rumble. "How did you come up with all of this?"

I hesitate, taking a long sip of my margarita to buy myself time. It occurs to me that Chad never asked me this question.

"It's... a long story," I say finally. "I started writing fanfiction when I was twelve. Then in high school, I joined the tennis team. I was terrible at it, but determined. Somewhere along the way, I started imagining what pro players might be like off the court, and, well... tennis fanfiction was born." I smile, shrugging. "*Fedal,* look it up."

He raises an eyebrow. "Fedal?"

"Federer and Nadal. Together. In a relationship. And I don't mean just an on-court relationship." Another gulp of my margarita. "Anyway, turns out, love and tennis make a pretty good combo."

His gaze doesn't waver. "And when did Chad show up?"

The mention of Chad makes me flinch, and I busy myself with nibbling on a tortilla chip. "Why do you care about Chad?"

His tone is quiet but firm. "Because he's the guy who convinced you you're not good enough."

I freeze, staring at him. How the hell does he do that—cut straight to the truth without even trying?

"Well," I say, exhaling slowly. "Chad and I went to grad school together. He showed up in my writing groups. He was the serious writer. The kind who called Hemingway *Papa,* if you can imagine, and thought every story needed to be about some tortured alcoholic having an existential crisis. He told me what I wrote was... fluff. He said *real* writers write literature. The kind that wins awards."

"The kind no one reads," Marco says flatly.

"Exactly." I laugh, but it comes out bitter. "I believed him for a while. Even tried to write something serious. But it wasn't very good. And Chad... he made sure I knew how much of a failure I was for sticking to romance."

Marco's jaw tightens, and when he speaks, his voice is low and deliberate. "Sounds like Chad was the failure."

The intensity in his tone sends a shiver through me.

"And for the record," I add quickly, my cheeks flaming, "no, we never did anything like page 69, or page 107, or page 124. Chad was very..." I hesitate, my cheeks flaming. "Unimaginative." *Why the hell am I talking about my sex life with Chad?*

Marco's gaze darkens, his voice dipping lower. "Unimaginative, huh? Then he didn't deserve you."

The space between us seems to shrink, the air thick with something unspoken.

"You don't have to prove anything to anyone," he says quietly, his words hitting me like a physical weight. "You're successful, Ami. Talented. And if Chad couldn't see that, then he's not worth a second of your time."

I swallow hard, my chest tight. This man is truly incredible. Hardened. Ruthless. Out of my reach.

But he's looking at me—like I matter. Like I'm more than enough. And it makes my heart ache in ways I'm not ready for.

"And Chad?" Marco adds, his voice softening just a fraction. "He's a fucking idiot for letting you go."

My breath catches. The weight of his words settle over me, warm and steady, a balm I hadn't known I needed.

"Marco..."

"Hmm?" His smirk returns, teasing but lighter now.

"You're... impossible."

His lips curve into a faint smirk. "I think the word you're looking for is *imaginative*."

35

MARCO

THE WARM NIGHT air clings to us as we drive through the quiet streets back toward the compound, the hum of the city fading into the background. Ami sits beside me in the passenger seat, her legs crossed, one hand lightly tapping her knee in rhythm with the music. The faint scent of jasmine drifts toward me—clean, familiar now, the kind of scent that lingers even after she's gone.

The moonlight streaks through the window, catching the messy waves of her hair and the faint flush still lingering on her cheeks from the margaritas. She looks like she belongs in one of her stories, effortlessly radiant, without trying to be. Soft, unrushed. Real.

She's midway through ranking margaritas, gesturing animatedly as she declares some hole-in-the-wall spot in Houston leagues above *Los Tíos*.

"'Best margaritas in the Southwest,' my ass," she quips, tossing her hands up for emphasis. "The ones at *Los Tíos* were fine, but they don't even compare to Julio's. The bartender? He's like a wizard. Lime, tequila, magic. Every single time."

"You're a smartass, you know that?" I say, glancing at her, my grip on the wheel relaxing as a small smile tugs at my lips.

She smirks, tilting her head. "And you're just figuring this out now?"

"No," I reply, the smile growing despite myself. "I figured it out the moment you opened your mouth."

Her grin widens. "And yet, here you are, willingly subjecting yourself to my charm. I must be doing something right."

"Charm might be a stretch," I tease, though there's warmth in my tone. "You remind me of another smartass, though."

Her brow arches, her curiosity sparking to life. "Oh? Who?"

I hesitate, the name on the tip of my tongue. But for some reason, I want to tell her. I want her to know.

"Elena," I say before I can stop myself. Her name slips out so naturally, like an echo I haven't let myself hear in years. "She was my sister." The words come out low, and something in my chest loosens just saying them.

The teasing leaves her face immediately, replaced by something quieter, more thoughtful. "Your sister," she says softly. "Maria told me a little about her. And Fidel mentioned her too. He said you don't really talk about her much."

My grip tightens on the wheel. "There's not much to say," I say, my voice steady but clipped.

"They both made her sound amazing," she says, her voice careful, measured. "I hope this isn't too personal, but... can I ask what happened to her?"

The question hangs in the air, heavy and intrusive, but not unwelcome. She isn't pushing, just waiting. There's something steady in her presence, something gentle but unyielding. Being around her makes it harder to bury the guilt. Harder to hide from the blame.

"She was nineteen," I say finally, my voice low, rough. "She was working late. She was a waitress at a diner. Called me, asked if I could give her a ride home."

Ami stays quiet, her stillness pulling the rest of the story out of me.

"I told her I couldn't," I continue, my jaw tightening. "I was in the Marines, home on leave from Afghanistan. Twenty-five, cocky, stupid. Out with some friends, drinking, fucking around. I figured she'd get a ride like she always did when I wasn't home."

The memory hits like a blow to the chest, sharp and unforgiving.

"And she did," I say, the bitterness in my voice cutting through the quiet. "She caught a ride with a coworker. But they never made it home."

I force the next words out, the weight of them pressing hard against my throat. "They were hit head-on by a drunk driver. Killed instantly."

I take a breath, trying to keep my voice even. "I went back to base two weeks later. Finished out my deployment. Didn't re-up. Seven years in, and I walked away. Couldn't wear the uniform anymore. Couldn't be that guy."

Ami lets out a soft breath, and when I glance at her, I see her hand hovering, like she wants to reach out but isn't sure if she should. And then she does, a light brush to the back of my hand that rests on the console. "Marco," she says, my name catching in her throat. "I'm so sorry."

"I should've been there," I say, the words scraping against my throat. "If I'd just done what she asked—if I'd put her first instead of screwing around—she'd still be alive."

Ami shakes her head, her gaze steady but full of something I can't name. "Or maybe you'd be dead too."

The words hit me like a gut punch, sharp and unexpected.

"What?" I ask, frowning.

"If you'd gone to pick her up, maybe you'd have been in the

car with her," she says, her voice steady but soft. "And maybe the same thing would've happened. Or worse. You can't rewrite history, Marco. You don't know what would've happened. You just..." She hesitates, her words careful, deliberate. "You can't carry that weight forever."

My jaw clenches, my grip on the wheel tightening. "It doesn't matter. What matters is I wasn't there. I let her down."

"You didn't let her down," she says, her voice firm but not unkind. "You were young, Marco. She was young. She called you because you were her big brother, not because she thought her life depended on it. And I'm sure she knew how much you loved her."

Her words scrape against the walls I've built around this part of me, peeling back layers I'm not sure I want exposed.

"Love doesn't mean anything if you don't show up when it matters," I mutter.

"That's not true," she says softly. "I know we haven't known each other for long, but... I see you. And I think you've spent most of your life trying to make up for something that wasn't your fault."

Her voice drops lower, gentler. "Marco, what happened to Elena wasn't your fault."

I swallow hard, my throat tight. "I'm sorry I'm going on about this. I've never really talked about it," I admit, my voice quieter now. "Not even with Fidel."

"Why tell me?" she asks, her voice barely above a whisper.

I hesitate, glancing at her. The moonlight catches her collarbone, her wrist, the curve of her jaw. Her scent is still there—subtle, clean, jasmine. Part of me wants to shut down, to bury it all again. But the way she looks at me—steady, patient, like she's not afraid of my darkness. It pulls the words out of me.

"Because... you remind me of her," I say finally.

Her breath hitches, her lips parting slightly as she holds my gaze.

"You remind me of... something good. And sometimes it's hard to find the good in my life," I finish, the words hanging heavy in the air.

We pull into the driveway, the mansion looming in the distance. I kill the engine, but neither of us move. The silence between us stretches, thick with things neither of us is ready to say.

"You know, you're not as tough as you think you are, Marco," she says finally, a small, knowing smile curving her lips.

I let out a low laugh, shaking my head. "Smartass."

Her smile grows, soft and teasing. "And you love it."

I don't respond. I don't need to.

But I sit there a moment longer, breathing in the silence. And her presence.

For the first time in a long time, I don't feel the weight of Elena's loss pressing quite so hard against my chest. And for that, I owe Ami more than I can say.

36

———

AMI

THE DOOR to my bedroom clicks shut behind me, and the silence presses in like a soft, weighted blanket. I lean against the door, closing my eyes and letting out a shaky breath. My heart is still racing from the drive back, from the way Marco looked at me, from the quiet intensity in his voice when he told me, *Chad didn't deserve you.*

That moment didn't just warm me. It's set something alight.

I cross the room in a daze. Moonlight spills through the gauzy curtains, casting soft, silver shadows over the bed, the armchair in the corner, the carefully curated warmth of this guest room. But none of it can distract me from the heat humming just beneath my skin.

Dropping my bag on the bed, I catch sight of myself in the mirror above the dresser. My cheeks are flushed, my eyes brighter than I remember them being, and my lips, still tingling from the way I'd bitten them while Marco spoke.

God, I need to get it together.

I turn away, kicking off my shoes and pulling my hair free of its messy ponytail. But as I go to grab a pair of pajamas from my suitcase, I pause. My mind drifts back to the car ride, to Marco's

180

quiet confession about Elena, to the depth of emotion in his voice when he talked about his sister.

He trusts me with that. He doesn't strike me as the type of man who opens up easily—or often. But he had. And the way he looked at me when he said, *you remind me of something good… it's* not just about Elena. It's not just words.

It's something more.

The way he made me feel about myself. He didn't just brush off Chad's shit; he annihilated it, as if it wasn't even worth the air it had taken to speak it aloud. *You're talented,* he said. *You're successful.* It was the kind of validation I hadn't realized I needed until it was already sinking into my bones.

And damn it, he's just *so* beautiful.

Not just the tattoos and the broad shoulders and the sharp lines of his jaw. It's the whole package: the calm confidence, the way he moves like he's the only man in the room, the subtle protectiveness in the way he guides me through a crowd. The sharpness of his mind, the unspoken grief in his eyes, the way his lips curve into that maddening half-smirk like he knows exactly what effect he has on me.

I run my fingers through my hair and then change into my pajamas. I've torn this room apart looking for a camera and come up empty. If someone's watching me, they're good. Too good. I'm done worrying about it.

I cross the room to the nightstand. My fingers hover over the drawer handle, my pulse quickening as I remember my whispered conversation with Natalie the night I'd arrived.

"Do you think they packed my vibrator?"

The memory makes me blush, but this time, there's no mortified panic—just a spark of something electric and undeniable. Slowly, I slide the drawer open and spot the familiar little velvet bag tucked neatly inside.

Of course it's tucked in the drawer. The staff here doesn't miss a single detail.

I pull it out, holding it in my hands for a moment as my thoughts spiral back to Marco. The way his hand brushed against mine in the kitchen. The way his fingers gripped my waist during self-defense training, steadying me like it was the most natural thing in the world. The way he always looks at me —like he's two steps ahead, but somehow still completely in the moment with me.

The heat in my chest spreads lower, warmth settling in my core, sinking deep until my thighs press together. A soft, restless ache hums there, demanding attention I've denied for too long. My breaths come quicker, and I feel an ache that's both maddening and impossible to ignore.

I pad to the bathroom, flipping on the soft light. The cool tile underfoot grounds me just enough as I set the bag on the counter and run the faucet, filling the sink with warm water. I carefully unzip the bag and pull out the sleek little device, glancing at my flushed reflection in the mirror. It's waterproof so I submerge it in the soapy water.

This is ridiculous, I think as I scrub the silicone casing. But the thought doesn't stop me. I wash the vibrator carefully, lifting my gaze to the mirror again. And there he is. Not really, but in my mind. The way his eyes darken when he looks at me. The way he sounds when he says my name.

The way he'd said, *"He's a fucking idiot for letting you go."*

No one has ever spoken to me like that before. Not Chad. Not anyone. And Marco hadn't just said it. He'd *meant* it. I could feel it in the weight of his words, in the steady conviction of his tone.

He makes me feel seen. Strong. Desirable.

And I want more.

I dry the vibrator carefully, setting it on a fresh towel. My skin prickles with anticipation as I carry it back to the bedroom, the ache inside me sharpening with every step.

Sliding onto the bed, I dim the lights until only the lamp's soft glow spills across the sheets. I settle back, heart racing, skin flushed, every nerve lit up like a live wire.

My fingers trace the smooth surface of the toy, pausing. This isn't something I do often, letting myself *go there,* fantasizing about a real man, letting my mind wander into dangerous, tempting territory. But tonight feels different.

Because tonight, the man I'm picturing is Marco. The warmth of his hands on my skin. The heat of his breath at my ear. The weight of his body pressed against mine. His mouth— *God, his mouth*—on my throat, his breath against my ear.

I close my eyes, letting the image of him fill every corner of my mind, every inch of my imagination.

And finally, I turn the vibrator on.

37

MARCO

THE GUARDHOUSE IS SILENT, save for the faint hum of the security monitors. I gave Fidel the rest of the night off, telling him I'd monitor security tonight.

I sit back in the chair, rubbing a hand over my jaw, trying to shake the tension that has coiled tighter and tighter since I left the restaurant with Ami.

I glance at the book sitting on the desk in front of me. *Volley Girl* by Amira Zadegan. Just seeing her name in bold across the cover makes something in my chest twist. I should've left it in the SUV, but no. Like an idiot, I'd brought it here. And then I'd opened it. And then I'd read page 124. Again.

The shower scene.

Her writing wasn't just good—it was *dangerous*. Every word, every vivid detail pulled you in, made you feel like you were there. Water streaming down their bodies, the heat of their need pressing them together, her legs wrapped tight around his waist as he drove into her. It was so raw and *alive*. I couldn't stop picturing it, couldn't stop imagining *her*. Ami.

She wasn't just a writer. She was an artist, one who knew exactly how to paint with words, how to make you feel every

184

ounce of tension, every gasp, every touch. And now she was invading my head, making me picture things I had no right picturing.

I toss the book onto the desk, letting out a slow breath, but it doesn't help. Not when I can still hear her voice from earlier in the restaurant, teasing and sharp, telling me how sex with her ex had been "unimaginative." Not when I can still see the way her lips had curved into a smirk when she'd talked about her explicit scenes—half teasing, half daring—like she thought I wouldn't be interested.

God, I want her.

I want her so badly it feels like a physical ache, one I can't shake no matter how hard I try.

I run a hand down my face, glancing at the security monitors in front of me. One by one, I click through the feeds—gates, perimeter, hallways, common areas—every part of the compound exactly as it should be. Quiet. Secure.

I don't need to check her room. I *shouldn't* check her room. It's off-limits, one of Raul's firm rules. The bedrooms have extremely well-hidden cameras. Only Fidel and I have access to those feeds. Because the private areas are to stay private, unless there's a damn good reason otherwise.

But then I think about dinner, the margaritas. She had more than one, and while Ami doesn't seem like the kind of woman to lose control, the thought of her alone, maybe unsteady, stirs something in me. Just a quick check, I tell myself. Just to make sure she made it safely to her room. Nothing more.

The excuse sounds thin even in my head. A mistake. A violation. Raul's rules about privacy aren't just guidelines. They're ironclad.

And I know it's not just to make sure she's okay. I want to see her. I want to watch her. And that's what makes me a piece of shit. Pretending there's some noble reason for doing something so fucking wrong.

I click on the feed to her room anyway.

The screen flickers, and there she is. I can see her, hear her.

Sitting on the edge of her bed, her hair loose around her shoulders, dressed only in a t-shirt and panties. My heart kicks up as I watch her pick something up wrapped in a towel and start drying it carefully. I lean closer, my eyes narrowing, trying to make out what it is.

When she pulls the towel away, my stomach drops.

A vibrator.

She holds it in her hands, examining it like she's considering her next move. My breath stalls as I watch her place it on the nightstand. I tell myself to look away, to shut the feed off, but I can't move. My hands freeze on the keyboard, my eyes locked on the screen.

Ami scoots back onto the bed, leaning against the headboard, her knees drawing up as she reaches for the hem of her oversized t-shirt, lifting it just slightly. Her movements are slow, unhurried, and impossibly enticing. My pulse thunders in my ears, and I swear under my breath.

This is wrong. I'm supposed to protect her. Not see this. Never this. She trusts me, and I'm betraying that trust in real time, watching her like this.

But I can't stop.

Her hands skim up her thighs, and my body tightens, every nerve in me screaming to look away, to stop invading her privacy. But I don't.

The soft glow of the bedside lamp casts her in a golden light, her skin luminous against the white sheets. My jaw clenches as I watch her shift slightly, her legs falling open just enough to make my blood run hot.

She doesn't move to pick up the vibrator again, not yet. But the way her hands linger on her own skin, the way her head tilts back against the headboard—it's enough to unravel me completely.

My hand drifts to the waistband of my trousers before I even realize what I'm doing. The ache low in my gut has become unbearable, and the thought of her—of her hands on herself, of the sounds she might make—pushes me past the point of no return.

I lean back in my chair, my hand moving of its own accord, opening my belt, my trousers, and slipping under the waistband, the ache becoming too much to ignore. On the screen, Ami shifts again, her legs drawing up a little higher, her t-shirt sliding further up her thighs. The slow, unintentional tease of her movements is driving me insane.

She still hasn't reached for the vibrator, but the way her fingers graze her skin—light, almost absent-minded, like she's still toying with the idea—makes my imagination fill in the blanks. The way she would look sprawled out on that bed, her head thrown back, her lips parting in soft gasps... God, I can hear her in my mind, the sound soft and breathless, just for me.

This isn't just attraction. It's something deeper, something primal, something I haven't felt in a long time. Something I didn't think I deserved to feel.

And there's no stopping it. Not now.

I reach into my briefs, grabbing my cock. My grip tightens as I watch her shift on the bed, her head tilting back, her fingers brushing over her collarbone and drifting lower, teasing herself like she isn't sure she should go further. My breath comes harder, my hand slowly stroking up and down, my chest rising and falling in time with the way her hands move—slow, deliberate, like she's savoring every touch.

I hear Ami let out a soft sigh, her chest lifting with the

sound, and I swear under my breath, my jaw tightening as I stroke my cock faster, the pressure building with every second.

I shouldn't be doing this. I shouldn't be watching her.

But fuck, I can't stop.

Her hand finally slips under the hem of her t-shirt, and my mind goes blank. Completely fucking blank. I can see the edge of her underwear now—simple, white cotton that somehow makes her look even sexier. I see her fingers slide lower, over her panties, and I imagine the way her body would react to my fingers, my touch. How wet she would be.

I bite down hard on the inside of my cheek, trying to ground myself, but it's no use. The only thing I can think about is her—how soft her skin would feel, how she'd taste, how she'd sound as I touched her, kissed her, made her come apart under me.

Staring at her on the screen, the image burns into my brain. I stroke faster, rougher, the fucking need clawing at me like it will never be satisfied.

On the screen, she suddenly freezes, her head snapping toward the door. My heart stops, my hand going still.

Ami glances around the room, her expression unreadable, and for one horrifying moment, I think—she knows. Think she can feel my eyes on her somehow.

But then she shakes her head, relaxing again, her hand falling away as she leans back into the pillows. She grabs the vibrator off the nightstand, turning it over in her hands like she's still deciding whether to use it.

I force myself to shut off the feed.

The screen goes black, and I sit there in the dark, my hand still wrapped around my iron hard dick, my breath coming hard and fast.

What the fuck am I doing?

I let out a shaky breath. My body still burns, my skin is still tight with tension, but I don't turn the screen back on.

Ami Zadegan is going to destroy me.

And for once, I'm not sure I care.

The black screen stares back at me, but it doesn't help. Shutting off the feed doesn't erase the image of Ami from my mind. It doesn't stop me from imagining the sound of her soft sighs, doesn't stop my body from responding, knowing that she's right there, touching herself on that bed.

Fuck it.

My hand slides over my length again, slower now, deliberate. My eyes drift closed as I lean back in the chair, letting the memory of her take over. The way her hair spilled across the pillow, the flush creeping up her chest, the slight part of her lips when she exhaled—it's burned into me, every detail vivid.

I can picture her there, her body arching under her own touch, her fingers dipping lower as she discovers exactly what she needs.

I tighten my grip, stroking my cock harder, letting my mind go. To the way she'd feel under me, her nails digging into my shoulders as she gasped my name. To the way her thighs would tremble as I pinned her down, showing her exactly how much she drove me out of my mind.

On the bed, in the shower, against the wall—I don't fucking care. All I know is that if I ever get the chance, I won't hold back. I'll give her everything. Take everything.

A groan escapes me, low and guttural, as the pressure builds, coiling tighter with every stroke. My breath comes faster, my hips shifting as I chase the release that has been building all damn day.

Ami's face flashes in my mind again—her lips parted, her head tilting back as she moans softly, lost in her own pleasure. Whispering my name. And that's it.

My body tenses, and the release rips through me, sharp and all-consuming. I bite back the sound rising in my throat, my grip tightening on my cock as the waves crash over me, relentless and unforgiving.

I stay there for a moment, chest heaving, my body still pulsing with the aftershocks. Not caring that I'm now covered in come. Slowly, I open my eyes, my hand dropping to my side as I stare at the blank screen.

But it's not over.

Even now, I can't stop thinking about her. Can't stop imagining what it would feel like to have her in my arms, to hear those soft sounds she made up close, to be the one driving her over the edge.

I should leave it there. I've already gone too far—invaded her privacy in a way I can't take back. But as I sit in the darkness, her image burned into my mind, my body still thrumming with need, I find myself reaching for the keyboard again. Just one more look, I tell myself. Just one more second.

But I know it's not true. I'm not in control of myself anymore. She is.

The screen blinks to life, and there she is, still on the bed. But now, the vibrator is in her hand, and she isn't hesitating anymore.

Ami's legs are spread slightly, her knees bent, and the vibrator is pressed between her thighs, the low hum of the device barely audible. Her head tips back against the pillows, her lips parting in a soft moan that I can feel in my chest.

My cock twitches again, painfully sensitive but already hardening at the sight of her. *Jesus Christ.*

Her free hand slides under the hem of her t-shirt, pushing it up to reveal smooth, soft skin. She isn't wearing a bra, and the sight of her bare breasts—her nipples hard, pebbled—hits me like a punch to the gut. She cups one in her hand, pinching and rolling her nipple between her fingers, her hips rocking against the vibrator as she lets out another soft, breathy moan.

Somehow I'm completely hard again, my hand instinctively wrapping around myself again as I watch her. There's no shame now, no hesitation. Just the overwhelming need to have her. To touch her. To make her mine.

She moves the vibrator in slow circles, her body arching slightly off the bed, her breaths coming faster. Her lips part, her brow furrowed slightly, and I can tell she's close. So fucking close.

And then I hear it, a faint whisper. "Marco."

The second my name leaves her lips, everything in me breaks. She's thinking about me. Wanting me.

She gasps, her body tensing, her back arching as her climax hits her. Her head tips back, her mouth falls open, and for a moment, she looks completely undone—wild, beautiful, and utterly out of control.

It's the most erotic thing I've ever seen. The most erotic thing I've ever heard.

My hand moves faster, chasing that second release, the sight of her pushing me to the edge all over again. It doesn't take long —my body is already primed, the need too intense to ignore.

When I come, it's harder than before, my head falling back against the chair, a low groan tearing from my throat.

I stay like that for a moment, catching my breath, the tension finally easing from my body.

I open my eyes and look at the screen again. She's panting, her chest still heaving. She looks beautiful.

I turn off the feed, shutting the monitor down completely this time. But she's till there—etched into my mind, my body, my blood. I crossed a line tonight. She would hate me if she knew.

But I already know. I don't give a fuck. I'd do it all again.

38

AMI

THE GYM IS quiet when I step inside, the faint hum of the air conditioning the only sound. Morning light streams through the high windows, pooling on the polished floor in soft, golden streaks. And there is Marco.

He's at the heavy bag, his back to me, shirtless and utterly focused. Every punch lands with a sharp *thwack*, his fists moving in precise, devastating arcs. The muscles in his back ripple with every motion, the ink of his tattoos shifting over his bronzed skin. He is power and control distilled into a single moment, and I can't look away.

My breath hitches, memories of the night before rushing back. The way my body came alive as I thought of him. The way his voice sounded in the car, low and rough, telling me *Chad didn't deserve you.* The way he looked at me, like I was something worth defending.

And now, watching him like this—raw, unfiltered, completely in his element—I feel it all over again. That heat. That pull. That maddening ache that refuses to be ignored.

I'm so lost in the sight of him that I don't notice he stopped. Marco turns, his dark eyes locking onto mine with a sudden intensity that sends a shiver racing down my spine. His chest rises and falls with steady breaths, his damp hair falling messily across his forehead. He wipes his face and chest with a towel, the movement impossibly casual but somehow intimate.

"You're early," he says, his voice low and steady, as if he hasn't just caught me staring.

I force myself to move, stepping fully into the room and dropping my gym bag by the wall. "Maria's in the library," I say, my voice a little too breathless. "Looks like it's just you and me."

His jaw tightens almost imperceptibly before he nods. "Alright. Let's get to work."

He pulls on a t-shirt as he walks toward me. The air seems to shift, growing heavier with each step he takes. His presence is magnetic, overwhelming, and it takes everything I have to keep from stepping back.

We start with drills, and Marco is all business. His voice is calm but firm, guiding me through each move with the kind of focus that leaves no room for argument.

"Your balance is off," he says, stepping closer. His hands find my waist, the calloused warmth of his palms burning through the fabric of my shirt as he adjusts my stance. "Center yourself. Here."

I inhale sharply, the heat of his touch sending sparks skittering across my skin. My heartbeat quickens, and I wonder if he can feel it, the way my pulse races beneath his hands.

"Relax," he murmurs, his voice softer now, almost coaxing.

"Easy for you to say," I shoot back, trying to mask the shakiness in my voice with sarcasm.

His lips twitch, just the faintest hint of a smirk, but he doesn't reply. Instead, he steps back, watching me with an intensity that makes my stomach flutter.

"You're getting better," he says, his tone quieter now.

I shrug, forcing myself to focus on the drill. "Maybe I have a good teacher."

His eyes stay on mine, something unreadable flickering behind them. "You're stronger than you think, Ami," he says, his voice low and deliberate. "You just don't know it yet."

The weight of his words presses against me, sinking deep into places I didn't know were vulnerable. He isn't just talking about the drills, and we both know it.

We move back into the exercises, but the air between us has changed. Every time he touches me—guiding my arm, adjusting my stance—it feels charged, like the space between us is alive with heat.

And then, stupidly, I bring up the Calderóns.

"So... the Calderóns," I say, trying to sound casual. "What's the deal with them? Are they—"

Marco freezes, his expression darkening instantly.

"Who told you about the Calderóns?" he asks, his voice cutting through the quiet like a blade.

I hesitate, caught off guard by the sudden shift in his tone. "No one. I just... notice things. Maria talks. People talk." I gesture vaguely. "I listen. It's what I do."

He steps closer, his presence suddenly overwhelming. "That's dangerous, Ami."

"What's dangerous is pretending I don't see what's happening around me," I shoot back, squaring my shoulders.

His hand comes to rest on my wrist, his grip firm but not harsh. "You're too smart for your own good," he says quietly, his voice low and rough.

I tilt my chin up, refusing to back down. "Maybe. But I'm here. I'm part of whatever's going on, whether you like it or not."

The tension between us crackles, and for a moment, neither of us moves. His eyes flicks to my lips, and I see it—the hesitation, the pull, the war he's fighting within himself.

And then, I close the gap.

The kiss starts slow, tentative, like neither of us fully believes it's happening. And then—he moves. It's not careful. It's not slow. His mouth crashes against mine before either of us can think.

His hand slides to the back of my neck, pulling me closer, all hesitation melting away. His lips are warm, firm, and impossibly commanding, and I can't stop the soft sound that escapes me when his other hand grips my waist, anchoring me against him.

Every nerve in my body lights up, my hands sliding up his chest, feeling the hard lines of muscle and the heat radiating off his skin. He kisses me like he's unraveling, like holding back is no longer an option, like every ounce of his restraint has just snapped.

And I want more.

I press closer, my fingers brushing the sharp edge of his jaw, feeling the faint scratch of stubble against my palm. His breath hitches against my mouth, and something about that—about knowing I can pull that sound from him—ignites a fire in my chest.

But then, just as suddenly as it began, he pulls away.

It isn't a slow retreat. It's sharp, abrupt, like he's just realized he's done something that can't be undone. His hands fall away from me, his chest rising and falling with uneven breaths as he takes a step back.

I open my eyes, breathless and dazed, to find him staring at me, his jaw tight, his expression torn between regret and something I can't name.

"This is a mistake," he says, his voice rough, almost guttural.

"Marco..." My voice is barely above a whisper, shaky and raw, but I don't know what else to say.

"I can't do this," he says, shaking his head. His gaze flicks to mine, dark, hollow, before dropping to the floor. "We can't be together."

Something sharp flares in my chest. Not hurt, not yet. It's fury that he kissed me like that and thinks he can just walk away.

"You don't mean that," I say, ready to fight back.

He doesn't respond. Instead, he turns on his heel and walks out of the gym, his movements stiff, deliberate, like he's holding himself together through sheer force of will.

I stand there, my heart pounding, my lips still tingling, my hands clenching at my sides like they don't know what to do now that they aren't touching him. The silence in the gym is deafening, pressing down on me, wrapping around the hollow ache in my chest.

I press my fingers to my mouth, the faintest trace of him still lingering there, warm and intoxicating. My breath comes out unsteady, and I swallow hard, willing myself to hold it together.

But no matter how hard I try, I can't shake the weight of what just happened—or the way it ended.

He kissed me like he wanted me. Like he needed me.

And then he walked away like none of it mattered.

39

AMI

The library buzzes with Maria's frenetic energy as she paces in front of the massive oak table, waving a printed manuscript at us. Sunlight streams through the tall windows, bathing the room in a warm glow, but Maria's presence eclipses everything else. She's in full creative mode, her face alight with excitement as she dictates notes to Rafe and Chuck with the authority of a general preparing for battle.

"No, no, no!" she exclaims, pointing dramatically to the page Rafe holds. "He wouldn't say it like that. He's an alien duke, not some awkward Earth teenager. He needs to sound commanding. Regal, but still..." She pauses, twirling a pen between her fingers. "Vulnerable."

Rafe, lounging against the edge of the table, raises an eyebrow. "Commanding *and* vulnerable? You're asking a lot from a guy with tentacles and a spaceship."

Maria shoots him a glare, her hands going to her hips. "The tentacles are secondary, Rafe. They're a metaphor for his complexity."

Chuck, seated with legs crossed in one of the armchairs, a

stack of pages on his lap, nods solemnly. "A metaphor for complexity. Makes sense."

"Don't you get it?" Maria asks, completely serious. "This is a love story, and the duke's dual nature—alien yet human, powerful yet tender—that's what Penelope falls for."

Rafe holds up his hands in mock surrender, though a grin tugs at his lips. "Alright, alright. I'll try it again. But don't blame me if it still sounds like something out of a bad sci-fi soap opera."

Maria crosses her arms and narrows her eyes, watching as Rafe clears his throat.

"Lady Penelope," he intones, his voice deep and dramatic, "I swear upon the twin moons of my homeworld that your radiance outshines even the fabled crystals of Zoronis."

Maria tilts her head, her expression contemplative. "Hmm. Better. But maybe less... fabled crystals, more... existential longing. He's not just a duke. He's a tortured soul."

Rafe groans, dragging a hand down his face. "Maria, he's got *tentacles.* How tortured can he be?"

Chuck cocks his head, considering. "I think the tentacles make him more tortured. It's a metaphor for his inner turmoil."

Maria beams, clearly pleased with his answer. "Exactly! Thank you, Chuck. Finally, someone who gets it."

Their banter fills the room, light and warm, but it barely registers. I sit at the far end of the table, cradling my coffee mug like it's the only thing keeping me tethered to the ground. Their voices blur into white noise as my thoughts circle back to the gym.

Back to Marco.

Back to the kiss.

My chest tightens as the memory surges forward, vivid and all-consuming. My lips feel tender and I swear I can still taste him. I can feel the way his hand gripped the back of my neck, firm and unyielding. The way his lips pressed against mine, searing and urgent, igniting something in me I hadn't felt in years. And then, just as quickly as it began, the way he pulled away.

"This is a mistake."

The words echo in my head, sharp and final.

What the hell was I thinking?

For one fleeting, reckless moment, I'd let myself believe the pull between us was real—the way he opened up to me about Elena, the way he defended me against Chad's memory, the way he looked at me. I thought it meant something. That I meant something.

But I was wrong.

I force down a sip of my coffee as I try to shove down the memory. Marco isn't interested in me. He can't be. I'm just an obligation—Maria's friend, Raul's guest, someone he has to look after because it's his job. The kiss was a lapse in judgment, a moment of weakness he clearly regretted the second it happened.

He doesn't get involved. Doesn't lose control. He executes orders and walks away.

And now, I feel like a fool.

"Ami!" Maria's voice cuts through my haze, yanking me back to the present.

I blink, realizing everyone is staring at me, Maria with her arms crossed, Rafe smirking like he just caught me daydreaming, and Chuck tilting his head in silent curiosity.

"Sorry, what?" I ask, forcing a smile.

Maria sighs, waving the manuscript at me. "I said, what do you think? Is the duke's dialogue believable, or does it need a rewrite?"

I stare at the pages in her hand, the words swimming in front of me as my brain scrambles to catch up. "Uh… I think it's good?"

Maria frowns, narrowing her eyes. "Are you okay? You've been weird all morning."

"I'm fine," I say quickly, setting my coffee down. "Just… tired."

Maria doesn't look convinced, but before she can press me further, Chuck leans back in his chair and grins.

"For the record," he says, "I think the duke's dialogue is fine. But if we're talking about authenticity, we should really address the logistics of alien anatomy."

Maria groans, but there's a faint smile on her face. "Not this again."

"I'm serious!" Chuck says. "If the duke has tentacles, does that mean he's got, like, suction cups too? Because that could really change the dynamic of the love scenes."

Rafe chuckles, flipping through the manuscript. "I think we've officially lost the plot."

Maria shakes her head, but there's a hint of amusement in her eyes. "You're impossible, Chuck. This is a love story, not a biology lesson."

"A love story with tentacles," Chuck quips. "I'm just saying, readers are going to have questions. Suction cup questions."

Their banter drifts around me, warm and familiar, but it feels distant. My thoughts keep circling back to Marco. The way he looked at me this morning, his dark eyes heavy with something I can't quite name. The way his lips lingered on mine, like he didn't want to let go.

And the way he had.

I tighten my grip on the coffee mug, ignoring the tightness in my chest.

Even now, sitting here with Maria and the others, I can't stop replaying the moment. Can't stop wondering what the kiss had meant to him.

To me, it had been everything.

To Marco?

I let out a slow breath, my gaze drifting to the windows where the golden light of late morning spilled across the floor.

It doesn't matter what it meant to Marco.

He walked away.

And the real question—the one I don't know how to answer—is whether I'll ever be able to face him again.

40

MARCO

THE NIGHT IS QUIET, the kind of night that usually settles me, the routine of patrol offering a strange comfort in its predictability. But not tonight.

Tonight my mind refuses to settle. It circles back, over and over.

Back to Ami.

To her lips.

To the softness of her skin beneath my hands. The way she'd leaned into me, kissed me, completely unguarded.

And then the way she'd looked at me when I'd pulled away —hurt, confused, betrayed.

I told myself pulling away was the right thing to do—for her, for me—but now I don't know. I thought the kiss was a mistake. That getting involved with her, someone who doesn't belong in my world, would be a risk to her, one I can't take. But the truth is, I didn't walk away because of the danger.

I walked away because I didn't trust myself. I walked away because I'm a fucking coward.

And now, patrolling the grounds, I wonder if I made a mistake pulling back.

When I spot the glow of the tennis court lights, my chest tightens. Although it's late, Ami is on one of the courts, practicing her serve. She's alone, her ponytail swinging with each motion, the thunk of the ball against the racket echoing through the night. She moves with a quiet determination, her body twisting and turning with each motion.

I stand back in the shadows on the veranda outside the gym, watching her in silence. She moves with an energy that's both focused and restless, like she's trying to work through something she can't say out loud.

Ami finishes, gathering the tennis balls into a basket, and then switches off the lights on the courts. We're immediately plunged into darkness, save for the faint glow of the compound's security lights. She begins climbing the gravel path toward the veranda where I'm standing.

I don't move, don't speak, letting the shadows conceal me as she approaches. She's so focused on putting the equipment away that she doesn't notice me until she's just a few feet away and I say her name. "Ami?"

"Jesus!" she yelps, nearly dropping the basket. Her hand flies to her chest, and her breath comes in sharp, shallow bursts. "Marco, for the love of God, do you *have* to keep scaring me?"

I step forward. "I didn't mean to scare you."

She rolls her eyes, brushing past me to set the basket down near the door back into the gym. "What are you even doing out here?" Her exasperation is clear.

"Patrolling," I say simply, my tone even. "What about you? Couldn't sleep?"

"Something like that." She lets out a short laugh, but it doesn't quite reach her eyes. "I was practicing my serve. Hitting something is good for stress relief."

Her posture is stiff, her movements clipped as she fusses with the equipment. She pulls her hair out of its ponytail and shakes her head, her hair going wild around her. I can tell she's avoiding looking at me, and the realization hits harder than I expected.

"Ami," I say quietly.

She stills but doesn't turn around.

"We need to talk."

At that, she spins to face me. "If this is about this morning—"

"It is," I say, cutting her off. "I need to apologize. For the way I acted. For walking away."

Her lips part, her expression guarded. "You don't have to apologize," she says, her tone clipped. "I should apologize. I pushed myself on you. You made it clear you're not interested."

"That's not it." The words come out before I can stop them.

Her brow furrows, confusion flickering across her face. "That's not it?" She sighs. "Then what is it, Marco? Because you're sending some very mixed signals here."

I exhale, dragging a hand through my hair. "I pulled back because I don't trust myself around you, Ami. You..." I hesitate, my voice rough. "You make me forget myself. That's not safe. For either of us."

Her arms cross over her chest, her stance defensive. "Marco—"

"This isn't just about me being some asshole with a gun," I cut in, my voice harder now. "This is about how I live. The risks. The violence. You've seen small glimpses of it, but you don't know what it's like to live with it every day."

Her arms drop to her sides, and she steps closer, her voice steady but soft. "Maybe I don't know everything, Marco. But I'm not blind. I see what's happening around here. I understand some of the risks. I'm understanding more every day."

How can she still care? After everything, after what I've already shown her?

I shake my head, the knot in my chest tightening. "You don't know what you're saying."

"Yes, I do," she says firmly, her eyes locking onto mine. "You're not even giving me a chance. You don't get to decide what I can or can't handle. That's *my* choice."

The weight of her words hangs between us, heavy and charged. I stare at her, the knot in my chest tightening.

"You don't know what you're saying."

She reaches up, her hand brushing against my jaw, her touch so light it almost doesn't feel real. "You're right. I don't know everything. But I want to. I want to take a chance with you. I want to risk being with you, Marco," she says softly. "I know so much already. And I'm still here. Isn't that enough?"

Something inside me breaks.

I close the distance between us, my hands coming up to cup her face as I bring my mouth to hers.

The kiss starts slow, hesitant, like we're both afraid to break whatever fragile thing is building between us. But when Ami's hands slides up my chest, her fingers curling into the fabric of my shirt, I give in. My fingers tangle in her hair as I deepen the kiss, pulling her closer until there's no space left between us.

She tastes like something sweet, and I can't get enough. Her body fits against mine like she was made to be there, soft and warm and perfect.

She pulls my shirt out of my trousers, her hands slipping under the hem, her fingers brushing over the bare skin of my stomach. The sensation sends a jolt of electricity through me, and I groan softly, my lips trailing from her mouth to her jaw, then down to her neck.

When we finally break apart, both of us breathing hard, I rest my forehead against hers, my hands still gripping her waist.

"This doesn't change anything. It's not a good idea," I say, my voice low and rough.

Her lips curve into the faintest smile, her fingers brushing against the back of my neck. "It is. And this changes everything."

I stare down at her, at the defiance and vulnerability in her eyes, and I know she's right.

"Take me somewhere we can be alone," she says, her voice even quieter now. "I don't want to talk anymore."

41

———

AMI

Marco takes my hand, his touch warm and steady, and leads me from the veranda into the gym building. We go down the hall between the locker rooms to a locked door marked "Massage." He takes out his phone and uses a security app to unlock the door, gesturing for me to follow him in.

The room is small but inviting, lit by dim, golden light. A low couch is tucked against one wall, and a massage table stands in the center. The air is cool, quiet—separate from the rest of the compound.

"This is a private room," Marco says softly. "No cameras. No patrols."

I barely register his words before his hand reaches up to tuck a stray curl behind my ear. His fingers linger for a moment, and then his dark eyes meet mine. "Ami," he murmurs, "I want you to know... I don't regret the kiss. Not for a second."

The knot of doubt that had been twisting in my chest unravels in an instant. Without thinking, I push him back toward the couch. He lets himself fall, his hands already reaching for me, pulling me down into his lap.

Straddling him, my knees pressed to either side of his hips, I reach for him, my hands sliding up his chest. His heat bleeds through the fabric of his shirt as I grip it, pulling him closer.

This time, there is no hesitation, no careful testing of boundaries. His lips crush against mine with a hunger that makes my head spin, his hands framing my face like he can't bear to let me go. I melt into him, my fingers curling into the fabric of his shirt as the rest of the world fades away.

It's just him. Just us.

When we finally break apart, our breath mingles in the small space between us. His forehead rests against mine, his hands sliding down to my waist, grounding me even as everything inside me burns.

"Ami," he says, his voice rough and unsteady. "I need to know... are you sure about this? About me?"

I cup his face with both hands, my thumbs brushing over his jawline. His stubble is rough under my fingers, a perfect contrast to the softness in his gaze. "I'm sure."

His jaw tightens, his expression flickering with something vulnerable. "Being with me is... not easy. It's a risk."

"I know," I say firmly. "I know what I'm walking into, Marco. And I'm telling you—I want this. I want you."

For a moment, he doesn't move. His dark eyes search mine, like he's trying to find some hidden truth, some reason to believe me. Then he exhales, the tension in his shoulders easing as his arms wrap around me, pulling me closer.

"I want you," he murmurs, his lips brushing my hair.

He pulls back, looking into my eyes. "If you want to stop, just say the word."

I trail my fingers over the tattoos etched into his forearms, tracing the lines of his story. "I don't want to stop."

His lips quirk in the faintest of smiles before he reaches for me again, his hands settling on my waist as he kisses me. This time, the kiss is slower, deeper, a deliberate unraveling of the space between us. His hands roam my sides, his touch igniting a heat that burns through any hesitation I might have.

I barely register him shifting me, laying me back on the couch, my head resting on one of the pillows. He presses against me and the world narrows to nothing but the weight of his body against mine, the warmth of his breath.

His mouth moves to my jaw, my neck, and I lean back to give him more access. *How does this feel so good?*

"Marco..." I start, but then he starts sucking on a pulse point on my neck and all coherent thought cuts off. He nibbles on my ear with a deep chuckle that reverberates against me, our chests so close.

"Less talking." He half whispers, half growls in my ear before biting my earlobe and I can hear the smile in his voice. Before I can say anything, he captures my lips in another kiss, sucking on my bottom lip and then flicking his tongue into my mouth.

I can feel his hair under my fingers as I scratch at his skull and down the nape of his neck. His hands are under my shirt, leaving trails of fire on my bare skin as they move up and down from my ribs to my hips in slow motion.

He pulls back, tucking one of my curls behind my ear as he looks into my eyes. "Ami, if we keep going..." Marco takes a breath, his hands gripping my hips a bit tighter. "Tell me now if you don't—"

"I do," I breathe against him, my thumbs rubbing up and down his throat. "God, Marco, you have no idea how much I want—"

He abruptly silences me, his mouth ravaging mine with renewed intensity. He lowers back down, his weight pressing into me, a tantalizing hardness pressing against my thigh. His lips trail down my neck, igniting uncontrollable pants from deep within me. One hand cradles the back of my head while the other teases at the waistband of my shorts. Fumbling blindly, I attempt to undo the buttons on his shirt, driven by an overwhelming desire.

"Off," I command with newfound boldness, tugging impatiently at his shirt. He gives me one last hungry kiss before grunting softly and sitting up to remove his holster and placing it on the floor. He reaches over his head and pulls his shirt off, tossing it aside.

I can't resist staring at his bare chest, taking in every scar, every tattoo. He chuckles, "Your turn." With a teasing tug at my t-shirt, he urges me to sit up as he slides his hands underneath and slowly pulls it over my head. Raising my arms obediently, I allowed the fabric to slide past me as he pulls my t-shirt off and tosses it aside.

I think I'll feel self-conscious but the way he looks at me, as if he can barely control himself, gives me the confidence to pull my sports bra off, tossing it in the direction of my t-shirt.

His eyes flick down to my breasts and he reaches out, slowly brushing one thumb across a sensitive nipple. A shiver runs through me as I close my eyes. Just his touch on my nipple is making me wet.

"You're so beautiful." His voice is a low murmur as he brings his hand back to cup my jaw, his thumb gently brushing against my lips.

His hand trails down to my throat, my shoulder, my arm, all the way down to my hand. Marco brings it to his mouth, pressing tender kisses to my fingers, my palm, my wrist.

I sigh, pressing up and into him for another kiss. Our tongues intertwine for a moment before he pulls back, resting his forehead on mine.

"Lay back," he murmurs in a husky, wanting voice. I follow his instructions, a sense of anticipation building up within me. Marco slowly moves down, knees on each side of me.

As his hands trail over my waist and into the waistband of

my shorts, he wordlessly asks permission to remove them which I give with a lift of my hips. He pulls off my shorts and my panties.

And then there I am. Completely naked. For a moment, I worry that I might not look good enough. Might not be what he was hoping for.

But Marco looks at me as if he wants to devour me.

He kisses my lips and then kisses a path down to my breasts, pausing to suck on one nipple and then the other. I can't help panting as I run my fingers through his hair. He hums against my chest, making his way down, swirling his tongue in my belly button, and then continuing down, down, down.

Marco's hands are on my thighs as he scoots back between them. He lowers himself between my legs, lifting my thighs over his broad shoulders, kissing and nipping at my inner thighs.

One of my hands fists into his hair, pulling, as Marco begins licking up and down my folds.

And then he gives a small kiss to my throbbing clit.

I feel a gush of wetness from my cunt, dripping between my thighs.

He begins gently licking my clit. And then sucking on it. Back and forth. Licking and sucking. Over and over.

I've never felt anything so intense. I pant. I moan. I utter unintelligible sounds as Marco licks and sucks and swirls his tongue through my hot, wet cunt, always returning to suck on my clit.

It's as if he knows exactly what I need, lifting his head to slide one finger inside me while his thumb begins maddening circles on my swollen clit. Our eyes lock as he gazes up at me, his name falling from my lips in a desperate plea for more.

Another finger joins the first, pumping in and out with a rhythm that matches the swirling motion of his thumb. The pleasure builds and I can feel myself getting closer to the edge.

"I've thought about this since the moment I saw you," he whispers, watching me closely.

"I'm so close…" My eyes scrunch closed and I throw my head back.

"Look at me," he demands. "Look at me when you come."

I lift my head and open my eyes, wanting to look at him. Wanting to do exactly as he tells me. I grip his hair as he removes his thumb, sucking on my clit again, his dark eyes never leaving mine, waiting for me to do as he said.

"I'm going to come, I'm going…" I pant, staring into his eyes.

And then—

Everything explodes.

Every muscle in my body convulses, as waves of pleasure roll over me, my orgasm hard and long. My cunt clenches on his two fingers, over and over, as they continue to pump in and out, as he continues sucking my clit. I can't control the intense pulses going through me. The shockwaves that keep coming. I can't breathe. My vision is blurred.

I can only wait for the pulses to slow.

And slow. And finally stop.

My vision slowly clears and I can see Marco's intense gaze still fixed on me. He slowly draws his fingers out, causing another throb of pleasure to move through me. With one more kiss to my inner thigh, he lifts my legs off his shoulders and sits back on his knees, staring at me as he puts his glistening fingers in his mouth and sucks them clean.

He pulls them out of his mouth and licks his lips. "You're perfect," he says as his lips quirk into a small smile.

I feel boneless and soft. Warm and relaxed.

I look down at Marco and I can see the bulge in his trousers. *Why are those still on?*

He crawls up to me and I grab his belt buckle. "These need to come off," I demand. It's his turn.

His hand covers mine, moving it down to feel the outline of his rock hard cock. "Yes, ma'am," he replies with a wicked smirk.

He stands and I can't help assessing him. As he begins to strip off his trousers, I see again how muscled he is, how impressive.

But before he can get completely undressed, his phone buzzes from the floor where he discarded it. He freezes for a moment, looking down at me with his trousers hanging from his hips, the tip of his cock just peeking over his briefs.

He lets out a heavy sigh and picks up his phone. "It's Fidel," he says. "I have to take this."

He answers the call and turns slightly away from me to speak. I can hear every word in the small room, the low rumble of his voice blending with Fidel's updates.

"You're sure about this?" Marco asks. "Better than eighty percent? Don't make me report this to Raul unless you're certain."

The call lasts less than a minute before Marco hangs up and turns back to me, the disappointment in his expression so clear it almost makes me laugh.

"Important intel," he says, running a hand through his hair. "I need to brief Raul. And what I want to do with you..." He trails off, his gaze flicking over me, dark and hungry. "What I want to do with you can't be done quickly."

I smirk, still feeling lightheaded. "I understand."

He begins to dress quickly, his movements efficient but tense. I stay where I am, too loose and content to move just yet.

When he turns back to me, fully dressed, I can see the frustration etched into his features. "Please, Ami. Don't look at me like that."

"Like what?" I tease.

"Like you want to be ravaged," he growls, stepping closer. His hands find my wrist, pulling me to my feet.

"I *do* want to be ravaged," I whisper, leaning into him, pressing my naked body against his fully-clothed one.

He groans softly, his forehead dropping to mine. "Next time," he says, his voice rough.

I wrap my arms around his neck, my breasts pressing against him. "Next time," I repeat, smiling.

He gives me one last kiss, deep and lingering, pulling me in close. I can feel his hard cock against me. God, I want him in me.

He steps away, heading for the door. He pauses, glancing back at me with a look that sends a shiver down my spine.

"Definitely next time," he says. Then he's gone, the door clicking shut behind him.

42

MARCO

THE DAWN LIGHT spills over the compound as I follow the gravel path toward the mansion, my steps measured, my mind anything but. It's not yet 5 a.m. but I know Raul is up. Like me, he rarely sleeps.

But my thoughts aren't on him. They're on Ami.

I know what I'm walking into. I want this. I want you.

I want it too. Her touch, her smile, the way she looked at me —like she saw something worth holding onto, even in the middle of this mess.

But the weight of what comes next settles heavy on my shoulders. The risks. The danger. The things I'm not sure I can protect her from.

I continue up the path, but stop when someone calls out for me. Fidel.

He catches up to me, his expression tight.

"Raul's not going to like this," he says.

Minutes later, we're standing before Raul, in his study. He sits behind his heavy oak desk, his sharp gaze on Fidel as he lays out the latest intel.

"I've been digging deeper into the Calderóns," Fidel says, his voice calm but edged with something hard. "Their movements, their money, their alliances. It doesn't add up."

Raul leans back, fingers steepled. "Go on."

Fidel pulls out his tablet, swiping to a set of financial records. "We know the Calderóns operate out of Del Rio, right on the border with Acuña, Mexico. They run low-level drug trafficking, weapons sales, extortion—the usual second-rate gang shit. But they've always been disorganized. And up until a few months ago, they didn't have the resources to plan anything bigger than a street brawl."

I frown. "They've got backing."

Fidel nods. "Confirmed. We've been treating them like a loud, reckless crew trying to punch above their weight. But their last few moves? Coordinated hits, planned diversions, higher-end hardware. It's not their style. This isn't them getting smarter. It's them taking orders."

Raul's voice is sharp. "We've discussed this, Fidel. I want to know—who's pulling the strings?"

Fidel exhales. "I don't have a name yet. But I've traced the money." He swipes again, pulling up a second document. "The Calderóns are suddenly pushing cash through a network of shell companies. Some based in Del Rio, others in Acuña. Most are listed as logistics firms, customs brokers, small import/export outfits. But a few of them are tied, either through ownership or transfer activity, to known cartel laundering operations."

He glances at Raul, then at me. "It's too clean. This isn't local turf-war money. It's cartel money. Someone's using the Calderóns as errand boys. Testing our defenses. Seeing where we bend. Or break." He takes a deep breath. "I think someone's made them promises to get them to do the dirty work. Maybe they've promised Diego the reins because they know they can control him."

Raul taps a finger against his desk, his gaze flicking between Fidel and me. "What do you think?" he asks me.

I consider for a moment before answering. "It makes sense. The Calderóns have always been reckless, but this is different. It does feel like someone else's plan. Like they're just following orders. And yeah, Diego might go for this if it means he ends up in power."

Raul nods, gazing at the ceiling. "They're erratic, but that actually works in their favor. We keep responding to their chaos, but the *real* threat is still in the shadows."

Raul exhales slowly, the weight of the revelation settling over the room. He looks back at Fidel, his gaze hardening. "So it appears we have a larger enemy positioning themselves against us, and we don't even know who they are yet."

Fidel tilts his head. "Not yet. But I'll find out."

Raul is silent for a moment before turning to me. "And our own security?"

"Locked down," I say. "We've increased patrols, tightened the perimeter, and doubled up on surveillance. If the Calderóns try anything at any of our locations, we'll see it coming."

Raul nods, his expression unreadable. "Good." I can see the exhaustion in his eyes as he continues. "We have another issue to discuss."

I stay silent, waiting.

"I've decided to let Maria attend Miss Zadegan's book signing today," he says, his voice calm but firm.

My shoulders stiffen, my mind immediately running through the logistics. A public event. A crowd. A thousand variables we can't control.

"A book signing? Are you sure that's wise?" I ask, keeping my tone neutral.

Raul's gaze sharpens. "Maria has been asking to go. She's been cooped up here, and frankly, this book signing provides a unique opportunity for her to move in public without drawing suspicion. It's a controlled setting, and with the right precautions, it's manageable."

Fidel raises an eyebrow. "And by 'precautions,' you mean...?"

"All of you," Raul says, his gaze locking onto mine. "I want the full team to accompany them."

I clench my jaw. Ami was already a target in ways she didn't fully understand, and Maria... Maria is Raul's daughter. His blood. The stakes are high.

"Yes, sir," I say, my voice steady despite the unease clawing at my gut. I expressed my hesitation. My place is not to question Raul's direct order further.

He leans back again, looking at me, the faintest flicker of something like approval crossing his face. "Good. This will make Maria happy so I trust you'll handle it."

Fidel smirks faintly, shifting his weight. "Looks like we're taking a field trip."

I shoot him a warning glance but say nothing. Raul dismisses us with a curt nod, and we leave the study in silence.

Fidel and I make our way back to the guardhouse. The morning sun is climbing higher and I can feel the weight of Raul's orders pressing down on me.

Ami's book signing. A public event. All eyes on her and Maria. It's a calculated risk—one Raul believes we can handle, but one that makes every instinct in me scream to lock them both away somewhere safe.

And Fidel's intel. Just as we guessed, the Calderóns aren't the real problem. They're a distraction. Something bigger is lurking beneath the surface, and we're running blind.

I clench my fists, exhaling slowly.

Ami.

I haven't been able to stop thinking about her. About the way she looked at me, the softness in her voice when she said, *I want you,* the way she touched me like I was something worth having.

But thoughts of the Calderóns slam into me. Wanting her doesn't change the danger. If anything, it makes it worse.

And now, I have to take her *and Maria* into a room full of strangers, in public.

I head for the armory next to the shooting range, jaw tight, prepping for whatever this day throws at us.

Raul trusts me to handle this.

Ami trusts me.

Failure is not an option.

43

———

AN EMAIL

Email from Net Sports Marketing to Email List Tagged "San Antonio Only"

Subject: 🎾 Just Announced: Amira Zadegan Tennis Fixation Book Signing @ Net Sports!

Calling all tennis fans, romance readers, and spicy sports fiction lovers—this Saturday is your lucky day!

We're thrilled to welcome bestselling author **Amira Zadegan** to our San Antonio flagship location for an exclusive **in-store book signing and fan meet-up!**
📚 **Event Details:**
🎾 **When:** Saturday, 11:00 a.m.
📍 **Where:** Net Sports – 8500 Blanco Rd, San Antonio, TX
🎟️ **Admission:** Free, all ages welcome

. . .

Ami is the powerhouse author behind the **wildly popular Tennis Fixation series**, which has sold over 80,000 copies worldwide and ignited a frenzy across BookTok, Bookstagram, and beyond. Whether you're obsessed with **Jack and Riley's enemies-to-lovers meltdown in** *Smash Girl* or still swooning over **Emma and Adrian's road trip fake-dating tension in** *Break Point*, this is your chance to:

    ✔ **Get your books signed** (all five titles available on-site!)

    ✔ **Meet Ami Zadegan in person**

    ✔ **Snap a photo** at our custom Tennis Fixation backdrop

    ✔ **Win exclusive giveaways** for romance readers and racket sport lovers alike

BONUS: The first 25 attendees will receive a **free** *Volley Girl* **tote bag** and be entered into a raffle for a **$100 Net Sports gift card.**

Whether you're a longtime fan or just discovering the series with *Volley Girl*, this is your chance to chat with the author who turned second serves and slow burns into a social media sensation.

No RSVP required—but come early! We're expecting a crowd (and yes, we're already stocked with extra Sharpies and sports drinks).

Play the game. Love the sport.

    —Team Net Sports

44

———

MARCO

WHEN WE PULL into the shopping center later that morning, the first thing I notice isn't the building itself. It's the crowd.

A line of people snakes out the front doors of Net Sports, winding all the way around the corner and spilling into the parking lot. They clutch copies of Ami's books, the colorful covers catching the sunlight. They hold tennis rackets and tote bags, chatting excitedly as they wait.

Maria squeals in delight from the backseat. "Oh my God, Ami! Look at this crowd! They're here for *you*!"

Ami leans forward, her eyes wide as she takes in the scene. "I... I didn't think this many people would show up."

It throws me for a second. She's successful, beloved. This crowd showed up for her. But the way she says it—it's like she doesn't believe she deserves any of it.

Just how deep did Chad's bullshit go?

I glance at her in the rearview mirror, catching the mix of awe and nervousness on her face. "Guess you underestimated yourself."

Maria practically bounces in her seat. "This is amazing! Do

you think this is what my book signings will be like? I'll have to talk to Natalie about hashtags and fan engagement!"

Ami shoots her a look that is equal parts amusement and panic. "Maria, your book signings will definitely be like this."

Maria just grins. "I *know.*"

I pull into a parking spot near the entrance, my eyes scanning the area as I cut the engine. The other Suburban parks beside us, and Fidel, Chuck, and Rafe climb out, moving seamlessly into their usual alert mode. Elias is already inside, having arrived several hours earlier to scout the location.

The crowd looks excited but orderly. No immediate threats. Still, I'm not taking any chances.

We've been treating the Calderóns like reckless idiots, but they're just a distraction.

That's what's been eating at me since the meeting with Raul. This isn't about some two-bit family trying to make a name for themselves in Del Rio. There's a bigger force at play—one smart enough to use the Calderóns' chaos to keep us off balance.

And here we are, out in the open, easy targets.

I don't think anything's going to happen today. But that's the thing about attacks. You never do.

And the moment we assume we're safe is the moment we're not.

I walk around to Ami's door, opening it and offering her my hand. She hesitates for a moment, her gaze flicking from my hand to my face before she places her palm in mine. Her touch is steady, but I can feel the tension in her grip, the quiet nerves bubbling beneath the surface.

As she steps out, her hand lingers in mine for just a second longer than necessary. When she finally lets go, her fingers brush against mine, the faintest contact, but enough to send that familiar spark skittering through me.

"You'll be great," I say quietly, my voice low enough that only she can hear.

Her eyes meet mine, wide and uncertain. "I hope so."

Maria pops out of the backseat, practically vibrating with energy. "Ami, they're going to *love* you! Just smile, sign some books, and maybe toss in a joke about tennis balls. You've got this."

Ami lets out a nervous laugh, smoothing her dress as her gaze drifts back to the line of fans. "No pressure, right?"

Chuck, Rafe, and Fidel position themselves near the entrance, their stances casual but deliberate as they scan the area.

They feel it too.

We didn't discuss it, but I can see it in the way they move—Fidel's constant scan of the crowd, Rafe's subtle shifting attention, Chuck's normally easygoing stance a bit more rigid.

We all know today is a risk.

I step closer to Ami, leaning in just enough to keep my voice low. "Stay close," I say, my tone firm but calm.

Her lips twitch in a faint smile, and for a moment, I see her shoulders relax. "I think I can do that."

As we walk toward the store, Maria loops her arm through Ami's, chattering nonstop about Insta reels, book clubs, and how to use "exclusive giveaways" to increase fan engagement.

I stay at Ami's other side, close enough to keep her in my line of sight, close enough to feel the quiet pull of her presence.

The crowd hums with excitement as we pass, their chatter rising with every step. And as Ami smiles nervously at them, I find myself hoping—no, *knowing*—that she's about to blow them all away.

45

AMI

THE CROWD outside Net Sports stirs with excitement as we approach the entrance. I've done book signings before, but never anything like this. The sheer size of the crowd takes my breath away, nerves twisting in my stomach.

A woman in a tennis skirt nudges her friend, the two of them whispering animatedly, their faces lighting up when they spot me. Further down the line, a teenage girl clutches a dog-eared copy of *Smash Girl* to her chest, bouncing on her toes like she can barely contain herself.

"She's here!" someone calls, and heads turn, voices rising in a low wave of excitement.

My steps falter, my stomach flipping with equal parts awe and terror. My instinct is to duck behind Maria, let her soak up the attention she seems so effortlessly born for. But before I can, Marco's hand settles lightly on the small of my back. His touch is warm and steady, grounding me.

"You've got this," he says quietly, his voice low and sure, just for me.

I glance up at him, and the memory of last night—the heat of his hands on my skin, the way he kissed me like I was something rare and precious—hits me like a slow, rolling wave. My skin flushes at the thought, heat crawling up my neck.

Focus, Ami.

Maria, of course, is thriving in the moment. She waves at the crowd with the kind of confidence that could start a cult, grinning like she's the one they're here to see. "Hi, everyone! Yes, she's here! Ami Zadegan, queen of spicy tennis romance, coming through!" She turns toward me with an exaggerated wink and mouths, "*Smile! Own it!*"

Chuck, who is holding the door open, gives me a playful bow. "After you, Your Highness."

I roll my eyes, but can't stop the small smile tugging at my lips. "Thanks, Chuck," I mutter, stepping inside.

Inside, the crowd noise follows us—laughter, footsteps, bursts of conversation—and a cool blast of air-conditioning, a welcome contrast to the warmth outside. Overhead, pop music plays softly, adding a light energy to the scene. A line of people weaves through the aisles, snaking between racks of tennis gear, pickleball paddles, and displays of colorful sports apparel.

At the back of the store, the staff has created a *Tennis Fixation* signing station. A table draped in a crisp white cloth stands ready, stacked high with every book I've ever written—*Volley Girl, Smash Girl, Ad In, Love All, Break Point*—their bright covers catching the light. Next to the table, a giant poster of the *Volley Girl* cover is propped up, my name emblazoned in bold letters across the top.

Maria spots it immediately and gasps. "Ami, look! It's you!" She whirls towards a staff member and grins. "This is genius!"

The young woman nods enthusiastically. "We're huge fans! We wanted to make this special."

Maria beams, soaking up the moment, while I try not to let the weight of it crush me. My nerves buzz, the pressure of all those expectant faces outside pressing against my chest.

This isn't a cozy bookstore with twenty people in line. This is an *event*.

"I don't know if I can do this," I whisper, mostly to myself.

But Marco hears.

"You can," he says, his voice calm and certain.

I look up at him, his dark eyes steady and unflinching. There's something in his gaze that makes me believe him, something that quiets the storm of doubt swirling in my chest.

"You'll be great," he adds, his hand brushing against mine, so brief it might have been accidental. But it wasn't. That small, fleeting touch sends a shiver of warmth through me.

Maria grabs my arm and tugs me toward the table, vibrating with excitement. "Come on, superstar. Let's do this!"

I let her pull me along, clutching the pen she hands me like it's a lifeline.

The first fan steps forward, a woman in a tennis dress with a friendly smile and a well-loved copy of *Break Point* and a new copy of *Volley Girl*.

"Hi," I say, my voice a little shaky but genuine as I force myself to focus.

"Oh my gosh, I'm such a huge fan!" she gushes, practically glowing. "My doubles partner and I read your books together. We even quote lines when we're on the court. You've made tennis so much more fun for us."

The tight knot in my chest loosens, and I find myself smiling back. "Thank you so much for reading," I say, and I mean it.

I sign her books, handing them back as she beams. "Good luck with the signing!" she says before stepping aside for the next person.

And just like that, the rhythm of the event settles in.

Reader after reader approaches, each with their own enthusiasm, their own story. There are women in tennis skirts and visors, men with pickleball paddles, teenagers clutching my books like they're treasures. Some ask me about the characters, others want writing advice, a few want tennis tips, and many just want to say thank you for creating stories about the sport they love.

Maria chimes in occasionally, her energy infectious, while Fidel, Chuck, Rafe, and Elias circulate, maintaining a subtle but watchful presence. Marco stays back, leaning against a rack of tennis bags nearby, his eyes scanning the room with quiet intensity.

Every so often, I glance in his direction, and without fail, his gaze meets mine. He isn't hovering, isn't overbearing. He's just quietly present. Steady. Solid. And every time, it sends a flutter through my chest, a reminder of last night and the connection we now have.

For the first time in my life, I feel like I'm in the right place, with the right person.

I'm not hiding behind my computer or watching someone else take the spotlight. This is *me*. My books. My readers. My moment.

Chad had made me feel small. Like my stories were silly. Like the success of my books was something to be embarrassed about.

But here I am—owning this moment, surrounded by people who actually see me. And I'm not shrinking. I'm standing tall.

And Marco—just a few feet away, watchful and steady—doesn't try to dim my light. He protects it.

For the first time, I'm not just writing the story.

I'm living it.

46

MARCO

THE STEADY MURMUR of the crowd fills the store—pages rustling, fans laughing softly, voices rising and falling in bursts of excitement. I keep my position a few paces from the signing table, eyes scanning faces, posture relaxed but ready.

On the surface, this is routine: public event, high-profile guest, controlled environment. But nothing about it feels routine to me. Not with Maria here. Not with Ami.

Raul approved this because Maria asked. Because she always asks, and Raul always gives in. I get it. She's impossible to say no to. But that doesn't make it less risky.

At least she's happy, holding court beside Ami, whispering jokes with fans, tossing her hair over her shoulder like this is her red carpet moment. She's radiant. Magnetic. She draws people in and somehow keeps them laughing, even under fluorescent lights.

But it's not Maria I'm drawn to.

It's Ami.

She's completely in her element, though I can tell she doesn't know it yet. She greets each person like they matter.

Listens like she means it. Smiles like she's grateful, not just for the praise, but for the connection.

The line keeps growing. Readers clutch books like they're sacred. Some wear tennis skirts and visors. Some carry stacks of Ami's books. A team of ladies in matching tennis outfits is in line. One guy in a neon headband just gave Ami a fist bump.

And she handles all of it with this quiet, unshakable grace.

Last night hasn't left my mind. The feel of her skin under my hands, the way she whispered my name, the heat of her body pressing into mine. But more than that, it's what came after. The way she looked at me like I wasn't broken.

I don't know what the hell to do with that.

"Perimeter's clear," Rafe says in my comm. "Chuck's holding back exit. Elias is posted by the register. Crowd's clean."

"Copy," I reply, eyes sweeping the room again. It's calm.

Maria throws me a glance and a cheeky wave. I give her a nod, but my focus shifts back to Ami. Her curls have started to slip loose, brushing her cheeks, and there's a flush to her skin. Not nerves now, but energy.

She catches me watching her and smiles. It's not the practiced smile she gives fans. It's something softer. A little vulnerable. Like she's still surprised I'm here.

I look away first. I have to.

Because if she keeps looking at me like that, I'll forget why I'm here at all.

She doesn't see what I see. This whole crowd showed up for her, and she still looks like she's waiting to be told she doesn't belong. I don't know what that bastard Chad did to her head, but I know this much—he made her doubt what she was worth. He made her believe she was small.

And now, here she is. Bigger than the fear. Braver than the lie.

"Boss," Chuck says through the comm, "still all clear. Crowd's moving smooth."

"Understood."

I exhale slowly, letting the tension ease from my shoulders. Everything is secure. The crowd is behaved. Maria is safe. Ami is safe.

And still, when I look at her, I can't shake the thought that has been gnawing at me since last night.

She deserves better than the life I can offer her. Better than the risks, the danger, the violence.

A good man would let her go.

But I'm not a good man. And I want her.

47

AMI

THE LAST OF the fans drifts toward the door, arms full of signed books, bookmarks, and tote bags stamped with Tennis Fixation quotes like *Love at First Serve*. The buzz of the crowd fades, replaced by the hum of the AC and Maria's voice, still going strong at the far end of the table.

She's in her element, hands flying as she describes her alien duke series to a teenage boy and his grandmother, complete with anatomically improbable appendages. Judging by their laughter and the sparkle in Maria's eyes, you'd think she was the headliner, not me.

Honestly? She kind of is.

I smile, trying to focus on her, on the warmth still lingering from the fans who waited for hours just to meet me. But my attention keeps drifting—back to the man leaning casually against a display of tennis bags.

Marco.

Arms crossed, stance deceptively relaxed. But I know that body by now, how tightly coiled it really is, how his sharp gaze never stops moving. Watching. Assessing. Protecting.

And every few minutes, his eyes find me.

When they do, it's like being touched. Not soft. Not sweet. But intense, steady, like he's searching for something in me I'm not sure I know how to give.

My chest tightens. I look away, busying myself with tidying bookmarks and cleaning up empty water bottles. But the pull between us is constant, like gravity. And I know I'll look at him again.

Then I hear it—the sharp, deliberate click of stilettos on tile. The sound cuts through the quiet, and before I even register her face, my body reacts. My stomach knots. My shoulders tense. Something in me braces.

Then I see her. Victoria Drake.

What the hell is she doing here?

The last time I saw Victoria was in New York, right before Chad dumped me and moved on to his so-called big-deal "literary debut." She'd been his agent then, smoothing his path to success. Or so I thought. She was with Hawthorne & Hawthorne, a huge New York literary agency, and I'd even been at some of the wining and dining when Chad signed with them, watching him soak up the attention like he'd already made it. And then one night, he decided I wasn't part of his success and we were suddenly over. I never understood why his career fizzled so fast after that, but I didn't care. At first, I was so hurt and then, eventually, so happy to be away from him that I never bothered to ask.

Victoria glides towards me like she's on a runway, tailored black suit hugging her like armor. Her jet-black hair is cut in a sharp bob, sleek and severe. Everything about her is precision-engineered, sharp and cold as polished steel.

Her gaze sweeps the room, zeroing in on me with terrifying efficiency. That smile—thin, calculated, all teeth and no warmth—spreads across her face as she crosses the store.

"Ami," she purrs. "How lovely to see you again."

"Victoria." I force a smile, my voice even though my pulse jumps. "What a surprise. What brings you to San Antonio? And... here?"

Her eyes flick to the empty book boxes stacked behind me, the scattered bookmarks, the line that only just dispersed. "I wanted to see it for myself," she says. "This... tennis phenomenon."

Her tone is smooth, almost admiring. Almost. But I hear the edge. The insult hidden inside the compliment.

"It's been a good day," I say, keeping my voice level despite the heat rising beneath my skin.

She steps closer. "Clearly. It's wonderful to see you thriving." She smiles, just a little too long. "But I didn't come here just to congratulate you."

Every muscle in my back tightens. "So why are you here?"

Her eyes gleam. "I wanted to talk about your next project."

I blink, caught off guard. Victoria had never shown the slightest interest in me or my writing before. Not when I was with Chad. Not when he left.

"You're... interested in my dark crime romance series?" The words leave my mouth before I can stop them.

Out of the corner of my eye, I see Marco's head snap towards me. His eyes narrow. His posture shifts—tense, alert, like he's suddenly not sure what he's guarding anymore.

Damn it.

Victoria falters. Just for a breath. But I see it.

Then her smile returns, silkier than before, and I know she's filed that little detail away. "No," she says slowly. "Though that does sound... intriguing." Her gaze sharpens. "I was actually referring to *Beneath a Persian Sky*."

The air sucks right out of my lungs.

I freeze.

How does she know about that?

My vision tunnels for a second, and I grip the edge of the table to steady myself.

Victoria's smile doesn't budge. "Chad mentioned it," she says, lowering her voice like we're sharing a secret. "He didn't give many details, of course, but it sounded promising. And once I realized it was your story—your family's story—I thought, well. It could be something extraordinary."

Chad's voice punches into my memory. Smirking, smug. *It's a vanity project, babe. No one's going to care about your grandparents' sad little immigrant tale.*

He made me feel like I was pathetic for even wanting to write it.

"I don't know," I manage, throat tight. "That one's... personal."

"Exactly." Victoria's eyes gleam as she leans in, her manicured fingers drumming lightly on the table. "That's what makes it powerful. With my help, a story like that—*your* story—could launch you to a whole new level. Bestseller lists. Awards. The works."

The temptation is immediate. Almost painful.

But something about her presence makes my skin crawl. There's a slickness to it, a subtle manipulation I recognize far too well.

Natalie and Crimson Quill believed in me when no one else did. Not Chad. Not Victoria. Certainly not the agents who ghosted me after I seeing the work I submitted.

Victoria slides a sleek black card across the table like it's a gift. "When you're ready for an agency of Hawthorne & Hawthorne's caliber," she says softly, "call me."

And then she turns and walks away, heels clicking their slow, deliberate rhythm all the way out the door.

I stare after her, heart pounding. The card sits between my fingers, cool and weightless and dangerous.

Marco's at my side before I even hear him move.

His presence is steady, grounding. But his expression is unreadable. His eyes burn into mine, sharp and dark and far too focused.

"You okay?" he asks, voice low.

I nod, slipping the card into my bag even though my fingers are still trembling. "Yeah. Just... surprised."

His jaw tightens. "Dark crime romance?" he asks, quietly, but there's something in his tone I've never heard before. A hint of... suspicion? Hurt?

I look at him, really look, and suddenly the secret with Maria feels heavier than it did a minute ago.

"It's not—it's just a project," I say quickly. "Something I've been toying with. Nothing real."

Marco doesn't move. Doesn't speak. But the line of his shoulders shifts, just slightly, like the weight he's carrying has changed shape.

Before either of us can say anything else, Maria bounces up beside us, completely oblivious.

"What's with Morticia Addams?" she asks, frowning toward the door where Victoria disappeared.

"Old acquaintance," I say lightly, forcing a smile I'm not sure I feel.

Maria shrugs and turns back to the table, already chatting with one of the Net Sports staff.

But Marco stays where he is, gaze still on me. Steady. Unrelenting. Quietly calculating.

And I know—this conversation isn't over. Not by a long shot.

48

AMI

THE LOW HUM of the Suburban's engine is the only sound as we drive back to the mansion, twilight bleeding across the sky. That perfect golden light has faded, giving way to muted purples and dusky blues.

Maria's passed out in the backseat, her head tilted at an impossible angle against the window. Somehow, even asleep, she looks completely unbothered. Meanwhile, I'm a mess of thoughts and nerves and questions I can't answer.

Marco drives, silent beside me. Steady. Solid. Hands on the wheel with that calm control he always has. But there's tension in the air—between us, inside me—like something unspoken is pressing down hard on my chest.

I try to focus on the book signing. On the fans with their bright smiles and the way they clutched their books like they were holding something magical. I should be celebrating. This was a win.

But my mind keeps looping back to Victoria Drake. To the calculating smile. To the name she dropped.

Beneath a Persian Sky.

The thought of that manuscript makes my stomach turn.

It wasn't just a story. It was me, stripped bare. A reflection of everything I'd never fully unpacked. The story of my grandparents, Iranian immigrants who raised me while my mom pushed through med school, residency, and into her career as a pediatric surgeon. She loved me, I think. But love wasn't the same as presence. Eventually, she got everything she wanted—her degree, her freedom, her space—but by then, we were strangers more than anything else. No father in the picture. No stories about him either, just a blank space where his name should've been.

So it was mostly just the three of us in that quiet little apartment, me and my grandparents, the sound of Farsi in the kitchen, stories of Iran in the air like fairy tales. My grandfather would tell me bedtime stories about Simorgh and firebirds, about jasmine gardens and narrow alleys lit by lanterns. My grandmother would hum lullabies while stirring *ghormeh sabzi*, the smell of herbs and turmeric settling into every corner of the apartment. Those stories felt more like home than anywhere else I've ever lived. They'd given up so much to come to the United States, all so my mother could succeed. And through their stories, I learned to ask the questions my mother never had time to answer: Where did I come from? Where did we come from? And why did I always feel like I belonged nowhere at all?

Beneath a Persian Sky was the closest I'd ever come to trying to make sense of it. Of my family. Of myself.

It felt too personal to share with anyone. Too raw. But once—naively—I did. I'd shown it to one person.

Chad.

The memory flashes sharp and cold.

He'd barely skimmed the pages before smirking, dismissing the whole thing. Said he hated it. Mocked it. Called it self-indulgent, sentimental, irrelevant. He said it like he was doing me a favor. Like stomping on my dreams was just another version of his tough love.

But he'd shown it to Victoria? Why?

I never submitted it. Never pitched it. Why would Chad tell her about it? Why would he share something he mocked? Something he said was worthless?

Chad was supposed to be the next big thing—book deal, interviews, all of it. Then it all just... vanished. No release. No explanation. And Victoria, who once gushed about his "raw brilliance," dropped him like he never existed.

At the time, I was so hurt to be cast aside by Chad. And then, at some point, I was just relieved. I realized that being away from him lifted some kind of weight I hadn't even known I was carrying. I could breathe again. So I hadn't wondered about him. Hadn't wondered what happened to his book. I told myself it was the publishing industry. Fickle. Unpredictable. But now... I wonder what actually happened.

I stare out the window, heart tight, watching trees blur by in the darkening light.

Across from me, Marco hasn't said a word. But I can feel him. Watching me even when his eyes are on the road. The memory of last night hums just under my skin—his mouth on me, the way he made me feel anchored and electric all at once.

But that warmth between us feels far away now. Like I crossed a line I didn't know was there.

I can't take the silence anymore.

"You've been quiet," I say softly.

His hands flex slightly on the steering wheel. "Just thinking."

"About what?"

A beat. Then another.

He doesn't look at me when he says, "About what you said to that woman at the signing."

My stomach knots.

"What do you mean?"

"Your dark crime romance," he says, his voice too calm, the

kind of calm that has sharp edges underneath. "What's that about?"

Panic prickles at the back of my neck.

"It's just an idea," I say quickly, too quickly. "Something I've been toying with. It's not serious."

He glances at me—brief, sharp. "Doesn't sound like nothing."

I exhale, trying to steady my pulse. "It's... a concept for a series," I admit. "Fictional. Inspired by... things I've observed."

His grip on the wheel tightens. "Things you've observed?"

"Maria's been open about her life," I say, trying to explain. "She told me stories about the family. It gave me ideas, but it's not like I'm writing an exposé." My voice wobbles as I rush to say the next part. "She encouraged it. I wouldn't have thought about it otherwise."

Marco doesn't respond right away. His silence is colder now. Heavy.

"Do you even realize what kind of target you'd paint on her if people thought your story was based on this family? On us?"

"No!" The word rips out of me, too loud in the quiet car. I glance back at Maria, sleeping in the back. I lower my voice. "It's not like that. I'd never do anything to hurt her. Or you."

He stares straight ahead, his jaw tight.

"I'm just a romance writer," I say, softer now. "My job is to entertain people. To make them feel things. It's fiction. It's an idea for fiction. That's all."

But even as I say it, something twists inside me.

They've welcomed me in, shared stories, trusted me—and I'm turning their lives into story fodder. For what? Sales? A fun twist on my usual brand?

I hadn't meant it to be exploitative. I didn't even think I was doing anything wrong.

But just because I don't mean harm doesn't mean I haven't caused it.

"This wasn't about spying," I say quietly, searching his face. "It's just... Maria made me feel like I could write something new. Something different."

Still nothing.

I press my hand to my chest like that might keep everything from unraveling. "I didn't think it would matter to you."

He flinches. Just slightly. But I see it.

"I would never betray Maria's trust," I whisper. "And I wouldn't betray yours."

His eyes stay fixed on the road. His silence cuts deeper than anger would.

The mansion comes into view through the trees, its dark outline glowing under soft lights. The Suburban glides into the drive and rolls to a smooth stop. Marco shuts off the engine but doesn't move. His hands still grip the wheel, knuckles white.

"You should've told me," he says finally, his voice low and even.

Guilt twists hard in my chest. "I didn't think it was relevant."

He turns his head, and the look he gives me is steady and unflinching.

"Everything's relevant, Ami. Everything here is built on loyalty. Trust." His voice drops. "And right now, I don't know if I can trust you."

I open my mouth. Nothing comes out. The words stick in my throat, trapped by my shame and fear.

Marco exhales, slow and sharp, his expression softening just a fraction. "Be careful," he says. "You're walking a fine line."

Then he's out of the car, door shutting behind him with a soft but final sound.

I sit frozen, his words echoing in my head. *I don't know if I can trust you.*

And suddenly, the quiet between us feels like a door closing.

49

MARCO

THE COLD GLOW of the monitors washes over the security room, painting flickering shadows across the walls. I sit back in my chair, eyes scanning the feeds—front gate, perimeter, the long stretch of private road beyond. Everything's quiet.

But the quiet doesn't feel clean.

There's a weight in the air tonight, something I can't shake. Part of it is Raul. Part of it is her.

I shift forward, elbows on the desk, rubbing the back of my neck as I watch the screens. Stillness doesn't mean safety. I know that better than anyone.

The day's been a storm I haven't outrun. The book signing. The way Ami looked at me after we'd been together—hopeful, hesitant. Like she wanted to say something but didn't trust herself to say it out loud. Or maybe she didn't trust *me*.

And being with her... Christ. It's burned into me. The way she touched me. The way she looked at me like I was something good. I've had women in my bed before. I've had comfort, distraction, even connection. But not this.

Now she's slipping out of focus in my head. Every time I

close my eyes, she's there. And every time I open them, the distance between us feels wider.

I shouldn't care. But I do.

Raul called me and Elias into the study earlier, after we'd returned from the book signing. Typical debrief. Businesslike. Controlled. His voice never raises, but it cuts when he wants it to.

"Let's start with current operations," he said, nodding to Elias.

Elias leaned forward, relaxed as ever. "Clubs and casinos are steady. Calderóns haven't scared the regulars off. My guys are keeping an eye on movement—suppliers, runners, anyone getting twitchy. There's noise, but nothing solid yet."

Raul listened, unreadable. "And Fidel?"

"On it," Elias said. "He's got their communications flagged. If they're planning something big, we'll know."

Then Raul turned to me. "Marco?"

"Security posture's holding," I told him. "No incidents today, but I'm sure they're watching us. Testing response time. Mapping routines. They're looking for soft spots."

He tapped a finger on the desk, thinking. "They won't stop until they find one."

No one says it, but we all feel it—something's coming. We just don't know when.

Then Raul gave us the real reason for the meeting.

"I' want to call a board meeting," he said. "Raul Jr. and Isabella from Houston. Carlos and Daniel from Austin. I want them all here tomorrow afternoon. In person. I want a full review of operations. We lock this place down—tight."

Elias let out a low whistle. "So all of the big guns."

Isabella Morales is RJ's right hand in Houston. Sharp, efficient, and a lawyer by training. She handles most of the day-today deals and negotiations. Daniel Castillo is Carlos's enforcer in Austin. His childhood friend, fiercely loyal, and not afraid to get his hands dirty when things go sideways.

"This isn't a reunion," Raul snapped. "It's reinforcement. No mistakes." He takes a breath, settling back into his usual calm. "Elias, make the arrangements."

"Yes, sir," Elias said.

I nodded. "Who else is attending?"

"You two," Raul said. "Fidel will monitor remotely, coordinate with Daniel during the meeting." Then, a flicker of a smile. "Maria will join us for dinner afterward. I want her spending time with her brothers."

And that's when my stomach drops.

If Maria's at dinner, Ami will be too. Maria will make it happen. She'll chirp and tease and pout until Raul and Ami give in. And they'll both give in when Maria gets that look.

Which means Ami—the one who doesn't know the rules, doesn't understand the stakes—will be sitting at Raul Sandoval's table, surrounded by lieutenants, captains, sons of the empire.

And I'll be watching her, wondering if she's taking notes for her "dark crime romance."

The words echo in my head.

At first, I didn't think much of it. Sounded like curiosity. A harmless creative itch. But now? Now it gnaws at me.

She's here, living inside Raul's world. Listening. Observing. Writing.

Does she know what kind of fire she's playing with?

And Victoria Drake. That cold, smiling vulture, showing up out of nowhere, dangling *Beneath a Persian Sky* like bait. Like a trap.

The way she said Chad's name—like it was nothing. Like it didn't turn my blood to acid just to hear it.

Ami doesn't know what really happened. She thinks Chad's betrayal ended with physical abuse and emotional scars. She doesn't know he *stole from her*. Doesn't know Victoria helped bury it.

Doesn't know I watched him slap her across the face and push her down, abuse her, like it meant nothing Like she was nothing.

And I haven't told her.

I've had that truth sitting in my chest for days, like a loaded gun I won't fire.

But now... I don't know what she's doing. I don't know *why* she's doing it.

Is she taking notes on me, too? On Raul? On all of us?

I don't believe she'd betray us. Not on purpose. But she's playing a game she doesn't fully understand. And this world doesn't hand out warnings. You get one move wrong, you don't get to play again.

The radio crackles—routine check-in from the outer patrol. I glance at the screen. Empty roads. Still shadows.

I should be thinking about the Calderóns. They're the real threat. But my head's full of her. Her voice. Her touch. Her silence about what she's doing. I don't know which is worse.

I hate how cold I was in the car. But if I let her in now, and I'm wrong—

I run a hand down my face.

I'm supposed to see threats before they happen. That's my job. But with her... I can't tell if I'm protecting her or walking blindfolded into something I can't control.

Raul's voice comes back to me.

No mistakes.

I stare at the monitors, watching the cold glow reflect off glass and metal. Nothing moves. But the silence feels like it's lying to me.

Ami's not a threat. Right?

She's the one thing I can't predict.

And in this world, unpredictability gets people killed.

50

A SECURE TEXT

Secure Message – Signal App

Timestamp: **20:12 CST**

Sender: E. Vasquez

Recipients: R. Sandoval Jr., C. Sandoval, I. Morales, D. Castillo, M. Cedillo, F. Cedillo

Encryption: End-to-End (Auto-Expire: 12 hours)

ELIAS:
SANDOVAL COMPOUND
TOMORROW – 18:00 CST
Agenda:
– Full operational review with R. Sandoval

– Mandatory in-person attendance

– Advance security briefing 16:00 (D. Castillo coordinate with F. Cedillo re: east-side coverage)

– M. Cedillo (security lead briefing @ 16:00)

– F. Cedillo (remote monitor, comms integration)

DINNER to follow with Maria and external. Full operational review. No personal devices. Do not deviate from cleared personnel list.

Reply to confirm.

51

AMI

The lounge just off the formal dining room looks like it was stolen from a movie set—something elegant and moody, the kind of place where impossibly beautiful people sip martinis, smoke cigarettes, and laugh at things that aren't actually funny. The lighting is warm and golden, designed to make everyone look like the best version of themselves.

Which is ironic, since I feel like the worst version of myself.

Soft music drifts from somewhere invisible. Waitstaff move silently, like they've been choreographed. Maria and I are lingering near one of the velvet-upholstered couches, waiting for Raul's so-called "board meeting" to end behind closed doors.

Criminal masterminds solving problems. Or maybe planning new ones.

Maria insisted I come tonight, though I still don't know why. I'm not family. I'm not part of the business. I'm a guest who keeps getting closer to things she probably shouldn't see.

I shift on my heels, resisting the urge to tug at the dress Maria picked out for me. It's a soft, slate blue. Simple. Classy. Expensive without trying too hard. She said it made me look elegant. But I just feel like an impostor, playing dress-up in a world where I don't belong.

And worse—I keep thinking about the women who *do* belong here. The ones who glide through rooms like this without flinching. The ones who know how to walk in stilettos without wobbling. The ones who fit next to men like Marco like they were carved from the same stone.

"Stop looking like you're at your own funeral," Maria mutters, elbowing me.

I blink. "What?"

"My brothers are going to love you," she says with a grin. "Try not to act like you're being marched to your doom."

"Your brothers?"

"RJ and Carlos," she says brightly. "They've been in the meeting with Papa. And as soon as they're out, you're meeting them. No arguments."

Before I can protest, the heavy double doors open, and the room shifts.

Raul steps out first, his presence changing the air somehow —denser, sharper. A waiter immediately hands him a tumbler of tequila and he takes a drink. His expression gives nothing away, but there's a weight in his posture that wasn't there before.

Elias follows, still wearing his usual smirk, but even he looks... frayed. There's tension in his shoulders, a slight squint like his headache's coming on hard and fast.

And then I see them. RJ and Carlos.

Maria's brothers are younger than Raul but just as commanding. RJ has a warm smile and the easy charisma of someone who knows exactly how charming he is. Carlos is a bit taller, more reserved, all sharp edges and quiet calculation. Both are dressed in perfectly tailored suits that whisper power, confidence, danger.

And then—Marco.

The sight of him hits like a sucker punch.

Charcoal suit. Red tie. Crisp white shirt that hugs his frame in all the right ways. But it's not just that he looks good. It's that he looks like he *belongs* here. Like he was born in a suit and raised in shadows.

His jaw is tighter than usual. His eyes darker. There's a tension in him tonight that even the clothes can't hide. His stubble is rougher, like he didn't bother shaving. His posture is locked down, coiled tight.

But it's not just him.

The whole team's been worn thin these past few days. When I see Chuck or Rafe in the library, they aren't cracking jokes. Even Fidel looks like he's been grinding his teeth lately. Something's building. I can feel it in the air, thick and electric. The calm before something sharp and ugly.

And then I see *her*.

The woman in red.

She's stunning. Breathtaking, really. The kind of beautiful that feels curated—perfect makeup, perfect hair, perfect everything. Her crimson dress clings like liquid fire, her black stilettos impossibly high. She moves like she's weightless, like she owns every eye in the room.

And she's on Marco's arm.

My stomach flips, then drops.

She leans into him, her laugh soft and musical. One of her perfectly manicured fingers brushes the fabric of his sleeve like she's done it a hundred times. Marco doesn't look at her, doesn't react. His focus stays on Raul and the rest of the group, jaw set, eyes unreadable.

But she looks at him like he's the only man in the room.

Maria grabs my arm before I can spiral further. "Come on!"

"Maria—"

"Nope!" she says, beaming. "Ami, these are my brothers. RJ,

Carlos—this is Ami Zadegan. The genius behind the books I won't shut up about."

RJ offers his hand immediately, that easy smile lighting up his face. "So this is the famous author. Maria's been texting about you nonstop."

I shake his hand, praying he doesn't notice how clammy mine is. "She exaggerates."

"Not even a little," Maria insists, squeezing my arm.

Carlos nods politely. His eyes are dark, cool, assessing. "Nice to meet you," he says, voice calm, low, and vaguely intimidating.

RJ raises an eyebrow. "What do you write?"

"Oh—uh—romance novels," I say, bracing myself for the smirk, the joke.

But RJ just nods, thoughtful. "Smart. People need something to believe in. *Donde hay amor, hay vida.*"

Maria lights up. "'Where there is love, there is life.' See? He gets it!"

I smile, but it feels thin. My attention keeps sliding back to Marco.

He's near Raul now. The woman in red is still tucked against him like she was made for that spot. She says something in his ear. I can't hear it. But I see the way her fingers graze his side, like she knows exactly what she's doing.

And he doesn't stop her.

My chest goes tight.

She looks like she belongs with him. In this room. In this world.

And me?

I'm just the girl who writes about love like she understands it. The girl who thought one night could mean something. Who thought *I* meant something to *him*.

A few days have passed, but that night still feels close. Since his hands were on my skin, his voice in my ear, his mouth on mine like I was the only thing anchoring him to the earth.

For a few fragile hours, I let myself believe it was real.

But now?

Now, I'm not so sure.

We've seen each other since then. Briefly. In passing. In the kitchen. In the gym during the self-defense sessions Maria insisted we keep doing. He's polite. Distant. Always somewhere else. And I don't know how to reach him anymore.

I reach for the champagne flute on the low table beside me, but my hand is trembling, and I set it back down before I spill it. I try to focus on Maria, on her brothers, on anything else. But my mind is spinning, fast and ugly.

Maybe it didn't mean as much to him as it did to me. Maybe I was just convenient. Temporary. Maybe I imagined the whole thing.

I feel humiliated. Small. Stupid.

Used.

And for the first time since I arrived, I start to wonder if I ever belonged here at all.

Just before I look away, I catch something. Marco's eyes flick to me.

Just a glance. Brief. Barely there.

But enough to make me freeze.

And then he looks back at Raul like nothing happened.

But I felt it.

I just don't know what it meant.

52

MARCO

THE HALLWAY to the west wing is quiet, the polished hardwood muffling my steps as I move through the mansion. Behind me, the faint hum of voices and clinking glass from the dining room fades into silence.

She slipped out as soon as dessert was served. I noticed. I've been tracking her all night, ever since I saw her in the lounge. That soft blue dress. Nervous posture. Eyes scanning the room like she was searching for the nearest exit.

She looked out of place.

And still, somehow, radiant.

I pause outside the library, exhaling slowly. I shouldn't have let the night get this far. Should've stepped in sooner. Should've stopped Isabella from—

I grind my jaw just thinking about it.

Dinner was a disaster.

The tension from Raul's meeting bled into cocktail hour. RJ and Carlos were confident that there's no immediate threat to Houston or Austin, but the Calderóns still seem to be pushing. Raul's last order to me was clear: *crush the Calderón problem before it spins out of control.*

I tried to stay focused. Sharp. Controlled. But my attention kept drifting—to Ami.

Maria had introduced her to her brothers like she was showing off her favorite treasure. And Ami, always polite, had smiled and played along. But I could see the tension in her spine. The way she fidgeted with her wineglass. She didn't belong here, and we both knew it.

I was halfway to her when Isabella intercepted.

"Two tequilas on the rocks," she said smoothly to the waiter, looping her arm through mine like it was hers to claim. When the drinks came, she handed one to me with a glossy smile. "One for you, one for me."

I took the glass out of reflex, already scanning the room for Ami. She was watching. Of course she was. And then—she looked away. Smile fading.

That twist in my chest hasn't left since.

Then—dinner.

Ami ended up across from me. Isabella took the seat to my left, practically glued to my side. Her cloying perfume clung to the air. Too sweet, too sharp. Every word out of her mouth was a performance.

"RJ and I have been working on the Houston expansion," she said, leaning closer. "Oil and gas contracts are tricky, but that's where I come in. I make sure everything stays above board. Don't I, RJ?"

RJ smiled without much warmth. "Couldn't do it without you," he said, bone-dry.

Then the moment I'd been dreading.

"What about you, Ami?" Isabella asked, her smile too wide. "What do you do?"

Ami's voice was even, but guarded. "I'm a writer."

"Really?" Isabella's eyes glinted. "Anything I would've heard of?"

Before Ami could answer, I cut in. "Ami is a very successful romance writer."

Her tone went sugary. "Romance. How... fun."

Ami's face flushed, and something in my chest went tight. Before I could speak, Elias cut in from across the table.

"She's extremely successful," he said lazily. "You should've seen her last book signing. Lines out the door. Readers grabbing her books like candy. But I'm sure all of those oil and gas contracts don't leave much time for real reading."

Isabella's smile wavered, her knuckles going white around her wineglass. She set it down, a little too quickly, wine sloshing near the rim. Her gaze flicked from Elias to me, then back to Ami—sharp, assessing. For a moment, she seemed to weigh her next move. But then she pasted on a too-bright smile, and changed the topic, asking Elias about recent Sandoval real estate acquisitions.

The rest of the dinner blurred. Ami barely looked at me. Her gaze stayed fixed on some point just past my shoulder, and when dessert hit the table, she stood and slipped out without a word.

Now, standing at the library door, I hesitate.

If she doesn't want to hear me out—if she's already done—I won't blame her.

But I have to try.

I push open the door.

She's by the window, heels kicked off, arms wrapped tightly around herself. The moonlight paints her in silver, catching the soft waves of her hair, the curve of her shoulder. But she's drawn in, closed off, like she's trying to disappear.

"Ami," I say quietly.

She turns, her expression guarded. "Shouldn't you be in the dining room? Isabella might be wondering where you are."

I sigh, dragging a hand through my hair. "Ami—"

"Don't," she says, shaking her head. "You don't have to

explain. I get it. There are other women. Probably lots of other women. Women like Isabella. Gorgeous. Smart. The kind who should be with you."

Her words hit harder than I expect.

"There are no other women. There haven't been for a while," I say, stepping toward her. "Isabella and I have never been anything. She likes to pretend otherwise, but I've never given her a reason to think that."

Ami glances away, arms crossing tighter. "Doesn't matter. I don't belong here anyway."

"I'm sorry," I say. "For tonight. For the last few days. For everything. Things with the Calderóns are heating up fast. I can't afford distractions. I know I've been distant. But not because you don't matter."

Her eyes lift to mine, hesitant. Searching. "Then why?"

I swallow hard. "Because you do matter. You matter too much. And if anything happens to you because of me..."

I shake my head. Can't finish the sentence. Don't want to imagine it.

I step closer, closing the distance between us. My hands find her arms—warm, delicate, tense beneath my palms.

"You're important to me now, Ami," I say softly. "More than I know how to explain."

Her breath catches. She stares at me for one long beat. And then her hands rise slowly, fingers curling around my wrists.

It's all I need.

I cup her face, leaning in. Our lips meet, soft at first, hesitant. But the moment she responds, the world narrows to just this.

Her. Me. This room. This moment.

When we finally pull apart, her cheeks are flushed, her breathing uneven.

"You mean more to me than I even want to admit," I say.

She doesn't speak, but her eyes shine—surprised, maybe. Or just open enough to believe me.

"Marco..."

And for the first time in what feels like days, I let myself breathe.

Nothing else matters in this moment. Not the Calderóns. Not the Sandovals. Not the weight of Raul's orders or the danger creeping closer.

Just her.

53

AMI

"Come with me," I whisper, my fingers still curled around his wrist.

His brow furrows, but only for a second. "Where?"

"Where we can be alone."

I don't wait for permission. I just lace my fingers with his and lead him through the dim hallway, up the grand staircase, toward my room. My pulse is loud in my ears, but I feel steady. Certain.

He follows without hesitation.

When we reach the door, I close it quietly behind us and twist the lock. I turn to face him in the soft glow of moonlight spilling through the curtains. His tie is slightly askew. His jaw tight. His eyes—on me.

"Here," I say, stepping in close. My fingers graze the sharp line of his jaw, the stubble rasping against my skin. "No one watching. No distractions. Just us."

His breath hitches, but he doesn't speak. He shifts slightly, pulling out his phone and tapping the screen before sliding it back into his pocket. "No one watching," he says.

"I want you to know I want this," I murmur. "I want *you*. All of you. Here. In this world."

He kisses me before I can say another word. Not urgently—*reverently*. Like he's tasting something rare.

I guide him backwards, slowly, until the backs of his knees hit the edge of the bed and he sits. I step between his legs, watching him watch me. My hands slide his jacket from his shoulders, let it fall to the floor.

I reach for the buckle of his holster. He grabs it before I can, smoothly removing it and placing it on the nightstand with the care of someone who's been trained to always know where his weapons are.

But tonight, I'm not the one who needs protecting.

I move in front of him, reaching for his buttons. He starts to help, but I shake my head.

"Let me."

He watches in silence as I unfasten his shirt, each button revealing more of the body I've been thinking about for days.

He shrugs it off, and I slide to my knees between his legs. I reach for his belt.

"Ami..." he starts, voice rough. "You don't have to—"

"I'm doing exactly what I want to do," I say, cutting him off with a look.

That's the difference.

I've never had this. This kind of control. This kind of want without fear or obligation. He's letting me lead—not reluctantly, but with quiet awe. This powerful man, who could silence a room with one glance, is here—open, waiting, *mine*.

I pull the belt free, unfasten his trousers, slide the zipper down. His cock is already hard, tenting his briefs, the tip peeking out—thick, flushed, waiting. I run my fingers along the waistband.

"I want all of this off. Everything."

He gives me a look like he's never seen anything like me. Then he kicks off his shoes and socks. He stands to push his trousers and briefs down, and my breath catches.

God.

He's beautiful. Standing before me while I kneel, it feels like I'm worshiping him—not out of obligation, but desire. His muscled frame. The ink that winds across his skin. The scars that mark where he's been. What he's experienced. I take all of it in, and all I want is more.

He sits again, and I stay on my knees. I reach for him, my palm wrapping around the base of his cock. It's heavy in my hand, warm and thick, pulsing with heat. I stroke him once—slow—watching the muscles in his stomach tense under my gaze.

A low groan escapes him, deep and ragged. His hips shift, like he's fighting the urge to thrust.

I lean in, let my breath ghost across the tip of his cock, and feel a rush of power at the way his abs tighten. God, he's beautiful. All hard lines and dark ink, every muscle honed to lethal perfection. And yet here he is, letting me take the lead.

I flatten my tongue against the base and drag it up the length of him, slow and deliberate, tasting salt and skin and him. He shudders, a sharp exhale breaking the silence.

His hand fists in the comforter, knuckles white.

I swirl my tongue around the head, teasing the sensitive ridge, and feel him twitch under my palm. I want to drive him crazy. I want to make him lose control.

When I take him into my mouth—just the first inch—he sucks in a sharp breath, the sound rough and raw.

"Fuck," he mutters, his voice low, strained.

I glance up, catch his eyes on me, dark and heavy, like he's fighting for every ounce of restraint. That look ignites something in me, a need to push him further, to show him what I can do.

I take him deeper, inch by inch, my lips stretching around him. The heat, the weight—it's almost overwhelming. I hollow my cheeks, sucking, and swirl my tongue around him, and his hips jerk, a low, desperate groan rumbling from his chest.

"Jesus, Ami," he breathes, his hand tangling in my hair now, not to force me, but to anchor himself.

But then his other hand lands on my shoulder—gentle, firm.

I pull back and look up, still holding him in my hand.

"You don't want—?"

"Oh, I want," he growls, leaning down so his mouth is just above mine. "But *right now*, I need to be inside you. I need to feel you come on my cock."

The heat in me pulses like a flare.

He kisses me, hard and deep. I taste the hunger in him. I feel his hands on my waist, lifting me, guiding me to my feet. I'm lightheaded with need.

His hands slide down to my hips, and he starts working the dress over them—slow, like he's unwrapping something he craves but won't hurry through. I lift my arms so he can ease it up over my head. The soft fabric slips to the floor, and suddenly, I'm bare beneath his gaze—no underthings. Nothing on but breath and heat and the weight of this moment. He doesn't rush. His eyes move over every inch of me like he's memorizing me. Like I'm something rare, and he wants to take his time.

"Ami," he whispers my name. "You had nothing on under this dress? All night?"

I give him a small smile. "I was hoping something like this might happen."

He pushes me gently onto the bed, and I grab his hand to pull him down with me. He moves between my legs, kisses me like he's mapping me. His mouth slides down to my throat, my collarbone, the tops of my breasts.

There's no urgency. Just awe. Adoration.

Then his lips find my nipple, and he sucks softly, then bites —just enough to make me gasp. His smile turns wicked against my skin, a dark promise.

I wrap my legs around him, hips lifting instinctively to meet his. His fingers find my entrance, slick and ready, and he groans, deep and ragged. "God, Ami," he mutters, voice thick with hunger. "So fucking wet for me."

Heat blooms in my chest, my thighs, everywhere. I feel powerful and vulnerable all at once. I reach down between us, find my clit, rubbing slow circles as he lines himself up. The head of his cock presses against me, and I feel the stretch as he slowly enters.

He looks down, eyes dark and wild. "Look at you," he rasps. "Taking me so perfectly."

"Please," I whisper. "I want to feel you inside me. All of you."

He pushes in—slow, so slow—and the stretch is everything. I arch, gasping, my hand falling away from my clit as he fills me completely, inch by inch. The sensation is overwhelming—slick heat, the thick slide of him, the way my cunt molds around him like it's where he's always belonged.

When he's deep in me, fully seated, he pauses, forehead pressed to mine, breath ragged. "Jesus, Ami," he groans. "You feel so fucking good. So tight."

I slide my hands up his sides, my body adjusting, welcoming him. I've never felt so full, so claimed.

"More," I whisper. "Please."

He pulls out almost all the way, then pushes back in, slow and deep, grinding his hips against mine. The rhythm he sets is torturous—steady, deliberate, each thrust sending a jolt of pleasure through me.

"Tell me what you want," he pants, his mouth at my ear.

"Harder," I breathe, arching up, my nails biting into his shoulders. "Please. I want it hard."

"Fuck," he mutters, his control slipping. He shifts, one hand gripping my thigh, pushing my knee higher, opening me up even more. When he thrusts again, he's deeper—so deep I can't breathe, can't think.

"Oh my God. Yes. There. Right there."

He grunts with each thrust, sweat dripping from his brow onto my chest, his jaw tight. "You're so fucking perfect," he growls. "So wet for me. Taking all of me."

My body is a live wire, every nerve lit up. The rhythm builds —harder, faster—and every stroke feels like it's splitting me apart in the best way.

"Marco, I—"

"Come for me," he orders, his voice a raw command that hits something deep inside me.

My head tips back, a broken sound tearing from my lips. My hand finds the sheets, clutching them, but I don't touch my clit. I don't need to. The way he's moving inside me—deep, relentless —is enough.

Pleasure winds tight, impossibly tight, then snaps—hard. I come with a cry, my body clenching around him, wave after wave crashing through me.

"Fuck, Ami," he groans, his hips stuttering. "You're so fucking beautiful when you come."

His pace falters, then he drives into me one last time, deep and rough, and I feel him come. Hot, thick, filling me. He curses against my throat, his body trembling with release.

It goes on and on—his orgasm drawing mine out, leaving me shaking, breathless.

We stay tangled like that for a moment, both of us gasping, sweat-slicked and trembling. He presses his forehead to mine, still buried deep. I can feel his heart hammering against my chest, his pulse echoing mine.

Eventually, he pulls out, collapsing beside me. I turn toward him, my body spent but alive, every inch of me humming with aftershocks.

His smile is soft. Easy. We lay there, neither of us moving. Then, his hand trails lazily across my hip, rests there, grounding me.

"You're so beautiful," he whispers.

I smile, brushing his hair back from his forehead. "So are you." He is. so beautiful.

He watches me for a moment, something quiet and raw in his gaze. "This isn't something I do. Letting someone in."

My heart pulls. I trace my fingertips along his jaw. "Me neither."

He leans in and presses a kiss to my forehead—slow, sure, real. Then he lies back, pulling me toward him, one hand resting on my thigh.

I close my eyes, my cheek pressed to his chest, listening to the steady rhythm of his heartbeat. My body aches in all the best ways. I can still feel the shape of him inside me, the weight of him, the heat.

But it's more than that.

For the first time, I didn't lose myself in someone else.

I found myself—in his hands. In his eyes. In my own goddamn pleasure.

And for once, I don't feel like I'm trying to belong in someone else's story.

This one? This is mine.

54

MARCO

THE FIRST LIGHT of dawn cuts through Ami's bedroom window, streaking gold across the sheets tangled around our legs. She's curled against me, warm and quiet, her breath soft where it brushes my chest.

I should have left by now. But I don't move.

I'm tired, but it's a good kind of tired. The kind that comes from a night of skin and sweat and need. She'd pulled me back again and again, wanting me inside her as badly as I wanted to be there.

My hand rests against the curve of her back. I can still feel her—everywhere. The shape of her body, the sounds she made, the way she looked at me like I was something solid in a world full of shifting ground.

For once, I let myself have it. No hesitation. No exit strategy. Just her.

It's not that the danger's gone. It's not that this world has changed. But maybe I have. Maybe I've finally stopped pretending that I can stay away.

Eventually, I slide out of bed. She stirs but doesn't wake. I dress quickly, quietly, grab my phone and turn the security camera back on. She'll never know about it, never know I turned it off last night. And that's how I want it.

When I close the door behind me, I'm not walking away from her. I'm just starting the day.

And it feels right.

Later that morning, I find her in the library with Maria. They're tucked into opposite corners of the same couch, laptops open, coffee mugs half-drained. Sunlight spills in through the tall windows. For a second, it looks normal, two women working on something they love.

Then I hear Maria.

"No, no, you don't get it," she's saying, eyes wide. "The duke *has* to kidnap her. He's an alien warlord. Abduction is part of the courtship."

Ami arches a brow. "That's your idea of romance?"

Maria puts a hand to her chest, scandalized. "It's *primal,* Ami. It's alien biology. You're denying the readers their pleasure."

Ami pinches the bridge of her nose. "I've lost control of this story."

I lean against the doorway. "That's the understatement of the year."

Ami glances up at me, and for a beat, neither of us says anything. Her eyes soften, lips curving into a subtle smile that's just for me. The memory of last night flashes between us like a secret.

Maria, oblivious, lights up. "Perfect timing!"

That puts me on alert. "What did I just walk into?"

She spins toward me with the energy of someone about to ask for a favor she already expects to get. "We're going to Luz tonight."

"No," I say immediately.

"Luz?" Ami asks, brows raised.

Maria turns to her. "One of the Sandoval nightclubs. *Our* nightclub."

She spins back to me. "You have to say yes, Marco."

"It's a risk," I counter. "Which means it's not happening."

Maria groans like I just canceled Christmas. "Marco, come on. It's Ami's book signing celebration. It's *Luz*. It's our club."

I shake my head at her but she waves a hand like I've missed the point entirely. "Papa's meeting last night went fine. The family's on the same page. The Calderóns are quiet. Things are calm."

"Calm doesn't mean safe."

"I already talked to Papa," she says, eyes wide with fake innocence. "He didn't say no."

I cross my arms. *"Una hija de papí."*

She shrugs. "Daddy's girl? Maybe? A little?"

I'm about to respond when Elias strolls in like he's been waiting for his cue.

"She's not wrong," he says, dropping onto the arm of a nearby chair. "Luz is ours. Our security. Our rules. No one keeps us from our own place."

I shoot him a look. "You're really backing this?"

He shrugs. "Think of it this way. If we can't walk into our own club with full coverage, we're already playing defense. This is about presence. Control."

He's not wrong. And if Maria's set on going, I'd rather build the perimeter myself than have her sneak out behind someone's back.

Ami's quiet through all of this, but I can feel her watching me. Not just listening—*reading the room*. She's waiting to see if I'll shut this down or make space for her to say yes to Maria.

I exhale. "Okay. Full team. Everyone geared. Elias, you'll run point. Rafe can handle the perimeter. Chuck and Fidel will stay on rotation. Inside and out."

Maria grins, already triumphant.

"And you two—" I look between her and Ami, "will stay in my line of sight. The whole night. Understand?"

Maria squeals, launching herself at me. "You're the best," she says, giving me a hug. "You won't regret this!"

"I already do," I mutter, but I don't stop her.

Ami's still watching me, arms folded, that half-smile tugging at the corner of her mouth. She looks amused. And a little surprised.

I give her a small nod. Just enough to say: *we're good.*

She nods back, and something sparks in her eyes.

We both know. This isn't safe. Or easy. But in my mind, she's mine. And she's not going anywhere without me.

55

AMI

THE BASS HITS ME FIRST—A deep, thrumming pulse that seems to vibrate through the soles of my heels and echo in my chest. Luz isn't just a nightclub. It's an experience. Dark, sleek, and pulsing with wealth and danger. Neon lights slice through the haze, flashing in rhythmic patterns that shimmer off gold-trimmed railings and a glossy black floor. A massive, modern light fixture hangs over the dance floor, casting shifting beams of violet, gold, and crimson on the crowd below.

A mural dominates the far wall—a towering purple leopard painted in sweeping strokes, its jade green eyes lit and gleaming, like it could leap off the wall at any moment.

The air smells like tequila, citrus, and something floral—maybe the surreal, oversized tropical bouquets placed around the room in glass vases. The music is hypnotic, a mix of house beats and Latin rhythms that make it hard to think clearly but easy to move.

Maria loops her arm through mine as the bouncer pulls back a purple velvet rope, grinning like she owns the place. Because she does.

271

Her silver sequined dress hugs every curve, catching the light like a disco ball designed for seduction.

"This is Luz. Isn't it amazing?" she yells over the bass, gesturing at the crowd like she's welcoming me to another universe.

"It's... unbelievable," I admit, nearly breathless.

"Ami," she says, tugging me closer, "just admit you're impressed. This is your night."

"My night?"

"Duh," she says, spinning in place as we step into the crush of bodies. "I told you. We're celebrating you! That signing was a smash and you're helping me write my dream book. You deserve a night out. We both do!"

I hesitate, glancing around. The energy is electric, no question. It's intoxicating, but not something I ever imagined myself choosing.

Though, to be fair, Maria started pushing me out of my comfort zone long before we even left the mansion. She'd burst into my room earlier this evening, arms full of slinky dresses, a mischievous grin on her face.

"We're celebrating your success," she announced, dropping fabric all over my bed. "And if we're doing it properly, you have to look like the queen you are."

I groaned, burrowing into my pillows. "Maria, I'm not the clubbing type. You must know that."

"Please. You packed for SpicyLitCon. You must have brought something cute."

"Cute for SpicyLitCon is not cute for—"

"Which is why I brought backup." She held up an emerald green dress that looked very, very small.

"Maria, I can't wear that. It's too—"

"Sexy?" she said, already grinning. "Exactly. We're showing off your tits and ass tonight, girl."

I buried my face in my hands. "This feels like a mistake."

"It's not. It's a makeover." She pulled me up by the wrists. "Ami, you've got curves people would kill for. We're going to put them to work. Trust me. You were a rock star at the signing, and tonight you're going to look like a porn star."

And somehow, she made it happen.

The dress hugs my body like it was poured on. Daring neckline, barely-there back, a hemline that makes me feel wild and expensive. Maria worked some kind of sorcery with my hair, curling it into soft waves that bounce with every step. My eyes are smoky and my heels make my legs look a mile long.

I don't just look different. I feel different.

As we move through the club, Marco's hand is on my lower back, his fingers brushing bare skin. Warm. Steady. Possessive in a way that makes me feel steady and claimed.

"Stay close," he murmurs near my ear, his voice low enough to cut through the noise and land straight in my spine.

I glance up at him, and the look he gives me—it sends a shiver through me.

It's quick, but it's real. His eyes drag down my body before snapping back to the crowd, like he's checking for danger and trying not to lose focus. But it's clear, he's seen me. *Really* seen me.

The way his jaw tightens? The pulse ticking at his temple?

He's affected.

And I feel it in every inch of me. Luxuriate in it.

Ahead of us, Chuck and Rafe move through the crowd with practiced ease—smooth, alert, deadly. Rafe drifts toward the bar, laid-back posture, eyes always scanning. Chuck' moves across the dance floor, tracking each person's movement like he's building a mental map.

Elias is near the entrance, speaking with a tall man in a fitted navy suit—likely the club manager. He's got a clipboard and a low fade, nodding as Elias speaks, everything about him polished and efficient.

Maria leads me toward a side staircase marked off by another thick purple velvet rope and a small sign reading VIP in gold script. A man in a dark suit stands beside it, arms crossed, keeping watch. Marco exchanges a glance with him and the guard nods once, lifting the rope, allowing us to pass. Maria leads me up the stairs with Marco and Fidel following close behind.

The VIP lounge is another world. Cooler air, thick carpet, plush furniture.. The music softens into something smooth and seductive, the bass a steady heartbeat. Everything here feels *intentional*. Power gathered under dim lighting.

Low tables hold ice buckets filled with high-end liquor and champagne bottles. Men in tailored suits lounge on white leather banquettes, sipping tequila from crystal tumblers and talking in low, conspiratorial voices. Women in low-cut dresses drape themselves across laps and arms, all legs and sparkling jewelry, wielding champagne flutes like weapons.

Maria drops onto a banquette, reaching for a chilled bottle of tequila in the ice bucket before her. She pours two glasses like she owns the world.

"This," she announces, holding her glass up, "is exactly what I needed." She turns to me with a grin. "And you, Ami, are welcome."

"Welcome?"

"For dragging you out of your shell and into this fabulous night, obviously." She gestures at me. "You look hot as hell. Admit it. You feel amazing."

I hesitate, but I can't help the smile. She's not wrong. I do feel amazing. Like I've stepped into a version of myself that's bolder. Braver.

"You do look incredible," Marco says, and the words land like heat on my skin.

I turn to find him standing beside me, eyes sweeping over me again, slower this time. His gaze is steady, his voice calm, but there's something in it—something sharp and hungry—that makes my breath catch.

"You clean up a little too well," he adds, almost to himself.

"Thanks," I say, trying not to sound breathless.

He leans in closer, his voice dropping low. "Just remember. This place isn't fiction. It doesn't always end the way you want it to."

I stiffen, his words cold water against the flush in my skin. But I meet his eyes and hold them.

"I know it's not fiction," I say evenly. "I'm not here to play pretend."

He watches me a moment longer. Then, with a slight nod, he straightens.

"Stay with Maria. Don't wander."

He gives Fidel another glance, then disappears back down the stairs—quiet, focused, all business again.

Fidel takes a position nearby, calm but alert.

I take a seat beside Maria as she hands me a glass. "He's so dramatic," she says, rolling her eyes. "Relax, Ami. You're safe. This is our place. And Fidel's got us."

I nod and take a sip. The tequila burns, then spreads warmth down my spine.

But my mind isn't on the drink. It's on Marco.

The way he looked at me. The heat in his voice. The tension behind his calm.

And the way he said *"don't wander"*? It wasn't just about safety.

It was about staying close—to him, to this, to whatever it is we're building.

56

AMI

"Drink up!" Maria shouts, downing her tequila in one smooth motion. Her silver dress flashes in the lights as she grabs my hand and pulls me to my feet. "Come on, Ami. We're dancing!"

The music is louder downstairs, the bass deeper. It throbs in my chest as we hit the floor, swallowed by movement and sound. Maria doesn't let go of me, tugging me into the wave of bodies already in motion.

"You're here, you look incredible, and we're going to have *fun*," she yells, spinning me under her arm.

The air is thick with heat and perfume and the pulse of music. Fidel is close by, on the edge of the dance floor—hovering, but not overbearing. He moves with purpose, a wall of calm in the middle of chaos.

Maria is pure joy—laughing, swaying, pulling me in for a ridiculous shimmy that makes me burst out laughing. "See?" she grins, twirling again. "You're glowing!"

"It's the lighting," I call back, even though I know it's not.

"It's *you*," she counters. "You're killing it."

And for once, I let myself believe her.

The floor shifts around us, every strobe flash like a shot of adrenaline. I'm sweaty, dizzy, free. Music pours through me like heat. And then—

A tap on my shoulder.

I turn to see three women, glittering with jewelry and excitement. The tallest—sleek brown hair, champagne flute in hand—gasps.

"Oh my God. You're Ami Zadegan, right?"

I blink, disoriented, and nod. "Yeah."

"I was at your signing the other day. At the tennis store," she gushes. "You were amazing. I can't believe you're here!"

Maria beams. "We're celebrating her success!"

"I *love* your books," another adds. "*Smash Girl* is my favorite. I've read it, like, five times."

I smile, still catching my breath. "That's... wow. Thank you."

"Can we get a pic?" the brunette asks, already pulling out her phone.

I nod, leaning in as she snaps a selfie. Her friends squeeze in tight, perfume clouding the space between us. "Thank you!" she chirps, eyes bright. "You're even prettier in person."

I feel dazed. Nothing like this has ever happened to me before. The girls vanish back into the crowd as quickly as they appeared.

Maria grabs my arm. "Oh my God, Ami! See? You're an icon! Let's grab drinks."

We weave through the crush of dancers toward the bar, Fidel following closely behind us. My head is still buzzing—not just from the music now, but from adrenaline, or from the fan girls. Or maybe its the tequila. Something warm and syrupy is spreading behind my eyes.

The bar glows in an amber light. Maria leans in, flagging down the bartender. "Two Cosmos!"

I blink, trying to reorient myself. "You picked those just because they're pink, didn't you?"

"They're pretty!" she fires back, grinning.

The bartender slides two perfect drinks toward us, garnished with curls of orange peel. Maria raises her glass. "To you, superstar."

I laugh and lift mine. "To both of us."

We clink glasses, but before I take a sip, a crash explodes behind us—sharp and sudden. It sounds like a bottle smashing into concrete.

I whip my head toward the sound. So does Maria.

Two men are going at it near the VIP stairs—shouting, shoving, a table toppling over. More glass breaks. People scatter, and security surges forward.

"Shit," Maria mutters, craning her neck. "What's happening? Is that guy bleeding?"

I set my drink back down on the bar. My pulse spikes, attention locked on the scene.

Security closes in fast. And so does Marco.

I spot him immediately—shoulders squared, movements precise, slicing through the chaos like he was made for it. Rafe is with him, jaw tight, hands loose at his sides.

Marco steps between the men, one hand raised. Rafe backs him up, their presence alone enough to make the fighting stop.

Maria leans in watching too. "Okay, okay. We're okay. They've got it."

And she's right. I see it—how quickly Marco commands the crowd without ever raising his voice. How people instinctively move out of his way. How the men stop fighting. I can't stop watching him. It's grounding. Comforting.

We both turn back to the bar, reaching for our drinks.

I take a sip. The Cosmo is cold. Sweet. Tangy with lime. I tip it back, finishing the rest in one smooth swallow.

The glass clinks softly on the marble bar. Maria's already flagging down the bartender for another round.

And I just stand there—warm, a little breathless, and thinking how I haven't felt this good in... God, I don't even know how long.

I'm in this gorgeous club with a woman who might be my new best friend. Three random strangers just recognized me on the dance floor and told me how much they love my writing. And somewhere in this room, there's an incredible man I can't stop thinking about—and maybe, *just maybe*, he's thinking about me too.

For once, everything feels like it might actually be working out.

The bartender slides over two fresh drinks. I take a long sip of the second Cosmo, chilled and sharp and perfect.

This whole night might just be perfect.

But then—something shifts.

It's a small feeling at first. A slow lurch, deep in my stomach. Like the ground beneath me isn't quite level anymore.

The room tilts. Just slightly. My legs suddenly feel uncertain. Like they've forgotten how to hold me up.

I blink hard.

The heat hits next—too much, too fast. My skin flushes, my arms go heavy. The music warps around me, thudding through a tunnel of cotton and light.

"Maria..." I try, but the word catches. My mouth feels wrong. Thick. Uncoordinated.

She turns to look at me, her smile slowly vanishing, replaced by a confused look. "Ami?"

I reach for the bar but misjudge the distance. My hand knocks against it clumsily. I try again to speak, but my tongue won't cooperate.

Maria grabs my arm. Her voice is sharper now. "Ami? What's wrong?"

The lights overhead fracture into halos. My legs feel wobbly, like they're about to give out beneath me.

"Something's... wrong..."

I hear my own voice like it's underwater. Far away. Warped.

Maria's voice rises, high and panicked. "Fidel! Fidel!"

Hands catch me—I don't know whose. Everything spins.

And through it all, just before the dark pulls me under, I see him.

Marco.

On the far side of the room, turning toward me. His face changes. His whole posture shifts—from command to something else entirely.

Something like fear.

And then. Nothing.

57

MARCO

"Marco!"

Maria's scream slices through the bass, panic sharpening her voice. I snap toward the bar and spot her, arms wrapped around Ami, struggling to keep her upright. Ami's head is slumped on Maria's shoulder. Fidel has one of her arms. Her legs can't hold her.

I move. Fast. I don't care who I shove aside. One moment I'm at the edge of the crowd. The next, I'm there.

My arm goes around Ami's waist, steadying her. She's limp. Her skin is clammy, her breaths shallow and uneven. Her hair sticks to her cheek. Her eyes don't focus.

"What happened?" My voice comes out hard and clipped, barely holding together.

Maria's face is white. Her hands won't stop shaking. "She said she didn't feel right," she stammers. "And then she just—collapsed."

My eyes flick to the bar. Two martini glasses. One still full. The other is nearly empty.

Rage punches me in the chest.

"Someone drugged her."

Maria stares at me. "What? No—what do you mean, drugged? How—"

"Not now." I shift my grip and scoop Ami into my arms. She doesn't stir. Her head lolls against my chest, and I hold her closer, tightening my arms like I can keep her safe retroactively.

Maria falls in beside me, clutching my arm. "Marco—she doesn't look good."

"She's breathing. That's enough for now. Let's move."

I tap my comm as we push through the crowd. "Elias. Someone dosed Ami. I need footage pulled. Every angle. Find the son of a bitch who did it."

"Already on it," Elias says, voice flat and focused. "I've got my manager scanning the bar footage."

"Good. I want eyes on that whole bar," I say. "Especially anyone behind it."

I keep moving, eyes scanning the crowd. "Chuck. Rafe. Meet me in the back hallway."

"Copy," Chuck answers.

I turn back to Fidel and lock eyes with him. "You don't leave Maria's side."

"I'm on her," Fidel says immediately.

Ami's weight isn't much. But she feels heavy in my arms in all the wrong ways. Fragile. Fading. I want to stop and check her pulse again, but there's no time. I just have to move.

Maria's voice breaks beside me. "This is my fault," she whispers. "I dragged her out. I begged her to come. I—"

"Maria." I cut her off, sharper than I intend. "Look at me."

She does. Barely holding it together.

"This isn't on you. But I need you calm. Can you stay focused?"

A tight nod. "Yeah."

"Good."

We push through to the back hallway. The music muffles.

Fidel swings open the door to the private offices. I don't wait. I carry Ami through and kick the first door open, laying her gently on the leather couch inside.

Maria drops beside her, gripping her hand. "Ami," she whispers, brushing damp hair from her face. "Hey. It's me. You're okay. You're gonna be okay."

I kneel beside the couch, two fingers to Ami's neck. Pulse is there. Weak. But steady. Her breathing's shallow, lips parted. Her eyes flutter but won't focus. Like she's trapped just under the surface.

"She's holding on," I say, low and even, although my blood's roaring.

Maria's lip trembles. "I should've stayed closer. I shouldn't have turned away."

"Stop," I say, firm but not cruel. "If you want to help, stay here. Talk to her. Keep her with us."

Maria nods. Swallows. Grips Ami's hand tighter.

"You're okay," she whispers. "You hear me, Ami? Marco's here. We've got you."

Ami stirs. Barely.

"Maria...?" It's a whisper, slow and slurred.

Maria leans in, her voice cracking with relief. "I'm here. Right here. Marco's handling everything. You're safe."

Ami mutters something I can't make out. Her eyes close again.

That's all I can take.

I stand. The control I've been clinging to nearly snaps. My hands curl into fists.

"Fidel," I bark. "Stay with them. No one comes in. Not staff, not security, *no one.*"

He nods once. "On it."

I meet Maria's eyes. Hers are red, but hard. "Marco," she says, voice tight, "whoever did this, you need to—"

"I know."

I slam the door behind me and stalk down the hallway.

"Elias," I say into my comm. "Talk to me."

"Got something," he says. "There's a guy—lingering near the bar just before the drinks were touched. Tall. Dark suit, no tie. We're grabbing him now. Pulling him to the back."

"Chuck. Rafe," I say, my voice flat and cold. "Back hallway. We're handling this."

"On our way," Chuck replies. Rafe doesn't even answer. He doesn't need to.

I roll my shoulders, forcing my expression blank.

But inside?

I only feel fire.

Someone thought they could poison her. Touch her. Leave her sprawled out like that while I was just a few feet away.

Someone thought they could get away with it.

Someone is about to learn the cost of their mistake.

58

MARCO

The door slams shut behind me, sealing off the pulse of the club. In here, it's quiet—the air already thick with the smell of sweat, blood, and fear.

Rafe and Chuck are flanking the guy in the chair. He's mid-thirties, maybe. Cheap black suit, slicked-back hair. His nose is broken—could be Chuck's work from the blood splattered in his beard. The guy's red shirt is soaked with sweat and blood. He reeks of piss and panic.

Elias stands directly in front of him, flipping his butterfly knife open and closed with a slow, precise rhythm. *Snick-snick. Snick-snick.* Calm. Focused. Enjoying himself.

"Talked to Tommy—my manager," Elias says, voice casual. "Says this one's been sniffing around for weeks. Watching the bar. First time he's had the balls to try something."

I step closer. The guy lifts his head and locks eyes with me. I see it—*the moment he understands.* He thought he could do it. Thought he wouldn't get caught.

He thought wrong.

"Tonight was your big move?" I ask. My voice is quiet. Cold. I don't need volume to make people scared.

"I—I didn't mean anything by it!" he blurts. "It wasn't personal!"

I lean in, grip the arms of the chair, and get in his face. "You drugged her drink. That's personal."

His breath stutters and he starts squirming. "I—I just thought she looked... easy—"

My hand flies forward. I grab his shirt and jerk him forward. My palm cracks across his face. Hard. Loud.

Blood sprays. He gasps.

"Say that again," I growl. "Go on. Say it."

He shakes his head, tears welling now.

"Marco," Elias says, brushing past me. His shoulder nudges mine—light, but firm. His knife still twitches in his hand. "Let me."

I let go and shove the guy back into the chair. Elias is very good in this type of situation so I let him go to work. The guy's eyes go wide when Elias crouches in front of him, blade gleaming in the overhead light.

"Here's the deal," Elias says, like he's talking over cocktails. "You're not smart enough to do this on your own. So tell me who sent you."

"I—I swear, no one—"

The blade kisses the man's ear. He stops breathing.

"I'm going to need a name," Elias says, tilting his head. "Otherwise..." A bead of blood slides down the man's neck. "I'll take something small to start."

The guy trembles. But he doesn't talk.

Elias smiles. "Chuck?"

Chuck comes up behind the guy's chair, grips his hair and locks his head in place.

"Thanks," Elias says—and starts cutting.

The first slice is slow. Deliberate. The scream that follows is ragged and loud and pointless. No one can hear him in here. Blood pours over his collar, down into his jacket.

"Wait!" he shrieks. "Wait, wait, wait!"

Elias pauses, knife still pressed to raw flesh.

"Someone paid me!" the guy sobs. "He gave me the stuff, told me about the girls—said to put it in the brunette's drink."

Elias doesn't move. "Which brunette?" His voice is soft. Polite. The blade presses deeper.

"I—I don't know!" the guy whimpers. "The one with the other one! I think he said both! Told me just make sure they drink it!"

I feel it in my chest—rage rising like fire. *Ami and Maria.*

"And you're telling me you don't know his name?" Elias asks, almost disappointed.

"I swear," the man babbles. "I don't! I just buy off him sometimes, y'know? Meth, mostly. I didn't ask questions. I just thought he hung out by the bar. Selling meth."

Elias wiggles the now half-sliced ear.

"Don't lie to me," he says. "I'm very good at spotting liars." Elias presses the knife down a bit, making a deeper cut.

The man shrieks again. His body jerks in the chair. Blood spatters the floor.

"Both girls," he chokes out. "That's all I know. I swear. Please —please, stop—"

Elias tilts his head, studying him like a bug on a pin.

"He said to do it during the fight," he blurts suddenly. "Said no one would notice."

My jaw tightens. There it is. The fight by the stairs. Loud, messy, timed to the second. Not a coincidence. Not a brawl.

A fucking smokescreen.

"Sloppy," Elias mutters. "But yeah. You might actually be too dumb to pay attention, get a name."

The man lets out something like a sob of relief.

Elias doesn't move.

"Still..." He moves the knife to the edge of the man's ear, carving a deep, clean notch into the cartilage. "Can't let you leave without a souvenir."

The man screams. Again.

Rafe doesn't blink. Chuck doesn't flinch. This is routine for them. Me? I want to break this guy's jaw with my fist. But I'm not here for catharsis. I'm here for information.

Elias wipes the blade on the guy's lapel and stands.

He grabs the man's chin and lifts it.

"If I see you here again," Elias murmurs, "you won't walk out next time. You won't even crawl."

The guy nods, sobbing. "Y-yes. I—I won't—I swear—"

Elias glances at me. "Your call, boss."

I stare at the man for a beat. Then: "Rafe. Chuck. Get him out. Make sure he remembers every second of tonight."

Chuck grunts and moves in. Rafe hauls him up like a sack of garbage. The guy's legs buckle, blood running down his neck. Doesn't matter. Chuck and Rafe drag him toward the door without sympathy.

It slams shut behind them.

Elias cleans his blade with a handkerchief and slips it back into his jacket like he just finished trimming a steak.

"Tommy didn't recognize him," he says. "Probably a temp. Errand boy."

"It's not random," I say. "The fight. The timing. The drug. This was planned."

"Calderóns," Elias mutters. "They're probing the fence. Looking for an opening."

I pause, jaw tightening. "And now we've got meth moving through our club."

The words taste like acid. We don't touch that shit. Not ever.

"Get eyes on every inch of this place," I say. "If Tommy doesn't lock it down, I will."

Elias smirks, faint and cold. "On it." He slips into the hallway, vanishing into the dark.

I turn toward the door. The one that leads back to Ami.

My hands are steady now. My fury is focused and razor-sharp.

This wasn't random. It was a warning. And warnings go both ways.

59

AMI

THE FOG in my head is starting to thin, but my body still doesn't feel like mine. Everything's heavy, uncoordinated—like I've been unplugged and only halfway rebooted. Even the soft cushion beneath me feels like it's holding me down. Every sound is too loud. Every light, too sharp.

Maria hasn't moved from my side. She's curled against me, gripping my hand like she's afraid I'll vanish if she lets go. Her sequined dress glints under the overhead lights, but the shine in her eyes is pure panic. Her mascara's smudged, her jaw tight. She's trying not to cry.

"You're okay," she whispers again, for the fifth... maybe the fifteenth time. "You're safe now. We've got you."

The door creaks open, and the air shifts.

Marco steps inside, and it's like the room reorganizes around him. He's quiet, but he carries weight, like gravity. His face is all hard lines and sharp control, his movements clean, deliberate. He doesn't say a word, not at first, but the tension in his shoulders says enough.

Fidel is close by, in position by the door, silent and still, like he's made of stone.

Marco's eyes land on me and stay there. He crouches in front of the couch, close enough that I can feel his heat. His hands find my knees. They're firm, grounding, real.

"Ami," he says. His voice is low, rough around the edges. "Look at me."

It takes effort to move my head, but I do it. My vision blurs, then sharpens. He's staring at me like I'm the only thing in the room.

"You're safe," he says again, softer this time. "We're getting you out of here."

I swallow against the dryness in my throat. "What... happened?" My voice sounds strange. Muffled. Like someone else is using it.

His jaw tightens. "Someone drugged your drink."

Maria lets out a shaky breath beside me and squeezes my hand tighter. "Marco," she says, and her voice is already breaking. "This is my fault. I shouldn't have—"

"It's not your fault," Marco cuts in, sharp but steady. "It's on the bastard who did it."

Maria opens her mouth again, but Fidel speaks first, his voice calm and low. "She's lucky. Whatever it was, it wasn't a full dose."

Lucky. The word settles in my chest like a weight. If this is what lucky feels like—disoriented, weak, like my limbs are full of sand—I don't want to know what unlucky would've been.

Maria lets out a brittle laugh, but it's jagged at the edges. "Lucky," she repeats. "I dragged her here. I should've stayed closer. I shouldn't have—"

"Maria," I manage, my tongue thick but cooperating. "You didn't do this. Someone else did."

She looks down at our joined hands. "I should've seen it coming."

I try to smile, though it probably looks more like a grimace.

"Next time, we're sticking to bottled water. That we open ourselves."

It's not funny. But Maria huffs a small, broken laugh, and the death grip on my hand eases a little.

Marco doesn't laugh. His hands tighten on my knees, just slightly. The pressure is light, but it cuts through the fog.

"This isn't a joke, Ami," he says. "It could've gone another way. Fast."

"I know." I do.

He stands up fast, and the movement makes my stomach dip. "We're leaving," he says, already scanning the room like he's checking for exits.

He turns to Fidel. "Stay right next to Maria. No one gets near her."

Fidel nods, calm as ever. "Understood."

Marco looks back at me, and something in his face shifts. It softens—barely—but it's enough to make my chest ache.

"Can you walk?"

I open my mouth, but Maria beats me to it. "She shouldn't," she says, glaring up at him. "She's not steady."

Marco mutters something I can't hear. Then he bends and slides one arm under my knees, the other behind my back.

"Marco—" I try, but the protest doesn't land. My body is already folding into his hold, drawn to the warmth of him. The steadiness.

"Save it," he murmurs into my hair. "I've got you."

The door creaks again. A man steps inside and lingers near the threshold—the manager, sharp navy suit, slick voice.

"Security's clearing a path out back," he says smoothly. "Elias wants to keep it quiet."

Marco gives him a sharp nod. I hear Fidel's voice, steady and just a little slower than usual. "Appreciate it, Tommy."

There's a pause. I clock it, even through the haze.

Fidel watches him a second too long.

Tommy looks back at him, at Maria, his face unreadable. Then he turns and walks out.

Maria pulls her arms around herself like she's cold. Her mascara is streaked and her heels wobble, but she follows us out, silent now. Hollow-eyed. Fidel walks beside her, arm around her shoulders, steadying her without saying a word.

The hallway is dim, the air cooler. My head rests against Marco's chest, and I close my eyes, just for a second. My fingers curl into his shirt.

I don't know if I'm holding on for him, or for me.

Maybe both.

At the door, he adjusts his grip, like he's making sure I'm not going to slip. His breath brushes the side of my face as he exhales.

"We're not coming back here," he mutters.

No one argues.

60

MARCO

THE COMPOUND IS quiet when we pull in. It feels like the silence is sitting on top of the place, pressing it down.

I kill the engine and climb out, rounding to Ami's door before she can move. She's already trying to sit up, her jaw set in that stubborn way she gets when she's hurting but doesn't want to show it.

Too late.

I open the door and crouch slightly. Her glare's already locked and loaded. "Don't," I say before she can get a word out. "You've done enough for one night."

Her eyes flash. "I can walk, Marco."

"I know you can."

I scoop her into my arms anyway. She doesn't fight it. Not really. She huffs and scowls, but her arms loop around my neck like muscle memory.

"You're impossible."

"Funny," I mutter, carrying her up the steps. "I was thinking the same thing about you."

She leans her head against my shoulder. I feel the tension in her body, the stiffness she's trying to hide. I can still smell the faint scent of jasmine in her hair. Still feel the weight of what almost happened.

What could've happened.

I adjust my hold as I push open the door.

Inside, Maria's already pacing in the sitting room like a caged animal, phone pressed to her ear, words flying out in rapid Spanish—her Raul voice. Damage control. She barely looks up.

Fidel's near the fireplace, arms crossed, watching her pace. He gives me a nod. I return it.

We head upstairs. Ami's lighter than she looks, but the weight of her in my arms isn't just physical. It's sharp. Heavy in a different way. I'm carrying the aftermath of someone else's choice. And if I hadn't been watching the room the way I was taught to…

She shifts against me, her voice small but clear. "Marco?"

I glance down. Her eyes are half-lidded but locked on mine.

"This wasn't random," she says.

It's not a question.

I keep walking. "No."

A beat of silence.

"They weren't just going after Maria."

I don't say anything. Just move up the stairs.

"So… it was me too."

I hear the words, but I don't react. Not on the outside. Inside? It hits me harder than it should.

"They know who you are now," I say quietly. "Maria's still their priority. But they're willing to use you to get to her."

To get to me.

She's silent. But I can feel the tension building in her limbs. She's holding onto my shirt again. Not tightly. Just… there. Like she's grounding herself.

"They don't care about collateral damage," I add. "They proved that tonight."

She swallows hard. "So I'm collateral damage."

I stop at the top of the stairs.

She's looking at me, and I know she's not asking for pity. She wants facts.

"They may think that. But you're not," I say. "Not to me."

We reach her room. I kick the door open with my boot and carry her straight to the bed. The lamp's still on. Soft light spills across her face, catching the faint smudges under her eyes, the crease in her brow.

I set her down gently, like she's made of glass, even though I know she's tougher than that. I adjust the pillows behind her, make sure she's settled.

"You need sleep," I say.

She exhales. "That's it? You just drop that on me and then tell me to go to sleep?"

I smirk, just a little. "Welcome to my world."

She doesn't smile, exactly, but the edge in her eyes softens. I should leave now. I should walk out and let her rest.

But I hesitate.

"Marco."

I glance back.

"You didn't have to carry me," she says.

My gaze holds hers.

"I know," I say. "I wanted to."

Her lips part, just slightly. She's not expecting the honesty. I didn't expect to say it.

I should tell her more. That she scared the hell out of me. That I watched her eyes roll back in her head and for one second thought I was too late.

But I don't. Because if I start, I won't stop.

"I have to meet with Raul," I say instead.

Something flickers in her jaw. But she nods. Quiet. Accepting.

I hover in the doorway longer than I should. I don't know what I'm waiting for. Permission? Forgiveness?

A sign that I'm not already in too deep?

"Rest, Ami," I say, low. "We'll talk soon."

I step out and pull the door closed behind me. I walk down the hall, past the portraits and the marble and all the quiet power this place holds.

And I know exactly what Raul is going to say.

That she doesn't belong here. That she's a risk. A weakness. That she has to go.

And the worst part?

He'll be right.

But none of that makes it easier. Because I don't know if I can let her go.

Even though I might have to.

61

A PHONE CALL

Intercepted Cell Transmission

Audio Transcript: "Tzuihuac" Communication, Intercept #1087
Analyst Comments in Brackets
Timestamp: 04:17 CST | Encrypted VoIP
Location: Unknown Warehouse, Del Rio
Status: Partially Decrypted/Translation from Spanish

Male Voice #1 – "Tzihuac": We launch Friday. First wave takes the east site—just enough fire to cripple. Then we bleed 'em on the second.

Male Voice #2 – Unidentified: The decoy?

Tzihuac: Small crew. Fast, loud, disposable. Make a lot of noise.

. . .

Unidentified: And the girl?

[STATIC – 4.2 SECONDS]

Tzihuac: Doesn't matter. The message is bigger than her. She's a symbol now.

Unidentified: They'll retaliate.

Tzihuac: That's the point. Let them waste their heat in the wrong direction. While we cut the pipeline.

[PAUSE – PAPERS RUSTLING]

Unidentified: He wants confirmation. He won't risk exposure unless this delivers.

Tzihuac: It'll deliver. Trust me. Two prongs. One burns the money. The other?

[LAUGH]

. . .

Tzihuac (cont'd): The north is a controlled fire. But the south...
that's to break the name.

[Analyst note – Spanish retained as heard: *para quebrar el nombre*. Translates literally as "break the name"; idiomatic meaning uncertain. Possibly refers to destroying legacy, honor or symbolic power.]

[END TRANSMISSION – PARTIAL FRAGMENT ONLY]

[NOTE: Full voice ID match pending. Suggest cross-reference with Los Tizones, Acuña side.]

62

MARCO

I SIT STRAIGHT-BACKED in one of the two leather chairs facing Raul Sandoval's desk, hands on my thighs, feet planted. Behind me, Elias, Chuck and Rafe stand like statues. Beside me, Fidel scrolls through his tablet, the screen casting cold light over his face.

Raul's study is dead quiet. No music. No voices. Just the soft tick of the antique clock on the far wall and the measured tap of Raul's ring—steady, controlled—against the desk.

He's calm, of course. Always is. Even now, with his empire on the verge of open war, the man is in a suit and doesn't have a single hair out of place.

"Fidel," Raul says, voice low but loaded. "Are we certain the Calderóns were behind the incident at Luz?"

"Yes, sir." Fidel doesn't hesitate. "Confirmed through surveillance, testimony, and chatter. The man we caught wasn't working alone."

Raul leans forward, eyes sharp. "Was Maria the target?"

Fidel gives a slight nod. "It's likely. But the instructions weren't clear. They may have been told to hit the woman with her. Maybe both of them. Either way, the goal was disruption. Public. Messy."

My jaw tightens. I already know where this is going.

Raul taps his ring twice against the wood. "They're probing for weaknesses."

"They found one," I say quietly. "They got too close."

Fidel swipes across his screen. "Intel confirms a two-pronged hit is in motion. The Calderóns are prepping to hit our southeastern warehouse—heaviest supply chain and most valuable asset. Simultaneously, we expect a secondary strike further north. Smaller crew. Distraction or decoy."

"They don't have the manpower for both," Raul says, not a question.

"No. They're stretched," Fidel replies. "If they're pulling this off, someone's backing them."

That hangs heavy in the room.

Raul's voice drops. "Who?"

"We don't know yet. But this kind of coordination? It's cartel-adjacent at the very least."

A beat of silence.

Then Raul sits back slowly, steepling his fingers. The quiet stretches.

"I don't like unknowns, Fidel," he says. His words are soft. But they land hard.

Then, after a beat—"Find out who it is. And find out what the fuck they want."

Fidel nods, already swiping through files with his thumb. But his jaw's tight. He knows time's running out.

Raul turns to me. "So. What's our response?"

I meet his gaze. "I take Rafe and six of our best to the warehouse. Lock it down. Full perimeter, inside and out. Elias and Chuck stay here, reinforce the compound. Fidel coordinates from the guardhouse. Remote eyes on both sites, drones included. We plug every hole before they find it."

Raul thinks for all of five seconds before nodding. "Approved. Take what you need. No fuckups."

"Understood."

Fidel rises, snapping his tablet closed. Chuck shifts behind me. Rafe cracks his knuckles once, then stills.

"Elias," I say, turning slightly. "Get the staff briefed and armed. Chuck, position patrols around the estate. Rotate frequently. No blind spots."

"On it," Elias says, already moving.

"You got it," Chuck adds, pulling out his radio.

As the room starts to empty, I turn back to Raul.

"You and Maria should stay close to the panic room until we confirm the strike zones."

Raul's eyes narrow. "I can protect my daughter."

"You shouldn't have to," I say evenly. "But you're their endgame. If they get to you, they win."

For a second, I think he's going to argue. But then he nods, slow and deliberate. "Caution is not the same as weakness. I know that. Do you?"

"I do," I answer.

His gaze drops to the map spread across the desk. "Then you also know what comes next. Show them what happens when someone comes for this family."

I nod, starting to rise.

"One more thing," he says.

I freeze, still half-seated.

Raul's voice is calm, but final. "Miss Zadegan."

I sit.

"She can't stay."

The words land harder than I expect, even though I saw them coming.

"She's a liability now," he continues. "The Calderóns know her face. They've marked her. She stays, she's a vulnerability. Not just to Maria. To all of us."

I lock my jaw. "Understood."

"Make her understand. Tonight."

I give a single nod. "I'll make it right."

It's an order. And I don't disobey Raul's orders. Even when I want to.

His eyes stay on me longer than I like. "See that you do."

I step out into the hallway. Rafe follows, silent, pulling the door closed behind him..

"She has to go," he says after a long beat.

"I know."

We reach the split in the corridor. Left leads to the armory and the men.

Right leads to her.

Rafe turns left. I turn right.

I head for her bedroom. And I dread every fucking step.

63

MARCO

THE HALLWAY outside her room is quiet. Still and heavy like the air right before a storm breaks. I stand there longer than I should, hand on the doorknob, jaw tight. I was a fool to think this could work—Ami, me, this world. No woman could ever survive the way I live. Any relationship with me is doomed before it even begins.

So I'll go in controlled, calm. No arguing. No damage. Make her understand. She needs to leave. I'll say whatever I have to say to get her out. Get her out of this life. Keep her safe. Follow Raul's orders.

I knock once, then push the door open.

She's on the bed, sitting cross-legged in oversized pajamas, glasses slightly askew. Her hair spills down over one shoulder, and there's a book in her lap she clearly hasn't been reading. When she sees me, something flickers across her face. Hope, maybe. Relief.

It doesn't last.

"You're back," she says. Quiet, guarded. She sets the book aside. She knows.

"We need to talk."

She straightens, spine stiff. "Let me guess. This is the part where you tell me I don't belong. That I should've left days ago."

I nod once. "You're leaving tomorrow."

There's a pause. Then a laugh. "Wait. What?"

"I'll have a car take you to the airport. Security will get you to the gate. You'll be safe in Houston."

Her eyes widen, disbelief sharpening her tone. "That's it? You've just decided I have to go." She rises to her feet slowly. "No discussion? No chance for me to have a say?" Her voice is now trembling. "You're making this decision all on your own?"

She lets out a harsh laugh, but it's brittle. "Was that your plan all along, or did Raul just give you your marching orders?"

She pauses, looking to me as if I might answer.

"Marco, this is the part where—if I meant anything to you, if *we* meant anything at all—you'd say something that sounds like you give a damn."

I don't move. Don't blink. Because if I open my mouth, I'll say the wrong thing.

"It's not about how I feel, Ami," I finally say, voice low. "It's about keeping you alive."

She crosses her arms, voice sharp now. "In other words, I'm just a problem to be solved."

I say nothing.

She takes a step closer. "So tell me, do *you* want me to go?"

I hesitate, but then say the words I need to say. "I need you gone," I say, quiet and brutal.

She doesn't flinch. But her face hardens. "Why?"

"Because you don't belong here," I answer. "You were never supposed to be here. And now you're a liability."

She glares at me. "You mean I'm not strong enough. Say it."

I hesitate. Then: "You're not built for this."

Her voice goes flat. "Built for this? Say it. You think I'm weak."

I run a hand through my hair, jaw tight. "I think you're not strong enough to survive this," I admit. "Ami, you may have survived other situations—bad ones. But this place—this is different. It's not about taking a hit and getting back up. It's about never letting your guard down. Never forgetting where you are or who's watching." I take in a deep breath. "This is a different kind of violence than any you've ever seen, deeper, dirtier. It gets inside you. It changes you. And you're not built for that."

Her breath hitches, but she stays silent.

"You left your drink on the bar, Ami," I continue, voice low and hard. "You didn't even think twice. Maria would never have done that. She knows better. But you..." I trail off, shaking my head. "It's not just about being careful. It's about knowing what can happen. And you don't."

I meet her eyes, cold but steady. "That makes you dangerous. To yourself—and to the people around you."

Her eyes lock on mine, her hands balled into fists at her sides. When she speaks, her voice is calm and low, but there's a slight tremble there too—like the ground's just dropped out from under her. "You think I'm not strong enough?" She takes a breath, her chin lifting. "Marco, I'm not here because I'm naive. I'm here because I want to be with you—here, in your world. I'm choosing this, choosing you."

I don't argue.

"And now what, I'm inconvenient?" she continues. "Too emotional, too soft? You're done because I'm too fragile?"

"It's not just that," I say, voice sharper now. "It's the way you look at this place, at all of us. Like this is some kind of backdrop. Like it's just research for your next fucking romance novel."

She blinks, her face paling.

"This is the real world," I go on. "It isn't fiction. You're playing with fire here, Ami."

I take a step forward, my jaw tight, ready to say the words I know will make this worse. "You came here—into a world you don't understand—and you thought it was inspiration. Material. Like it was research for a fucking dark crime romance."

She shakes her head, her words a whisper. "I never—"

"You don't get it," I say, voice flat. "This is real. Violence. Blood. Betrayal. It's not a goddamn story. People bleed here. People die." I keep going because I have to. "You could die."

Her voice is quiet but shaking. "You really think I stayed because I just wanted to write about this?"

"I think you stayed because you don't understand."

She squares her shoulders, eyes blazing even as tears gather. "I don't believe you. That's not enough to push me away. You have feelings for me. I know you do. Tell me the real reason. Tell me why you're sending me away. Because I can survive. You know I can. And I'm not leaving unless you tell me the truth."

Silence.

"Say it," she says. "Say what you really think of me. Tell me why I can't survive here."

I meet her eyes. "Chad."

She blinks, caught off guard. "Chad? What does he—"

"I saw the video. University of Texas. Him slapping you. Pushing you. Leaving you on the ground."

Her mouth opens, but nothing comes out. She just stares at me, eyes wide, lips trembling.

I press on, each word like a nail in a coffin. A knife through my heart. "I pulled your background when you got here. I needed to know everything. The footage was buried. But I saw it."

Her breath hitches. "You... saw it?" she says. She stares at me like she doesn't know me at all. "And you didn't say anything?"

"My job is to protect Maria. Protect the Sandovals," I say

quietly. "I needed to know what you might bring into this house."

A silence stretches between us. She shifts, like the weight of what I've said is finally sinking in. Her hand drifts to her chest, pressing over her heart.

When she speaks again, her voice breaks. "So that's it? You saw something violent and humiliating, and your conclusion was... she's a liability?"

I swallow hard, but she's not done.

"You didn't feel angry. Or protective. Or anything human. Just 'traumatized, weak, cut her loose.'"

I clench my jaw. "I saw it. Saw you. And I did what I had to do."

Her eyes flash. "Oh my God. You don't care about me. About what happened to me. I wonder if you're even capable of human feelings."

It's time to tell her everything. I know this will hurt, but maybe, one day, it will make her stronger and maybe she'll see it as a gift.

"I didn't tell you what else I know. About Victoria Drake," I go on, getting it all out. "She dropped Chad because he plagiarized *Beneath a Persian Sky*. That's your book, right? He stole it from you—and you never noticed. Never even suspected. So she's circling now because she knows you're the real talent."

She shakes her head, tears building in her eyes. "Stop."

But I can't. I've already torn the wound open.

"He took your words. Your story. Threw you away after. And you never even knew. Never even saw what was happening in your own world."

Her hands cover her face, shaking. "I'm an idiot." Her breathing is shallow, rapid. "And you just... didn't tell me? Didn't think I should know? Let Victoria talk about my book and you didn't tell me what she did? What Chad did?"

I pause, jaw tight. "I'm not here to fix things for you."

Her hands drop and she looks up, eyes hard as she locks on mind. "No," she says, a hitch in her voice. "You're definitely not."

She takes a deep breath. When she speaks, her voice has turned cold. "Let's talk about you now, Marco." She wipes the tears from her eyes as she continues. "You've clearly been profiling me. Gathering data like you're preparing a fucking threat report. I'm too weak. Too soft. Not assessing the threats in my own world. And so you're done."

She turns away for a second, breathing hard. Then turns back, fury burning bright.

"But you think I haven't noticed the way you treat me? Like I'm a *situation* to manage? A *threat* to neutralize?"

I open my mouth, but she barrels on.

"Every word from you is calculated. Measured. Like feelings are a weakness you can't afford."

"I'm trying to protect you—"

"No, you're trying to control me." Her voice rises, cracking just slightly. "Like you control everything else. That's what this is really about, isn't it?"

She's trembling now, fists clenched, but her voice is hard.

"You saw what Chad did. What Victoria did. You knew what they stole from me. And you didn't tell me. You watched me doubt myself. Question my worth. And you said nothing."

Her face twists, grief and fury bleeding into every word. "Why would you tell me? You don't care about anything as trivial as feelings. You just assess the threat. Take orders. Follow the mission. And then you shut down so no one ever sees the real you."

She drags in a breath, like she's choking on the truth. "And when I finally got too real for you—too *weak*—you decided I didn't belong."

Her voice goes so low, it's a whisper.

"You aren't protecting me. You're following orders. And telling yourself that those are the same things."

I look down at the floor, unable to meet her gaze. And she drives the knife in.

"That's right, Marco. I've assessed you, too."

I look up and her gaze is like ice as she twists the knife.

"You think you can save everyone if you don't let yourself care. That if you stay frozen, never feel anything, no one you care about will die. That's what happened with her, isn't it?"

My stomach locks. "Don't."

"Elena," she continues. "You cared about her, but you couldn't save her. And now, somehow, you've convinced yourself that if you never care about anyone again, you'll never fail like that again. That you'll never feel that kind of loss."

She shakes her head, eyes burning.

"Jesus, Marco. If that's what you came up with after Elena's death—if your answer was to shut down and turn into *this*— then something is seriously broken inside you."

"That's not—"

"No," she cuts in. "You're telling yourself that pushing me away is the only way to protect me. But it's not about me, is it? It's about you. You're terrified. If I get hurt, you'll have to feel it. And you can't handle that."

I exhale, sharp and shallow.

She steps in closer, voice low and final.

"You think you didn't save Elena," she says, her voice low, "and maybe you'll carry that for the rest of your life. But do you honestly think this—*this*—is what she would've wanted for you?"

Her eyes shine now, not just with hurt, but with fury.

"For you to turn yourself into an unfeeling machine? To stop caring? To push people away just so you'll never have to feel that kind of pain again?"

I stay silent. Because I can't say no.

"This isn't about saving *me*, Marco," she goes on, her voice sharper now. "Don't pretend it is. You're not doing this for me. You're doing this for *you*. So you don't have to care. So you don't have to hurt."

She steps closer, voice dropping into something dark and true.

"Fuck my feelings, right? And honestly, fuck Elena's death too. Because if this is who you've become in the aftermath—someone who can't love, can't let anyone love him—then that's what really died that night."

Silence.

And then, her voice drops to a whisper.

"Was any of this even real?"

Her eyes are wide, shimmering with tears, fixed on me like they're searching for something—anything.

I want to say yes. I want to tell her I've never felt anything more real than her. But I say nothing.

And that's answer enough.

She exhales, slow and shaky. "Right. Just fuck the stupid writer and move on."

Her voice cracks, but she doesn't look away.

"You were right. I don't belong here," she says. "I don't know what this was between us, but whatever it was, it's done. Please, just go."

I turn for the door. Grip the knob.

I don't look back.

I step out, shut the door behind me, and lean into the silence.

She thinks I chose this. That I never cared.

But the truth is worse. I do care.

And I'm still letting her go.

64

———

AMI

I HEAR the click of the door as it shuts behind him.

I don't move. Just stare at the door Marco left through. My arms are wrapped tightly around myself, but it's not helping. Nothing is. The air in the room feels heavier now. The glow from the lamp is too dim, too yellow, like even the light has given up trying.

He's gone. Not just physically. He left in every way that matters.

Because he knew what Chad did to me—knew even more than I did—*and said nothing.*

I lower myself to the edge of the bed, my hands gripping the blanket like it might hold me together. My stomach twists so hard it hurts, like grief and shame and disbelief are all tangled up in my ribcage.

Marco watched that video. He saw Chad slap me. Saw him shove me to the ground. Saw him leave me there.

And he said nothing.

He let me go on thinking I was the problem. That I hadn't tried hard enough. That I hadn't been good enough, smart enough, *serious* enough.

And still said nothing.

I press my palms to my eyes, forcing back the heat. The humiliation is worse than the heartbreak.

And that wasn't even the worst of it.

He knew Chad stole from me. Knew Victoria helped him. That they took *Beneath a Persian Sky*, the book I buried, the one I told no one about. Marco knew what they did. And still, he said nothing.

I let out a dry, brittle laugh that barely sounds human. *Do I have a type or what?*

First Chad. Now Marco. Men who look at me and see something they want to take, to use. And apparently, I just hand it over.

My hands curl into fists in my lap. I don't even know if I'm more hurt or furious. Both, probably. And underneath it all, this suffocating ache that won't let go.

He saw the worst things that ever happened to me, and his conclusion was: *she's weak. She's soft. She doesn't belong here.*

Not *she survived.* Not *she deserves better.* Not *she matters.*

And then, after all of that—after what we shared—he had the nerve to say it.

"Like it's just research for your next fucking romance novel."

My breath catches in my throat, and something inside me cracks.

He thought that's what this was. That I was using him. Using Maria. Using *all* of this—for some twisted story idea.

I shake my head, vision blurring. "That's what you thought of me?" I whisper. "After what we said. What we did. You thought that I was *using* you?"

God.

I'd have to laugh if it didn't hurt so much. I gave him everything—let him see parts of me I've never shared with anyone. I fell for him, *hard*, and he looked at all of it and thought: *she's using us.*

I press a fist to my mouth, swallowing a sound that's not quite a sob. This isn't just heartbreak. It's betrayal. And it's shame.

Because some part of me still wants him. Even now.

How fucking pathetic is that?

I stare across the room, eyes landing on my half-zipped suitcase in the corner. I never fully unpacked. Some part of me must've known I wasn't going to stay.

And now?

I'll leave tomorrow. Get on a plane. Go home. And try not to hate myself for falling for a man who never once gave me the benefit of the doubt.

Not when it mattered.

I pull the blanket over my legs, curling in on myself like maybe I can disappear.

I should be angry. I should be strong. But right now, I just feel *wrecked.*

Because I let someone get that close. And when it counted, I thought he saw me—really saw me—

And then he decided I wasn't worth keeping.

65

MARCO

I DIDN'T LOOK BACK.

After I closed the door on Ami, I walked out of the house, and into the back of the SUV waiting to take me to the warehouse. Didn't pause. Didn't think. Didn't feel.

Couldn't.

Not with an op already in motion.

I shoved it all down—the words I hadn't wanted to say out loud, the way she'd looked at me like I'd broken her—and slid back into the only version of myself that makes sense.

Controlled. Focused. Useful.

Because orders are orders. And distraction gets people killed.

Now, headlights slice through the dark as we approach the warehouse—a squat, jagged silhouette against the moonlight. It's supposed to be a secure shipping hub, the southeastern asset Fidel had flagged. But the air already feels wrong. Sharp. Electric.

Beside me, Rafe checks his weapon with quick, practiced hands, his eyes locked on the building.

"Too quiet," he mutters. "We should've already made contact. This feels like a trap."

"Probably is," I say.

The SUV slows to a crawl. The driver kills the lights and rolls to a stop at the loading bay. A second SUV pulls up behind us with the rest of the team.

I'm out first, boots crunching against loose gravel. The men gather in close. "Stay tight," I say, my voice low but carrying.

The heavy steel doors groan as we force them open. We move in fast—six men behind Rafe and me, splitting into formation. Rafe and I push forward through the shadows, weapons drawn. The interior reeks of oil and rust, the scent thick in the back of my throat.

Moonlight streams through the windows, casting long shadows over crates stacked high against the concrete walls. Firearms. Explosives. Military grade hardware. The warehouse is an asset we can't afford to lose.

"Fan out," I signal. "Sweep and clear."

Rafe breaks right with three men. I go left with my unit. The warehouse is silent. No footsteps. No voices. No resistance.

That's when the trap snaps shut.

An engine roars, and a black van smashes through the loading dock doors like a wrecking ball. Metal shrieks. Wood explodes. Crates splinter into debris as the van barrels through them. Shouts ring out as armed men pour out from the van— rifles raised, full body armor. Six, seven, maybe more.

"Contact! Nine o'clock!" I bark into my comm, diving behind a steel support beam as bullets light up the air. Sparks fly off concrete. A round tears through a crate beside me, splitting it open.

The Calderóns didn't come to rattle us. They came to bury us.

"East side hot," Rafe calls out, his voice loud but steady. "Four targets flanking. Trying to pin us in."

"Suppress the van!" I shout, leaning out and firing a controlled burst. One target drops. Another scrambles for cover. "Keep them pinned!"

My comm crackles to life—Fidel's voice, sharp and urgent.

"Marco, we've got a problem here. The mansion's under attack. This—" a burst of static, "—warehouse is the diversion."

A chill shoots down my spine.

"How bad?" I ask, although I already know.

"Bad. Power's down. Generator's hit. Raul's holding the first floor, but Maria and Ami are upstairs—heading for the panic room, I think. We're not going to make it if you don't get here fast."

Another round slams into my cover. I grit my teeth, heart hammering.

"Where the hell are Elias and Chuck?"

"Dispatched to the casino—other side of town. They were pulled out before the strike. Misdirection. It was coordinated."

Goddammit.

This wasn't just an assault. This was a chess move. And we walked right into it.

I fire another burst and drop a second Calderón before slamming the rifle against my shoulder and barking into my comm. "Rafe—we're pulling out. Back to the compound."

Static crackles through my earpiece and Raul's voice suddenly cuts into the channel. Fidel must've patched him in. "Marco, get back here. They're inside." His voice is calm, despite the gunfire I can hear in the background.

"Hold them," I snap. "We're en route."

"Move fast," Raul says. "We're running out of time."

Gunfire rattles through the comm—too close.

I break cover and move. "Rafe, status!"

"They're breaking. Numbers are light. Two left near the van."

The shooting slows as Rafe's team mops up the last of the Calderón men.

"Clear," Rafe calls out a moment later.

"Move!" I bark. "Let's go."

We're sprinting, loading into the vehicles. I'm already behind the wheel before the doors shut. I slam the gas, the SUV jerking forward with a growl of the engine.

Fidel's voice cuts through again. "Raul's pinned near the stairs. Staff are holding the lower floors, but they won't hold forever. You need to move."

I push the SUV harder, faster. Every turn is a blur.

Then Raul's voice comes again, lower. Harder.

"Marco, this isn't a raid. They want Maria. They'll take her."

And Ami.

That's the part he doesn't say—but I know it.

My hands tighten on the wheel. My jaw locks.

The Calderóns lured us out. Played us. Scattered our people. And now they're coming for the only two things that matter.

If I'm even a second too late—

They'll pay for that mistake. In blood. Every last one of them.

66

AMI

THE POWER GOES OUT JUST after 1 a.m.

One second I'm pacing my room, replaying every awful thing Marco said—every awful thing I said back—and the next, the lights snap off and the house plunges into silence.

I freeze. I know enough about the situation to know that's not good.

And then I hear it—shouts from downstairs, sharp and panicked. The staccato burst of gunfire.

The house is under attack.

Maria bursts into my room, a gun in her hand. Her eyes cut through the dark, sweeping the corners. Her sequined pajama set glints faintly in the hallway light, absurdly glamorous and terrifying all at once.

"Shoes. Now," she snaps, already heading for the door.

I scramble for my sneakers, my hands shaking.

"I don't know what I'm doing," I whisper, because it's true.

Maria's voice is calm, razor-sharp. "Stay behind me. We're going to the panic room. Papa will meet us there."

I nod, even though my knees feel like they're made of jelly.

The hallway is dark, everything reduced to shifting shades of black. Faint red emergency lights glow along the baseboards, giving the house an eerie, underworld feel.

My breath is tight in my chest.

This isn't a book, I think. *This is happening.*

Every step I take pulls me further into the dark, toward the danger waiting there.

Then a sound ahead—too close. A creak. A shift. Something big moving. A man coming toward us, gun raised.

Maria doesn't hesitate.

She fires.

The gunshot splits the air, deafening in the confined hallway. The bullet punches through the man's chest and I see a spray of blood in the air for a heartbeat before he crumples to the ground.

We continue on, stepping over him. The smell—gunpowder and coppery blood—hits me instantly. My stomach clenches as I hesitate.

"Move!" Maria grabs my wrist, dragging me forward.

I stumble but keep going. I turn to look back, just for a second. I see the man's blood spreading, soaking the carpet.

Ahead, another shadow surges toward us, gun raised.

My breath catches, panic clamping down—

Then Raul steps into view. Calm, deliberate, his movements cut through the chaos. His sharp gaze sweeps through the darkness, lands on us. He lowers his gun.

"Keep moving," he barks. "Panic room. Now."

Maria snaps into step behind him. I follow, heart hammering.

Gunfire and shots downstairs grow louder. Closer.

I think we're almost there when a single shot rings out, close by. The loud crack of it explodes in my ears.

I see Raul stagger. His shoulder slams into a wall, a grunt ripping from his throat. Blood blooms across the sleeve of his white shirt, vivid and shocking.

"Papa!" Maria's scream is raw, high-pitched. She raises her pistol toward someone in front of her, fires—

And misses.

The man coming toward us doesn't slow. His steps are heavy, deliberate, gun trained on Maria.

"I've got you, sweetheart," he growls, stepping into the emergency light. His face is young but worn, sweat-streaked and wild-eyed, the edge of mania dancing in his voice.

"You thought you could hide behind your father's name? Behind these walls?"

He takes another step forward, gun unwavering. His grin is too wide.

"This is bigger than you. Bigger than him. This is history. And I'm the one making it."

Then he's louder—shouting now, as if claiming the moment for himself:

"Tonight, the Calderóns rise again. I lead them now. Not the old men. Not the cowards."

He lifts the gun, aiming at Raul. "I am Diego Calderón. And this is the beginning of everything."

I understand now. This is the man who ordered Maria's kidnapping. And he's not just dangerous—he might be insane.

Panic claws at my chest. *This is where I die because I was too weak, too soft.*

And then—a calm voice cuts through the chaos in my head. A voice only I can hear.

Marco.

"Don't think. Move. Trust your instincts."

Diego is focused on Maria, ignoring me. So he doesn't notice when I step into his path—fast, close—getting inside the arc of his reach before he can raise the gun.

His wrist jerks upward, and I react. My hands snap to his forearm, just like Marco taught me. *Pivot. Twist.*

"Redirect the line."

His eyes meet mine, shocked, surprised, as his gun slips free and clatters to the floor.

I don't think. I don't hesitate. I just react.

He lunges at me. I drive my knee into his groin. Hard. He crumples forward, gasping. I grab his head and bring my knee up again—into his face. A sickening crunch, and he drops to the ground.

A breath. Two.

He groans, bloody teeth bared. "You fucking bitch—"

Then Maria steps up beside me, points her gun at his face—and fires, twice.

The shot cracks through the hallway.

Diego Calderón doesn't get up.

The world tilts, but I keep my balance. Barely. My hands are shaking. My body's shaking. But I'm still standing.

I took him down. I did that.

The thought spins inside me. I wish I could tell Marco.

Maria grabs my arm. "Help me. Papa's hit."

I turn, and Raul's there, slumped against the wall, blood soaking his shoulder. His jaw is tight, his skin already gone gray.

He meets my eyes. Gives me the smallest nod.

Good job.

It rattles something loose in my chest—pride maybe? But there's no time for emotion.

We hoist him up, drape his arms over our shoulders, and half-carry, half-drag him down the hallway. His blood seeps into my clothes, hot and slick and real.

Gunfire bursts below again—closer now. Voices shouting in Spanish.

We round the final corner. The panic room.

Maria punches the keypad. The door hisses open. We drag Raul inside just as shadows fill the end of the hallway behind us.

Shots ring out. The door slams shut with a deep, metallic clunk. The lock engages.

And then—silence.

Not safety. But something like it.

Maria drops to the floor, her pistol still in her hands. Raul leans back against the wall, grim but breathing.

And me?

I slide down beside them, my back against the cold metal door. My hands won't stop trembling. I can't catch my breath. I close my eyes. Try to focus on something, anything.

Marco's voice echoes in my head. *Trust your instincts.*

I did.

Maria looks over at me, her voice hushed, awed. "I think you just saved us."

The words hit hard. Because maybe Marco was wrong about me. Maybe I am strong enough for this world.

But the images won't stop—Diego Calderon's face destroyed by Maria's gunshots, blood pooling on the carpet beneath him, the violence I can't scrub from my mind. Now I see that strength alone isn't enough to survive here. It's also about who you're willing to become. And I'm not sure I could ever become that person.

67

MARCO

THE MANSION RISES through the smoke like a broken crown, windows shattered, walls scorched, a van still burning near the fountain, painting everything in flickering orange light.

I kill the engine and jump out. My boots hit blood-slick stone.

The air stinks of smoke, metal, and scorched fuel.

"Eyes up," I snap, rifle already raised. Rafe moves beside me, his jaw tight, scanning fast.

"Fidel. Talk to me."

His voice crackles in my ear, sharp and controlled. "Kitchen's clear. Staff locked down. Two injuries confirmed. West wing is a war zone. Raul and the girls are in the panic room. Someone's hit. They're not communicating."

The last part punches a hole in my chest.

Just the three of them. Ami's up there. Unprotected. Surrounded. Maybe hurt.

"Chuck and Elias?" I ask.

"West wing. Holding. Calderóns tried to push through in another van." There's a grim satisfaction in Fidel's voice. "Detonated in the driveway as soon as they rolled in. Van's toast, and so are most of the targets."

Rafe checks the blown-out remains of the van as we pass. "Timing was perfect."

"Fidel. Stay locked down," I tell him.

Fidel hesitates a beat. Just long enough to notice. Then: "Move fast."

No shit.

I look to the rest of our team, out of the SUVs now and circled around me. I meet each man's eyes as I give them their orders. "Sweep the perimeter of the house. Half left, half right— no one gets in or out. If they're Calderón, shoot on sight."

"Copy that," one of them responds, voice tight. They split up and move.

I turn to Rafe. "We're sweeping upstairs."

We sprint through the main doors—half-blown off their hinges. Glass crunches underfoot. The emergency lights flicker, casting the grand hallway in blood-red pulses.

This house, always pristine, now looks like a war zone.

Gunfire pops to the west. Controlled bursts. Elias and Chuck still fighting.

"Come on," I bark to Rafe, cutting through smoke and debris toward the stairwell. We round the corner and drop into the fight.

Chuck is crouched behind a shattered sideboard, his rifle laying down cover. Elias is posted farther down, pinned but breathing. Across from them I see three Calderóns, dug in tight, firing low and hard toward the base of the stairs.

"Flank right," I order Rafe, breaking left. We don't need to talk strategy — we've done this move too many times.

I catch two in a crossfire. Rafe gets the last.

"Clear!" Chuck yells, panting as he stands. "Took your sweet damn time."

"West wing secure?" I ask, scanning the bodies for movement.

"For now." Elias wipes blood from his hands onto his trousers. "They hit us hard."

"Hold this position," I say. "No one gets upstairs but us."

I'm already moving. The stairs are wrecked, spattered in blood, railing shattered, walls pocked with bullets.

The scent hits me halfway up, blood, gunpowder, scorched wood. But another layer, too. One that grabs me by the throat.

A faint scent. Jasmine.

Ami.

At the top of the stairs, two bodies slump in the hall. Both Calderóns. Both shot and taken down clean.

By Raul? Maria?

The panic room's just ahead. I rush to it and press my hand to the steel door, grounding myself for half a second.

"It's Marco," I call.

A beat passes. And then the lock disengages. The door creaks open.

And they're alive.

Raul is slumped against the far wall, a tourniquet cinched around his upper arm, soaked through. Pale, but focused. Maria stands at the door, pistol limp in her hand. Her eyes find mine, wide and hollow. And then she looks away.

And Ami—

Ami's on the floor against the wall. Knees to her chest. Blood on her shirt. Hands shaking just slightly.

But she's seems steady, uninjured.

She meets my eyes. And I stop breathing. She survived.

"Ami." My voice cracks.

I cross the room and drop to a crouch in front of her. "Are you hurt?"

She shakes her head. Her voice is quiet but clear. "No. Raul's hit, but... I'm fine."

She's not. Not really. But she's here. She's whole.

Raul coughs, clears his throat, then speaks from the wall. "She saved us."

I look over. His face is pale, but his eyes are hard.

"She took down a Calderón, disarmed him, and cleared the hallway. Gave us enough time to move."

I look back at Ami. She doesn't smile. Doesn't cry. She just shrugs. "I just did what you taught me. Bought some time."

Maria snorts—a sharp, wet sound. "You did a hell of a lot more than that. You protected him." Her chin jerks toward Raul. "You protected me."

I study Ami's face. And it hits me harder than any of the gunfire outside.

She *could survive* here. Not in theory. Not in some wishful fantasy.

I see how wrong I was about her. She could hold her own. She was right about that. And that's what makes this so much worse.

Because if she stayed, it would mean a life of violence. Death. I would watch as her innocence got stripped away, piece by piece.

I can't ask her to do that. I can't ask her to live this life with me, live with blood on her hands. I can't.

Our eyes meet. She knows. I know.

There's no victory here. No happy ending.

I reach for her without thinking. Then stop myself. My hand drops.

"Ami—" I start.

But she cuts me off.

"It's okay," she says. Not angry. Not hurt. Just tired. Resolved. "I know."

I nod. Once. The tightest movement I can manage.

Behind me, Raul winces as he shifts upright. I move toward him, needing something to do. Something I can fix.

"We'll get you patched up," I tell him. Businesslike. Detached.

I don't look back.

I walk out of the panic room.

I walk away. From her.

68

___

AMI

THE LIBRARY HUMS with quiet motion. Low voices murmur as Dr. Rodriguez and his assistants move between the injured, their hands steady but quick. Bandages unravel, gauze presses down, antiseptic bites at raw skin. The smell of it, sharp and clinical, helps to smother the tang of blood, smoke, and adrenaline that still hangs in the air.

Sunlight spills through the tall windows, streaking the floor in gold. The library is too bright. Too clean. Like this part of the house hasn't realized what happened yet.

I sit stiffly in a velvet chair near the corner, a cold mug of coffee in my hands. I'm not drinking it. I'm just holding it, gripping the ceramic like it might keep me from unraveling.

Everything in my body feels tight and loose at once. My limbs heavy. My nerves raw.

Twelve hours ago I was at a nightclub. Laughing. Dancing. Pretending I was part of something. That I had someone.

Now I'm sitting in a war zone, trying not to think about how much blood I saw last night. How much of it was on me.

Across the room, Dr. Rodriguez works on Raul. His shirt's off, his wound bandaged. Maria sits beside him, patting his hand, brushing his hair back, her fingers shaking just slightly.

She's trying to be strong. But she looks different today. Dimmed. Quieter.

Raul catches my eye.

"Ami."

It startles me. He's never used my first name before.

I look up. "Yes?"

There's something in his expression I didn't expect. Not suspicion. Not scrutiny.

Respect.

"You have my gratitude," he says. His voice is low but certain. "What you did last night saved lives. You protected my daughter. And me. That matters."

His words hit harder than I expect. Like they're pushing into a place I've been trying to keep numb.

I think of that hallway again. Diego Calderón's gun on Raul. The panic in my chest as I moved toward him. The feel of Raul's blood on my hands as we dragged him to the panic room. A reminder of how easily it could have ended differently.

It didn't feel like heroism. It felt like desperation. Like survival at any cost.

"I just... did what I had to do," I murmur.

Raul shakes his head once. "No. You did what you chose to do. And not everyone would've made the same choice."

I don't know how to respond to that. It doesn't feel like praise I deserve.

"I helped last night," I say finally, staring into the coffee I'm not drinking. "But... that's not who I am. Not really."

Maria turns sharply toward me. Her face twists, surprised, hurt.

"I can't stay," I say gently. "You know that. This world, this life... it's never going to fit me. You belong here. You were made for it. I... wasn't." My throat feels dry and tight as I swallow down my tears. "I have to leave."

She doesn't argue.

She stands. Crosses the room. And kneels at my feet.

Her hand finds mine, steady and warm.

"You're strong Ami Zadegan. So strong. And you're my friend," she whispers. "I'm going to miss you."

My throat clenches. I force a shaky smile.

"We're still writing your book," I say, squeezing her hand. "You're not getting rid of me that easily."

She sniffles, nodding, and stands. She helps Raul to his feet. He pauses just long enough to give me a short nod—quiet, formal, but honest.

They leave without another word.

And the library is quiet again. No gunfire. No sirens. Just the soft rustle of movement and low voices.

I let out a sigh.

And then I feel it—that pull. I glance toward the door.

And Marco is there.

He stands just inside the threshold, half in shadow, half caught in the morning sun. His profile is beautiful and strong— sharp jaw, straight nose, a mouth that's too serious for this moment. His shirt is rumpled, sleeves rolled to the elbow, streaked with blood and dirt. A gun is in the shoulder holster slung across his chest, a second gun tucked at the small of his back, the hint of menace clashing with the faint vulnerability in his eyes. He truly looks like something out of a dark crime romance novel, a conflicted, morally gray hero, dangerous and heartbreakingly real.

He speaks briefly to Raul. They exchange a few clipped words. Then Raul walks away.

Chuck appears behind Marco. Marco says something to him in a low voice. Chuck nods. Then he's gone too.

Marco turns toward me and, although the room is full of people, there's only us.

He crosses the room to me, and then crouches down. He looks... tired. Not just physically, but tired deep in his bones.

"You okay?" he asks.

I nod. "You?" I ask back.

His jaw flexes. He doesn't answer right away.

"I'm fine," he says eventually. But his voice is raw. Worn thin. He looks away. Then back.

"Chuck's packing your things," he says. "You don't need to see the rest of it, what's out there." He gestures toward the carnage that I know is outside the doors. He hesitates, then says it. "It's better this way."

I nod. "You were right. It's time for me to go," I say quietly.

His gaze flickers. He wants to disagree. I can see it. But he doesn't.

"Fidel's booked your flight. Chuck will get you to the airport."

I nod again. My throat's tight. My hands are cold.

He hesitates. Then reaches out. His fingers brush against mine. Just a touch. Just enough to remind me what it felt like to have him.

"Take care of yourself," he says.

"You too," I whisper, my voice breaking as tears prick at my eyes.

He holds my gaze for a second longer.

Then stands.

And walks away.

No last look. No changed mind. No movie ending. Just the echo of footsteps. And the heavy, hollow space they leave behind.

I close my eyes. Let the quiet settle.
This is the end of whatever we were.
And even though I'm leaving—
I know I'll carry him with me for a long, long time.

69

MARCO

Two Weeks After the Siege at the Sandoval Compound

THE HUM of the security monitors fills the guardhouse, a low, steady rhythm beneath the quiet. Fidel sits at the desk, arms crossed, the blue glow from the screens casting shadows across his sharp features. On one monitor, the mansion's front lawn stretches in perfect symmetry—freshly trimmed, even if the edges still bear signs of upheaval. Another shows the warehouse, loading dock rebuilt, its exterior half-painted, scaffolding still in place, all of the inventory inside transferred to a secure location. The damage to the Sandoval empire is being erased, bit by bit. Like nothing ever happened.

The Calderóns are finished, their organization in ruins. Whatever was left in the aftermath of their attempted coup has been destroyed by Raul. Thus, business for the Sandovals has returned to some version of normal.

But I know better.

Two weeks isn't nearly enough time to forget the blood, the chaos, the stench of gunpowder. To forget how close we came to complete destruction and disaster. I can't let my guard down.

Leaning against the doorframe, I cross my arms and watch as Fidel taps at the keyboard, his focus absolute. The cameras shift, sweeping across the perimeter in smooth mechanical movements. Everything is locked down. Secure.

"Still obsessing?" Fidel asks without turning around. His tone is light, but the edge is unmistakable.

"Not obsessing," I reply evenly. "Just staying sharp."

He snorts, glancing over his shoulder. "You mean waiting for the next threat to show up so you can throw yourself at it like a human battering ram and ignore everything else."

I ignore the jab and step further into the room. "You've got too much time on your hands if you're coming up with metaphors like that."

Fidel smirks, but his expression softens as he turns the chair to face me. "First, it's a simile, not a metaphor. And second, the Calderóns are done. The compound's secure. Maria's writing that ridiculous alien Regency romance novel, and Raul's already back to business. Everyone's breathing easier—except for you."

I don't respond.

Instead, my gaze locks onto one of the monitors showing the mansion's west wing. The worst of the interior damage is patched now, though scaffolding still lines the halls and painters move methodically along the walls, erasing what's left of the chaos.

But in my mind, I still see the bullet holes. The bloodstains. The chaos.

"I don't breathe easy," I say finally.

"No shit," Fidel mutters, shaking his head. "You've been running at full tilt since we were kids, Marco. Always the one jumping into the fire to put it out." He leans forward, resting his elbows on his knees. "But I've never seen you like this. It's like you're waiting for the world to explode."

I exhale, my jaw tight. "Maybe I am."

Fidel's brows draw together, his sharp eyes narrowing. "This about the Calderóns? Or about Ami?"

Her name hits like a punch to the gut, but I don't flinch. "It's not about her."

"Bullshit." Fidel leans back in his chair with a quiet laugh. "You've been like a goddamn ghost since she left. Don't think I haven't noticed."

I clench my jaw. "She's better off away from this. From me."

"Really? That's what you're going with?" Fidel shakes his head, letting out a sharp exhale. "Because I'm pretty sure she was good for you, Marco. And for the record? I liked her." He pauses, his voice quieter but firm. "She reminded me of Elena."

The name hits harder than Ami's. A tight, familiar knot twists in my chest.

"Don't," I say, my voice low.

"Why not?" Fidel presses. "We never talk about her. Not really. And maybe we should. She was my sister too."

I turn away, staring at the monitors. "There's nothing to talk about."

"You mean there's nothing *you* want to talk about." His voice softens, but the insistence remains. "You've been carrying this guilt for fourteen years, Marco. Ever since that night."

The memory claws its way up. I try to shove it back down but I can't. And for the first time ever, I don't want to.

"I should've picked her up." My voice is rough, strained. "She called me. Asked for a ride. I blew her off. If I'd gone to the diner, she wouldn't have gotten into that car. She wouldn't be dead."

Fidel stands, closing the space between us. "The guy who hit her was drunk out of his mind. He ran a red light going eighty. You think you could've stopped that?"

I look away, my throat tight. "I don't know. But I could've done something."

Fidel lets out a slow breath, rubbing a hand over his jaw. "Elena was stubborn as hell. You know that better than anyone. She made her own choices. And yeah, it sucks that one of them cost her life. But that wasn't your fault."

"I was her brother." The words scrape out like broken glass. "It was my job to protect her."

"And you did." Fidel's voice sharpens. "You were always there for her, Marco. You were always there for me. For mom. Always. But you couldn't control everything. You still can't."

He pauses, his voice quieter. "You can't save everyone."

The words settle like lead in my chest.

"And Ami?" Fidel continues, his tone gentler now. "She's like Elena was. Strong. Stubborn. Determined to live her own life. You didn't push Ami away to protect her, Marco. You pushed her away because you're afraid of what it means to let someone in. To let yourself want something. Because if you lose her too—"

The confession slips out.

"I wouldn't survive it."

Fidel nods slowly, his gaze steady. "You lost her, Marco. You lost Ami. And yet, here you are. Still breathing."

Ami's face flashes through my mind. The sharp wit. The warmth. The way she made me feel like maybe, just maybe, there was something in this world worth risking everything for.

Fidel lets the silence stretch for a long moment, then shakes his head, smirking faintly. "You really are an idiot sometimes, you know that?"

I shoot him a look, but he just chuckles, arms crossed.

"She might have loved you, Marco. And if I'm not mistaken, you might have loved her too. So maybe instead of sitting here waiting for the world to end, you should figure out how to get her back."

I stare at him, something shifting inside me.

He turns back to his chair, sitting to stare at the monitors. "You know, I read her book."

That gets my attention. "What?"

"*Beneath a Persian Sky.* The full manuscript. I pulled it off her laptop. The one she brought in for me to look at after she took out that kidnapper with it."

"You read it?" My voice comes out sharper than I intend.

He shrugs. "It was just sitting there. Figured I'd see why Chad wanted to pass it off as his own."

"And?"

"And I think it's good," Fidel says simply. "Beautiful, actually. Romantic in a way that doesn't make me want to light myself on fire. But also... it's angry. Not on the surface—but it's there. You can feel it, buried in the story. Like she was trying to write something about her family, about herself, that she never got to say out loud."

My jaw tightens. I stare at the monitors, but I'm not seeing anything now.

"She never got to publish it," I say quietly.

"Nope." He turns to me, expression suddenly serious. "Chad and Victoria did such a number on her she probably thought she never could. Too bad."

A long beat passes.

"You still have it?" I ask.

Fidel doesn't hesitate. "Yeah. Full manuscript. Metadata intact. A few early drafts. Some deleted notes she probably didn't mean to keep, but they're there." He digs around on his desk and then hands me a stack of paper.

"Here's a printout. Take it. Read it for yourself."

I take the pages Fidel hands me. "Thanks."

Then I get up and leave.

Fidel doesn't call after me.

———

Three Weeks After the Siege at the Sandoval Compound

I've read the whole thing now. Twice. It's rough in places, unfinished. But the heart of it—the voice? It's unmistakable.

It's her.

And now that I've read it, I can't let it stay buried.

I thought about it. How to fix this. How to give her book back to her. I don't know much about books, about publishing. But I know about taking people down with information they thought they'd buried.

I took my idea to Raul. He didn't ask for details—just said to handle it. Quietly. But completely. Said we owed her. That was all I needed.

I find Fidel in the server room, cables everywhere, three monitors glowing with code. He doesn't hear me come in, not until I say, "I need your help."

He spins his chair halfway, brows lifting. "With?"

I pull a folded page from my back pocket and set it on the desk. It's handwritten notes. Names. Dates. A rough plan with the only details I know.

"I want to give her something," I say.

Fidel blinks. "What do you mean?"

"Chad took her story. Victoria made sure no one knew. I want to make sure the world hears it. From her. Not them."

He picks up the page. Studies it. "So you want to build a case against them."

"I want to make it impossible for them to deny what they did. And if we destroy them in the process, even better."

He nods slowly. "You want it anonymous?"

"Yeah. She can tell the story her way. But I want the truth to be undeniable. This isn't about me."

A pause.

Fidel looks up. "You still think she's better off without you?"

My chest tightens. I don't answer.

Instead, I ask, "Can you do it?"

Fidel smiles and then turns back to his keyboard. "You know I can."

Five Weeks After the Siege at the Sandoval Compound

The dossier is finished.

Emails. Internal notes from Chad's publisher. The draft history of *Beneath a Persian Sky*. The flagged plagiarism matches. The timeline. The screenshots. The video clips. Even a few images from Ami's original outline, with her handwriting in the margins.

It's all here. Clean. Precise. Devastating.

We're in the guardhouse again. It's late. Rain ticks against the windows.

Fidel pulls up a secure portal, types in a generic subject line: *For your consideration. Source protected. Truth intact.*

He hovers over the send button, then glances at me.

"You sure?"

I nod.

He hits send.

The message vanishes into the void, headed for Lena Chen-Byers, investigative journalist, *Final Cut* magazine.

No signature. No trail. Just the truth, weaponized.

Fidel leans back. "You think she'll know it was you?"

I shake my head. "Doesn't matter."

A pause.

"She might not take you back, you know."

"That's not what this is."

Fidel studies me for a long moment. "You're doing this anyway."

"Yeah."

Silence.

Then, softly, "Okay."

I smile at my brother, something I haven't done in a long time.

I turn to the window and watch the rain blur the view outside, the compound still and silent around us.

I couldn't save Elena. I couldn't stop Chad. I couldn't hold on to Ami. But I can do this.

And for now, that's enough.

70

AMI

Eight Weeks After the Siege at the Sandoval Compound

THE APARTMENT FEELS SMALLER NOW. Not cozy. Compressed. Like the walls are closing in, trying to squeeze the air out of me.

I'm curled up on the couch in the same sweatshirt I've worn three days in a row. Maybe four. My laptop's shut on the coffee table—dead weight I can't bring myself to open. A mug of coffee sits beside it, stone cold.

The silence is loud. And I can't tell if the ache in my chest is grief or guilt or just the echo of something that used to feel like purpose.

I haven't written a word in weeks.

The cursor on that damn dark crime romance manuscript blinked at me for an hour last night. Or maybe it was two nights ago. Doesn't matter. Every time I try to pick it up, it feels like I'm putting on someone else's skin. Someone who doesn't exist anymore.

My phone buzzes, slicing through the quiet.

Natalie.

For a second, I think about letting it ring. But then I sigh and answer. "Hey."

"Honey, you sound like you've been living in a cave," Natalie says, voice bright but edged with concern. "Tell me you've showered today."

"Define 'today.'"

There's a pause. Then a softer version of her voice slips in. "How long are we going to do this?"

I pick at a loose thread on my sleeve. "I'm fine."

"Okay. You're fine." She takes a deep breath and then changes gears.

"Hey, here's something you might find interesting. I got a call this week. From *Final Cut*. The magazine. They want to talk to you."

My stomach drops. "What? Why?"

"They're working on a piece—big feature. Plagiarism in publishing, institutional cover-ups, how the industry protects the wrong people. Victoria Drake and Chad are both on their radar."

I sit up, tension crawling up my spine. The plagiarism. Did they know about what Chad had done to me? How could they know?

"And they want to talk to me?"

"Apparently, they've got evidence. They know about your story. Other people too. They've uncovered emails, patterns— things that match your experience."

I had told Natalie what I'd learned about Chad and Victoria, about the plagiarism. But hadn't told her how I'd learned it. I hadn't wanted to relive the pain of that final night with Marco again.

I swallow hard, already regretting the question I'm about to ask, knowing that it may, at some point, force me to confront that pain head-on.

"So they want to interview me? For the article?"

"Off the record, at first. You don't have to say yes, but it's legit. High-profile. They've clearly done their research."

I frown. "What kind of research?"

"They wouldn't say much. But they knew things. Things I've heard behind the scenes. Rumors. Things I didn't think were public."

The back of my neck prickles at that. But I push past it.

"They say they want to show how broken the system is," Natalie says more gently. "How easy it is for authors to be taken advantage of, to get erased. And how hard it is to get your work back once it's stolen."

The silence stretches.

"And you think I should talk to them?"

"I think it could help a lot of people," she says. "Writers like you. And maybe—just maybe—it helps you take your story back."

The words land hard. Take back my story.

The idea sparks something in me, a very small ember, flickering back to life. I stare at the laptop. At the cold coffee. At this version of myself I didn't realize I'd become.

"Also," Natalie says quickly, like she's scared she's lost me, "I've been thinking. About your next project."

"Please don't say dark crime romance."

"I'm saying *Beneath a Persian Sky.*"

My chest tightens.

"Natalie—"

"I know. I know it hurts. I know it feels radioactive. But it's yours, Ami. It always was. And maybe now... with the timing of this *Final Cut* story, maybe it's time to take that back, too."

I close my eyes and press my palm to my forehead, grounding myself.

"This is a beginning, a change," she says gently. "Not the kind you might have wanted. But maybe the one you need."

The words settle like a quiet truth.

I exhale slowly. "Okay."

"'Okay' you'll think about it?"

"'Okay' I'll think about it."

She pauses. Then, softly: "I'm proud of you, Ami. After all you've been through, you're allowed to be tired. But you're not done."

The call ends. And I stare at the blank laptop screen.

Maybe I'm not done.

Maybe I've just been waiting for the story to come back to me.

71

AMI

Nine Weeks After the Siege at the Sandoval Compound

THE RESTAURANT IS DISCREET. One of those upscale places tucked into the top floor of a boutique hotel downtown—linen napkins, low music, and panoramic views of the Houston skyline through frosted glass windows.

The kind of place that never needs to advertise because everyone worth knowing already knows.

I sit at a small table in the back, palms flat against the table-cloth, trying to look calm. I've already ordered a sparkling water I haven't touched.

I don't know what I'm doing here.

Natalie said it was off the record, exploratory, no pressure. But even she sounded nervous when she told me who was coming.

Lena Chen-Byers.

Pulitzer Prize-shortlisted. Broke the Buckminster College academic fraud scandal two years ago—the one that took down the chancellor and half the board. Her byline has appeared on half a dozen *Final Cut* pieces that blew the roof off institutions no one thought could be touched.

And now she wants to talk to me.

I straighten when I see her walking toward the table—sharp navy blazer, fitted jeans, heels that look functional but designer. Her hair's pinned up, glasses perched on her nose, a leather-bound notebook tucked under one arm.

No assistant. No entourage. Just her. Controlled, calm, practiced.

She offers her hand. "Ami Zadegan? Thank you for meeting with me."

"Of course." I shake her hand and gesture to the seat across from me. "Thanks for... reaching out."

She smiles warmly. "I read *Volley Girl*, by the way. To prepare for this interview. Get some insight into you."

I swallow and take a breath. "And what did you think?" I prepare to hear the worst from this top-notch investigative journalist.

"Well, let's just say, if that's what's actually happening out on the tennis courts, I think I've found my new sport." She gives me a wink. "I downloaded the rest of the series last night."

I laugh and relax just a bit. I think I like Lena Chen-Byers.

She smiles again and continues. "I'm going to be up front with you, Ami. As Natalie may have told you, we've been working on this piece for a long time. The publishing industry. How it really works. Trying to piece it all together." She shrugs. "But it never quite gelled into what we wanted, what we knew was happening. So we shelved it." Her eyes locks on mine and her smile sharpens. "But then your story came to us and, suddenly, it gelled."

I nod, trying to keep my expression neutral. Because something about her tone catches me. She's not curious. Not here to ask me what my story is. She's confident. Like she already knows all about me, already knows what I'm going to say. I don't think she's here to ask me questions. She's here to confirm information she already has.

A feeling of discomfort moves through me. Does she know everything about my relationship with Chad? Does she know about the abuse?

Lena opens her notebook but doesn't look down. She studies me for a moment, then says, "What happened to you and your writing isn't rare. Sadly. But the level of documentation we received on your case—the depth, the clarity—that was unprecedented. All of it confirmed so many things we had suspected but had been unable to prove with hard evidence. Honestly, I thought this piece was going to be permanently backburnered. Thought it might never come out. And then someone gave us a complete picture. Contracts. Drafts. Internal memos. Legal notes. A complete evidentiary package."

Something twists in my stomach.

"Complete?" I echo.

She nods once. "Yes. Honestly, what we've been given is... breathtaking. Surgical in its precision. Whoever gave us this information knew exactly what mattered. And how to prove it." She gazes up, a flicker of something like admiration crossing her face. "It's complete,... elegant."

A beat of silence stretches between us. I know she's now talking about Chad. About Victoria. About the plagiarism.

"Who gave you this 'evidentiary package'?" I ask, even though I'm already scared I know.

Lena tilts her head. "A confidential source. Anonymous. Off the record. But what they gave us was extraordinary. Not just Chad Bennett's theft—incredibly brazen by the way—but Victoria Drake's cover-up. Her pattern. And once we had her, we were able to trace a dozen other cases where she and others at her agency suppressed or erased female collaborators in favor of marketable male names."

My throat goes dry.

"They gave us a version of *Beneath a Persian Sky* that predates Chad's attempt to publish by nearly two years," she continues. "Watermarked. Metadata intact. Complete."

My pulse spikes. "But... that version..."

"Yes, not something that could've been pulled from a public drive," she says gently. "It's your work, but the file was extracted from a secure backup. Full metadata. Unaltered. Time-stamped. It's about as close to irrefutable as you can get."

My breath catches. That file, all of my work... it was on my old laptop. The one with all of my files. The files Fidel downloaded when he couldn't repair my laptop.

At the time, I barely registered it. Never wondered if Fidel might have kept a copy of my files. For himself. For the Sandovals. But of course he did.

Now I see it clearly. Lena Chen-Byer's backburnered story, suddenly coming together. That could only happen if someone not only had my files, but also managed to get inside Lena's files. To hack into the entire *Final Cut* system and not only learn about this story, but figure out what they needed to make it happen.

This isn't luck. This is precision. Intent. Someone went looking, not just for what Chad had done, but for proof they could pass on. The kind of proof that stands up to journalistic scrutiny. The kind no one can talk their way out of.

And that same someone found out exactly where to send it. Someone who could slip into the systems of multiple national investigative publications, sift through what they were working on, and leave—without a trace.

And I know, deep in my gut, only one person had the determination—and the power—to make something like this happen.

Marco.

Lena keeps going. "There are also email chains. Victoria expressing concern over how different Chad's draft is to a manuscript he previously submitted. She had questions. Lots of them. She knew. And she still signed off."

I stare at her, the buzzing in my ears louder than the soft jazz playing overhead. My hands are folded on the table in front of me but I drop them to my lap to hide the way they've started to tremble. My chest feels tight with a mix of disbelief and fierce gratitude.

This isn't journalism. This is a targeted hit.

Marco didn't just believe me. He went to war for me. With the full force of the Sandoval machine behind him.

He let me leave—but he wasn't going to let Chad beat me. He wasn't going to let Victoria win. He provided a way to take them both down. For good. For me.

Lena watches my expression shift but doesn't interrupt. Instead, she says, more softly now, "Your name never came up in any of our previous documentation. You had been completely hidden. It wasn't until this that we could prove the plagiarism pattern. That we learned about you." She takes a sip of water and then continues. "And whoever sent this wasn't interested in credit. They just wanted to expose the truth. Believe me, we've tried every hacking trick we know. But we can't figure out who they are."

Of course. Because Marco would never want credit. He wouldn't care about that.

He just wanted me to *have* it. Have my story.

"Why do you think this is happening now?" I ask, my voice smaller than I mean it to be.

Lena pauses. "Maybe whoever gave us all of this thought it

wasn't too late. That what was taken from you could still be given back."

I look down at my hands, shaking under the table. I think of him watching me leave that morning, silent, unreadable. And now I understand.

He wasn't letting me go because he didn't care. He thought he had to let me go because he cared too much.

Lena lets the moment stretch. Then: "This piece is going to change things, Ami. We're naming names. Showing receipts. Victoria Drake, the agency she works for, they won't be able to hide behind contracts or a PR team anymore. I'm pretty sure they'll be over after this."

Lena looks at me carefully. "Do you want to speak on the record? We can keep it anonymous. Or we can print your name, your words. It's entirely up to you."

I think about everything I've lost. Everything I almost stopped fighting for. And what I've just been handed.

Truth. Power. *Proof.*

I meet her gaze. "I'll talk."

Her smile is small, but it reaches her eyes. "Great. This is going to move fast. We've been building the story for a long time —you're the final confirmation."

She holds my gaze a beat longer. "Your story is what will make people listen. It's going to make people care. You're going to help a lot of people, Ami."

My story.

We talk for nearly an hour. She takes notes, but mostly, she listens. And as we talk, it becomes clear just how detailed the file she was given really is. She knows everything—about the emotional abuse, the gaslighting, the unraveling of who I used to be.

But she never asks about the physical abuse. I can tell she

doesn't know about it. Doesn't know about the video. About Chad slapping me. And the rest.

And for that, I'm grateful.

We close the meeting. She leaves me with a card, and a promise to send me the piece before it goes live.

I don't leave right away. I stay by the window, staring out at the city. My chest aches. But it's not grief. Not fear.

It's something heavier.

Hope.

72

AMI

Two Weeks After the Interview

My phone buzzes for the fifth time in two minutes.

Texts. Missed calls. Emails. Twitter tags. A flood of unfamiliar names in my DMs. I haven't even read the article yet, but the world apparently has.

I keep ignoring the screen, until I see Natalie calling.

I answer on the second ring.

"Okay, do not panic," she says without preamble. "Or do panic. I'm panicking, so you're allowed."

My stomach flips. "What happened?"

"What happened? Ami, the article dropped an hour ago and it's already on fire. *Final Cut.* Headline spot. They pushed it to the top of the homepage with a *trigger warning,* Ami. Twitter is a war zone. BookTok is in full meltdown. I'm getting emails from journalists, publishers, podcast hosts, random book club presidents. You are everywhere."

I sink onto my couch, blinking at the still-loading *Final Cut* link on my laptop.

"I haven't read it," I mumble.

Natalie sucks in a breath. "Okay. That's fine. But when you do? Be ready. Lena didn't pull punches. She didn't need to—the documentation speaks for itself."

I nod, even though she can't see me.

"And," she adds, her voice softening, "you come across like the hero of a revolution. Quiet but furious. Honest. Brave. People are going to rally around this."

My chest tightens. "I don't know if I want them to."

She doesn't respond right away. Then: "Too late."

A pause. "PublisherCon just reached out," she adds, more carefully now. "They want you on a panel. The mainstage one. The topic is 'Plagiarism and Power: Who Gets to Tell the Story.'"

I let the words settle. Let them scare me. Thrill me. Stagger me.

My story.

And this time, with my name on it.

————

Three Weeks After the Interview

I'm lying on the floor of my apartment, scrolling through TikTok with one hand, eating cereal straight from the box with the other. I haven't slept much.

A video auto-plays—one of those "drama explained" BookTok recaps in enthusiastic voiceover.

"...so after the *Final Cut* exposé confirmed that the now-canceled Chad Bennett plagiarized *Beneath a Persian Sky*—a manuscript that he stole from author Ami Zadegan—we learned today that he's been officially terminated from his position teaching remedial writing at Santa Rosa Community College in New Mexico..."

I nearly choke on a frosted mini wheat.

The video keeps going:

"But it's not just him. Victoria Drake? Out. Her agency? Imploding. Turns out this was part of a pattern—uncredited female authors, hidden drafts, editorial gaslighting. Yikes."

A jump cut to another creator holding a stack of my books:

"She's the moment. She's the voice. She *is* the main character."

Hashtags scroll across the screen:

#AmiWasRight   #BeneathAPersianSky   #TennisFixation #ReadHerNotHim #WritingIsAFeministAct

My name trends for the right reasons and also the wrong ones, depending on who's talking.

I close the app and open my email. There are interview requests. Panel invites. A long, lovely message from a woman who used to work for Victoria and wants to apologize.

Later that night, I record a podcast episode with a host I trust —someone who's been advocating for authors of color and marginalized writers for years. She's kind. Thoughtful.

Somewhere near the end, she asks:

"The piece references and quotes from a set of documents. Files, internal emails, early drafts. Some of it was clearly from encrypted sources. Do you know who provided that?"

I hesitate.

But I don't lie.

"I don't," I say quietly. "It came anonymously. But whoever it was... they gave me something I thought I'd lost forever. My story. My name."

I pause, voice softening.

"If they're listening... I just want to tell them, thank you. I will never, ever forget you."

———

Four Weeks After the Interview

Natalie calls at 8 a.m. sharp, which tells me something's up.

"You have to stop sleeping like a civilian," she says without even saying hello. "You're in your phoenix-rising era now. Get up."

I groan. "Why?"

"Because PublisherCon *confirmed* you for the panel. And a dozen agents have emailed me asking about *Beneath a Persian Sky*. Big names. Real offers. Multiple zeroes."

I sit up, dazed. "Seriously?"

"Seriously." She takes a breath. "Also, digital editions of all *Tennis Fixation* books are charting again. *Volley Girl* hit the top 10 on Amazon. For all categories, Ami. All. And Net Sports wants another event—Houston flagship this time. They want you next Saturday."

I blink. "That's a lot."

"I know. It's beautiful chaos. But there's something else."

I hear her shifting in her chair, bracing herself.

"Everyone wants *Beneath a Persian Sky*. Now that they know about it, they want your story. And Ami... I have to ask because Lord knows I'm a good businesswoman. Would you consider letting Crimson Quill publish it?"

Silence stretches.

Then I ask the question that's been hiding in my chest since this started.

"Would *you* want it?"

A beat. Then Natalie lets out a choked laugh. I think she might be crying.

"God, I was hoping you'd ask. Ami—yes! Of course we want it. It's amazing. It's your heart on the page. We'd be honored."

I smile, slow and quiet and real.

"Okay," I say. "Then let's do it."

73

A SOCIAL MEDIA POST

Transcript from TikTok User @bookriotqueen

[UPBEAT POP MUSIC PLAYING UNDER VIDEO]

@bookriotqueen (speaking to camera):

Okay, BookTok, we need to talk about Ami Zadegan—yes, *that* Ami Zadegan.

If you've been living under a rock, here's the deal:

She's the author of the *Tennis Fixation* series.

She just got publicly vindicated for having her manuscript *Beneath a Persian Sky* stolen and passed off by that slimeball

Chad Bennett.

The exposé went nuclear. The receipts were RECEIPTING.

And guess what? She's doing a signing *this Saturday.* In person. In Houston.

[2 SECOND PAUSE]

I don't think y'all understand—

She's not going to be doing tiny in-store events much longer. This woman is about to blow up like Taylor Swift during Reputation. You want a signed copy? You want your moment?

Get. In. Line.

Also? Her new book will be devastating. The drama is delicious. I'm not saying it's giving *Smash Girl* smut energy, but I *am* saying bring your waterproof mascara and don't say I didn't warn you.

[HASHTAGS IN NOTES:
    #BeneathAPersianSky
    #AmiZadegan
    #BookSigningAlert

#BookTok
#Tennisfixation
#Tennissexation
#JusticeForAmi
#ThisIsHerVillainOriginStoryButMakeItFeminist]

[CUT TO MONTAGE - Tennis Fixation book covers and fan art that is not safe for work]

74

MARCO

The Day Before the Houston Net Sports Book Signing

FIDEL SITS behind the desk in the guardhouse, bathed in blue light, typing one-handed while sipping from a chipped coffee mug with the words *I Hack, Therefore I Am* printed on the side. He's calm. Focused.

I'm not.

I lean against the wall, arms crossed, eyes locked on a west-facing camera feed. Clear skies. Clean roads. Nothing moving.

But still—I wait.

Fidel doesn't look up. "You're not going to say it, are you?"

I raise an eyebrow. "Say what?"

"You've been hovering behind me for fifteen minutes without blinking." He glances at me now, expression dry. "If you want an update, just ask."

I stay silent, and he snorts. "Fine. Don't ask. You're lucky I love drama."

He taps a few keys, dragging a window onto the main screen. It's a PDF—legal language, red stamps, digital signatures.

Zadegan, Amira – Copyright Reassignment Approved

Final Ruling: Full rights to Beneath a Persian Sky officially restored to original author.

"The Copyright Office's decision," Fidel says flatly. "Chad's out. Pretty sure he's so cancelled he won't even be able to get a job flipping burgers. Victoria and her agency are circling the drain. Four of her biggest clients dropped her yesterday. The publisher has quietly pulled her next big thing from distribution. Books are coming off shelves left and right. It's a PR nightmare. Total collapse."

I exhale, slow and tight. "And the doc dump?"

He nods. "People are wondering but everyone assumes it's an anonymous whistleblower. Well-timed. Elegant. Ruthless. Very 'us.'"

His mouth twitches.

"Does she know?"

"Ami? Not sure," Fidel says. "But she's not stupid. She's probably figured it out."

I let that sit.

Ami Zadegan. The woman who walked away from this world before it could ruin her. The woman I let go because I didn't know how to keep her safe.

"She deserves the win," I say quietly.

"She earned it," Fidel replies. Then, after a pause: "You helped her get it."

I shake my head. "I didn't do much. Just helped make sure the truth landed where it needed to."

Fidel leans back in the chair, folding his arms. "You know, for someone who regularly walks into ambushes like it's just a cardio workout, you're weirdly afraid of letting anyone love you."

I shoot him a look. He grins.

"I'm just saying. You didn't see her after the interview. Or the article drop. Or any of the online stuff she's done since. She isn't broken. She looks focused. Excited even. And yeah—maybe a little wrecked. But not fragile. Not even close."

He swipes to a different tab. An image of a storefront appears. Bright awnings. Huge glass windows with displays of tennis gear. Signs advertising a book signing.

"Which brings us to tomorrow," he says. "She's doing a signing at Net Sports. Houston store. Starts in—" he checks his watch, "—twenty-two hours and sixteen minutes."

My pulse spikes, but I keep my expression neutral. "She wouldn't want to see me."

Fidel snorts. "Maybe. Maybe not. No idea." He pushes back from the desk, heads for the door, but pauses in the frame. His voice is quieter now.

"But if you don't show up, you'll never know. And that'll be on you."

Then he's gone. The hum of the monitors returns, low and steady.

I don't move. Not yet. I don't think I can face her without fucking it up.

But maybe he's right. Maybe I don't need a war to prove what I'm willing to protect.

Maybe I just need to show up.

75

———

AMI

THE LINE STRETCHES out the door.

Readers clutch books to their chests—*Smash Girl, Love All, Ad In*—and scroll through their phones, already tagging videos with the event's official hashtags. A few flip through copies of *Final Cut,* pointing at photos and passages from the article. There's laughter. Buzzing excitement. One woman stands near the front of the line, sobbing quietly with a copy of *Break Point* pressed to her cheek.

I sit behind the table, smile in place, pen in hand.

I'm tired. But this time, it's not from hiding.

"Thank you so much," I say, signing another book. "I hope you enjoy it."

A teenage girl grins. "I'm writing my own novel now. I never thought I could, but after everything you said—"

She doesn't finish, just presses her hands together in a silent thank-you.

And then it happens.

I can't explain it. But I feel it. The energy in the room tilts on its axis. The air shifts. Conversations falter. Whispers spread like wildfire. A ripple of gasps sweeps through the crowd, punctuated by the unmistakable clicking of phone cameras.

I glance up, my pen hovering mid-air.

And I see him.

Marco Cedillo.

He strides through the crowd with all the presence of a storm rolling in—silent but impossible to ignore.

He isn't dressed like the heroes in my books, no leather jacket or artfully distressed jeans. No. Marco wears a dark suit tailored to within an inch of its life, the open collar of his crisp white shirt adding just enough edge to make him look dangerous. There's probably a gun under his jacket. Probably two.

But it's not the suit. It's not the tattoos curling out of the collar.

It's him.

The gravity of him. The focus. The absolute certainty.

The way he moves. The sharp intensity in his gaze. The way his eyes are focused on mine.

The crowd is losing it.

"Oh my God," someone whispers. "Who *is* that?"

"Did someone summon Jack from *Smash Girl*?" another murmurs.

"He's not Jack. He's better than Jack," a woman breathes. "I mean, look at him. *Look. At. Him.*"

Marco's eyes stay locked on mine. He walks like the room belongs to him and I'm the only thing in it that matters.

I forget how to breathe. My pulse flails. My brain—usually sharp, snarky, and ready for battle—fizzles into white noise.

He stops in front of the table, his lips twitching into that maddening, faint smirk of his. The one that destroys me.

"Ami." His voice is low, smooth, but loud enough for everyone to hear.

The entire store goes silent.

Not a cough. Not a rustle. Even the air conditioning seems to have stopped.

My mouth opens, but no words come out. After what feels like an eternity, I croak, "Marco. Uh... this is a surprise."

His brow lifts. "That's all you've got?"

I flounder. "Well... what do you expect me to say? You walk in here looking like... that." I wave vaguely at him, my brain too fried to be articulate. "And now the entire store is waiting for you to do something ridiculously cinematic."

The smirk widens.

A quiet laugh rumbles in his chest. "Ridiculously cinematic?" he repeats, his voice practically a purr. "How about this?"

Before I can react, he's moving around the table, fluid and deliberate, like the whole scene has already been choreographed in his head.

And suddenly, he's in front of me.

Pulling me gently to my feet.

The crowd inhales in sync. One unified intake of breath.

His hands are warm on mine, his voice low, rough, and unwavering.

"I want to make sure you know. Even if you never want to hear anything from me ever again."

He pauses—just long enough to let the words land.

"You walked away because I made you think I didn't feel anything. For you. For us. But the truth is—I was drowning in it. In how much I felt for you. You were right to walk away. What I said to you was unforgivable. And you didn't deserve any of that. You were right to walk away." His voice softens. "But I now know I wasn't ready for someone like you, Ami. I didn't deserve you."

My breath catches. His dark eyes are locked on mine. I couldn't tear my gaze away even if I wanted to.

"I used to think strength meant control. Silence. Shutting everything down. Then you showed up—with your chaos, your stories, your impossible courage—and suddenly I couldn't shut down. You made me feel. You made me want more."

Another pause.

"Ami Zadegan, you're the most extraordinary woman I've ever met."

He takes a breath. "You don't owe me anything. But I needed you to know. You made me better. You made me want to be better. I'm yours, if you want me."

Somewhere behind him, someone whispers, "Oh my God." Another chokes on a sip of iced coffee. A third lets out a small gasp. It's total silence... with just a bit of sobbing.

I can't move. Can't breathe.

And then he says the words that shatter everything. The words I've wanted from him, feared, imagined.

"I love you, Ami."

My heart pounds, everything cracking open inside me.

I tried to let him go. I told myself it was for my own good. But the truth is staring me in the face. Undeniable. Inescapable.

I love him, too.

I have since the moment I first saw him at La Cascada all those months ago. When I should've been terrified of the stone-faced, dangerous bodyguard. But I wasn't.

"Marco," I whisper, "you're insane."

His grin tips into full, devastating territory. "Probably."

And just like that, I break. Tears stream down my face. I can't stop them. Happy tears.

I say the only words I can say. The only words I want to say. "I love you, too."

The crowd takes in a breath as one. A beat passes. And then the room erupts into cheers. They're actually *cheering.* Phones flash. Someone shouts, "This is going viral!" A woman near the front fans herself with a copy of *Ad In.* "My God," someone murmurs. "It's like watching a romance novel come to life."

And then—Marco kisses me. Like we're the only two people in the world.

76

AMI

Five Months Later

THE BOOKSTORE BUZZES with lively energy, the kind that happens when excited readers and their favorite author are in the same room.

Maria stands at the podium, radiant in a sky blue dress that shimmers under the soft lighting. The Velvet Chapter, an indie San Antonio bookstore, has been transformed into an intergalactic Regency dream. Posters of her brooding alien duke —with glowing eyes and a jawline sharp enough to cut glass— line the walls. Stacks of her books, their glossy covers gleaming, fill every table.

Maria waves to the crowd, her grin contagious, as the manager of the store gushes through the introduction of "Mercede Sanchez," the pen name Maria has adopted. She looks like she was born for the spotlight, and the audience adores her.

Behind me, Marco's arms tighten, his chest warm and solid against my back. He's so much more openly affectionate now, a shift that has taken time. But I've learned to savor these moments, his steady presence grounding me, the quiet reassurance in the way he holds me.

"Look at her," Marco murmurs, his voice low against my ear. "She's killing it."

"She really is," I say softly, my heart swelling with pride as Maria beams like a queen surveying her kingdom.

Around the room, the Guard Dogs are subtly stationed, their sharp gazes constantly scanning. Chuck is seated in the audience, casually chatting up a woman who looks like she just stepped off the pages of *Vogue*. Through Marco's comm, I hear Chuck casually brag, "The glitching cloaking device? That was my idea."

Maria steps to the microphone, confidence radiating off her.

"Before we dive into the story of *The Dark Duke*," she begins, holding up the book with dramatic flair, "I want to dedicate tonight to two very special people."

Her eyes find Raul, seated in the front row, his posture relaxed but watchful.

"First, my father. Your support means everything to me, Papa."

The crowd claps politely, but Raul's small nod speaks volumes. Maria had once worried he'd disapprove of her writing, but tonight, his pride is unmistakable. Right now, the crime lord looks every bit the proud father.

"And second..." Maria's gaze sweeps the room until it finally locks onto me. "Ami Zadegan."

Oh, no.

Every head in the room turns, and I feel my cheeks flame.

"Ami, you are my mentor and my inspiration," Maria continues. "You *saved me* in more ways than you probably realize." A sly wink, and I know exactly what she's thinking. "Without your brutal honesty, this book would still be a chaotic mess of voice memos and sticky notes."

Laughter ripples through the crowd, followed by a wave of applause.

Marco leans down, pressing a kiss to my temple. "Told you. You're a big deal," he whispers.

Maria opens her book, flipping to a marked page as her grin turns mischievous. "Now," she announces, "I'll be reading one of my favorite scenes. And fair warning—it might be a *little* spicy. But let's be honest, that's exactly what we're here for, right?"

The crowd laughs, nodding eagerly. Through Marco's earpiece, Chuck's voice chimes in: "Yes, Mercede. That's *exactly* what we're here for."

Maria clears her throat and then begins reading, her voice rich with theatrical flair:

"The duke's six-fingered appendages quivered with restrained desire as Lady Penelope stepped into the chamber, her diaphanous gown clinging to her every curve like a second skin. His dual hearts thundered, their rhythm betraying the conflict within..."

The audience sits transfixed, hanging on Maria's every word. Even I have to admit, she's good.

She reads through her piece dramatically, looking up to make eye contact with the audience at the spiciest parts. She's truly in her element. When she finally closes the book with a flourish, the crowd bursts into applause and laughter.

Even Raul, seated in the front row, stands and claps, his normally impassive face softened with pride.

"She's a force of nature," I say, smiling as Maria basks in the moment.

"She really is," Marco murmurs, his lips brushing against my ear. "But she's not the only one."

As the applause swells, Maria steps back from the microphone and moves down from the stage. She makes her way to Raul, who pulls her into a rare, quiet hug. A proud father, in full view.

Fidel stands beside him, his posture casual, but his eyes are on Maria. He says something low, just for her. Whatever it is makes her smile, wide and genuine and a little shy. She swats his arm gently.

The applause dies down, and Natalie steps up to the podium. "Ladies and gentlemen," she begins, her voice warm and commanding, "Crimson Quill Press is so fortunate to have been the first to publish the incredible Mercede Sanchez. And I know you'll join me in our excitement as I proudly announce that Mercede's next masterpiece is already in the works and slated for release in eight months. Mark your calendars now so you're ready to grab *The Stellar Sovereign*."

The applause surges again, louder this time—cheers, whoops, whistles from the back. Maria lifts her chin, radiant, waving to the crowd.

The applause swells again, and Marco leans down to whisper, "When *Beneath a Persian Sky* comes out, I want to see you up there, too."

I smile faintly. "We'll see."

I see Natalie step from the podium and have a word with Elias. Then she's weaving her way through the crowd toward us. Her warm smile widens as she approaches, her gaze flicking to Marco's arms wrapped protectively around me.

"Well, if this isn't the happiest-looking couple in the room," Natalie teases lightly. "Mind if I interrupt for a moment?"

"Not at all," Marco says smoothly, his voice carrying that easy authority I've come to know well. His arms don't move, though, staying firmly in place around me.

"Ami, I've been meaning to tell you—the trade reviews for *Beneath a Persian Sky* are incredible. NetGalley readers love it. I'm thinking we may get *New York Times* and *USA Today* buzz."

My breath catches, a mix of disbelief and elation rushing through me. "Are you serious?"

"As serious as a dual-hearted alien duke," she says with a grin. "It's stunning work, Ami. Truly. I'm so proud of you."

Marco's hand tightens on my waist. "Told you," he murmurs again, his voice brimming with pride. "And now, if you'll excuse us, Natalie." He takes my hand. "Miss Zadegan," he continues, his voice still low. "I need you to see you privately. In the manager's office."

"Marco Cedillo," I whisper, my heart racing. "What are you thinking?"

His grin widens as he guides me thought the crowd. "Let's just say I'm curious about what Tara and Ronan were up to on page 142 of *Break Point*."

Heat creeps up my neck, but I can't stop smiling. "You've read *Break Point*?"

"Baby," he says, his voice low and full of promise, "I've read all of your books. And every compromising position you've ever described is on my 'To Do with Ami' list."

I laugh. "Lead the way, bodyguard."

And for the first time in my life, I feel completely safe, utterly adored, and deeply, irrevocably loved.

77

FIDEL

THE GUARDHOUSE IS SILENT, but my mind isn't.

I should be sleeping. The reception Marco and Ami hosted for Maria in their new Riverwalk apartment ended hours ago. The compound is quiet. Secure. Marco and Ami are gone. Chuck and Rafe are keeping Maria safe inside. Everything is as it should be.

And yet—I'm still sitting here.

I lean back in my chair, staring at the security monitors, my fingers tapping idly against the desk. Outside, the Sandoval estate is a fortress again. The damage completely repaired. The grounds quiet.

The Calderóns are history. Gone.

And that's the problem. Because I can't let it go.

Marco was right. They shouldn't have been able to do what they did. Diego Calderón was a reckless pawn, nothing more. Maria put him down during the siege—fast, clean.

But it still doesn't add up. He didn't have the brains or backing to pull off what he did on his own.

After their attack on the Sandovals, it hadn't been difficult to destroy their infrastructure, take out their leadership, erase them completely. They didn't have much in the way of assets. And they were reckless. Sloppy. The kind of men who got themselves killed trying to punch above their weight. But somehow, they'd breached our defenses. Infiltrated the compound. Caused chaos.

Which means someone gave them an edge. Someone bigger. Someone smarter.

I pull up my files—again—the fractured, encrypted Calderón communications I've spent the past several months piecing together. At first, the patterns seemed random. But recently, I've noticed a name, buried deep in the code.

Los Cuervos.

A cartel. Lesser known. Not operating in the U.S. Ruthless, organized. Silent, but growing.

I'm sure of it now—they hadn't just funded the Calderóns. They had used them.

I tap a key, pulling up intercepted messages. Not with the Calderóns. About the Calderóns.

The words stare back at me, cold and calculated.

Create distraction. Collapse the weak links. Calderóns expendable.

My jaw tightens.

Expendable.

They had been pawns in a bigger game.

The next message hits harder:

Sandovals vulnerable. Pressure him through her.

Him. Raul.

Her. Maria.

I sit forward, my fingers tightening into fists.

It wasn't just Raul they wanted to weaken. They knew. Maria was his greatest strength. And his greatest weakness.

Then the final message lands like a gut punch:

Secure the asset. Use her to dismantle him.

Asset.

That's what they called her. Like she was a bargaining chip. Like they thought they could take her.

A slow, deep breath fills my lungs, but it doesn't push back the rage that flares in my chest each time I read the messages.

I should tell Marco. Or Raul. Or both. Let them know I don't think this is over.

But I don't.

Not yet. I'm not sure. This is my problem to solve first. I don't know enough. Not yet.

I need to keep digging. Find the missing pieces to fit the puzzle.

Marco and Ami have earned their peace. I'm not going to drag them back into the fire.

Not until I'm sure.

I switch screens, pulling up surveillance photos of suspected Los Cuervos members. The images are grainy, but one detail stands out in every single one.

A tattoo.

A black crow, wings spread. I see it inked on men. On their hands, their wrists, their necks.

I stare at it, the image burning into my brain.

Something about it has been nagging at me for a while. *What is it about that fucking tattoo?*

I tap a key, flipping through months of files. Searching. Scanning. The back of my mind is screaming at me.

And then it comes to me—the night at Luz.

The night Ami was drugged.

I hadn't watched the security footage in months.

The video loads. The bar comes into view. The man lingering too close to Ami and Maria.

Something about that night... what is it?

I decide to review all of the footage from that day, not just time surrounding the drugging. Everything.

I start early, fast-forwarding through the setup. Bartenders. Barbacks. Waitstaff. Cleaning. Stocking shelves. Preparing to open.

I see Tommy Dawson—the manager—pass through several times. He's gone now. Left town. Disappeared shortly after that night, probably worried there'd be consequences for his serious fuck-up. And he was right. Marco would've made sure of it.

And then—I pause.

That afternoon. Club still closed. Tommy at the bar, talking to two men. I zoom in.

Neither of these men is an employee. One of them is one of the assholes who started the fight that night. I remember his face from the aftermath. Broken nose. Blood on his shirt. Playing drunk when security dragged him out.

The other one—my blood runs cold—is the guy who drugged Ami.

Tommy hands one man a small package. Probably the rohypnol. Then slides an envelope to the second. It has to be cash. It's fast. Efficient. Coordinated.

He claps them both on the back like he's sending them off to work a shift.

And that's when I see it.

A tattoo. A black crow in flight.

Right there. On the back of Tommy's hand.

Tommy.

Who was managing Luz.

Tommy, who had been so helpful pulling security footage for us that night. Who had come to the back office and stared at Maria.

Tommy, who had only been running Luz for a few months before the drugging happened. Who gave two men two jobs— one to start a fight, the other to slip something into a drink.

And who then disappeared right after.

Tommy—the link I've been looking for.

A slow, grim smile tugs at the corner of my mouth.

Found you.

If Los Cuervos thought they could use Maria to break this family?

They were wrong. Dead wrong.

GLOSSARY

Below is a quick reference for non-English words and slang used throughout *Guard Dog*.

- Donde hay amor, hay vida. - Where there is love, there is life.
- Ghormeh sabzi - A traditional Persian stew made with fresh herbs (parsley, cilantro, fenugreek), kidney beans, and tender chunks of meat, usually beef or lamb, simmered together with dried limes and turmeric. This dish is a staple of Iranian cuisine.
- Jefe - boss
- Librería Vida - Bookstore of Life
- Los Cuervos - The Crows
- Los Tios - The Uncles
- Los Tizones - The Embers
- Luz - light
- Niña - girl
- Papel picado - Traditional Mexican folk art made by cutting intricate designs into tissue paper. Often used as festive decorations for holidays and celebrations.
- Pendejo - asshole, dumbass (derogatory)
- Simorgh - A benevolent, mythical bird from Persian mythology, often depicted as a majestic, peacock-like creature with the wisdom of ages. The Simorgh symbolizes strength, healing, and the bridge between earth and heaven.
- Una hija de papí - a daddy's girl

ACKNOWLEDGMENTS

Guard Dog is my very first novel and it could never have happened without my family and friends. Thank you to everyone who helped me, encouraged me, and made me feel like writing this book was something I could do.

To my husband, thank you for always letting me do my thing and for listening to me, even when I say things like, "if you really want to money launder, you have to get into crypto." Your support is the foundation this dark-crime-romance-with-rom-com-elements empire is built on.

To my daughter, thank you for introducing me to a whole new world. You started this when you handed me that first tennis romance. And from there it was fantasy romance, monster romance, hockey romance, mafia romance, and all the rest. I appreciate that you acted completely unsurprised when I decided to write my own story with guns, tattoos, bodyguards and intense sex.

To my sisters, thank you for reading early drafts and giving feedback with near-professional composure. Your ability to read and comment on explicit sex scenes composed by your big sister without gagging is appreciated.

To my sons, thank you for always believing in me no matter what I take up next and acting like I can do anything I set my mind to.

And finally, to you, the readers, thank you for stepping into the morally gray shadows with me. I hope *Guard Dog* wrecked you in all the right ways and you'll continue on this journey with me. Because there's definitely more to come!

A NOTE FROM THE AUTHOR

So You Made It to the End…

I hope that Marco and Ami's story gave you everything you came here for: fierce loyalty, deep healing, smoldering tension, and love that defies the odds.

But the Guard Dogs' story is just beginning…

Book 2: Watch Dog follows Maria and Fidel as they crash into a whirlwind of cult fandom, high-stakes hacking, film deals, fake dating, and one very sexy leather mini-skirt.

If you want to be the first to know when **Watch Dog** is released—or get sneak peeks, bonus content, and behind-the-scenes chaos from the entire **Guard Dogs** world—please join me at:

https://KattAndrews.com/newsletter/

Yes, there's a mailing list but I promise to never, ever spam you (because I hate it too). Come for the bodyguards. Stay for the found family, forbidden love, and just the right amount of explosions.

Here's to romance, revenge, and the people who'd kill for you -
Katt Andrews